A Widening War

At Home and At sea, 1806

Revised version

by

John G. Cragg

©2023 John G. Cragg

A Widening War: At Home and At Sea, 1806

Copyright © 2021, 2023 by John G. Cragg

All rights reserved.

.

Dedicated to

The Memory of

Charley Cragg

1995-2021

A man who loved the sea

Table of Contents

Chapter I	1
Chapter II	15
Chapter III	29
Chapter IV	49
Chapter V	61
Chapter VI	75
Chapter VII	95
Chapter VIII	113
Chapter IX	131
Chapter X	145
Chapter XI	167
Chapter XII	185
Chapter XIII	207
Chapter XIV	229
Chapter XV	243
Chapter XVI	257
Chapter XVII	273
Chapter XVIII	299
Chapter XIX	315
Chapter XX	331
Chapter XXI	349
Author's Note	359
Glossary	363
Main Characters	367

Preface

This book is a work of fiction, both in terms of events and of characters. It follows on from the first five volumes in this series, *A New War: at Home and at Sea, 1803, A Continuing War: at Home and at Sea, 1803-4, A War by Diplomacy: at Home and at Sea, 1804, A Stalemated War: at Home and at Sea, 1805* and *A Changing War: at Home and at sea, 1805-II.* They are available at Amazon.com and other Amazon sites by searching for my name or the title. The present tale takes place in 1806. A great many things have changed in the more than two centuries that have elapsed since that date, including items and phrases that may be unfamiliar to many readers. To help those who are curious, a glossary is provided at the end of the book. Items in the glossary are flagged on their first appearance in the text by an * as in, for example, tack*.

This revision corrects some mistakes in the first edition and add some material that was left out of the previous version by mistake.

As always, I am indebted to my wife, Olga Browzin Cragg, for her encouragement and meticulous help in trying to make the manuscript readable.

Chapter I

"The Crown calls Daphne Giles, Countess of Camshire," Sir Peter Solvisti, the barrister representing the Crown, announced to the judge. The cry was taken up by an usher inside the courtroom and others outside it, "The Crown calls the Countess of Camshire." One of the Court's functionaries knocked and opened the door to a small room. "My lady, they are calling you."

Daphne rose from the chair where she had been waiting nervously. She was not looking forward to testifying against her husband's prize agent, Randolph Edwards. She had known Mr. Edwards ever since she had married Giles less than three years ago. Her husband's formal name was, of course, Captain Sir Richard Giles, Earl of Camshire, Viscount Ashton, KB. She had completely trusted Mr. Edwards to look after her husband's interests. Only in one instance had she had reason to doubt his probity. That had occurred when she was trying to dispose of the house of ill repute that Giles had acquired as part of the estate of his half-brother, the previous Viscount Ashton. Now she was testifying about discovering how Mr. Edwards had been cheating his clients out of substantial amounts of prize money. Giles had been supposed to be the one testifying, along with several other victims of the agent, but they had all been sent to sea on an urgent expedition two weeks before the trial was to start. As a result, Daphne had been called upon to testify about how the fraud had been discovered and to explain its nature.

Daphne followed the official out of the room, trailed by her lady's maid, Betsey. Daphne was wearing a black walking dress, cut in a contemporary but unremarkable style, with only a small amount of white lace at the collar and cuff. Only those touches revealed that it was not truly a mourning gown worn to mark the death of her husband's father, the late Earl of Camshire. The late Earl's wife, now the Dowager Countess of Camshire, Lady Clara, had refused to go into mourning, a decision which her son, Daphne's husband, agreed with. Daphne wholeheartedly supported her mother-in-law in not mourning her despicable father-in-law. Still, Sir Peter had strongly suggested that she did not want to shock the jurors in the trial by too blatantly flouting convention. The jurors, he had claimed, were drawn from London's business and professional classes, and they were a very conservative lot. They would already be horrified that a Countess, wife of a renowned naval captain, would have anything useful to say about a criminal charge, and he would prefer if Daphne did not further shock them when undoubtedly they all knew that she should be in mourning.

Betsey left Daphne at the door to the courtroom and was whisked upstairs to the public gallery, where a place was being held for her by one of Lady Struthers' senior housemaids. The housemaid would be on hand when Daphne's testimony ended to escort her to the carriage and then to Lady Struthers's house in Mayfair. At the same time, Betsey would remain in the courtroom so that she could recount all that went on following Daphne's testimony. Lady Struthers was Giles's aunt, with whom Daphne was staying while she was in

London, and a pillar of London's aristocratic society. Daphne thought that she was perfectly capable of finding her way by herself to the front steps of the Old Bailey Courthouse, where her coach would be waiting for her, but Lady Struthers would not hear of it. That was not how ladies behaved! They must have a maid with them when out in public! Daphne respected her aunt too much to dispute this dictate while she was staying at Struthers House, her uncle's mansion in Mayfair.

The usher led the way to the double doors of the courtroom, opened one side, and whispered to someone inside. Then he stepped aside to let Daphne enter, saying, "Lady Camshire, my colleague will show you where to go."

Daphne glanced about her. The courtroom was large and well illuminated by large windows. The judge, wearing a large, very old-fashioned wig, sat behind an elevated semicircular affair with other bewigged figures beside him, well spaced out with plenty of elbow room. The 'bench' had a solid, finely crafted wooden barrier so that only the top part of these men could be seen.

Below the judge's bench was a semicircular table where still more bewigged men sat, ready to write. Across from them was a raised platform, almost as high as the judge's, where Daphne's acquaintance, Mr. Edwards, was standing behind a wooden railing. He was her husband's prize agent who had acted in that capacity from before her marriage. Mr. Edwards had performed a wide variety of other services for Giles. She realized that Giles would need a new agent if this trial proceeded in the way she expected. With him away for an indefinite period, quite possibly garnering more prizes, she had better find out which ones were the best. It might even fall to her to select one if Giles sent prizes home before he could come himself.

The usher accompanied Daphne to the foot of a curved set of steps leading up to another elevated box. One of the many bewigged court officials took over when she reached the top of the stairway. He asked her to state her name. His request took her by surprise, though she should have anticipated it. Of course, she knew that witnesses had to swear to tell the truth, but they also had to state who they were before taking the oath.

"Daphne Giles — Countess of Camshire."

Daphne wasn't used to her new title, let alone naming herself with it. 'Countess of Camshire' was her mother-in-law's name, or so it had been until very recently. At least she hadn't stumbled completely and named herself 'Daphne Moorhouse.'

The usher then presented Daphne with a book and asked her to repeat an oath after him with her hand on the Bible. After that formality, she had a moment to look around as Sir Peter stood up and shuffled some papers before proceeding. Opposite her was an elevated box containing twelve men sitting in three rows of four, with each row a bit higher than the one in front of it. That must be the jury. The men in the jury box looked to be older shopkeepers or superior tradesmen, all dressed as if they were going to church.

To Daphne's left was another elevated box called, Daphne understood, 'the dock.' Mr. Edwards was standing in it. Daphne was surprised to see that a large mirror hung over the dock, tilted to reflect extra light onto his face. To her left were the judge's bench and the semicircular table where Sir Peter was adjusting his gown before looking up at her.

"Lady Camshire, I understand that the Earl of Camshire is a naval captain."

"Yes, he is."

"And he has been one for some time?"

"Of course. He started as a midshipman, the third son of an earl who had no intention of supporting him, but he is now a post-captain and has been one for some considerable length of time."

"He has been very successful in the matter of prize money, has he not?"

"Yes, he has been lucky in that regard, especially in taking or sinking enemy warships, though he has also done well in capturing enemy trading vessels. Those prizes are the source of the funds he used to purchase our estate, Dipton Hall."

"Is it true that his prize-money accounts are handled by the prisoner in the dock, Mr. Edwards?"

"Yes and no. Mr. Edwards is in charge of receiving the funds and, in some cases, for representing Captain Giles – Lord Camshire much prefers to be addressed as 'Captain Giles' in anything related to his naval service – at hearings or other such events to determine the legitimacy and value of prizes. He then reports the results to Captain Giles.

"Your husband is often away for long periods at a time, is he not?"

"Yes, he is. We have been lucky in that, recently, his voyages have lasted only a few months, but it is quite possible that he will be away for years."

"Is he away now on naval matters?"

"Yes, he is."

"So, what happens to these reports when your husband is away?"

"They come to me, and I go over them. Then I decide what to do with the funds when they are received. His Majesty's Government is not known for settling its bills promptly."

Daphne's remark prompted some vigorous nodding among the jurors.

"Are you telling me that *you* are handling these accounts?" Sir Peter feigned amazement and doubt about Daphne's dealing with business matters, even though he had been over her testimony with her before the trial, and her words came as no surprise to him.

"Yes, of course. Captain Giles is away, so I naturally deal with all these matters. I am sure that there are many men here whose wives manage their accounts."

Several men in the jury box nodded their heads in agreement. Daphne had been told by the Crown solicitor that juries were made up of men of property in London, with most idle men of fashion succeeding in avoiding jury duty even if they were not nobles. The legal status of the wives of the jurors, which seemed to presume incompetence in monetary matters, was the same as that of the wives of aristocrats. However, in practice, they were much more likely to take an active role in their husbands' affairs than were the wives of the gentry.

"So you received the report on the French frigate, *Nereid*, which the Earl of Camshire captured on his last voyage?"

"No. Captain Giles was at home when that arrived. He passed it on to me, saying, 'Here, Daphne, you had better take this. Until I am through with sea service, you are in a better position to deal with our finances than I am, and there is no point in my getting in your way. It is, of course, an enormous sum, but I am still surprised how much the government fees and Mr. Edwards's commission have eaten up my three-eighths share of the prize money.'"

"Is this the report, My Lady?"

Sir Peter reached up to hand Daphne a sheet of paper.

"Yes, it is."

"Please tell the jury what it says?"

"All right. It is labeled as 'Settlement of prize money for the French frigate *Nereid*.' It is dated the 21st of December of last year. Then it lists the prize money arising from the Admiralty buying *Nereid* in as £8,870/0/0. The next line is for charges made by the prize Court and other official charges amounting to £1237/9/8, which is subtracted from the first line to give a sum of £7532/11/4. That sum is identified as 'Proceeds for disposal.'

"The next line is said to be Captain Giles's share being 3/8 of the previous figure or £2,758/14/4.

Following that is Mr. Edwards's commission, which is ten percent, amounting to £275/17/8. The final line is £2,422/4/8, which the paper states was deposited to Lord Camshire's account at Coutt's Bank."

"Did you see anything strange about this statement at the time you received it?"

"No. It looked just like previous ones Captain Giles had received."

"And which you had examined?"

"Yes, that is what I meant."

"But you did discover something wrong with this one, didn't you?"

"Yes, but not immediately."

"Tell the jury how the error came to be discovered, Lady Camshire."

"Well, after Captain Giles and I had gone over the mail, we joined my father and my uncle for luncheon. They had come over to Dipton Hall for that purpose. At table, I mentioned that we had received the information on my husband's prize money for the French frigate. In fact, I happened to mention the exact figure of £8,870 and added that there were fees to be deducted before the net figure was calculated. Then, Captain Giles would only receive three-eighths of the latter figure, which is, as I mentioned a few moments ago, £2,422/4/8. That is a larger fraction than successful captains usually receive because, when *Nereid* was captured, *Glaucus* was sailing under admiralty orders, so there was no admiral to get a one-eighth share."

The men in the jury box appeared to be following all this with great interest. Of course, it would seem to them to be a vast sum if any of them were ever to receive so much.

"Yes, my Lady, and then what happened?"

"My Uncle, George Moorhouse, said that something couldn't be right. He had said that he had read in the Naval Gazette that all the fees had been paid before the figure of £8,870 had been arrived at so that he didn't see how there could be an extra charge."

"How would your Uncle George know about that?"

"Uncle George is the owner of a gunsmith establishment in Birmingham. He has been fascinated with my husband's career ever since I married him. He likes to follow all the naval news that might contain information about Captain Giles. The results of prize courts or ways of paying for captured vessels particularly fascinate him. My uncle also has a prodigious memory for figures and how to calculate others based on them. He told me that he had seen a report on what had happened with *Nereid* and how Captain Giles – or Viscount Ashton, as the paper called him – had captured her. The article mentioned both the gross figure that she fetched and what the net figure was after all charges had been leveled. The £8,870 was that net figure. I don't remember the exact gross figure. I understand, Sir Peter, that you will be introducing it sometime in the future."

"My Lord," said the Crown Barrister, "I shall indeed have a witness who will introduce those and other relevant documents, which will establish the veracity and validity of Lady Camshire's testimony.

"Now, Lady Camshire, what happened after that?"

"Well, I was bothered by my uncle's claim, of course, but I had a very hard time believing that Mr. Edwards was cheating us somehow. Two days later, my father asked my husband and me to dine at Dipton Manor."

Daphne looked directly at the jury box as she said, "Dipton Manor is my father's house, where my Uncle George also lives; Dipton Hall is my husband's estate.

" It can be a bit confusing, I am afraid," she added smiling at the jury.

"Anyway, Sir Peter, Sir Titus Amery was visiting my father. Sir Titus is a High Court judge, but he is often seconded to the government on various law-enforcement matters. I mentioned the discrepancy my uncle had discovered. My uncle sent for the relevant papers. His manservant produced them, and Sir Titus said that he would look into the problem. That is as much as I know about the matter. I wrote to Mr. Edwards asking for an explanation, but I did not receive a reply. Instead, I learned that he had been arrested and that I was called upon to testify here today."

Sir Peter turned to address the Court, "My Lord, that is all that I have to ask this witness."

Daphne prepared to leave the witness box. "One moment, please, my lady," said the judge. "Mr. Baleweight may have some questions for you."

A large, swarthy man rose from the lawyers' table. He was wearing a black robe and a white wig, just like Sir Peter, but somehow they looked ominous on this barrister.

"Lady Camshire, I find it hard to believe that a countess would have such a good head for figures. It is not what one expects at all."

"Why ever not, sir? Do you think one has to be addle-pated to marry an earl?"

Even the judge had to hide a chuckle at that reply.

" Anyway," Daphne continued, "I haven't always been a countess. Before I married, I was just plain Daphne Moorhouse. My father had realized that I had better competence for dealing with numbers than he did, so after a while, he let me handle all the accounts for our estate of Dipton Manor. Somehow, I have taken on the same task for all of the Earl of Camshire's estates and other business while he was still Viscount Ashton. We are going to have to find a reliable manager to help now since his properties are so much more complicated as the result of the death of my father-in-law."

"You amaze me," said Mr. Baleweight. "Surely facility with numbers is not part of the education of ladies."

"I am not aware of what constitutes the usual education of ladies. I see no reason why basic arithmetic should not be considered essential for everyone. In my case, my father stressed logical thinking, including some mathematics, and when my governess was inadequate in that area, he dismissed her. I am sure that my experience is not completely atypical, especially among young ladies who are destined to be more than ornamental appendages of their husbands."

Daphne rather regretted that she had allowed Mr. Baleweight to get under her skin quite so easily but felt better when she noticed that several of the jurymen were nodding their heads as if they agreed with her. It wouldn't hurt to have Mr. Edwards's barrister look foolish.

"I see. So you had the acumen to believe that you had discovered misdoing by Mr. Edwards."

"You are twisting my words, sir," Daphne replied immediately, even as Sir Peter was rising from his feet to cry, "I object, my Lord."

"I am afraid, Sir Peter, that your witness has already forestalled your objection," the judge replied. "I believe that Lady Camshire had something further to add. Lady Camshire?"

"I was about to say, my Lord, that it was my Uncle George who found that the report didn't make sense."

"Ah, ha!" cried Mr. Baleweight. "Surely, we should be hearing this from Mr. Moorhouse rather than from Lady Camshire."

"My Lord," Daphne interrupted, again forestalling whatever Sir Peter was about to say as he rose to his feet and tugged on his gown before objecting. "My uncle has suffered from a seizure which has left him unable to talk or to walk. He can still write with one hand, more legibly than most gentlemen whose notes I have perused. My uncle's brain, however, is perfectly lucid, so he communicates by writing, but he is not physically able to testify here."

Sir Peter, at that point, finally got to say something. "My Lord, the Crown will be calling witnesses to testify to the rules involved in the payment of prize money. Lady Camshire is testifying as to how Mr. Edwards's crimes were first discovered."

"Mr. Baleweight," the judge said while trying to suppress a grin. "Do you have further questions for Lady Camshire? Perhaps you would like to see if she can demolish you just as effectively again?"

"No, my Lord, I have nothing further."

"Then, thank you, Lady Camshire, for appearing here today," the judge said. "I know that many of our noble ladies find excuses for not testifying when they should."

Daphne was surprised at the judge's remark. Surely, she had had no choice but to testify. Though Lord Struthers had rather mysteriously offered to get her exempted from the ordeal, and Lady Struthers had said that she had never heard of a lady of Daphne's rank being required to testify in open criminal court, Daphne had presumed that it was her duty to testify and had never even thought of finding some way to avoid the ordeal. Of course, Daphne wouldn't have testified if Giles had been available, but he had been sent away in his frigate, *Glaucus,* in a great hurry soon after it had been announced when the trial of Mr. Edwards would be held. Uncle George, who had a great deal of experience dealing with the government, had been certain that Giles had been ordered away so that he could not testify, a suspicion that seemed to be confirmed when both Captain Bush and Captain Bolton had also been sent on the same mission.

Chapter II

Lady Struthers's maid was waiting for Daphne at the door of the courtroom, and her carriage was at the curb in front of the courthouse. There was a lot of activity on the street, Old Bailey, which was being hindered by her coach, but no steps were being taken to move along her conveyance. Daphne had already discovered when she had had a viscount's coat of arms on the door of her carriage that the coachman could stop anywhere he liked; this would be even more the case when the coat of arms belonged to an earl. However, the large vehicle could only move at snail's pace, for the streets were very busy. People on foot or in sedan chairs wove their way through the jams of horse-drawn vehicles and were able to reach their destinations much quicker than did the passengers in carriages or hackney cabs. Today, the pace seemed to be particularly slow. How in the world could she get to her next appointment before dinner time?

"Do you know what is going on, Mary," Daphne asked the maid.

"Oh, my lady, they are getting ready for a hanging tomorrow. Very important one. I imagine they expect a big crowd since there hasn't been a hanging there for two weeks, and six people are scheduled to swing—a woman among them. "

"Will you be attending it?"

"Oh, no, my lady. Lady Struthers won't allow any of us to go to hangings, not under any circumstances."

"A good rule, I think." Daphne had no intention of trying to undermine her aunt.

After ten minutes, the coach had moved less than ten yards from the spot where they had boarded it. Daphne was losing patience. She knocked on the roof, and a footman immediately jumped off the rear of the carriage to see what was needed.

"Help Mary and me out of the coach, George," Daphne ordered the footman, "and get us two sedan chairs."

George had no difficulty in summoning two empty chairs that had been waiting outside the courthouse for business. While an earl's coach in the city was guaranteed to snarl traffic, a countess and her maid in sedan chairs were bound to produce large tips. With luck, she might even want to be accompanied by the footman as well.

Daphne was quite happy only to have sedan chairs for herself and the maid Mary. Off they went. It was not far to their destination in Chancery Lane in which her solicitor's office was located. Indeed, the decision to abandon the carriage meant that Daphne was early for her appointment with the lawyer. She was sure being early didn't matter. She had already learned that countesses, particularly well-heeled countesses, always found that lawyers and doctors and other professional men were never busy when they came calling. A few moments when less profitable business was sent to wait, and she was always ushered in to see the man. What happened when two high ranking members of society wanted the services of a professional man at the same time was not something she had yet discovered.

Daphne's expectation was met without a hitch. The minute Mary announced that Daphne's presence in the offices of Snodgravel, Whistlethwaite, and Gardiner arose from a desire to see Mr. Snodgravel, a clerk bounded to the partner's office door and returned very quickly to usher Daphne into the lawyer's office. As she was being bowed in, she had the distinct impression that she heard the latch on the other door in the office click closed while Mr. Snodgravel pushed some documents aside, with one of them falling on the floor as he did so.

"Lady Camshire," the lawyer greeted her, "I am surprised, but very glad, to see you. I understood that you would be testifying in Court, in the Old Bailey, today."

Daphne was not surprised by the greeting. Various newspapers had been following the case closely, and they had noted the very unusual event of a countess, particularly a rich and well-known countess, testifying in Court. The papers had also indicated that the aristocracy usually found ways to avoid such a duty. It was, therefore, news when it became known that the new Countess of Camshire was not avoiding her duty. Indeed, Lord Struthers had somehow arranged that it became common knowledge that she was testifying not because Mr. Edwards had been stealing from Giles but because the theft had been from other heroic officers for whom the reduction of their prize money would be much more serious.

"I was," Daphne replied. "It took less time than I expected, and then I took a sedan chair here. The crowds around the courthouse were too thick to allow my carriage to make reasonable progress. They were getting ready for a hanging tomorrow at Newgate Prison, I am told, and that was the reason for the jam-up."

"Of course, yes, there is a hanging scheduled for tomorrow. I had not thought about how that might impinge on the Court's activities. Six felons are to swing if their sentences are not commuted at the last minute," commented the lawyer.

"I thought that executions in London took place at Tyburn, wherever that is. I have heard of it ever since I was a little girl, and my nanny used Tyburn as a ridiculous threat when I was naughty."

"Yes, executions used to take place at Tyburn, but not for years and years now. I can remember my father taking me to a hanging there when I was a very young boy. It was quite a festival in those days. A huge mob accompanied the carts in which the condemned men and women rode until we reached Tyburn, where the gallows were ready for the condemned. Quite a carnival, I must say!

"I never got to observe a traitor being hung, drawn, and quartered," Mr. Snodgravel continued with a relish that Daphne thought was vulgar. "I am not even sure when that last one occurred. They were also held there, I believe."

"Where is Tyburn, Mr. Snodgravel?"

"It's at the end of Oxford Street, right at the end of Mayfair. I think that is why they moved the gallows to

Newgate. Mayfair expanded and crossed Oxford Street, and the rowdy procession with a lot of undesirable people in it was too close to the rich people's addresses. Anyway, hangings are much less popular entertainments than they were then, though I am told they still attract quite a crowd. Of course, there are fewer now since so many felons get sent to Australia instead of being hanged. Your Mr. Edwards may well have that happen to him."

"He is not *my* Mr. Edwards. And I was only testifying because Lord Camshire was ordered to sea."

"Yes, I heard about that. Edwards seems to have a lot of people in high places who do not want him to turn them in because he is hoping to get out of being hanged. However, I am sure, my lady, that you did not come here to discuss executions.

"Now, about Lord Camshire's will – the late Lord Camshire's will and the disposal of his property. I still get confused when one client suddenly takes a former client's name, and we have to talk about both individuals' affairs."

"Call my husband 'Captain Giles' if you want, and you can call me 'Lady Daphne.' Let's just get on with it."

"Very good, my lady. We've had word from the Diocesan Court of Canterbury about the main points we raised. There are several important aspects of the probate proceedings."

"Yes?"

"First, concerning the property in Norfolk. You know, the one where the late Earl's mistress is living.

The title is not in her name, even though he left it to her in his last will. Indeed, it is still part of a larger estate which he bought and then borrowed heavily on. It is virtually worthless to you if Captain Giles decides to pay the debts on the property. Anyway, the late Earl forgot the terms of the entail* established by his father. He couldn't leave the property to her. It goes to Captain Giles.

"Unfortunately, it will be up to Captain Giles to evict that woman. The longer she stays there, the harder it may be to get her out. In situations like that, where people are allowed to continue to occupy the premises for any length of time, evictions become more complicated to execute, especially as local magistrates become more unwilling to enforce orders from distant courts. I suggest that you arrange to have the eviction as soon as possible. I have sent full details to my correspondent in Norwich, whom I believe you have used in the past. If you wish, he can approach the magistrates to have her evicted. Your presence, of course, is not required, though you should get more details about the property before you decide how to dispose of it. On the other hand, you may also be more effective in persuading the local authorities to execute the eviction notice if you are on the spot than if the order comes as an instruction from some faraway place. Incidentally, my cousin's son is a captain in the Wiltshire Militia and is stationed in Norwich now. I can send him a note to be on hand with some of his men when the eviction occurs. Often there is trouble when people established in an area are removed from premises that they think, incorrectly, that they own. I don't know how this woman is viewed in the area."

"Can I attend the eviction? Can the Dowager Countess of Camshire?" asked Daphne.

"I suppose both of you can, but I would advise against it, though, as I say, having you in the region could facilitate any steps that need to be taken."

"I would think you would be against it, Mr. Snodgravel, but Lady Camshire may want to gloat over having her husband's – uh – concubine thrown out of the place he gave her. Go ahead with getting the eviction organized, but be sure to let me know when it will occur."

"Let's see. It will, of course, take some time to arrange all this. And for you and the dowager countess to travel to Norfolk."

"Can the arrangements be made for the event to occur a week Thursday?" Daphne asked.

"Ten days from now?– Yes, I am sure they can. If you are leaving London on Monday morning, with relays of horses, you could spend the night in Cambridge and then proceed to Norwich the following day. Long days, but you could relax in Cambridge for a day – an interesting place, it is. I can recommend the Sun Inn opposite my old college, Trinity. I can give you a note to the Head Porter, who can arrange to show you around the College if there is no special festival going on. Then another long day to Norwich. There are turnpikes for that route, so it is quite easy to traverse, even at this time of year. There are no good roads from Dipton to Norwich which do not go through London."

"Please arrange for the eviction to take place, then, Mr. Snodgravel."

"There is also some other major news," the lawyer resumed. "It concerns the entails that the late Earl tried to slap on properties that he did not inherit but acquired. Those properties are covered by the entails that required the properties to be passed intact to his son. Some of the late Earl's entails that would require Captain Giles to leave them to his son were not valid – that is what happens when you try to get legal work done on the cheap. Your husband, Lady Giles, is free to sell them if he wishes. That was a ruling of the diocesan court. You don't have to worry about the details, Lady Camshire – uh – Lady Giles. It is a mixed blessing for they are mostly so laden with debt as to be virtually worthless. The late Earl had speculated quite extensively in property, often disposing of properties and buying them even though the dispositions were, in principle, forbidden by the entails that forbade him to sell properties he acquired. I don't actually know at this time how many he sold despite the entails, but that is water under the bridge. I don't believe that it is worth pursuing the matter. I have prepared a list of the properties that are now owned by Captain Giles with a notation of the ones that are not covered by the entails. I imagine that you will want to pass the documents on to your agent – when you find a new agent."

Mr. Snodgravel was quite right. In the past, Daphne would have been likely to pass such a list on to Mr. Edwards and await his evaluation and recommendations. She would only deal with urgent matters; others could wait for Giles's return. She should look into agents even before Giles got back so that his continuing affairs could be looked after properly.

"Thank you, Mr. Snodgravel. Let me study this, and I will communicate what further service you can be to my husband. Incidentally, do you have any recommendations for an agent to replace Mr. Edwards? Please think about it and let me have your suggestions."

Daphne used another pair of sedan chairs to take Mary and her to Camshire House, which was located in Mayfair on an even more fashionable square than Struthers House. Well, maybe not more fashionable yet, but that would undoubtedly change when she and Giles moved there, and Camshire House was once more the London residence of the Earl of Camshire. It had been rented by the late Earl to an industrialist parvenu, but the renters had been shunned by their neighbors, who felt that they lowered the tone of the neighborhood. Not surprisingly, the tenants thought that they would be more comfortable in a less fashionable square.

Daphne was not at all sure that she wanted a London house, but realized that she would have to have one – at least if she wanted to accompany her husband when he attended Parliament. The prospect was not all grim, especially not for the winter months when usually Parliament started meeting. There were plays and concerts and far more balls than in the country, and she suspected that there might be interesting gatherings of people who went in for serious conversation rather like the group she had been introduced to in Birmingham.

Moving into Camshire House was not as straight forward as Daphne might have hoped. She realized that she was not prepared to turn the needed renovations and redecorating of the mansion over to one of the many fashionable firms who would be delighted to present her with a house all ready to move into, though one that ignored her own tastes. Instead, in her usual way, Daphne was taking a more hands-on approach. Today she was meeting with the architect she had hired, together with a builder and her half-niece-in-law, Catherine, who was married to Captain Bolton, another client of Mr. Edwards who had been mysteriously ordered to sea on an urgent basis before the trial of Mr. Edwards. Catherine had shown herself to be very adept at making rooms as bright and cheerful as possible. The consultation should not take long. Daphne was, indeed, only checking that what she had wanted was being included in the final plans.

Some modernization of Camshire House was certainly needed, though there was little about the basic house that a thorough cleaning and painting of the walls and other decorations wouldn't deal with. New, more modern furniture would have to be made, but the house should be ready by early spring if the orders were placed soon. There was little she could do about the paintings in the house before then. Her father-in-law had sold all the valuable paintings before he rented the house, but Daphne thought it would be better to take time to find replacements for the horrible pictures he had picked up. She would have to investigate getting more works by the current school of painters, who Catherine told her were outstanding, but that could wait.

The only reason to have a London house, Daphne had been told, was to take part in the Season, which ran roughly during the period when the Parliament was in session. Its current session had recently started, but Daphne had been assured that there was lots of time before the Season got going fully, possibly not until April. Her mother-in-law and Lady Struthers had strongly suggested that Giles's ease in being accepted into the House of Lords in a way that would ensure his influence would be greatly enhanced if the Earl and Countess of Camshire played a prominent role in the Season. Strangely this was true whether her husband was a Whig, a Tory, or someone with no fixed allegiance. Of course, since he had been called away to sea, he had not yet taken his seat in the House of Lords.

The social doings that paralleled the meetings of the legislators were as effective in influencing the details of legislation as were the calm or rowdy get-togethers in the various Gentlemen's clubs that occurred at the same time. It was also, Lady Struthers suggested, the only way that ladies had any chance of furthering their own ideas or aiding their husbands to achieve their ends. Daphne must not miss the opportunity by remaining in Dipton during the Season. Lady Struthers had offered to help with these endeavors, including allowing Daphne to use Struthers House as the center of her activities connected with the special time until Camshire House was ready. However, there was no doubt that a freshly refurbished mansion thrown open for a ball would guarantee that Giles's name would be on every tongue. It would announce that, in future, the behavior and, so, the influence of the Earl of Camshire would be quite different from that of the previous holder of the title.

Daphne was somewhat doubtful about how much time she and Giles would really want to spend in London, but he was a man who took his duties very seriously. If that included his sitting in the Lords, then she could see where having a brilliant London House would further his desires. She had taken the task in hand as soon as the need was made clear to her. With today's choices made, there was every reason to hope that the house would be ready by the middle of May. A June ball would be just the right event to get the new Earl of Camshire's place in London Society established securely.

That left her with the problem of servants, but preliminary work on staffing Camshire House had begun. The recent tenants had taken their servants with them, but that didn't matter much. Betsey had learned in conversation with other senior servants in houses on the square that they had not been up to the expertise that would be expected in an Earl's household. Giles had obtained the three pillars of the staff at Dipton Hall from this very establishment when his father had closed it for financial reasons. Her butler, Steves, and her housekeeper, Mrs. Wilson, had both adapted to country ways with enthusiasm and had no desire to return to the capital. However, they still had useful contacts and had agreed to help choose the senior staff, though not on this particular visit. Getting servants would have been so much easier if Mr. Edwards had not shown himself to be so dishonest. This aspect of losing his services simply demonstrated again how urgent finding an able and reliable London agent had become.

It did not take Daphne long to make sure that all the plans for the house were being carried out without further difficulties arising. Soon she left again. It was only a short walk to Struthers House. She wondered if Betsey would be back from the trial yet.

28

Chapter III

"Seven bells of the morning watch*," Lieutenant Daniel Stewart cried as he turned the glass. The ship's bell was not rung, so the passage of time had to be communicated orally. H.M. Frigate *Glaucus* was in heavy fog with almost no wind. Nearby were two other British frigates. The trio was roughly ten miles off the north coast of Spain, close to Finnestere, the point where the land turned sharply left to go down to Lisbon, Cadiz, and Gibraltar. The fog had cleared briefly during the night, which allowed the Master, Mr. Brooks, to determine their latitude from the North Star. How close they were to Finisterre was not yet known. Captain Giles had ordered that they should not ring the bell as long as the fog lasted, and the order also applied to the other two frigates. He wanted quiet so that any enemy ships that approached would not be warned of the presence of warships in the area.

Giles had had the ship cleared for action at six bells. Clearing in darkness was partly an exercise to keep everyone on their toes, but it also prevented very nasty surprises when the sky started to lighten with the impending dawn. It was always possible that an enemy had gotten close to *Glaucus* in the night without being discovered before it was within cannon range. However, Giles also suspected that any ship approaching the shore on a foggy, moonless night might hesitate to come too close to land in the hours of darkness. Still, it was as well to be prepared when the black of the night turned into the gray of the day with not much more visibility. If enemy ships were in the area, they might emerge from the fog with little warning. Giles wanted to be ready. He had ordered the others in his little squadron to be prepared too. He had also ordered the squadron to head east under very reduced sail during the night, and then they would go west during the day, wind and weather permitting. That way, they would not be bypassed by the ships they were waiting to capture in the dark.

Lieutenant Stewart thought he heard a muffled sound from behind him. If he was right, it shouldn't be one of the other frigates, which had been well ahead of *Glaucus* the last time they had hit an open spot in the fog about an hour ago.

It was finally getting lighter; dawn could not be far off, Mr. Stewart thought. The unidentified sound came from straight behind them, muffled and indistinct. It came again; he was sure of it. Then it repeated a third time, slightly louder. That was followed by an unmistakable shout that sounded like '*Mierde*.' That sounded a bit like *Merde*, whose English equivalent had produced a tongue lashing from Mr. Brooks, the Master, while Mr. Stewart was a midshipman but whose meaning was entirely clear to the acting lieutenant. Mr. Stewart beckoned the midshipman of the watch* to him.

"Mr. Bush," the lieutenant said in a whisper. "Go to Captain Giles and tell him that I hear a Spanish ship close astern of us. Go very quietly."

Giles came on deck a few minutes later. "What is going on?" he whispered to Mr. Stewart.

When the situation had been explained, he thought for several moments. Then some more noises came from behind *Glaucus*. "Mr. Bush, get Mr. Miller – quietly, quietly."

When the two officers arrived, Giles gave his orders quickly. They were to take the longboat, which was being towed behind the frigate; they were to select some reliable sailors to row the boat with muffled oars and some marines; then, they were to investigate the nature of the vessel producing the noise. Despite trying to be silent, it was quite possible that whoever was in the fog behind *Glaucus* would be ready for a boarding party. If it looked as if boarding would involve a serious fight, they were to come back without trying to board. Giles reckoned from the sounds that they had heard that the stranger would be within easy range of his long guns, so it was pointless to risk losing men trying to board against significant opposition when it was quite likely that *Glaucus* could deal with any well-armed ship that might be buried in the fog. Although everyone tried to be quiet, there was a bit of noise as the crew who were chosen for the expedition assembled, the longboat was pulled up to *Glaucus,* and they boarded her. Giles feared that the element of surprise might be lost because of the unavoidable noise, though there were no more sounds from the nearby ship that might indicate that its crew was preparing to welcome visitors. The loaded boat pulled away, and the sound of muffled oars faded quickly.

Giles and the rest of the crew of *Glaucus* waited impatiently for news of the expedition. Time crawled, even though it was only a few minutes since the longboat had vanished into the fog. Giles hated the helpless waiting that always occurred when a boarding party was sent away at night or in fog. He wished that he had done what he often did: lead the foray himself.

Then there came a loud shout out of the fog. "*Quien va alla?*"

"It means, 'who goes there,' in Spanish," Mr. Brooks announced.

"Or in Portuguese, I believe," added Mr. Macreau, the second lieutenant who was French.

A muffled shout followed, mixed in with a variety of noises that the waiting crew of *Glaucus* could not decipher, with two exceptions. A pistol shot stood out above the others, and, a moment later, it was followed by a loud clang of metal that might have been two cutlasses striking each other. There followed a set of muffled thumps and voices raised in what sounded like curses, even though the words could no be discerned.

More anxious waiting followed for the men on the frigate. Giles noticed that the fog was starting to thin. It quickly dissipated in the strange way of fog banks to reveal a brig* about a cable and a half away. *Glaucus*'s longboat was beside the ship, and several men were on deck, most of whom came from *Glaucus*.

"The man who looks to be giving orders is Mr. Miller," announced Mr. Stewart, who had the best eyes among the officers and was all too willing to remind the others about it. On the strange ship, a heated discussion was going on between Mr. Miller and a well-dressed man, who, despite fine clothes, had the look of a seaman. Both men were gesturing towards the fog from which the brig had just emerged. It was evident that *Glaucus*'s lieutenant had secured the brig, though its nationality and nature were not evident to the naked eye. Just as Giles was starting to fume that his subordinate seemed to feel no urgency about telling his captain what was going on, the fog rolled back some more so that another ghostly ship appeared and soon could be seen clearly. What in the world was going on? It was clear from his gestures that Mr. Miller had not yet noticed the other ship. Certainly, he was taking no steps to secure the newcomer. This wouldn't do!

Giles ordered that his barge be prepared. He guessed that his coxswain, Carstairs, had anticipated the order since, in moments, the barge was ready, with the crew armed in case the new ship turned out to be hostile. Though he was tempted to go himself, Giles sent Mr. Macreau instead. It would do the young lieutenant good to have the experience, and he was the one among *Glaucus*'s officers who was most likely to understand what was said in Spanish, of which Giles had at most a minimal understanding.

Off went the captain's barge pulling hard for the second ship. Giles tried to contain his frustration at not knowing what was happening. Why did Mr. Miller seem so unconcerned about the appearance of the second ship? Was the first ship friendly or hostile, and if the latter, why was it not more evident?

The mystery of the second ship deepened as some pistol shots rang out, followed by the unmistakable clang of swords or cutlasses. These did not last long, and Giles could make little of the action even though he was staring at it through his telescope. However, the fighting seemed to be over; Mr. Macreau was shaking hands with one of the men on the second vessel's deck. Then Giles realized why the reaction of Mr. Miller to the appearance of the second ship was so strange. The two ships were still on the edge of the fog bank. Between them, the fog extended enough towards *Glaucus* that they could not see each other even though Giles could see them both.

It would be too complicated to signal to them what was going on, especially as Giles was not sure how adept the men he had sent were at reading complicated flag messages. Impatience got the better of him; he would investigate himself, leaving only Mr. Stewart and Mr. Brooks in charge of *Glaucus*. A careful look forward showed only the solid fogbank; heaven only knew where the frigates accompanying *Glaucus* were.

"Mr. Bush," Giles called the midshipman. "Get the jolly boat ready. You can take me over to those two ships so that I can determine what is happening."

Mr. Bush showed no surprise that his captain would leave his ship to investigate what other officers had done rather than to wait for them to report to him. That may have been because the only ship he had served on was *Glaucus,* so he was not aware of how unusual, indeed improper, was what his captain was proposing to do. Acting lieutenant Stewart also considered the captain's request and the proposed action unsurprising; he had also been with Giles ever since he had first gone to sea. Only Mr. Brooks knew how unusual Giles's suggestion was, but he also knew that the captain's unconventional ways were successful more often than not. He was quite sure that the Admiralty would take no action even if something went wrong with the venture since Giles was a popular hero and now a powerful peer of the realm. Secretly, Mr. Brooks knew that if he were ever to become a captain – a very remote possibility – he would act in the same way as Captain Giles.

Just as all the other officers had expected, Giles got into the jolly boat as soon as it was ready, giving no orders for one of his subordinates to carry out whatever task he had in mind, but, instead, telling Mr. Stewart that he was in temporary command of the frigate. He told Carstairs to head for the first of the strange ships.

Mr. Miller was in the waist of the first vessel, near where *Glaucus*'s longboat was tied. He was conversing with one of the seamen of the strange ship while a couple of other strangers were standing freely in a group with some of *Glaucus*'s men. Somehow, Giles had the feeling that they were trying to help Mr. Miller understand what was said. Mr. Miller broke off and came to the rail as the jolly boat slid into place alongside the ship.

"What is going on that has taken you so long, Mr. Miller?" Giles asked irritably.

"Sir, I was trying to determine what the situation is here before going back to *Glaucus*," the first lieutenant told his captain.

"And what *is* going on here?"

"Well, sir, it took quite a bit of sorting out, but I think I am on top of it now."

"Yes?"

"This is a Portuguese ship, sir, the *Santa Clarissa* from Oporto. She was captured by pirates – I think that is what *corsario* means – last night. The ship has a cargo of wine, I think. I suppose that must be port wine. I believe that the pirates are Spanish."

"Did you secure the cargo so that our people can't get at it?"

"Yes, sir, but not quickly enough. Some of the Spaniards had already broken into the hold, and our fellows found a few bottles, which they drank. I suppose we will have to flog them when we get them back to *Glaucus*."

"Possibly." Giles was, in fact, sure that that would not happen. The responsibility had been Mr. Miller's, whom he could not flog. Unfortunately, the men would have to lose their rum rations for a couple of weeks to bolster Mr. Miller's authority. Giles only considered flogging appropriate for the most serious crimes, certainly not to cover an officer's mistake.

"Is the ship now secure?" he asked.

"Yes, sir. I was just finishing preparations for fighting off the pirates if they should reappear from this fog. Then I was going to report to *Glaucus*. As far as I can make out, the pirates are Spanish, but Spain isn't at war with Portugal. So I presume that the situation is one of piracy rather than the work of a privateer."

"Probably. We spotted another ship nearby – behind that fog bank. Mr. Macreau seems to be in control of it. That is my next stop. Make sure that this ship is secure and leave Mr. Dunsmuir in charge when you return to *Glaucus*."

If Giles didn't seem to be too pleased with Mr. Miller's behavior, it was because he was actually furious. His first lieutenant should have taken charge of the ship and returned to *Glaucus* much more quickly. He wondered what he would find when he visited Mr. Macreau and the next ship. Mr. Macreau had more initiative and perception than Mr. Miller, so maybe he could be more informative.

The boat rowed around the edge of the fog bank, which, if it was moving at all, was drifting very slowly. The other ship came into view, and Giles directed Mr. Bush to head right for it. Mr. Macreau was at the railing as the jolly boat slid up to the ship.

"Thank heavens you've come, sir," the lieutenant said. "There are too many enemies here for me to send any of my small contingent back to *Glaucus* to report."

"What is the situation, Mr. Macreau?"

"This ship is the *Santa Marta*. She's a Spanish privateer. She captured the other ship, a Portuguese merchant ship that was going to the Isle of Man with a cargo of wine from Oporto. *Santa Marta* took her prize, which is the first ship we spotted from *Glaucus*, called the *Santa Clarissa,* off Cape Finisterre. *Santa Marta* was taking her prize into Ferrol. The privateer captain must have figured that the wine would find a good market in a naval port.

"The captain showed me his letter of marque, sir, but I don't think that Spain is at war with Portugal. Doesn't that make it piracy?"

"I am afraid that I just don't know. I saw you shaking hands with some man."

"That was the Portuguese master. He was very grateful that we had captured the pirate ship – that's what he called her – and insisted on shaking my hand."

"I'm not sure what to do with him or his ship and cargo," Giles mused. "Is the prize of a captured pirate a prize for us when we capture the pirate? She would not be if the *Santa Clarissa* were a British ship, or we were formally allies with Portugal, but we are not, so that is not the case. However, I think we should let her go. I hate to do it since she is bound for the Isle of Man, and the only reason to ship wine to that benighted island is so that smugglers can take it to England. Whatever *Santa Marta*'s status is, she should be a prize for us. Because of this damned fog, the other frigates are not in sight, so we won't have to share with them. What a mess! It's not fair, but I can't flout the rules, especially not when the case of Mr. Edwards is still pending, as far as we know.

"Now, Mr. Macreau, this is what I want you to do. Take the officers and the petty officers of the Spanish ship over to *Glaucus*, leaving enough of our people on it to keep the Spanish crew secured until I can send more men. Mr. Bush, you are in command of the *Santa Marta* for the time being. I will take the captives from the Portuguese ship back to their vessel

Giles's mind was working furiously as he was rowed back to the *Santa Clarissa*. He was sure that there was some opportunity here that he had yet to recognize. It wasn't that the ships that he had taken were worth very little as prizes. It was that he felt he was missing some strategic possibility arising from the two ships. By the time the jolly boat reached the Portuguese ship, he had sorted out his thoughts. He would try to use the *Santa*

Clarissa to determine whether the ship that was his target had already reached Ferrol.

Glaucus's presence off Point Finisterre had arisen from orders given to him just after Christmas. According to the First Lord of the Admiralty, Lord Hatcherley, a packet ship had arrived in Liverpool from Jamaica a few days earlier. One of the messages that the ship carried, which the First Lord did not show to Giles, said that a spy in Cuba had reported that a Spanish galleon had arrived in Havana with a cargo of treasure, primarily gold but also some silver and precious gems. The ship was not the usual galleon – not surprisingly, Giles thought, since they had long gone out of style — but was more of an armed merchant ship or possibly a small frigate. The report was vague. However, the Admiralty was sure that the Spanish had no ships of the line in the Caribbean, so the treasure ship would not be more powerful than *Glaucus*.

The critical aspect of the information, according to the First Lord, was that the vessel had not been due to sail from Havana for at least two weeks after the spy's report had been sent from Jamaica. The Spaniard was said to be making for Ferrol rather than Cadiz since Cadiz might still be blockaded by the British. There would still be time to intercept the treasure ship if immediate steps were taken to do so.

The upshot of the meeting at the Admiralty was that Giles, together with Captain Bush, a long time friend, and Captain Bolton, who was married to Giles's half-niece Catherine, were ordered to form a three frigate squadron to patrol the approaches of Ferrol to stop the treasure ship from reaching harbor. The whole assignment and the information it was based on sounded strange – fishy is how Daphne had described it when she heard about it. Daphne made Giles even more suspicious about the assignment when she remarked that it seemed strange that three of the prominent captains who the papers had reported were victims of Mr. Edwards had been sent to sea immediately after it was announced that they would testify at Mr. Edwards's trial. Giles smiled fondly as he remembered how Daphne had decided that she would testify in his place, even though such behavior was unheard of for noble ladies.

However, the problem remained as to whether there was a treasure ship at all, and if there had been one, had it sneaked past his frigates at night or in the fog? With the long winter nights and with the unsettled weather since his squadron had arrived off Cape Finisterre, it would be quite possible that the Spanish ship had reached its destination without him being any the wiser for its passage. So far, there had been very little traffic in and out of Ferrol that had been visible to Giles. He really wanted to see what was in the harbor that was so well screened by the land around the narrow inlet where the port was located. The Portuguese ship might hold the answer. She could go into the port and sell her cargo there. An observer that accompanied her could see whether any ship from Havana had arrived recently.

Would the risks of such a venture be worth the possible returns? It would do no harm to have an up-to-date evaluation of what ships were in the major Spanish base, even if there was no sign of the treasure ship. Ferrol was an impractical place to blockade, and Giles had had severe doubts about his task. If already there was what looked like a likely candidate for the treasure ship in the harbor, he would be justified in abandoning the mission sooner rather than later. Of course, if there was not, that would not indicate that there was a treasure ship still to be caught. Quite possibly, it had been a figment of some spy's imagination, or the ship had been prevented from leaving Havana by a re-evaluation of the situation, or it had gone into some other Spanish port. Giles had no idea how the news of the Battle of Trafalgar might have altered Spanish plans or when they would have heard about what, from the Spanish point of view, was a disaster that had affected their naval forces at least as much as the decimation of the French fleet had weakened France.

Giles was about to turn to the Portuguese captain to discuss his plan when he remembered that Mr. Macreau had said that none of them spoke English. Restoring the vessel to its captain would have to wait until he had a chance to talk about his plans. That would require the presence of Mr. Macreau.

After more to-and-froing among the vessels, Giles met in his cabin on *Glaucus* with the Portuguese captain, whose name was Sebastien Barbas, and Mr. Macreau. Though Mr. Miller had returned from the *Santa Clarissa* with a sample of her cargo, Giles thought it would be wise not to serve it to her captain and instead offered claret. He started the conversation aggressively.

"Captain Barbas, I see from your log that you are headed to Douglas on the Isle of Mann with a cargo of Oporto wine."

"Si," responded the Portuguese captain. Mr. Macreau saw no need to translate the single word.

"The only reason to bring wine to the Isle of Mann is to supply smugglers," Giles stated.

After Mr. Macreau had translated this statement, it produced a long speech from Captain Barbas. When he paused for breath, Lieutenant Macreau translated, "He says it is not illegal to carry wine to Douglas. Even though the Isle of Mann is part of Britain, it is a free port. People like him only sell their wine there, and someone else has to smuggle it into England. The smugglers all say that all the risk is on them, not on the ships that bring the material into the port, so they pay us a much lower price for our cargo."

"I see," Giles responded. "I think, Captain Barbas, that you are mistaken. However, we can take your ship to an English port and see how the revenue service rules about it. Of course, you would have the opportunity to appeal any ruling, and the service would also have such a right, so you could not expect a speedy decision. It is a very fair way to resolve my dilemma, wouldn't you agree? A bit slow, of course, but a few bribes can speed that up for you, I am sure."

Giles leaned back in his chair, smugly looking as if he had conferred a great benefit on the other captain. Captain Barbas did not seem to agree, not surprisingly because he would know that, what with delays and legal costs and the need to grease various palms, Giles's suggestion would ruin him, even if, at the end of the process, he was allowed to keep his ship.

As expected, this little speech produced a long and emotional tirade from the other captain. "He says," reported Mr. Macreau, "that this is piracy. It is not fair; he has every right to take the wine to the Isle of Mann. You should be strengthening the long bond of support between Portugal and England, especially now with Spain and France against us."

"Please tell him that I sympathize with him, but I don't have any choice. I can't just let him go on his way since I know what will happen to his cargo if I do. Of course, if he were going somewhere else, even Spain, I could turn a blind eye to it, provided I had some way of knowing that that was what he had done. Even if he were going to a Spanish port, it would be all right since no blanket blockade against Spain has been announced as far as I know."

Giles had no idea what sort of legal ground he was on here, but, hopefully, it wouldn't matter. This time the harangue from Captain Barbas was quite a bit shorter.

"He wants to know what you have in mind," reported Giles's lieutenant.

"Tell him that I want to know what vessels are in Ferrol, especially if there are any that look like they have just had a long voyage across the Atlantic."

Captain Barbas spoke passionately when this remark was translated to him.

"He says it is too dangerous for him to act as a spy."

"Is it? I only want him to take you far enough into the port so that you can determine whether there are any likely vessels there. Ferrol is not where ships from the Spanish colonies usually go; Cadiz, or even Cartegena, are the usual destinations. So it should be possible to recognize any ship that has just crossed the Atlantic in winter. I was thinking of sending a midshipman in the *Santa Clarissa* to scout out the harbor and then have him rowed back in a boat that Captain Barbas could trail behind her."

"Sir," said Mr. Macreau even before he translated Giles's explanation, "I think that I should be the one to make the observations. I have far more experience than any of the midshipmen and can communicate easily with Captain Barbas."

"If you wish, yes, you can, though it is not an undertaking without its hazards."

A few more exchanges were needed to flesh out the plans. Captain Barbas would carry Mr. Macreau and two seamen into Ferrol and take them as far into the harbor as Mr. Macreau wished. Then they would take *Santa Clarissa*'s smallest boat and row back to where *Glaucus* could pick them up. If Captain Barbas tried to capture the British party to gain favor with the Spanish, Mr. Macreau would state that the Portuguese captain had thought up the spying idea in the first place. That would be enough to get him shot along with Mr. Macreau.

The day was progressing. If she left now, there would be just enough time for *Santa Clarissa* to get to her new destination while there was still sufficient daylight left to enter the port. The fog was thinning, and a wind had come up that would soon sweep it away. If *Glaucus* sailed in the other direction, it would be unlikely that any watchers on the shore would realize that the Portuguese ship had been in contact with the British squadron.

Giles stayed on deck until *Santa Clarissa* was hull down, heading towards the land, which was only now appearing from the fog. Maybe his ruse would work. There was nothing further that he could do about it now. He had been tempted to lead the excursion himself. Indeed, until very recently, he would have done so, but criticism from superiors, the horrified look that he always got from Mr. Brooks, and the disappointment he saw on the faces of his subordinates when he announced that he would be leading some venture that they were quite capable of handling had led him to be more cautious on this occasion. However, he missed the thrill of doing something that was not expected of a staid post-captain.

Was he becoming one of those unimaginative senior officers whose lack of daring had always irritated him? Daphne would be disappointed if he lost his spontaneity, but she had never wanted him to take on risks that he could delegate to his subordinates. Had the perfidy of Mr. Edwards, for so he thought of the actions of his agent, taken the edge off his enjoyment of his profession? Certainly, he felt little of the usual exuberance he used to when planning an unconventional foray. Or was it that his responsibilities ashore had expanded greatly as a result of his father's death? Even before that event, Giles was starting to feel a little guilty about how many tasks Daphne had to perform that would have fallen to him if he were not at sea. All the business of sorting out the tangled situation with the many entailed, but almost worthless, properties that went with the Earldom of Camshire was now falling to her. The fact that he was sure that she was much better at understanding and resolving such problems was irrelevant; husbands, not wives, were supposed to handle all business matters. Furthermore, the problems arising from his father's courtesan, which unquestionably he should be the one to handle, and certainly not his wife, were falling on Daphne's shoulders. More than ever, he missed her. She had even had to testify in court for him against Edwards, and, of course, it was Daphne and her uncle who had found out about the stealing, not Giles. God, he was lucky to have her!

Thinking about Mr. Edwards and the trial reminded Giles that today was when Daphne was scheduled to testify. How had she fared? Had she been treated with proper respect? Her latest letter had told of the date of the testimony and how uncomfortable she was to bear witness against a man she had previously regarded as a friend. He wondered how Daphne's appearance in court had gone. And would Edwards get his just desserts? Had Giles been sent to sea in an attempt by people with influence to protect some shady charácters whose involvement in criminal activities Edwards might use to save his neck if the trial went against him? What had happened to the happy, restricted life at Dipton that Giles had hoped for when he married Daphne and which he had promised her. Giles was afraid that she would revel in the life of a countess no more than he would enjoy being a wealthy earl. But, enough of this rumination. He must write to her. How much of his gloomy thoughts should he confess to her? They held nothing about their thoughts and feelings from each other, usually, and he wouldn't now. However, he would try not to reveal at great length how very unsettled he felt.

48

Chapter IV

Lieutenant Etienne Macreau stood beside the wheel of the *Santa Clarissima*, which her captain, Sebastien Barbas, was holding. Macreau knew little of the ways of merchant ships, and he did not know if the captain being the helmsman was standard practice on them. It certainly wasn't in the Royal Navy. He had never seen Captain Giles at the helm of *Glaucus*, and, for that matter, Etienne had never steered the frigate himself. Captain Barbas certainly knew what he was doing. Lieutenant Macreau realized that the captain was extracting every bit of force from the light wind.

"We'll be in Ferrol harbor long before dark, Etienne," Captain Barbas remarked as they passed the first headland leading to the harbor. "Keep your eyes skinned so that you can see all parts of the anchorages as we proceed. The dock I am going to is very deep into the harbor, though the inlet goes a good deal farther. You should be able to see all the vessels that are at anchor before we tie up.

At least, that is what Lieutenant Macreau thought that Captain Barbas was saying. Lieutenant Macreau had to guess at the exact meanings of many words. He didn't understand Portuguese and had only a smattering of Spanish, so he guessed some of the meanings of the captain's remarks based on similarities to French. Captain Barbas was no more fluent in French than Lieutenant Macreau was in Portuguese. Nevertheless, they had succeeded in getting to know each other on a first-name basis.

"We are arriving at the right time, at least, since the tide will be rising for a few more hours," Captain Barbas continued. "There is a moderate current going into Ferrol on the rising tide and a very strong one coming out with the ebb." At least, that is what Mr. Macreau understood him to say, though his guesswork was aided by the fact that Mr. Brooks, the master on *Glaucus,* had mentioned the currents and had been pretty sure that they would be suitable for leaving the harbor during the middle of the night. It helped that Captain Barbas liked to take his hands off the wheel momentarily to illustrate what he was saying with his hands.

Santa Clarissa turned to larboard* as they passed the headland to head up a narrow inlet. Ahead Lieutent Macreau could see a town and the masts of many ships at anchor or at docks along the waterfront. The wind was blowing from the west so their ship could run right up the inlet without tacking*. Before long, they came abreast a major fort standing guard over the port; the muzzles of its large cannon seemed to be aimed right at *Santa Clarissa.* That reminded him that he should be concentrating on his mission, not idly gazing at the sights of the Spanish port.

There were quite a few warships at anchor in the port. Mr. Macreau counted three line-of-battle ships. Had they been among the few Spanish third-rates which had escaped from the Battle of Trafalgar, he wondered, or were they ones that had never been in the battle at all? Around them were sprinkled several smaller warships: four frigates, small ones, and some brigs and still lesser vessels. He noticed that the ship nearest the entrance to the port, and some distance from the next warships, was one of the frigates. She was larger than the other frigates, a thirty-six. She appeared to be almost brand new, with hardly any of the signs that she had been exposed to the winds and waves that rapidly marked wooden vessels as having had even one cruise.

Mr. Macreau continued to examine the shipping as *Santa Clarissa* went deeper into the port. He noticed that none of the major ships showed any signs of recent battle repairs. It was safe to conclude that they had not seen any action at Trafalgar. That was not surprising. Even with major battles like Trafalgar, it was usual for only a small fraction of a country's major vessels to participate.

The lesser naval vessels looked more experienced and weather-beaten than their larger consorts. Some of them had been to sea quite recently and for extended periods of time, too. However, none of them looked as if they had recently crossed the Atlantic in winter. Of course, the report had said that the Spanish treasure ship had not been a naval vessel and was sailing alone, a strange arrangement for transporting valuable cargo. Etienne Macreau had thought it a fishy story when he first heard it, even before he realized that Captain Giles also had doubts. Allegedly, the enemy had taken this approach of getting their riches home because it was so unexpected.

Mr. Macreau continued to study the shipping anchored in the harbor and tied up to docks at the inlet's edge. None looked as if they had crossed the Atlantic recently, though he realized that among the many smaller vessels, many were large enough to ship a large fortune in precious metals. Whether they could safely face the ocean in winter was another question.

The late afternoon sunset had already occurred before *Santa Clarissa* pulled up to an empty spot on one of the docks near the end of the harbor. "We had to come this far because it is the only facility that is suitable for unloading alcohol," is what Mr. Macreau guessed that Captain Barbas meant as their mooring lines were thrown to idlers on the dock. "The tide will be turning in half an hour, Etienne, so if you wait an hour, you should be able to sneak out of here unnoticed. I hope the fog does not return."

Time seemed to drag for Mr. Macreau and the sailors with him as they waited for the time to be ripe for leaving. Then they climbed down into the ancient rowboat, unshipped the oars, and set off to leave the harbor. The fog had not returned, and there was a sliver of a moon to give them some illumination. They kept close to shore; there would be nothing unusual in a small boat rowing in a busy harbor. All went well until they were past the town and were approaching the large fort that Mr. Macreau had noticed from *Santa Clarissa*. He decided to keep close to shore, where they could not be seen by sentries patrolling the battlements of the fort. This seemed to be a good idea until disaster struck.

The current was now running rapidly, carrying the boat along quickly. Suddenly there was a thump as they hit a submerged rock. The boat stopped abruptly, with the rowers thrown backward off their benches. Mr. Macreau found himself kneeling on the bottom of the boat. Even as he crawled forward to help the rowers recover, he felt water seeping into his trousers. The boat was filling with water. They would have to beach it as soon as possible. Etienne immediately turned towards the shore.

The water reached the gunnels of the boat while it was still several yards from the beach. It would have sunk, except that, instead, it grounded on the bottom. Giles and his two seamen had no choice but to abandon the wreck and wade ashore. Luckily, they had managed to get beyond the foundations of the fortress to a place where there was a small beach. Already, being soaking wet with the temperature only a bit above freezing had them shivering and their teeth chattering.

Just as they reached the sand, the stranded sailors heard noises of people crashing through the bushes that covered the hill rising from the beach around the edges of the fort. Their presence could not be an accident. Some over-zealous sergeant must have heard the noise when Mr. Macreau's boat had struck the rock and sent men to investigate.

"Hide," Mr. Macreau whispered to his men. They had hidden behind some bushes when four soldiers emerged onto the beach. The Spaniards were armed with muskets that had bayonets fixed.

"Hay un bote por alla," said one of the newcomers.

'Bote' sounded a bit like 'bateau' and 'boat' to Lieutenant Macreau. Their sunken craft had been spotted.

"Donde estan los hombres?" was the next remark.

'Hombres' sounded somewhat like 'hommes,' the French for 'men,' Mr. Macreau thought. Was the Spaniard wondering where they were?

The soldiers started to walk along the edge of the beach, looking towards the bushes to see if they could see any sign of the people from the boat. Even in the dark, they were bound to spot the wet tracks left by the ship-wrecked sailors. Mr. Macreau bent down and felt for a suitably sized stone. He had a good reason for this apparently strange act. Etienne had spent part of his youth in a small Hampshire village where his family had lived after being taken in by a cousin married to the lord of the local manor. They had had to flee France during the terror following the French Revolution and had been lucky to have a helpful relative in England.

While in England, Etienne had developed a passion for the strange English game of cricket. The emigré had, indeed, become a very effective bowler. Now he would substitute the stone for the cricket ball and Spanish soldiers for wickets.

"I'll take out the lead soldier," he whispered to the others. "Then each of us can take one of the others. Use your knives. We want no further noise, if possible."

The Spanish soldiers were approaching. Through the bush that he was hiding behind, Etienne could see that they were in single-file, all looking closely to see if they could spot anything. The lead one stopped and held up his hand for the others to gather, where he pointed to something on the beach. He must have spotted the wet tracks that Etienne and his men had left as they scurried for hiding.

"Mire este!" the leading Spaniard called to the others. Etienne had no idea how to translate the words, but their implication was clear. He could wait no longer. He stepped from behind the bush where he had been hiding and threw the rock at the Spaniard's head. His aim was true: the rock hit the soldier in the head with a solid thump. The man collapsed immediately.

Etienne took no time to admire his success. "Attack!" he roared and sprang at the next soldier in line, drawing his knife as he went. He stabbed the startled man in the throat, producing a torrent of blood, much of which splashed in his face. Wiping his eyes with the still soaking sleeve of his jacket, he looked to see how the others had done. They had been equally ruthless with their soldiers, who were all lying dead on the ground with their throats slit. Etienne turned to finish the man he had stunned with a rock. It wasn't necessary. There was enough light to show a big dent in the man's head, and a quick check revealed that he had no pulse. While he was doing so, his two companions were rifling through the pockets of the dead Spaniards. It was inevitable, of course, especially when these two sailors had been chosen for their ruthlessness. They were only in the navy because their sentences to hang for armed theft had been commuted to service in the Royal Navy.

"We must get away from here as quickly as possible," Etienne told the other men. "These people will be missed, and it will not go well for us if we are caught."

The lieutenant had noticed what looked like a small fishing village that they had rowed by just before they came to the fort. If they could get there before the alarm was raised, they might be able to steal a boat in which to escape. However, to do so, they would first have to go around the fortress. Heading off into the interior did not strike him as a good idea, however. The moon was fast disappearing in the west. It would be all too easy to get turned around if they simply plunged into the forest that came down to the shore here. However, a moment's thought persuaded him that there must be a path from the beach to the gates of the fortress for the soldiers to have arrived so promptly at the shore after hearing the noise marking the destruction of their boat.

Etienne's had no trouble finding the path along the side of the fortress. The three men stumbled up the narrow track and arrived at the corner of the outer wall. Here there was a better path leading to what Etienne supposed must be the main gate. No one challenged them as they moved along, keeping as close as they could to the walls of the fortress. From above them, on the ramparts, they did not hear any noises indicating that the walls were patrolled. That surprised Etienne. With British warships lurking offshore, he would have expected more careful guarding of the stronghold. After all, British sailors were known to raid enemy fortifications from the sea.

The road beyond the main gate of the fortress was much better than the path that Etienne's group had been using. It soon joined an even better road that promised to run along the edge of the inlet in the direction of Ferrol, though it could not be a direct route to the town since there was an arm of the inlet between them and the port. As the road passed the fortress, it curved a bit to be near the edge of the cliffs that characterized this small bit of the coast, but, before long, they reached a place where it swerved inland. There they found a cart track that led towards the water. As Etienne had hoped, this track proceeded down to the beach where the small fishing village was. He was afraid that some people might be about who would prevent their stealing a boat, but the only thing to do was investigate.

They descended the track cautiously, prepared to slip into the bushes that lined their route at any sign of anyone else being nearby. The track didn't actually go to the beach; instead, it went behind some modest huts that faced the inlet. Some of them showed lights through cracks in their shutters. Etienne and his men crept past all the huts and then turned right to go along the side of the last one. When they reached the beach, they found several dinghies pulled up above the high water line, while some bigger craft were in the water moored to buoys.

In the dark, there was no time to select the best of the dinghies. The one nearest to where the group from *Glaucus* had emerged onto the beach was the best one, especially as there were no more boats further along the beach away from the huts. The moon was setting, but it still gave enough light for Etienne to see that there were two sets of oars in the boat. Gesturing to his men to take the two stern corners of the boat, Etienne positioned himself at the bow and signaled that they should slide the boat to the water. At first, when the boat was still above the high water mark, it was heavy going because the boat was putting up substantial resistance to being shoved over the rocky beach. However, when they got to where the last tide had come, the shingle of the beach became slimy, and the boat skidded along easily. In minutes it was floating.

The three men scrambled in, with Mr. Macreau taking a position in the stern while the others grabbed oars to pole the boat into deeper water. Then they put the oars onto the thole pins and started to row back to where their previous craft had gone aground. This time, however, Etienne stayed much farther away from the shore as they passed the fortress. It would be bad luck if they were spotted from the ramparts, but not as bad as if they hit another rock. As they went by the fortress, Etienne saw several torches on the firing platform and a couple down on the beach. No doubt, the soldiers they had killed had been found, and a lively discussion about the situation was in progress.

The moon had set. The current was running even faster than it had been the last time they had come this way. A lot of flotsam was moving seaward around them. Etienne ordered the men to stop rowing and to turn their faces away from the fort. Hopefully, the torchlight would weaken the ability of anyone looking from the fortress to spot them, or, at least, it might make the Spaniards mistake them for just some innocent debris floating out on the tide. There was no shout from the ramparts to suggest they had been spotted. Once they were well past the fortress, Etienne ordered that the rowing resume.

The activities involved in getting away from the fortress had helped somewhat in drying out their clothes, but they were still damp. Etienne realized that he would be wise to rotate the rowers and take his turn at the oars. Roughly every quarter of an hour, they did this. As a result, they kept up a rapid pace, though after having switched places a dozen times, they were all getting exhausted. The current that had been aiding their progress was slackening, judging by how fast the dim outline of the shore seemed to be changing.

Although they were now nearing the entrance to the inlet, they could not rest on their oars, though they did not have to work quite as hard. Unfortunately, the tide had turned. Before long, they would have to fight the flood tide. Mr. Brooks had told Etienne that the current in Ferrol tended to be stronger when the tide was ebbing than when it was rising. Something to do with the large amounts of water coming into the inlet from rivers flooding with the winter rains. Even so, if they rested on their oars now, they would lose part of the progress they had made, and it would be more difficult for *Glaucus* to pick them up. Etienne was confident that dawn would find *Glaucus* in sight, ready to rescue them.

Their rowing slowed. The man who was not at the oars fell asleep. They were hardly holding their place against the current. The sky in the southeast started to lighten. Out to sea, the brightening sky revealed the outlines of a frigate. They could recognize that outline anywhere: *Glaucus* was at hand. As they watched, she reset her mainsail, which had been backed to hold her in position, and adjusted the other sails. The light wind carried her to them.

Chapter V

The coach lurched as one of the wheels dropped into a pothole. Despite its being a new traveling coach of the latest and most expensive character, the four occupants were jostled together. Daphne could only hope that the footmen had been able to hang on outside. All they needed after the long day was to have to stop and attend to an injured servant. Luckily, no one outside had fallen off. The coach continued on, swaying alarmingly at times.

"It won't be long now, mama," Daphne said to Lady Clara. Only recently had she started to call Lady Clara 'mama,' which sounded much better than 'mama-in-law.' "It won't be long now. That was the last posting-inn, and we left there over an hour ago. We'll soon be in Cambridge, and we will spend a day there before proceeding to Norwich."

They had been traveling since before sunup. The weather had been foul all the way, while the lengthy rainy period, which they had been enduring for weeks it seemed, had left the turnpikes in less than pristine condition. Now the daylight had been gone for some time, and the journey seemed endless. They had exhausted all subjects of conversation hours ago. While

Lady Clara had been able to sleep despite the motion of the carriage, Daphne had not.

Daphne had been busy since she had testified in the Old Bailey. She had made a rushed trip to Dipton because she had to pick up Lady Clara for the trip to Norfolk and because she wanted to see her children. She knew that most of the nobility would think nothing of leaving their children to be taken care of by their servants while they were away for long periods, but Daphne was not comfortable about doing so. It turned out that the best roads to get from Dipton to Norfolk ran through London so that they had broken their journey for a couple of nights with Lady Struthers. That break had made the journey to Norfolk seem entirely worthwhile to Daphne.

Lady Struthers had two main passions in life besides attendance at court. One was musical concerts, and the other was learned lectures. On the second night that Daphne and Lady Clara were staying in London, a mathematician was giving a talk on recent advances in geometry at one of the lecture series to which Lady Struthers subscribed. Daphne was self-taught in geometry, having no formal training in the subject. She had come upon a translation of Euclid's treatise on geometry in her father's library. The book had engaged her interest though it had never been read since she had to cut the pages. Daphne had found the step-by-step, rigorous nature of the demonstrations of propositions fascinating, as was the way that the establishment of one proposition often built on earlier ones. Her interest in mathematics had lain dormant since she had married Giles. Daphne asked to join her mother-in-law in going to the lecture when Lady Struthers mentioned the subject. Unlike Lady Struthers, who cited the topic as a reason for her not to attend that evening, Daphne very much wanted to hear a lecture on mathematics. Lady Clara begged off, claiming fatigue, although the real reason was complete disinterest in mathematical matters. Nevertheless, Daphne decided to go by herself.

The lecture was on a method recently developed by the French mathematician Legendre for rigorously analyzing the connection between two related sets of measurement. The lecturer called the technique 'least-squares.' Daphne wasn't sure that she understood all the steps in the proofs but thought she could work them out later at home, and she felt that she might have a use for what she had learned as a way for summarizing the results of some of the changes that she had initiated in the fields at Dipton. After the lecture finished, Daphne asked a few questions of the lecturer, who promptly encouraged her to take an interest in one of the mathematical societies. Daphne was flattered by the indication that the mathematician thought that she would benefit from such activities. She said that she would consider doing so when she was in London.

The invitation opened Daphne's eyes to further benefits of living in London that were not available in Dipton. She didn't mind that the rather condescending tone of the mathematician made her suspect that he was as interested in getting a noble patron for his club as in recognizing her mathematical abilities, but that didn't matter. She knew she had a head for mathematics. She would enjoy learning more, and she was sure she could do so readily, even if everyone presumed that, at most, women could only dabble ineffectively in serious matters. She had plenty of time on her hands in the evenings when Giles was away, especially in winter, when neighbors' visits were rare, and she no longer had Giles's half-sister and nieces staying with her at Dipton Hall, which had necessitated social times after dinner. Running over in her mind some of the thoughts inspired by the lecture made the time pass more quickly as they neared Cambridge at the end of the long, tedious day.

Daphne had not done much traveling before this trip. Birmingham and London were the only cities with which she had any acquaintance since her forays to Portsmouth and Chatham with Giles had involved no exploration of the towns. She was looking forward to seeing Cambridge and Norwich on this trip.

All her life Daphne had heard about the universities and the cities in which they were located. Many of the young men she had met were students at these places of learning. Her father had been at Oxford and, as Daphne had learned recently, was typical of graduates of that institution in looking down his nose at Cambridge, which he believed to be inferior. However, she now realized that that was largely prejudice. Lord Struthers had been at St. John's College in Cambridge and was convinced that Cambridge was infinitely superior to Oxford. Lord Struthers had also claimed that the town was full of interesting sites to explore, waxing quite poetic about the beauties of the place, though he confessed that, as a woman, the colleges might be closed to her. Daphne had a whole day to get a taste of the university town and hoped to make the most of it.

Any anxiety about where to stay in Cambridge or the reception she might encounter had been set aside by Lady Struthers's arranging for a groom to go ahead to arrange for accommodations at the Sun Inn. Lady Struthers had said that that hostelry had the best reputation in the town. It was in Trinity Street, very close to her husband's old college, a virtue that Lady Struthers clearly thought was important.

When the carriage finally clattered into its yard, the Inn was indeed warm and welcoming, though exhibiting what Daphne thought was most overdone servility over the arrival of a countess and a dowager countess. The rooms were comfortable, and the separate dining room and parlor which were provided were warm and brightly illuminated. The meal that was served had several removes*, and the wine was of high quality. However, Daphne and her mother-in-law did not linger over the meal, and when they ascended to their rooms, they found that the beds had proper warming pans placed in them.

Daphne dismissed Betsey quickly and could only stay awake long enough to pen a short letter to Giles. Being in Cambridge made her wonder if he would have liked to study there or at Oxford instead of picking up most of his education as a midshipman on vessels in active duty. How much richer would his life have been if her husband had enjoyed serious study instead of the rather helter-skelter education directed by the captain and the master of whatever ship he was in? She gathered that his formal shipboard studies had concentrated primarily on navigation and the mathematics needed for that purpose, taught as standard rules whose basis in a wider area of mathematics he had only learned later from Daphne. Geography had, of course, been learned as much from observation and the tales of shipmates as by any systematic study.

Giles, however, did not seem to be much more ignorant than many of the university graduates she had sat next to at dinner; a university education did not guarantee table conversation that was based on reading or keen observation of anything around them. Her husband could certainly hold his own with any of them. Well, she looked forward to seeing many of the town's features tomorrow, even though, as a woman, she would never have been allowed to participate in its intellectual endeavors.

The following day was sunny, with only puddles to remind one of the foul weather of the day before. Daphne and Lady Clara ventured out of the Sun to explore a bit of the town, with their maids trailing along behind them, together with a guide that they had hired to explain to them what they were to see. The guide was a young gentleman, Mister Forsythe, who revealed, when Daphne questioned him, that he had been a student at Queen's College. He had not found satisfactory employment when he left. As a third son, he could expect nothing from his father. He was acting as a guide until something better turned up. He had no wish to be someone's curate, and the chance of getting a living if he was ordained was non-existent.

They emerged from the Sun Inn into a narrow street, with some shops in it. Across the street was a gatehouse and the east end of a church with a large gothic window. Many young men were walking quickly, or even running down the street while others were strolling. They all wore open, black gowns about knee length that flapped about as they moved. Mr. Forsythe stated that gowns were required of University members, with the gowns revealing to the initiated which college the man belonged since each college's gown was made with subtly different patterns that were unique to each college.

"That chap is from Jesus, and the one behind him is from Trinity Hall," the guide stated, though he did not indicate what aspects of the gowns provided the information.

"That is Trinity Collge Gatehouse and Chapel," announced Mr. Forsythe, pointing across the street. "Trinity is the largest of the colleges. You should not confuse it with Trinity Hall, which is nearby and is very much smaller. Sir Isaac Newton used to have his rooms in that tower. Of course, I cannot take you into the college."

"Is St. John's College near here?" asked Lady Clara. "My sister's husband was a student there."

"Yes, it is just down the road. You can see its gate over there. My tour will come back that way after seeing some of the more important places," replied Mr. Forsythe.

They turned left to proceed along the narrow street. The party had not got very far, with Mr. Forsythe explaining that they were passing the side of a college called 'Gonville and Keys,' though the second half of the name was not spelled as it sounded, when they came to the corner of the street where there was a bookshop. Mr.

Forsythe stated that it had been there since very early times, but what interested Daphne was that it must have volumes on agriculture that were unfamiliar to her. Nothing would do but that they go in, despite Lady Clara's indication that nothing could interest her less.

Unfortunately for Daphne's explorations of the available titles, they were met at the door by a shop attendant, who did not seem to be very happy to see them, even when Mr. Forsythe happened to use the ladies' full titles. He insisted on accompanying them as they explored the shop, keeping up an annoying commentary on the books and regularly stating that they had only a very small collection of novels or other frivolities that the ladies might like. His annoying patter didn't deter Daphne — she proceeded to examine books that interested her and soon had selected three.

"What do you have on mathematics," Daphne asked the hovering shopman, whose arms were full with the three heavy tomes she had already chosen, even though they had yet to be bound with proper covers. He led her over to another section of the shop, where a rather rotund older gentleman was perusing the shelves. The stranger was also wearing one of the ubiquitous open black gowns, though one of greater length than the ones the students had been wearing. He looked up when Daphne appeared with her companions.

"Forsythe!" he exclaimed. "What are you doing here. I thought we sent you down."

"Professor Milner, you did, but I am now acting as a guide."

"To these two ladies?"

"Yes, sir. Lady Daphne Giles, Countess of Camshire, and Lady Clara Giles, Dowager Countess of Camshire, may I introduce Professor Milner, the University Professor of Mathematics."

"I am honored to meet such distinguished ladies, but I am surprised to find you in the mathematics section of this bookstore."

Daphne explained how she had been at the mathematics lecture recently, was intrigued by the lecture's subject, and was hoping to find suitable books so that she could learn more about the subject. This revelation led to a discussion of the proposed method of summarizing the relationship between different measurements. Professor Milner's attitude changed from the rather condescending tone with which he had greeted the ladies to serious discussion of the problem.

"I must say, I am amazed to find by chance a lady so able in mathematics. I thought I knew all the lady mathematicians in England."

"Oh, I would not call myself a mathematician, Professor Milner," Daphne replied. "I have had very little systematic training in the subject, though I have worked my way through Euclid. In fact, that is why I am in this section to see if I could find some books so that I could have a better understanding of the subject."

"Let's see what they have. Yes, here is one that would be relevant. It is on the calculus covering the subject rigorously from the beginning. With your knowledge of Euclid, a rare understanding these days, I must say, you should have no difficulty following the arguments in the book."

Professor Milner quickly chose two other volumes that he thought that Daphne might like. "I warn you, these books are not easy reading, my lady, not like novels that ladies seem to enjoy so much," he declared.

Before Daphne could comment on this remark, Lady Clara replied to it. "I am the one who is partial to novels, Professor. Lady Daphne likes more serious books. She has just purchased a couple of works on agronomy."

"I apologize for any hint of condescension, my lady. It is, however, rare to find a woman, and a countess at that, who is interested in mathematics and who has such perceptive insights. Now, if you wish, I would enjoy showing you my college, from which I am afraid Mr. Forsythe is banished."

Mr. Forsythe was also dismissed from further guiding of the ladies. Professor Milner led them down the street, which they had already been following, pointing out many features, mostly connected with various colleges or the University. Then they turned into a large towered gatehouse, similar to the one they had seen at Trinity College and that both ladies had seen at St. James's Palace. It turned out that Professor Milner was also the president of this college, so that he could show them all its interesting buildings from the inside as well as the outside.

Following a dish of tea in the President's Lodge, Professor Milner took them over a curious wooden bridge into meadows on the other side of the river from the colleges, and they strolled along with a series of views of several different colleges. Lady Clara was charmed by the various sites and the bits of information about them that Professor Milner imparted. Daphne was more excited by what they discussed in terms of mathematics. The man was a born teacher, and she learned as much from her questioning him about what she had gleaned from the lecture as she had from the lecture itself. Their walk took them slowly along the river until they reached another bridge, over which the professor led them, saying that it entered Trinity College. After passing through two striking, but quite different, courts and the impressive gatehouse of the college, they found themselves back at the Sun Inn.

Professor Milner then excused himself, saying, "I would ask you ladies to dine, but, unfortunately, my college is holding a feast tonight, and I have to be in Hall for it."

Instead of going into the inn, Lady Clara suggested that they head up the street to the next college, St. John's. At the gatehouse there, she explained that her brother-in-law had been an undergraduate at the college and that they would like to see the college buildings.

"What is your relative's name, madam?" the porter asked.

"Ian Gillespie."

"Of course, Lord Struthers. A very distinguished graduate of this college."

The porter then hailed a man whose long black gown indicated that he was a fellow of the college rather than a student. " Dr. Fell, this is Lady Clara, the Dowager Countess of Camshire, and her daughter-in-law, Lady Daphne, the Countess of Camshire. Lady

Clara is the sister-in-law of Lord Struthers, who was an undergraduate here before your time. They would like to be shown around the college. Could you do it?"

"Of course, I'd be delighted to. Ladies, please come this way through the gatehouse into the first court, which we call, rather unimaginatively, 'First Court.'"

Dr. Fell was not the best of guides and seemed rather awed by being in the presence of two countesses, but he did show them as much of the college as they wanted. It was only when they were returning to the Sun Inn that Daphne expressed her amazement at having two of the scholarly dons being so willing to act as their guides.

Lady Clara laughed and said, "You will have to get used to it, Daphne. All sorts of institutions are shamelessly on the lookout for additions to their endowments. Colleges like this one keep track of who has graduated from them and done well, and they are always on the lookout for chances to make a good impression. Don't be surprised if Professor Milner or someone from his college should happen to solicit funds from Richard, and you can expect St. John's College to do the same. You'll just have to get accustomed to it and take advantage of their willingness to be of help."

That night in her letter to Giles, Daphne told him a great deal about what she had seen. She waxed enthusiastic about the possibility that their son, Bernard, might attend Cambridge when the time arrived. What would his character be like, she wondered? Would he be better off at a large college like Trinity or at one of the smaller ones? Implicitly, she presumed that her son could study wherever he wanted. She remembered to add that, of course, it would be up to Giles to decide which University his son should attend, and it would also be up to her husband to pick the college. Though she wrote that proviso in her letter, Daphne had no doubt that she would influence the choice when the time came, possibly even determine it.

Chapter VI

The two Ladies Camshire departed the next day for Norwich. The weather now was fine, and they bowled along the turnpike much more comfortably than on their trip to Cambridge. Daphne was fascinated by the flat country they passed through, which was so different from the hilly land around Dipton. Enclosure of farming land was almost complete here, so there were many small fields separated by hedgerows. Even in winter, she could see evidence of how they were used for different crops. Many of them had cattle or sheep grazing in them. While the fields looked much like many that she was familiar with, there were subtle differences. Was that because best agricultural practice differed on different soils, or was it that tradition arbitrarily dictated what was grown? Maybe her books on agronomy would enlighten her on the reasons for them.

Night had fallen before Daphne and her mother-in-law reached Norwich. The carriage turned into a busy coaching inn on the market square where their local solicitor, Mr. Chapman, had made all arrangements for their arrival and stay. A splendid dinner was soon laid on for them in a private dining room. The ladies retired early, wanting a good night's sleep before the exertions of the morrow.

Mr. Chapman turned out to be a rotund man of middle age, notable for the red nose of a frequent drinker. He met with Daphne and Lady Clara in a parlor set aside for their use while staying at the inn. After introducing himself and exchanging the usual, empty initial conversation, he turned to business.

"Ladies, I have received the writ for the eviction from the local magistrates, even though we have yet to receive in full the probate results from the Diocesan Court of Canterbury. I am afraid that the officials had little respect for the late Earl and had no objection to evicting his concubine from the property. I have arranged for the parish constable to meet us at the drive to the house at one o'clock, together with several bailiffs I have hired. Also, Captain Snodgravel has his militia company bivouacking in one of the fields — your fields — near the drive.

"I hope it all goes smoothly, but there may be some trouble."

"Oh?" Daphne asked.

"Yes. There are two sources of possible difficulty. The first is that Mistress Cogswell has taken a new lover who spends all his time at Gracy Grange — that is the name of the house she is occupying. The second is a dispute over who actually controls the property. That is somewhat complicated, but if you wish, my lady, I can tell you the essence of it now."

"Yes, please, Mr. Chapman."

"Sir Thomas Hitchens has a small estate near here. He is an excellent agriculturist whose property is too small to give much of a return or to benefit fully from more modern farming techniques. Sir Thomas's lands adjoin Gracy Grange, whose lands are more extensive. For years the previous owner of Gracy Grange had put no money into maintaining the property, so it was almost worthless when the late Earl purchased it. He paid almost nothing for it and was able to borrow from several institutions, mainly based on the acreage of his acquisition. I imagine that the lenders expected him to spend the money on improving the yields of the properties. However, the Earl then spent no money on the fields. The late Lord Camshire did, however, spruce up the residence and installed Mrs. Cogswell in it. He next turned around and leased the property to Sir Thomas, but not in the usual form. What he did was sell Sir Thomas a ninety-nine-year lease on the land, including the house, with the proviso that the Earl could use the residence and the land immediately around it until the Earl died, in which case it was to revert to Sir Thomas's control. The unusual thing was that the rent on the property was prepaid, and there would be no additional amounts required until the lease expired. I suspect, Lady Clara, that you will be delighted to know that your late husband has treated Mrs. Cogswell even more shabbily than he has you since she thought that she was to inherit the property on his death, or at least the part that contains the house."

"So, are you saying, Mr. Chapman, that while my husband may now own the property, effectively, it is completely controlled by this Sir Thomas Hitchens?" asked Daphne.

"No, that is not quite the end of the complications, which now swing in your favor. You see, because the land is entailed to be passed to your husband, Lady Camshire, the late Earl could not grant a ninety-nine-year lease for it to anyone. Any lease that was made would have to terminate either when the period was up or when the late Earl died, whichever came first. Despite there appearing to be ninety-five years still to run on the lease, it ceased to exist the minute your husband died, Lady Clara. So, legally, the whole property now belongs to the Earl of Camshire free and clear — and so, Lady Daphne, you have control of all decisions that have to be made about it until Captain Giles returns. And you, Lady Clara, get six shillings eight pence in the pound of any net income that it generates."

"So, what is the other problem?" asked Lady Clara.

"No sooner had the late Earl died than Mistress Cogswell, as might be expected from her profession, took up with a very rich factory-owner in Norwich, a Mr. Herbert Jarred. He moved into Gracy Grange with Mistress Cogswell, who is now his — ah — concubine. She and he thought that the Earl had promised her the property in his will, as indeed he did, even though it was not his to dispose of as he saw fit. The property in question is the same residence at Gracey Grange that the Earl of Camshire said would be included in the ninety-nine-year lease of the property on his death. So Mr. Jarred believes that his concubine owns the house in which he receives her favors while Sir Thomas Hitchens believes he has an equally strong commitment, in writing no less, that he would have the use of the place for a very extended period. In law, neither of them has a valid claim, but neither recognizes that fact at present.

"With the will so in variance with the entails that are registered against the properties, the two local gentlemen involved – and their tenants – feel that they have been cheated and that the law is being used to steal from them. I must say that I am sympathetic to their claims, the late Earl was certainly dealing with each of them in bad faith, but the law is clear. The land is your husband's property unquestionably, freehold, Lady Camshire. Both the will, in this instance, and the leases are invalid. Neither of the parties is happy about your taking over the property, and they are prepared to try to prevent it, using their laborers and other tenants rather than the law. So I am glad that we have the militia backing us up. We may be in for a nasty confrontation when we try to claim the property. Are you sure, ladies, in light of these developments, that you want to witness the eviction of Mistress Cogswell?"

"Yes, I do," said Lady Clara. "I want to call out this hussy and let her know who is behind having her thrown out of the house and, quite frankly, gloat that things are no longer going her way."

"As you wish, my lady. I am also rather looking forward to this," the solicitor replied, much to Daphne's surprise. Mr. Chapman had not struck her as a belligerent person.

They set off in Daphne's carriage, with fresh horses supplied by the posting inn. They pulled up at the drive to Gracy Grange sometime before one o'clock. Mr. Chapman's dozen men were waiting on the side of the road at the entrance to the property, which was marked by an open wrought-iron gate. On the field just inside the gate, a militia company was bivouacked, with a sergeant drilling the soldiers in a space that they had left free of tents. The officer in charge was on horseback and rode over to Daphne's carriage when he saw it arrive.

"Captain Nathaniel Snodgravel of the Wiltshire Militia at your service, my lady."

"Thank you for coming, Captain Snodgravel," Daphne replied. "I am very relieved to see you and your men here. Tell me. What is the situation?"

"Well, my lady, it is a bit complicated. Two groups oppose your taking possession of your property. The first supports Mistress Cogswell, who claims that the late Earl of Camshire left her the property in his will and had long promised it to her for the services she rendered him. I am afraid, my lady, that those services were of a most improper nature."

Much to Daphne's surprise, for she had presumed that little could shock a military officer, Captain Snodgravel blushed bright red while blurting out the last sentence.

"You need not be concerned, Captain," said Lady Clara. "I have long known the disgraceful role that strumpet played in my late husband's life."

"Mrs. Cogswell claims that the property was left to her in the late Earl's will. Is that correct, Mr. Chapman?" asked the militia officer.

"No, sir. The land was entailed, and the entail prohibited the Earl from bequeathing it to anyone. It would pass automatically to his closest legitimate male relative, in this case, the present Earl of Camshire. Mrs. Cogswell has no standing."

"I am afraid that she is not taking this ruling lying down. Her present lover, a Mr. Jarred, claims that the late Earl had given the property to Mrs. Cogswell, and so it hers. That commitment, he claims, predates the lease given to Sir Thomas Hitchens. Mr. Jarred is no gentleman, but he has assembled a group of his quarry workers to enforce his concubine's claims. There is another group near the house, led by Sir Thomas, mainly farm workers and tenants. Sir Thomas claims that by the terms of a lease he bought from the late Earl, the land is his to farm or use in any other way he wants for the next hundred years. I presume that that claim is also invalid, Mr. Chapman?"

"Yes, it certainly is, in law. As you know, the land is entailed, and it could not be rented out except on a fee-simple basis that would terminate on the death of the late Earl. Sir Thomas also has no claim on the land."

"That is what my uncle indicated, Mr. Chapman. So do you have your bailiffs and the writ you want to be enforced?"

"Yes. Since we are all here, I will endeavor to serve it now."

"Good. As you know, I can't intervene until they refuse to accept the writ or refuse to comply with it. I will form up my company so that we are ready to intervene if necessary."

"Very good, Captain Snodgravel," said the lawyer. "My ladies, I will walk down the avenue with the bailiffs I have hired to enforce the orders. You may find it safer to follow in your carriage at some distance in case things turn nasty. Tell your coachman to turn around if there is any trouble."

Mr. Chapman and his bailiffs set off along the drive towards the residence and the two groups of hostile men. Daphne and Lady Clara got into the carriage, which proceeded at walking pace behind the solicitor and his assistants. As they neared the Gracy Grange mansion, they heard a loud, verbal dispute break out between two groups on opposite sides of the drive.

"Get the blazes out of my house, you whoremonger, and take your doxy with you." A man, well-dressed in the country fashion, bellowed across the roadway. Daphne presumed that he was Sir Thomas Hitchens.

"You sniveling piece of pig-dung, get off Mrs. Cogswell's land," a rotund man on the other side of the drive yelled back. He must be Mr. Jarred since behind him stood a middle-aged woman in a day gown that indicated that she was no maid or working woman. Daphne presumed that this must be Mrs. Cogswell, even though she had a hard time seeing her as an alluring or exotic courtesan.

"It's not her land, you miserable molly-boy," Sir Thomas shouted back. The Earl rented it to me, and he kept the mansion only during his lifetime. He's dead, so you are trespassing."

"The devil I am. Mrs. Cogswell had a document signed by the Earl that transferred the land to her on his death. Made proper, signed, and witnessed proper before he died."

"Made it yourself, did you, you whoreson? What makes you think you can move with your whore into a property fit only for a gentleman? Get out now!"

"I'd like to see you make me. You are the one who has to get off my land, you clodhopper."

"Clodhopper, am I? Well, here's a clod to send you on your way, you muffdiver."

With that, the squire picked up a clod of earth and hurled it across the driveway. His supporters followed suit, pelting their opponents with mud balls. It didn't take long for the men on the other side to retaliate. However, instead of mud-balls, they picked up rocks. Their response was initiated by Mr. Jarred, who threw the first stone.

Mr. Chapman and his bailiffs halted as missiles hurtled between the two sides. Shouted orders came from behind the carriage in which Daphne and Lady Clara rode, and in moments soldiers ran by each side of the carriage. The rocks and clods of earth continued to be heaved across the road. One stone hit Sir Thomas on the head; down he went unconscious, collapsing like a rag doll.

Captain Snodgravel rode his horse past the carriage to join his men and bellowed, "Wiltshire men, halt. Aim above their heads. Fire!"

The muskets crashed out in a ragged fusillade. The opposing men stopped hurling missiles at each other as they turned to see who was attacking. Captain Snodgrass wasted no time in shouting to his men, "Fix your bayonets and advance."

The two fighting groups did not wait to discover whether the militiamen would use their weapons. On both sides of the driveway, the combatants turned and ran. It was one thing to support your employer in a dispute with another who was infringing on his property; it was quite a different matter to be shot by the militiamen or, worse still, hanged for insurrection. The only people left on the battlefield were the fallen Sir Thomas on one side of the drive, and the couple who, Daphne figured, must be Mistress Coswell and her lover. That pair were standing staring at the militia company, apparently not knowing what they should do next.

Mr. Chapman resumed his march towards the mansion with Daphne's carriage following. Captain Snodgravel ordered his men to form up in parade-ground fashion and stand easy, though he did dispatch a sergeant with two privates to examine Sir Thomas.

The lawyer came up with Mistress Cogswell and pulled out a paper with seals dangling from it.

"Rosalie Cogswell, I am here to enforce a writ of the magistrates of Norfolk requiring you to vacate these premises in compliance with the ruling of the Diocesan Court of Canterbury. The writ requires you to leave immediately, taking only your personal effects since it is presumed that everything in these premises belonged to the late Earl of Camshire and therefore are now the possessions of the present Earl of Camshire."

"You can't do that," protested Mr. Jarred. "Mrs. Cogswell has a lease that I obtained from the late Earl for these premises."

"Your 'lease' ended with the death of the Earl. It is now the property of the present Earl," declared Mr. Chapman. "Since the late Earl had only a lifetime interest in the property, your lease no longer applies. The present Earl has no desire to rent to you or to your fancy woman.

"Mistress Cogswell, you may take only your personal items from the house and things that you can prove belong to you. Mr. Taker and Mr. Snatch, the bailiffs, will help you select your items. That cart brought by the rioters who have disappeared can be used to transport whatever you may have.

"Mr. Jarred, you have no longer any business here. I order you to vacate the lands of Gracy Grange immediately."

"Not so fast, Mr. Chapman," intervened Captain Snodgravel. "Sergeant Shorthouse has reported to me that Sir Thomas is dead. Since, Mr. Jarred, you are the person who threw the first stone, a lethal weapon as the scripture indicates, and you were also participating in a riot, you must be bound over for trial at the next assizes on charges of murder and inciting a riot. Sergeant Shorthouse, take your platoon to the gaol in Norwich with Mr. Jarred on charges of manslaughter and inciting a riot. Tell them that I will be along later to validate the arrest and charges.

"Sergeant Underhill, please arrange for Sir Thomas's body to be transported to his residence. Lieutenant Stockly, the company will now return to our camp. See to it."

As his underlings hastened to carry out his orders, Captain Snodgravel turned to Daphne and Lady Clara. "My ladies," he said, "I trust that that has resolved any difficulties you might have encountered in establishing your right to this property."

"Thank you, Captain," replied Daphne. "Your aid and that of your men have been invaluable. If you are free tonight, I hope you will dine with us at the inn in Norwich this evening and bring one of your lieutenants."

"I would be delighted, my lady."

"Good. Mr. Snodgravel, I trust that you will also dine with us."

"Gladly, my lady."

"If it is convenient for her, you may bring your wife as well."

"Thank you, my lady. I know that she will be delighted," the lawyer replied. "I believe, my ladies, that we are finished here. My men will supervise Mistress Cogswell's departure, and I will leave a couple of them to take care of the place until you decide what to do with it. You may wish to leave now."

"Daphne, I would like to stay to see that vulture depart," said Lady Clara. "It's the nearest I will ever get to revenge on her."

"And I am curious to find out what has been added to our properties," Daphne replied. "Let's take the carriage to the front door."

The carriage drew up in front of the entrance to the residence. It was a substantial building of a style that would have been in the latest fashion only forty years before. Daphne and her mother-in-law entered the mansion.

"This place is much better furnished and kept up than Ashbury Abbey," Lady Clara declared bitterly, referring to the major seat of the Earls of Camshire. "He had money to waste on his doxy but wouldn't do anything to maintain my home. That bloodsucker must have taken all the money he had not already wasted, and there must have been much more of it than he ever let me know. Now, at least, I can make sure that she doesn't abscond with anything that should have been mine."

Lady Clara took up a position at the bottom of the staircase. Before too long, two of the bailiffs came down the stairs with a large, heavy trunk.

"Show me what is in that trunk," Lady Clara ordered.

"It only contains some clothes," Mistress Cogswell protested.

"Open it anyway," Mr. Chapman commanded.

Lady Clara had her maid sort through the collection of ball gowns, day dresses, and other garments that filled the trunk. Nothing else was found. A second trunk was carried down by the bailiff, supervised by Mistress Cogswell. It was said to contain outer clothes and boots. The maid was able to find nothing amiss. Then came the third trunk.

"That's the last of them. Do you want to check it too? I saw it being filled, and it is full of women's private garments. Most embarrassing to watch it being filled, it was." One of the bailiffs who was carrying the load declared.

"I suppose not," Lady Clara instructed.

"Betsey," Daphne said at the same time, "Check that trunk very carefully."

Daphne's order was much more definite than Lady Clara's. The men put the trunk down and unfastened the lid. Betsey started to carefully remove the separate layers in which garments had been laid in the trunk. First came nightdresses, some very plain, some made of satiny materials with embroidery. These were followed by shifts; again, some were plain, and some were embroidered and enhanced with lace in ways that suggested they were meant to be seen. Several layers of stays* preceded ones of petticoats. These all took up somewhat over half the trunk.

At that point, the nature of the clothing changed. Now came much flimsier garments, that in Betsey's opinion, at least, would not provide much warmth and seemed to be quite indecent in how they might reveal glimpses of the body if they were not properly covered. Some were diaphanous or made out of lace alone with good-sized holes that would allow whatever was beneath to show clearly.

Lady Clara and Irene, her maid, looked at these items with curiosity and appeared to find them shocking even though they were not quite sure what they were. Daphne had no such problem. When Lady Clara wondered what they could possibly be used for, Daphne informed her mother-in-law that they were the stock-in-trade of the occupants of the better bordellos regularly visited by members of the gentry. Her feigned disgust at the garments suggested that she thought that only the most fallen of fallen women would wear such apparel, even though secretly she had already adopted similar, though much more finely made, apparel when Giles was home. She had discovered that he enjoyed finding her dressed in the most suggestive and titillating apparel. The problem of acquiring such shocking garments without her purchases being known to all the gossips in London Society was easily solved by using a seamstress who made the lingerie for the demi-monde. No respectable woman would venture into such a place, so her secret was safe since Betsey knew better than to gossip about what happened in her mistress's bedroom. Betsey feigned considerable embarrassment at being required to handle what her mistress had described as a whore's working garb but bravely continued the exploration of the trunk. She removed several layers of these strangely salacious garments before, at the bottom of the trunk, she found a large, elaborate jewel box.

"Open it, Betsey," commanded Daphne.

The maid complied. Inside was a jumble of jewelry. Necklaces, rings, earrings, broaches, even a tiara, studded with diamonds, emeralds, sapphires, pearls, and other gems.

"Those are mine," protested Mistress Cogswell angrily. "They were given me by Camshire and other gentlemen."

"Were they?" Mr. Chapman broke in. "Can you prove that they are yours? Letters, receipts, something that tells us that they do belong to you and not to the late Earl?"

"Of course not. One doesn't ask for a document giving transfer of gifts from one's admirers. Surely the fact that I have them shows that they are mine."

"But do you have the records, madam? The jewelry has been found in the late Earl's residence. They – and you – are not mentioned in his will. The presumption at law is that they belong to his estate or, in other words, to the present Earl of Camshire, whose power of attorney is held by the Countess of Camshire, who is present. The fact that you went to such lengths to hide the jewels in your trunk suggests that you knew that they did not belong to you. The chest in which they were found may also be presumed to be the property of the present earl. The other contents of this trunk would appear such that they can be considered to be your own, though I am not sure of the status of the unusual items that can only be considered to be tools of your trade. Do you think that we should retain them, Lady Camshire?"

"No," said Daphne. "I have no use for them, and I would not like to deprive Mistress Cogswell of the means with which she can earn her living by praying on the carnal wants of depraved gentlemen."

"Then, Mistress Cogswell, you may take the trunks but not the jewels. One of my men has brought a cart. He will be happy to transport your belongings to Norwich. For a fee, of course," said Mr. Chapman.

"One last thing, Mistress Cogswell," Daphne spoke up. "I will not need your servants. You may take them with you. I expect that you will have to pay them if you are not continuing to employ them. In any case, I expect them to be gone as soon as they gather their possessions. Mr. Chapman will, of course, check that they are taking nothing that does not belong to them."

"My lady," one of the men who was dressed as a butler, "none of us want to keep serving Mistress Cogswell. We would all rather have the money she has failed to pay us these last few weeks than continue to serve her. We only stayed because, if we left, we could not hope to get a character or a full settlement of what is owed us. In fact, we were paid by Lord Camshire – the late Lord Camshire – rather than by Mistress Cogswell when we were paid at all."

"I see. So your unpaid wages are a debt of Lady Clara's husband. Well, as representative of the Earl of Camshire, I will have your back wages paid," declared Daphne. "Indeed, until I know what we are going to do with this property, all of you can retain your positions."

"Thank you, my lady. We all appreciate your generosity."

"I believe that we have seen everything we need to here. Mr. Chapman, we will see you this evening."

In the carriage heading back to Norwich, Lady Clara remarked, "Daphne, that was a very satisfying visit, I must say. It may not be Christian to gloat, but I really enjoyed how you threw that hussy out of her house with hardly more than the clothes on her back. Especially as her new protector is likely to have to pursue whores as a convict in Australia if he isn't hanged. It was marvelous to find her jewel case and appropriate it. But why did you invite Mr. Chapman to dinner?"

"He and Captain Snodgravel have been very helpful to us. It is to encourage them to help us further that I invited them and Mr. Chapman's wife to dine with us. After the reputation that Camshire seems to have got for himself, the more we can get people to think that the present earl is quite different, the better. Not only do we need Mr. Chapman to be especially helpful and thoughtful, but we also want the word to spread about how different we are. I am sure that his wife will do that for us. Remember that we still have to deal with the properties and false leases that your husband granted. Mr. Chapman tells me that there are three other small properties in Norfolk, at least, that need to be dealt with, as well as other places. We may also find it useful to be able to call on the militia to deal with any situations resembling the one we just encountered. I suspect that your late husband's death has left many people so much in the lurch that we may find the militia useful to keep the peace."

"Are there really still other estates that Camshire acquired? I never heard of any properties he owned except for Ashbury Abbey, and Ashton Place, and, of course, Camshire House in London. Oh, and also Green's Club, which used to be our London House, and he said he couldn't sell it."

"I am not sure that anyone knew how he had been using land in his dubious money-making schemes for a long time," Daphne replied. "I am not entirely clear as to how it worked exactly, partly because, I suspect, the lawyers do not completely understand how he could get money from his purchase of properties. I think that somehow your husband bought run-down properties, then sold leases on them that extended long into the future, probably with some promise to share in needed improvements, and then borrowed even more money based on the supposed value of the leases. He then puechased new properties with the proceeds and so kept the process going. I don't fully understand it all, but I am sure it will come crashing down soon. In Giles's absence, I'll have to try to make sense of how to straighten it all out without it ruining us. That's one of the reasons for needing to cultivate a more favorable opinion of ourselves with the local gentry and professional people. A bit of goodwill may go a long way, I hope."

The dinner was a success. Daphne had no difficulty charming the lawyer and the militia officers, but Mrs. Chapman was more of a struggle. She was extremely diffident in the presence of two titled ladies. To Daphne's surprise, Lady Clara was able to unbend and get the woman to talk about her children and her hopes for them. The Chapmans had two sons and three daughters. Still, Mr. Chapman's success in his profession meant that his wife was sure that he would secure good articling positions for his sons in other solicitors' chambers and provide dowries such that her daughters could marry into at least the same level of society. Once the flood-gates had opened, Lady Clara only had to make brief comments to keep the flow of conversation going.

Lady Clara's success was confirmed as the guests left. By some oddity of the construction of the inn, Daphne and she could hear Mrs. Chapman's boisterous endorsement of the evening: "That Lady Clara is not at all what I expected. She is such a good listener and so sympathetic to my problems. Not treating us at all as if we were beneath her. And the Countess of Camshire seemed to be having very lively conversations with you two gentlemen."

Lady Clara raised an amused eyebrow to Daphne. "I see that you were right about the effect of asking them to dinner. I had never considered the use of being gracious to people of inferior rank to further our own ends. I also never thought about how they would feel about our making it clear where they actually stood."

Before going to bed, Daphne wrote her nightly letter to Giles detailing the events of the day. On business matters, she was careful to minimize the difficulties and to stress that she was sure that he would handle all these matters more effectively than she could if he were home. That led naturally to several paragraphs detailing how she missed him and hoped his cruise was going well. She did happen to mention the special garments that had been found in the trunk, commenting that they were far inferior to what he could expect her to be wearing when he got home..

Chapter VII

Giles returned to his cabin when *Santa Clarissa* vanished from sight. Was he doing the right thing sending Mr. Macreau to Ferrol? It was dangerous, all right. Was it worth risking his lieutenant? Yes, it was. Information about a major Spanish base, one which could not be assessed by ships at sea, was well worth having, quite apart from the question of whether the elusive Spanish treasure ship was in harbor. That consideration didn't stop Giles from going over and over again in his mind his order, even though he knew that the result would be the same if he had to make the decision again.

Glaucus's crew knew that their captain was troubled when the sounds of his violin started to escape from his cabin. He was playing the slow piece by that German composer whose name started with 'Beet,' so that's what they called the music he was playing. The crew preferred reels or gigs or something else that would get your toes tapping, but *Beet* was better than nothing.

Giles's letter to Daphne that night was longer than usual, for only there could he express his doubts about what he had decided to do. That job finished, he slept soundly until he was woken, as he had ordered, shortly before first light.

Giles dressed quickly, accepted a mug of coffee, which his servant had brewed, and went on deck. Mr.

Stewart was the officer of the watch, but Mr. Brooks was, in fact, sailing the frigate.

"Good morning, Captain," the Master greeted Giles. "I believe that we are roughly in the spot where you wished us to be, though it will take more light to verify our position. What little wind there is is blowing west-northwest. The mainsail is backed, and we are waiting for more light to tell us exactly where we are."

"Is there any sign of Mr. Macreau."

"No, sir. If he is wise, he will hug the coast until he can see out to sea."

"And there has been no sign of our other frigates?"

"No sir,"

As the darkness eased, Giles looked over the stern. "Ah," he said, "there is one reason why we have seen nothing of Captain Bush or Captain Bolton." A solid fog bank lay offshore a mile or so away.

"Captain," came a hail from the masthead, "there is a small boat close to the shore, ten points off the larboard bow."

Giles raised his telescope, lining it up in the indicated direction. Yes, there was a small dinghy, but it was not the one that *Santa Clarissa* had been towing when they had last seen her. Nevertheless, it was one they must go to since Mr. Macreau was slumped in the stern sheets*. Even as Giles watched his subordinate, the lieutenant caught sight of *Glaucus* and must have ordered his two seamen to start rowing. They took up the stroke, but it was clear that they were exhausted.

"Set the main," Giles bellowed. "Helmsman, course south by west. Mr. Stewart, make for that rowboat."

It seemed to take forever for the two vessels to close with each other in the very light breeze. Finally, the dinghy was alongside. The three men were helped onboard by eager hands. Giles was not the only one who had been worried about their shipmates venturing into an enemy stronghold.

Lieutenant Macreau reported to his captain. One look at him told Giles that he was freezing. His clothes had not dried fully, and his teeth were chattering uncontrollably.

"Get some dry clothes and warm food right now, Lieutenant Macreau," Giles ordered. "Your report can wait a while: there is nothing we can do immediately about what you have found out." A glance at the other men from the dinghy revealed that Carstairs had taken them in hand to get dry clothes and some food.

"Mr. Miller," the Captain called. "Those men deserve an extra tot. Right now."

The first lieutenant seemed displeased by the order, but he knew better than to argue with Giles when the captain adopted such a decided tone of voice. Instead, he ordered, rather sulkily, "Bosun, see to the Captain's orders."

Half an hour later, Etienne reported the Captain's cabin. Dry clothes and a hot meal featuring bacon and eggs, available because *Glaucus* had not been long from port, had done wonders to his appearance. Despite being up all night, Mr. Macreau appeared to be ready for anything. Giles reflected wryly for a moment on the resilience of youth, even though he was only seven years older than his subordinate. The Master was already in the cabin, having been asked by Giles to attend and to bring the chart of Ferrol harbor that he had copied from Admiralty sources before they sailed. It was a very up-to-date chart since it came from one of the Spanish ships captured at the Battle of Trafalgar. The chart had a notation that it had been updated from direct observation only a month before that disaster had befallen the Spanish.

"What have you discovered, Mr. Macreau?" Giles asked

Etienne recounted his adventures, starting when *Santa Clarissa* had turned eastward to enter Ferrol Inlet. Giles wanted details. Just what had Etienne observed about the fortifications? Exactly where were the naval ships anchored? How ready to sail did they seem? What about the merchant ships in the harbor? When Etienne finished, Giles reflected for a few minutes.

"So none of these ships looked like they could have made a recent crossing of the Atlantic?" he asked Etienne.

"No, sir. Though many had been at sea recently, none appeared to be large or strong enough to have survived a crossing from Havana. They did not look as if they had very worn or very new rigging."

"Well, that's disappointing, I suppose. We will, unfortunately, have to keep waiting for that supposed treasure ship to arrive, though I do wonder if there ever was one. Now, what about this new frigate you saw. You say that it is anchored here?" Giles pointed to a place on the chart.

"As near as I can figure on the basis of only sailing past her. I am sure that she was lying on a line between the headland over here and that church tower marked on the map as an important landmark. At least, I guess that is what I saw, though it doesn't look like the churches I have seen in England. But I can't be sure just how far along that line she lies. That is true of the rest of the ships as well. Their positions relative to that frigate and the town are, I think, about correct, but they may be closer or farther from the town than I placed them."

"I understand. Now, you only saw one man on board here?"

"Yes, sir. It surprised me since the ship looked ready to sail."

"Why do you think that, Mr. Macreau?"

"Well, sir. Her yards are crossed, and the sails furled on them. Her boats are stacked on deck, though one was in the water, trailing behind her on a painter. It's strange, though. I only saw one man aboard her. He was looking over the quarterdeck* rail, looking bored. Just a harbor watch, I would guess."

"I am also interested in that first ship-of-the-line you mentioned. You said that her yards were sent down, didn't you?"

"Yes, sir. And her topmasts."

"So, she is not ready to sail?"

" No, sir."

"Did you observe any crew members on board her?"

"Yes, sir. But not very many. Three or four sailors were lounging about, on the quarterdeck, sir, not forward. There was also one other man who looked like he might be a petty officer."

"But no officers?"

"No, sir."

When Giles and Mr. Brooks had finished asking about the ships in Ferrol Harbor, Giles enquired about the rest of Etienne's adventure. The two senior men listened in fascination as he outlined what had happened as he and his two seamen had got away from the port. The account was interrupted only once by Mr. Brooks.

"Where did you say this hidden rock was, Mr. Macreau?" the Master asked. "There is none marked on the chart."

"It was right about here, Mr. Brooks," Etienne answered.

"Good. The knowledge may never be any good to us, but I will mark it anyway. Thank you. What happened next?"

Etienne resumed his story and continued until he reached the point where *Glaucus* appeared in the dawn light.

"Now, Mr. Macreau," Giles said, "when you had to kill those soldiers – good thinking on your part, incidentally – did you happen to empty their pockets?

"Yes, sir, the men got everything of value from them, almost as soon as they killed them. I'm sorry about that, sir. It isn't the proper way to treat fallen enemies."

"Maybe not, Mr. Macreau, but I doubt that you could have stopped them. Anyway, I am glad they did. If you had left any valuables on their bodies, it would have been very suspicious. This way, they may well presume that it was brigands who assaulted their men. Even if they found your boat, it did not look like anything that a naval raid would use. I think it very unlikely that they will be watching out for us when we go to take that frigate of yours."

"Take the frigate, sir?" said Etienne in puzzlement.

"Yes, of course, Mr. Macreau, it is far too good a chance to ignore. We should be able to snag her and get her out of the harbor before the Spanish are much the wiser, and I would be surprised if any of their other ships are ready to sail immediately."

"Can I go on the cutting-out* expedition, sir?"

"I think you can. Right now, go and get some sleep. We'll meet at six bells of the afternoon watch in my cabin.

Etienne was the last officer to join the captain's meeting later in the day. He had slept solidly and was only late because the wardroom* steward had failed to wake him at the right time. He was fully rested and ready to participate in whatever the captain had in mind.

Giles opened the meeting as soon as Etienne had found a place.

"You all know that Mr. Macreau visited Ferrol yesterday. The chief purpose of his mission was to see if the Spanish treasure ship that we are awaiting had somehow snuck past us. He found no evidence that it had, so I am afraid we and the other two frigates will have to stay here for a while longer. In the course of his visit to the harbor, Mr. Macreau noted that there were several Spanish naval vessels in the port. He acquired valuable information about the Spanish strength there, which we will forward to the Admiralty at the first opportunity. However, that is not why we are meeting.

"One of those ships is a new frigate. It is lying closer to the mouth of Ferrol Inlet than any of the others. Mr. Brooks has brought a chart of the inlet. Mr. Macreau, please show us where the frigate is."

Etienne stepped forward and looked at the chart which the Master had spread out on Giles's table. Since he had already determined with Mr. Brooks where the Spanish ship lay at anchor, he had no hesitation at pointing to the place.

"It is about here, sir, but I am not sure of precisely where she is anchored.."

"And where is the Spanish ship that is nearest to her."

"That would be about here," the lieutenant replied. She is a ship-of-the-line but not ready for sea."

"Of course," Giles agreed. "I believe that that frigate would do better as part of our fleet than of the Spanish one. I intend to make that a reality tonight.

"It is a pity that the other frigates of our squadron have disappeared, so we can't call on them to help us. I will take all our boats. I'll have my barge. Mr. Miller and Mr. Macreau will be in charge of the other two boats. Mr. Stewart, you will be in command of *Glaucus* while we are gone. We will not be taking any marines, Mr. Macauley. We'll need all the sailors we can take in order to quickly set the sails or tow her out if there is no wind.

"Besides taking the frigate, we will try to board the ship-of-the-line and set her on fire. We'll time the fire so that it diverts the Spaniards' attention from our capturing the frigate. I am sure we all agree that the

Spanish don't need that ship-of-the-line, so we will be doing them a favor destroying it."

As Giles intended, that remark produced a laugh that reduced some of the tension that was inevitably felt when a daring mission was being proposed.

"Based on Mr. Brooks's estimates," Giles resumed, "and what Mr. Macreau observed last night, I expect that the current will be reversing at seven bells of the first watch. You should be in charge of the Spanish ship sometime before that, preferably by six bells. That way, you can slip the Spaniard's anchor a bit before the current changes while she is still lying with her bow pointing towards the entrance to the inlet. Unfortunately, there will be a moon, so we can't get *Glaucus* as close to the frigate as I would hope before we have to start rowing. So, we will man the boats and set off at four bells of the first dog watch.

There were no questions when Giles finished speaking. This was not surprising. The captain was known for faultless planning, while *Glaucus* had been on enough cutting-out actions that all the officers were experienced in what was involved.

The expedition went almost exactly as planned. The boats left *Glaucus* at the designated time, and the current carried the little flotilla of rowing boats into Ferrol Inlet without incident. It was still running when Giles's signaled all the boats to assemble half a cable away from the first target. There was no sign of a crew on board the Spanish frigate while she had been moored far enough from the shore that they had heard nothing to suggest that they had been spotted by anyone on land. In that, they were lucky.

There was no wind so far, and the sky was clear so that the inlet was well lighted by the moon. The only problem for the boats commanded by Mr. Miller was that they had to be extra careful not to make noise when approaching the frigate, which was their target. They could only hope that there would be no alert lookout to shout a challenge that would be heard clearly from the town and other ships. There were only a few clouds in the sky, and the half-moon was shining brightly. They would just have to hope that no curious people on shore might be looking over their area of the inlet and think it strange that there was a little flotilla of rowing boats in the harbor. That danger was somewhat alleviated as Giles's barge left the others to row towards the larger battleship.

The final leg of the trip to capture the frigate was easy. The current carried the boats toward their prey, with only a few strokes of the oars being needed to maintain their course. Giles's barge had farther to row. He could expect to arrive at their pray later than the others, but that was no problem. Giles would not mind having someone on the larger ship reveal their presence if, for some reason, noise from the frigate got their attention.

Mr. Miller's boat, as planned, skimmed past the bow and the waist of the Spaniard and hooked on where some of the most nimble of the sailors could climb up the side to disappear onto the quarterdeck. The other boat arrived at the waist of the frigate only moments later; its crew swarmed aboard, looking for Spaniards to silence. No enemy was found amidships while, on the quarterdeck, two elderly sailors had been looking out over the stern rail, smoking their pipes and talking amiably. They didn't notice that there were intruders on their ship until two of Miller's men slit their throats.

A thorough search revealed only one other Spaniard on board, a seaman who was fast asleep, a man whose drunken torpor meant that his life was spared as the sailors who found him speedily bound and gagged him so that he would prove no hindrance to their plans. Luckily, Mr. Macreau discovered the source of the Spaniard's drink before his crew did and set James Jenkens to stand guard over the stash of wine. Jenkens was known for his rigid religious beliefs that prohibited him from imbibing alcohol. This oddity had earned him the nickname Saint Jim. Any other crew member put in charge of the wine could be expected to begin his charge by determining the quality of the drink by the most obvious method.

The search of the frigate for other Spaniards was quickly completed. All that was discovered was that the name of the frigate was the *Santa Bartholomaeus*. Why no other crew members were on board remained a mystery. No English frigate moored at Sheerness or Spithead would let all the officers and most of the crew be away.

The first part of the plan had been executed flawlessly. Since the men from *Glaucus* had to wait for the change in the current, there was plenty of time to get ready to sail. Nevertheless, Mr. Miller thought that the preparations should be made as soon as possible, even though the current was holding the frigate tight to its anchor so that they would not be able to sail for some time.

To carry out the preparations needed before *Santa Bartholomaeus* could sail, Mr. Miller started bellowing orders to get the topmen aloft to be ready to unfurl the sails and other crew members to prepare to slip the anchor. Horrified, Mr. Macreau tried to quiet his superior, reminding him that Giles had stressed that there was to be no unnecessary noise.

"Don't try to give me orders," was Mr. Miller's response. "One can't get underway quietly; you know that. The need for quiet disappeared when we captured this ship."

Mr. Miller demonstrated his belief by bellowing some more orders.

Giles's barge had reached its target and was searching for the easiest place to board her when Mr. Miller's bellow echoed around the harbor. "Get us hidden under the stern," he immediately ordered Carstairs. They waited for several minutes to hear sounds from above them, but none came. Surely any watchmen would be curious about the English shouts echoing around the harbor. However, there was still no sign of life on the ship-of-the-line that Giles intended to destroy. After waiting for a couple of minutes, Giles ordered the barge to move around to the side of the ship where his crew could swarm up the tumblehome* to reach the deck. Once on board, they set out to explore the mystery of the lack of response to the English bellow that surely anyone on deck would have heard. It didn't take them long to solve that mystery.

On the quarterdeck, behind the mizen mast, four men were stretched out. Lying near them were not one but two bottles. Giles's nose told him that they had contained brandy. A further search revealed that there was no one else on board. Giles's plan had been to set the ship on fire just before the frigate was to sail so that it would act as a diversion. Now it was more urgent to get the ship burning to divert anyone who was coming to see what was happening on the frigate which Mr. Miller had capturd.

The sixty-four gun warship had the appearance of not being properly dismantled when the yards had been taken down. The sails had not all been stowed or removed, coils of rope littered the deck, and there was a lot of miscellaneous ropes and other debris lying around. Giles was puzzled. Was there something so wrong with the ship that it was being decommissioned? Well, possibly burning her was a needless undertaking, or the state of the warship might be a reflection of the lack of morale among the Spanish Navy after having been forced into a disastrous battle by an ally that many in Spain, Giles knew, disliked intensely. Whatever the reason, he was now on board her and would set her on fire even if the Spanish did not value her greatly.

Giles ordered his crew to make piles of combustibles at various spots on the deck where a fire would most likely be transmitted to the tarred rigging. Then he went below. There in the captain's cabin, he found more indication of a dispirited abandonment of the vessel. The material not carefully stowed would help get the ship to burn quickly and fiercely so that there would be no chance for the Spaniards to dowse the flames. Before leaving, he checked the magazine. Unbelievably, the Spanish had left a great many barrels of gunpowder in place, as if the boats with which the Spaniards were removing the explosives from the ship had become full before all the explosives had been taken, and then they had forgotten to come back for them. Giles had intended to burn the ship, hoping that the Spaniards would not be able to douse the flames in time to save their ship. Now he could blow it to kingdom come.

The next job in preparing to destroy the ship was to string slowmatch to the various places where he wanted to start fires. The fuses all led to the place where his boat was tied. All was set. Giles looked to the shore and saw that there was activity there, probably from people who had been roused by Mr. Miller's unfortunate shouts, which involved the launching of several boats. They, no doubt, were about to investigate those maddening bellows.

Things were looking up for the frigate's escape. The wind, which had been distressingly calm, was now blowing from the southeast, ideal for getting the captured ship out of the inlet. While Giles intended to ride the ebbing current to get away from the town, it would give the same aid to any boats pursuing them. However, the boats which were about to converge on the frigate might be diverted by setting the sixty-four on fire. He lit the slow match, checked it was burning, and told Carstairs to row toward the frigate.

The crew of the captain's barge pulled steadily towards the frigate. Giles's attention was spread between the ship they were leaving and the flotilla of boats heading towards the frigate. Suddenly flames sprang up from the sixty-four's deck as the slow match reached one of the piles of combustibles that he had gathered. It took no time at all for the approaching flotilla to notice the flames and swerve towards the burning ship.

Giles's rowers were also diverted by seeing the flames behind them eased their stroke.

"Keep pulling," the Captain ordered. It would become part of his later legend that he said this in a normal voice as if they were enjoying an uneventful row on the Serpentine and not fleeing a ship that might blow up at any moment.

It took a seemingly endless time for the fire to reach the magazine. When it did, the main deck of the large ship seemed to push upwards before being sent violently into the sky by a giant flame. Moments later, a huge bang caught up with the barge, deafening everyone on board. It was followed by a large wave that threatened to swamp Giles's boat. When it passed, the crew resumed their methodical rowing. It was not for English sailors to screech the way they could hear the Spanish townsfolk whose boats had not been swamped by the effects of the explosion.

Legend would have it that Giles stared calmly forward as the Spanish ship blew up so spectacularly. In fact, he stared at the mayhem he had produced with as much amazement as anyone else on his barge. It was Carstairs who recovered first and ordered the rowers to take up the stroke.

Mr. Bush, who had been charged with readying the anchor on the Spanish frigate, tried to report that the anchor was buoyed, possibly so that the frigate could venture out of the base and return with a minimum of hard work as her training voyages took place close to Ferrol. Where that crew might be remained a mystery, but it was no concern of Mr. Bush. His problem was that no one seemed concerned about his finding because the Spanish ship-of-the-line had blown up.

The first person who was interested in Mr. Bush's news was Captain Giles, who climbed to the deck of the frigate eager to get her underway as soon as possible. It was quite clear that he felt that the frigate should have sailed the minute the tide turned. The plan had been for the frigate to sail as soon as she could. If Giles were not yet on board, his barge would meet up with her somewhere down the inlet.

The report on the anchor was good news for Giles. Had *Santa Bartholomaeus* been anchored in the usual way, getting underway would have involved either raising the anchor or cutting the anchor line, both of which would have been noisy and time-consuming undertakings that would be certain to alert the port to the news that the new frigate was about to join the Royal Navy.

The current had almost stopped flooding; it was on the turn. Giles was about to order the designated rowing crews back into the boats to start towing the frigate out of the harbor when he noticed a light southeast breeze had sprung up. As long as the wind was strong enough relative to the current that the *Santa Bartholomaeus* had steerage way, there would be no need to use the boats.

The tricky time for getting underway was here. Giles wanted to unfurl the sails when the mooring rope went slack, making sailing away no problem. Too soon, and the rope would stay taut, almost impossible to free without desperate strokes from an ax; too late, and the ship would ride over her anchor, making it more difficult to pull away, and possibly spin around so that it faced the wrong way. When the critical time came, Giles recognized it. He gave his orders to loose the sails and set them, even as the mooring line came slack enough that it could be unfastened without trouble and thrown overboard. *Santa Bartholomaeus* smoothly sailed forward while the mooring disappeared astern of her. His crew had executed their tasks perfectly; the frigate had become a British prize, and the Spaniards still seemed to be oblivious to her change of ownership. The enemy remained entirely concerned about the burning remains of their destroyed warship.

The wind and the current took the captured frigate down the inlet. She turned north at the appropriate moment and encountered the long Atlantic swells outside the harbor as she was born to sail. In the moonlight, there was no problem meeting with *Glaucus*. All that remained was to select a crew for the newly acquired British frigate, which everybody was already calling *St. Bart*. Then Giles could return to his own ship.

"Well done, Mr. Miller," Giles cried in a voice loud enough that every man on board could hear him. "The men have performed admirably. I am told that St. Jim has found some wine, and while it is not our peoples' favorite beverage, I am sure they will all enjoy a glass.

"Mr. Macreau, since you discovered where this ship was anchored, you can command her as we leave this port. I cannot see the other frigates who are part of our group, can you? Since they are not in sight, we won't have to share the prize money with them."

That produced a cheer from the crew, but Giles wasn't sure whether that was because they were about to enjoy the Spanish wine or because they would enjoy three times as much prize money for capturing the *Santa Bartholomaeus* as they would have received if the other British frigates were in sight.

Back on board *Glaucus,* Giles went to his cabin immediately but not to sleep. He wanted to tell Daphne about the adventure they had had. In writing this news, he again felt guilty about leading the expedition. He should have stayed home and let Mr. Miller command. He hadn't because he hated to dispatch half his crew on a risky adventure without going himself. He had, at least, had the first lieutenant take part in the cutting-out expedition. Maybe that might help his chances of being promoted. Of course, those chances would have been better if Giles had not taken command of the venture. Or maybe not. Miller's error in shouting orders up into the rigging might well have sunk the whole venture if he hadn't been stopped. Mr. Miller was definitely a bit of a disappointment. Giles would dearly like to see him promoted so that he would be off *Glaucus*, but not at the cost of needlessly jeopardizing the rest of his crew.

What a relief it was to be able to tell Daphne all these things, if not in person, then at least in a letter! How long would this senseless mission drag on? Furthermore and more generally, was it time for him to give up *Glaucus* and go ashore?"

Chapter VIII

Two weeks had passed since the raid on Ferrol, two weeks of boredom for Giles and the sailors of his little fleet. Soon after taking the Spanish ship, the fog had at last dissipated, and he had been reunited with Captains Bush and Bolton. Giles had kept *Santo Bartholomaeus,* the Spanish frigate he had captured, with them rather than sending her to England.

All three frigates of the original flotilla had sailed from England with full crews so that each ship could fight both sides* if needed. Giles had manned the captured frigate with a quarter of the sailors on each of the ships under his command so that now all four had the same size crews, enough to be wholly effective in battle. He gave the command of *Santo Bartholomaeus* to *Glaucus*'s First Lieutenant, Mr. Miller. He was the senior lieutenant in the group. The appointment and his role in the Spanish ship's capture might help advance his promotion to commander, which Giles wanted. Of course, Mr. Miller would have his difficulties getting his crew up to fighting trim: each ship had sent a disproportionate number of the King's hard bargains* to the captured vessel.

Keeping the Spanish frigate with them rather than sending her home had strengthened the ability of the little fleet to intercept the treasure ship if it ever showed up. It also diminished the chance of the frigates' permanently losing significant numbers of their crews, a danger that all too often attended ships' sending in their prizes unaccompanied by the capturing vessel. All three British frigates had stable crews who had been with their ships for some time; their captains were loath to lose the men to ships that had been less successful in recruiting valuable hands.

While waiting for the Spanish treasure ship, Giles's squadron had taken and sunk a number of merchant ships trying to get into or out of Ferrol, allowing their crews to row ashore before their vessels were destroyed. Sinking the ships did not sit very well with the captains and sailors of the other frigates who had a greater need for even small amounts of prize money than did those on 'Lucky *Glaucus*,' but Giles had been adamant. If there were a treasure ship, and if she were accompanied by other vessels, he did not want to fail in carrying out his orders because his ships were undermanned. Already enough enemy trading ships had been sunk that his squadron would have been almost stripped of midshipmen and master's mates, and, furthermore, they would now be seriously short of topmen if he had sent his captures to an English port. He wouldn't see any of them for a very long time — if at all.

Giles decided that this would be the last day on which they would wait off Ferrol for the treasure ship. He thought that it could now be presumed that she had never existed at all or if she did exist, that she had not sailed for Ferrol. He wasn't pleased with his suspicions about his mission. Corruption, he knew, was endemic in the government, but he had no idea that it could extend to inventing a false mission just to protect a scoundrel with close connections with some people of power. He would much prefer to believe that the Spaniards had changed their minds about sending their treasure at such a dangerous time. But would anyone in Havana have the authority to reverse orders that must have come from the highest levels in Cartagena?

Giles was equally horrified in considering the alternative possibility that the mission had been invented to keep him from voting in the House of Lords contrary to the scoundrels' interests or his directing Members of Parliament who were in his control to cause trouble for their pet projects. Giles wouldn't mind getting home now and putting a spike in their nefarious schemes if, indeed, his journey had been ordered to protect their plots.

The Frigates were strung out in line abreast* with roughly ten miles between them. *Santo Bartholomaeus*, which the crews had dubbed '*Saint Bart'*, was the southernmost one with Cape Finisterre off her larboard quarter. *Glaucus* came second, followed by Captains Bush and Bolten. It was a clear day, with a weak winter sun shining but producing little warmth. At around four bells of the forenoon watch, Mr. Bush, who was midshipman of the watch, reported that *Saint Bart* was signaling.

"I think that she is saying that there is a ship in sight," the midshipman reported to Mr. Macreau, "though two of the flags are wrong, or else the message is gibberish. — Ah, here comes the direction, I believe, south by southwest."

"I see. You'd think that Mr. Miller would have instilled greater competence in that midshipman; he's had him for some time."

The midshipman in question had been the youngest one on *Xerxes*, Captain Bolton's Frigate, and had not been considered the brightest of the young gentlemen serving in the squadron.

"We had better inform the Captain about this strange sail, though I am not sure that there is anything he will want to do about it," Etienne continued. "See to it, Mr. Bush."

"Aye, aye sir," said the midshipman. "Just a minute, sir. *St. Bart* is signaling again, 'Another sail spotted to the south by southwest.'"

"Now we definitely have to tell the Captain. Fitzgibbon," Etienne addressed a master's mate who was on the quarterdeck, "please tell the Captain that *St. Bart* is reporting two sails to the southwest."

Giles came on deck as quickly as he could. He listened calmly to the reported signals and then promptly made his decisions.

"Signal to *St. Bart*, 'Investigate.' Signals to Captains Bush and Bolton, 'Alter course to south by west. Keep same distances between our ships.'" Giles instructed the midshipman. "Mr. Macreau, alter course to south-southwest. Set the royals. We'll go and have a look at what is happening."

Pandemonium broke out briefly on *Glaucus*'s deck as the topmen rushed to the shrouds*, and other crew members went to their places to adjust the many lines controlling the sails. In minutes, however, order was restored as the frigate settled onto her new course.

The extra sails were unfurled and sheeted* home as *Glaucus* speeded up. It was as if the frigate also welcomed the chance of doing something other than patrolling off the coast, waiting for a ship that never came.

"Get aloft, Mr. Dunsmuir, with the telescope," Giles ordered. "Report on the other frigates."

The senior midshipman, a youth of only seventeen years, hastened to the shrouds and raced aloft. Once settled at the main royal mast crosstrees*, he looked ahead in his telescope. It took him only a moment to find the upside-down image of *St. Bart*. She was on the same course as *Glaucus*. Even as Mr. Dunsmuir watched, her royal sails started to appear. He swung his telescope in the other direction, using his left eye to catch sight of the frigate to the north of him, on which he then focused the telescope. Captain Bush's frigate, *Xerxes*, sprang into view. She was on the same course as *Glaucus*, and she, too, had set her royals. Captain Bolton was still out of sight over the horizon.

The midshipman settled down to keep an eye on the distant ships. The lookout, a topman called Jenkins, seemed entirely at home balancing without noticeable effort in the unstable area whose primary purpose was to provide the fittings from which the royal yard was hung. Time seemed to drag for Mr. Dunsmuir with nothing much to do except keep an eye on the horizon. He knew that Jenkins had better eyes than he did and would no doubt see anything of interest before he would.

A good half hour passed before there was anything more to report from the masthead. *Glaucus* was gaining on *St. Bart* and was out-sailing *Xerxes*. Then Jenkins touched Mr. Dunsmuir's arm to get his attention, and gestured with his chin. The midshipman first scanned the horizon and saw a hint of something a long way away. He brought his telescope to bear. As *Glaucus* rose to the top of a wave, he could make out a sail — no three overlapping sails — on the horizon. They disappeared as *Glaucus* sank into a trough in the waves, only to reappear when she rose again. He formed a speaking trumpet with his hands and bellowed to the quarterdeck, "Deck there, sail on the horizon, two points off the larboard bow. She is a large ship with three masts."

"Look at the cut of her sails, Mr. Dunsmuir," Jenkens said. "I swear that they are Dutch cut. Not at all what I would have expected to see out here."

The midshipman studied the distant sails through his telescope, but he didn't know what to look for that would distinguish a sail of one nation from another.

Only a minute or two passed before Mr. Dunsmuir's attention was caught by another sail on the horizon. As nearly as he could tell, it was on the same course as the other one. It, too, revealed itself to be a ship-rigged vessel.

The chase went on and on, with *Glaucus* catching up with *St. Bart,* which, in turn, was closing the distance to the unknown ships. When the hull of the distant ship appeared for several moments on the crest of a wave,

Jenkins remarked, "She looks like an East Indiaman, sir."

"Are you sure, Jenkens?"

"Pretty sure, sir, though not entirely. I have never seen an East Indiaman that wasn't English, but I'm told that the Dutch have some. Maybe that's what those ships are, sir."

Mr. Dunsmuir transmitted this information to the deck.

"Do you know, Mr. Brooks, if the Dutch have East Indiamen?" Giles asked the Master.

"Yes, sir, they do. They carry valuable cargoes from their spice islands. The Spanish, the Portuguese, and the French also have some East Indiamen, I believe. The Dutch ones have a reputation for being slow."

"So, if Mr. Dunsmuir is correct, these could be French or Dutch ships trying to get to their home ports."

"Yes, sir. I believe some of the foreign East Indiamen even paint themselves, just as ours do, to look like line-of-battle ships, though they have many fewer guns on board and lighter ones, and their crews are not usually practiced in firing them. A well-managed frigate should have no problem taking one, while two frigates would easily overwhelm both of them."

"Are you suggesting that *St. Bart* and *Glaucus* should attack those ships when we come up to them rather than wait for *Xerxes* and Captain Bolton in *Flicker*?"

"Yes, sir. *Xerxes* is not gaining on us, and *Flicker* is even farther away. They may not come up with us or our targets before sunset, I'll be bound."

"Exactly my thinking, Mr. Brooks, Exactly! Mr. Fisher, signal to *St. Bart*, 'Wait for me.'"

Even as the midshipman of the watch readied his flags to send the message, the situation changed. The easternmost of the ships they were chasing suddenly turned so that her course settled on east-southeast by south, and she started to diverge from the track of the other ship. Clearly, their prey hoped that one of the ships could escape while the British frigates were engaged with the other one. Giles was having none of that.

"Mr. Fisher," Giles said to the midshipman, "Cancel that last order. Instead, signal *St. Bart* to pursue the easternmost ship."

Another hour passed before Giles gave his next order. "Mr. Stuart, clear for action."

Glaucus was approaching the Dutch ship from its starboard quarter. They were now near enough that Giles could read the name, *Huis van Oranje*, on her stern. It would still be some time before *Glaucus* could engage her. Giles glanced towards where *St. Bart* was approaching the other Dutch East Indiaman. That merchant ship was huge, and she was painted to look like a man-of-war. In particular, there appeared to be two levels of gunports, emphasized by two black stripes along her side with white rectangular markings punctuating them at regular intervals to display where the gun ports were. They were still all closed.

The two distant ships must be getting close enough to each other that an engagement would commence at any moment. Giles put his telescope to his eye to see in much finer detail what was happening. He had hardly focused on the frigate before he saw clouds of smoke come billowing up from her larboard side. There was no doubt about what had happened. *St Bart* had opened fire on the Dutch ship. Giles kept his telescope focused on the battle. He could see no immediate results from the frigate's broadside, but as the smoke cleared, he noticed that the Dutch ship had opened its gunports, though only four of those painted on her side actually opened. Giles was not surprised, East Indiamen were armed sufficiently to see off pirates or small naval vessels, but a full broadside of large guns would greatly reduce her ability to carry cargo, as would having a crew large enough to fight an engagement in the way that a third-rate naval ship would. Usually, only a few of the 'gunports' had a gun behind them, and, in most cases, that gun was far smaller than the mammoth cannon that a third-rate naval battleship would carry.

As Giles watched, the stranger fired her four guns. They must have been quite substantial, judging by the amount of smoke they produced. At first sight, the Dutch cannonballs appeared to have done no damage, and *St. Bart* sailed along unaffected by the fusillade. That impression, however, turned out to be false.

St Bart's main mast started to sway alarmingly, and in minutes it went by the board. The frigate slewed around so that now none of her guns bore on her prey, and she was drifting helplessly. The Dutch ship sailed on, showing no signs that Giles could see of the frigate's broadside having done any damage. That a properly set-up frigate, crewed by experienced sailors, even though they had worked together only for a short time, should be so easily put out of action was distressing, to say the least. He turned back, disgruntled, to his own encounter with a Dutch East Indiaman.

Giles had positioned *Glaucus* just where he wanted her, off the starboard quarter of *Huis van Oranje* where his frigate could not be reached by any of the guns of her opponent unless the Dutch ship had a very wide range of fire for her stern guns, a most unlikely possibility, just as, almost certainly, the guns were at most nine-pounders. Giles's chosen position was ideal. *Glaucus* could not be hit by any of the guns carried by the *Huis van Oranje,* and any attempt by the Dutch ship to change course would make her a better target for the English frigate without ensuring that any of her guns would yet bear on her attacker.

"Larboard bow cannon, aim for the middle of the quarterdeck rail," Giles bellowed to the men at *Glaucus*'s unusually powerful and flexible bow chasers. "Fire when you bear."

Only a moment was required for the gun crew to use their crowbars to alter the aim of their cannon and another moment so that the gun captain could judge the pitching of his own ship and that of his opponent. Still, there was certainly a large element of luck when the first shot hit the rail, sending deadly splinters streaking all over the quarterdeck. The gun crew cheered their success without losing any time as they loaded their cannon again.

The Dutch captain must have accepted the situation as hopeless, despite the success of his partner in dealing with *St. Bart*. He stepped up to the halyard of the flag and severed it with one stroke of a knife. At the same time, he roared, "Ik geef me over! Je me rends!"

Giles had no idea what the first phrase might mean, but he was pretty sure that the second one meant, "I surrender."

"Cease firing." Giles roared. Work at the bow chaser ceased immediately. "Mr. Macreau, take the longboat with a squad of marines and thirty of our best shiphandlers to board that Dutchman and accept her captain's surrender. Then take command of her. Mr. Dunsmuir, please accompany Lieutenant Macreau. Once I see that the Dutch ship is secure, I will take *Glaucus*, without waiting any longer, to see what can be done about the ship that crippled *St. Bart*. When you have sorted things out, go over to *St. Bart* and wait for me with her.

Meanwhile, *Huis van Orange* had turned so that she lay across the wind and backed her mainsail. Mr. Brooks, seeing that Giles was distracted, took it upon himself to follow the larger ship around and back *Glaucus*'s mainsail so that she maintained her position out of the range of the Dutch ship's guns in case the enemy tried to renege on their surrender. However, *Huis van Orange* tried no such tricks. Mr. Macreau and Mr. Dunsmuir were greeted on board, and it was a matter of little time for them to take control of the ship and send its officers across to *Glaucus*. Then off the frigate sailed, now heading towards the other East Indiaman.

Giles was surprised at how little more distance the other ship had put between them while he had been engaged with taking her mate. *Xerxes* was now closer to her. If the Dutch ship turned to larboard Captain Bush would come up with her sooner. A turn to starboard would shorten Giles's chase to catch her. The two frigates were, in effect, herding the East Indiaman south as they slowly caught up with her. Her fate seemed certain, except for one difficulty. The day was advancing inexorably, and the winter sun would set early. The moon would rise many hours after dark. That would give their target a long period to lose her attackers if they didn't catch her by nightfall. If at least one of the British frigates was not within a long cannon shot of the target by the time the short afterglow following sunset had darkened, then their target might easily escape their clutches in the dark before they could find her again by moonlight.

"Mr. Stuart," Giles called to the acting lieutenant. "Send up the skysail masts, yards, and sails."

It was usual not to have the skysail spars ready in winter and especially not to employ them at night. But this situation was exceptional; *Glaucus* would gain speed in these light winds with the additional sails pushing her along. It also gave the crew something to do as everyone on board the frigate waited to come up with the Dutch ship. After the additional sails had been set, *Glaucus*'s speed increased by at least half a knot. It was not much, but it might make a difference in the time remaining before darkness closed in completely.

Giles stared longingly at the other ship. Could he just make out her name on her stern? He focussed his telescope. Yes! Fancy lettering sprang into sight. *Rembrandt*. She was named for the Dutch painting. Giles knew that he was greatly admired by Mrs. Bolton, his niece. What would be her reaction if he could boast that he had captured the *Rembrandt*?

Slowly, agonizingly slowly, the distance between the two ships closed. *Xerxes* would not arrive in time. Would *Glaucus*? She was getting steadily closer to the fleeing East Indiaman, but the sun was on the horizon and would soon sink below it. Giles had cleared for action some time previously, but that action would be fruitless if the frigate's cannon could not reach their target.

"Larboard bow chaser: fire across her bow," Giles ordered. The gun had already been loaded and run out. The gun captain waited for the bow to rise, and, just before it reached its zenith, he pulled his lanyard. While this was going on, the last sliver of the sun disappeared below the horizon. In the dusk, Giles could see the spark just before the cannon roared out, and the gun surged backwards. A moment passed. Where would the cannonball fall? There was the splash, well ahead of the bow of the East Indiaman. Giles waited for there to be a response from the target vessel. He was now sure that he could take her, but would she also realize that her position had become hopeless? Would she surrender or turn to starboard, hoping that her few guns could disable *Glaucus* as she had *Saint Bart*? Giles wasn't worried about having the Dutch ship fire at his frigate since he could match any moves she made to try to make her guns bear, but he had to know if more gunfire from *Glaucus* would be needed to make her yield.

The answer came quickly. The man who had been standing by the wheel of the East Indiaman, likely her captain, turned and fiddled with a cleated line. In a moment, the large Dutch flag flying from the staff on her taffrail* came down. The response to a shouted order, which the man bellowed, seemed to be the lowering of the flag that flew from the masthead. Then the wheel of the Dutch ship spun to turn her to starboard. Giles presumed that *Rembrant* was turning across the wind to stop by backing her mainsail. Giles instructed Mr. Brooks, who was more expert in ship handling than his captain, to slide *Glaucus* up alongside the other ship so that they could grapple her as she came to a stop.

The maneuver went off without a hitch, and lines were thrown to join the two vessels together. The East Indiaman seemed to tower over the frigate. Luckily, the master had positioned *Glaucus* so that the battens that went up the side of the larger ship were positioned in the middle of the frigate's quarterdeck rail. Giles could board his capture in as simple and dignified a way as possible when he climbed the ship's side.

Once having bowed to *Rembrandt*'s captain as a way to accept her surrender, Giles faced the language problem. He hadn't thought to discover whether any among the crew of *Glaucus* spoke Dutch. It was immediately obvious that the Dutch Captain knew no English, and *Rembrandt*'s crew was mainly composed of lascars. Somewhat in desperation, Giles called to the East Indiaman's crew, "Do any of you speak English?"

A tall, thin man who was wearing a turban stepped forward.

"Yes, sahib. I am fluent."

"What's your name?"

"Rajit Khan, sir. I am First Mate of this ship."

"Very good, Mr. Khan. Please explain to the Captain — incidentally, what is his name?"

"Captain van Leiden, sir"

"Tell Captain van Leiden that his ship is now a prize of my British ship and that we will be taking her to England with us. Unfortunately, you will have to accompany us, though, as civilians, I doubt that you will be imprisoned in England."

Giles had to wait for *Xerxes* to join them before he could arrange for crew to take *Rembrandt* to England. He had already lost a quarter of his crew to manning *St. Bart* and then some more for *Huis van Orange*. Now he would draw on *Xerxes* instead of weakening his ship anymore.

While waiting for the other frigate to join them, Giles had Mr. Khan show him the ship's documents. He discovered that her cargo consisted of spices, silks, and gems. The latter were locked in a special part of the hold with a heavy lock whose key was kept in Holland. Even without the gems, the cargo would bring a fortune when it arrived in London. Together with the value of the Dutch ships themselves, the captains of the four frigates would be sharing a very large fortune. Of course, Giles would have to take his little fleet to England for that to happen. He wondered if Mr. Miller would participate in the captains' shares of the prize money, or would he count only as a lieutenant. It was probably the former; it seemed unfair since his contribution to the capture had been negligible when he should have been able to accomplish the capture using *St. Bart* without further help.

Thinking about the value of the prizes they had taken reminded Giles of one of the most difficult aspects of his previous voyage to stop piracy against the East India Company. One of the problems he had had to deal with was the passengers who had been carried by the ship he rescued on that occasion. Did this Dutch ship also have passengers? Or the *Huis van Orange*? He had been so rushed after his first capture had surrendered that he had learned nothing about her. Just as well, too: *Glaucus* had only just succeeded in capturing *Rembrandt* before he would no longer be able to see her.

"Mr. Kahn," Giles asked, "are you carrying any passengers?"

"Yes, sir. We have three couples who decided to risk passage with us rather than to remain in Batavia. Captain van Leiden had them confined to their cabins on the larboard side when it looked that you would be attacking. They had been a nuisance when we fought off that other frigate of yours."

"Well, let's leave them there until we have this all straightened out."

Giles returned to the deck to find that *Xerxes* had arrived and that Captain Bush was being rowed across in his barge.

"Welcome, Sir Toby," Giles announced.

"Lord Camshire, I see that you have seized another prize," Bush replied. "Can I assist you, sir?"

"Yes, you can. I don't have enough men to operate *Rembrandt* and still be able to sail *Glaucus* effectively. I already had to provide an adequate crew to *Huis van Orange*. I need a lieutenant to command *Rembrandt* while we get her to England, a midshipman, a master's mate, a dozen marines, and two dozen sailors. That should do the trick."

"Aye, aye, sir. I'll send over my second lieutenant and my senior midshipman and the others."

"Good, we can ease the loss of men a little when we come up with *Flicker*. I am sure that Bolton will be happy to do his share.

"That reminds me," Giles added as he turned to face *Glaucus*.

"Masthead," he bellowed. "What do you see of *Saint Bart*?"

"She lit a masthead lantern at sunset, sir. I can still see it. Another lantern has joined her. And a third one is going towards her."

"*Flicker* must have arrived. The other light should be *Huis van Orange*" Giles remarked. "Well, Toby, after we straighten out the crew assignments here, we will join them. I am now convinced that the Spanish treasure ship never existed, so we can sail for home with our captures."

It had been a long, tiring day, and there were still many chores for Giles to perform before his squadron set sail for home. Even so, he added to his letter to Daphne before he climbed into his hanging bed. He might well give it to her in person this time, but even then, he knew, she cherished his writings made at the close of his day, whether it had been a dull or adventurous time.

Chapter IX

Daphne sat back from the desk in her morning-room at Dipton Hall and rubbed her neck. She had been going over accounts and letters regarding the various properties that Giles now owned and those of her father and her uncle. She realized that her doing so was ridiculous. She and Giles were rich beyond anything she could have imagined when she had married him, and yet she was working at mundane tasks more than she ever had. Most of the nobility relied on agents or lawyers or some such men to do all the detailed work of managing their estates, but, somehow, Daphne could not give up the in-depth knowledge that came from direct examination of the information that flowed from their operations.

At least, she had taken a more reasonable approach to the tangle of properties that her late father-in-law had left in Norfolk. There she had put Giles's Norfolk affairs in the hands of her lawyer, Mr. Chapman, and an agent who had come highly recommended, a Mr. James Forsythe, the second son of a local baronet. She also had capable agents for managing the routine matters having to do with Dipton Hall and Dipton Manor and the other properties that Giles had acquired in the neighborhood. But still, she reviewed their reports in detail and those of her uncle's business in Birmingham and information about Ashton Place. This reflection reminded her that she had kept putting off a visit to that property even though she had long been curious about the inheritance that had fallen into Giles's lap when his eldest half-brother had died.

Daphne's reverie was broken by Steves, her butler, entering to announce that Major Stoner would like to see her. Major Stoner was married to Daphne's sister-in-law Lady Marianne. He was also in charge of the operations of the canal-boat enterprise that Daphne had founded, in Giles's name of course. Probably that undertaking was what he wanted to discuss, but, even so, his visit would be a nice break. In fact, it turned out that he wanted to discuss something quite different.

"Lady Daphne," the Major began after the usual pleasantries had been exchanged, "about the Hunt race."

Daphne had no problem knowing what the Major wanted to talk about. Ever since they had moved into Dipton Manor, Giles and she had hosted the Ameschester Hunt Ball to mark the end of the hunting season. The Hunt Ball had started as a fairly modest affair, but word had rapidly spread far and wide that it had been a superlative event and the following year had seen a much wider attendance at the Ball. This year, it promised to be even more popular among the very best people. This was also true of the Hunt itself, which threatened to be unmanageably large. Daphne wasn't at all sure that she hadn't enjoyed the first Ball more with its having fewer of the pretentious people who seemed mainly concerned with establishing their high status. But she would make the best of it, laying on special facilities and entertainment for the ladies who would come with their husbands but had no intention of riding to hounds. As always, Daphne figured that if she was going to do something, even something for which her enthusiasm was decreasing, she would do it as well as she could. Whether she would ride in the hunt would depend on how overcrowded it was.

Giles and their stablemaster, Mr. Griffiths, had developed an interest in horse racing. They had not reached the point of having horses to enter in the famous thoroughbred races, but they were developing a very able and well-trained group of hunting horses. Those steeds would be suitable for cross-country races and even the more formal races, involving set jumps, that were being termed misleadingly 'steeplechases.' They had thought that such a race starting and finishing at Dipton might be a splendid addition to the Hunt Ball festivities and put Dipton Hall on the map as *the* place for obtaining hunting horses.

In Giles's absence, it had fallen to Major Stoner to organize the race, even though he was very busy with other matters. There was some sort of problem down at the start of the canal in Harksmouth, which was interfering with the amount of legal cargo arriving at the port, probably because it was being diverted to the smuggling trade instead. In the absence of both Giles and Captain Bush, who had been roped into the surprise mission to Spanish waters, it had fallen to Major Stoner to find out what the problem was. Daphne presumed that he was about to renege on arranging the race.

That was not the Major's intent. "My Lady — Daphne — I wonder if I might prevail upon you to help with the course to be specified for the race. The President of the Hunt, Mr. Summers, is so miffed at your and Captain Giles's generous support of the Hunt, which he feels has shown up his inadequacies, that he won't help me, saying, "Since it's Lord Camshire's idea, Lord Camshire can make all arrangements for the race. I would greatly value your advice since your knowledge of the area around Dipton is much greater than my own."

"Of course, I'll help. What do you have in mind?"

"Well, I have selected a suggested route, though, of course, people can vary it as long as they go to each of the checkpoints in the right order. The checkpoints are all little churches, though, around here, we seem to have church towers rather than steeples, but they serve the same purpose as beacons along the route. I want your advice on whether the course is too long or too difficult, especially to try to avoid having any very tricky shortcuts that the inexperienced might take and get injured."

"I suppose that it would be most helpful if we rode the possible course together to look for hazards," Daphne broke in when the Major seemed to be getting stuck. She knew that he had trouble asking her for favors.

"Well, yes, that would be very helpful, but I hate to ask when you are so busy."

"Let's get it done now. There is enough daylight left to get around the likely course before dark. Major, please ring for Steves."

When the butler appeared within moments of being summoned, Daphne gave her orders crisply, "Steves, send word to the stables to harness Serene Masham. Have Cook prepare a light, cold colation for the Major and me as quickly as possible.

"Now, Major, while we wait, fill me in on the problem with the canal barges."

The Major, as always, knew how to report succinctly. The basic problem was simple. Trade for the first ports on the canal, especially in spirits but also in wine, had tapered off alarmingly, while they were able to sell almost none of their imports in Harksmouth, where they were landed and taxed. Some of the ships coming to them from France had suspiciously small cargoes, and the area was again flooded with contraband. The only explanation that occurred to the Major was that the smugglers were no longer being harassed. Somehow they were getting the magistrates and the Revenue Service to turn a blind eye once again to their nefarious activities. They were organizing the scattered remnants of their old smuggling operations into effective, illegal cliques and networks of the sort that had been destroyed by the earlier actions taken by Giles and Daphne together with their associates.

"I'm planning to go to Harksmouth as soon as the preparations for the Hunt Race are finalized. I don't know what I can do about the situation that far away, but I can't do anything without understanding it better," the major concluded.

"Yes. That's a good idea. Then we may be able to count on Sir Titus Amery or someone else to straighten things out," Daphne replied.

After quick lunch, Daphne changed into her riding clothes, and she and the Major mounted their horses, which had been brought to the portico. Both their horses had been acquired from the predecessor of what was now called the Dipton Hall Stables, a horse farm specializing in hunters. They had been bred and trained by Mr. Griffiths, who was now the stablemaster at Dipton Hall. Both were excellent horses, but there was no doubt that Daphne's hunting mare, Serene Masham, was the more able of the two, and Daphne rode her more often for recreation and more daringly than the major rode his hunter. As a result, Serene Masham was undoubtedly the better steed.

Daphne and the Major trotted along, chatting about obstacles and things to watch out for in setting the course. It was truly a steeplechase, or rather a church-tower chase since towers rather than steeples were the feature of parish churches in the Ameschester area. At each of these churches, someone would be stationed to record when horses passed that point, and only horses that had been recorded at each church could win the race. Daphne and Major Stoner were on the lookout for innocent-looking jumps that were, in fact, hazardous and shortcuts that would appear to be so very attractive that they were unlikely to be resisted even though, in fact, they led only to swamps or other impossible terrain. These places would then be marked with signs before the race was held. Luckily all the landowners along the route that Major Stoner had selected were willing to have the race go over their land, so no special warnings were needed at places where racers might be tempted to cross forbidden land.

Daphne and Major Stoner were on the last stage of the course, the one from Upper Dipton back to Dipton when they came to a gate in a high hedge, which had been left untrimmed for some time so that, even on horseback, it was hard to see what was on the other side. It was not safe for someone to decide that the cart track that the gate crossed would lead to a useful shortcut and could be jumped with impunity. On the other side of the gate, the cart track, Daphne knew, dipped into a hollow while executing a hard right turn. Looking over the gate from the place that a rider in a hurry might decide to jump the obstacle, Daphne couldn't see what sort of a hazard might lie on the other side. She had never had occasion to jump the gate, but she felt suspicious about its safety.

Major Stoner claimed that the gate was not a danger if someone wanted to try for a shortcut that way, so no special warning would be needed that it was not, in fact, a good way to go to reach the next church even though it might look tempting. Daphne was less certain. She seemed to recall from visiting the spot during a harvest season when the track was in use — the land was held by one of Dipton Manor's tenants — that just beyond the gate, where the path could not be seen when approaching the obstacle, the land dropped off nastily while the track turned sharply to the left and was not level. Inviting riders to jump the gate could easily lead to disaster.

"Major, that gate might appear to lead to a shortcut to the next church, don't you think?"

"I suppose so. Isn't it?"

"No, it isn't. In fact, besides not going in the right direction, it is dangerous in ways that are not evident if you are racing along. It is actually a very difficult jump, even when you know the lay of the land well."

"Nonsense, I think you are being overly cautious, my lady." Major Stoner declared. "It looks simple enough to me. Let me demonstrate."

Before Daphne could stop him, the Major put spurs to his horse and headed for the gate. The horse trusted its rider, and when asked to jump the gate, it did. The animal would expect to go straight forward after a jump, as was usually the case, unless guided otherwise by its rider. If the land on the other side presented any difficulty to a smooth landing, disaster was likely. Despite Daphne's warning, the Major gave no directions to his mount, not even definite ones to go straight. In such a situation, the horse followed its own inclination, or rather, its instinct and training. As it cleared the gate, Major Stoner's horse did just that and swerved to the left as the safest way to handle the unexpectedly difficult ground. The Major was not ready for the sudden change in direction. He pitched out of the saddle, sailing headfirst straight down the steep slope at the side of the track. An outspread arm tried to catch a rock as he landed, and that probably saved his life. However, it had the effect of swinging him around. While his head suffered a bang on some loose earth lying where he landed, his foot hit a jagged and immovable rock sticking up a bit from the ground. A bone in his leg broke as it hit the rock before he came to a stop, lying on his back with his feet pointing down the hill. Relieved of its rider, the Major's horse took off along the track at a gallop.

From the other side of the gate, Daphne couldn't see what had happened to Major Stoner, but she heard the noises that indicated that things had gone wrong. She guided Serene Masham to the gate, but she could see nothing useful, though she heard the other horse thundering away. Daphne needed to get to the other side of the gate at once. She guided Serene Masham in a circle away from the gate and then set her to the jump. Serene Masham was more sure-footed than any other horse that Daphne had ever ridden. With Daphne knowing the land and giving Serene Masham her head, the filly easily cleared the gate and veered onto a flat place to stop.

Daphne slid from the saddle. After a few steps, she spotted the Major flat on his back. She scrambled down the steep hillside to him. He was unconscious but breathing, and his pulse was firm. There was nothing that she could do for him without help; she didn't even want to raise his head to slip something softer under it in case the major had damaged his neck. She climbed back to the gate.

"Betsey," Daphne called to her maid, "Major Stoner is injured. Go to Dipton Hall and have Steves send for Mr. Jackson to come to examine the Major as soon as possible. He also needs to send several men to carry the Major. Oh, and they will need some material to make a stretcher and someone to round up and ride the Major's horse to Dipton. Now, off you go — just standing there looking concerned isn't going to help anything."

Daphne returned to Major Stoner. He was still unconscious, and there was nothing she dared do to make him more comfortable. It was lucky, she thought, that he was not bleeding or thrashing about. She just hoped that help would arrive soon. Having Betsey with them had been lucky, possibly even a life-saver. If she had not been there, Daphne would have been faced with the dilemma of whether it would be better to stay with the Major until someone happened to come by or to leave the injured man while going to seek help.

Daphne did not usually take Betsey with her when riding in Dipton. She regarded the custom of having a lady's maid accompany a socially significant lady whenever she ventured out of doors by herself or in the company of a gentleman — especially in the company of a gentleman — as being ridiculous. The idea that her reputation as a chaste woman would be compromised by not having a maid trail along behind her struck Daphne as silly. Any maid who told tales about her mistress would be turned out immediately without a reference; she wouldn't risk her position to indulge in salacious gossip.

While it might make sense in London, where the accompanying maid could be useful for carrying packages or hailing cabs, a footman would serve the purpose better and protect the lady far more effectively than a maid. Daphne usually rode by herself or in the company of others without worrying that not having a maid would ruin her reputation, but Major Stoner's wife, Lady Marianne, though she had spent much time in army camps where propriety often got short shrift, was now a stickler for proper behavior. It was not that she didn't trust her husband or her half-sister-in-law, but she didn't want any malicious tongues to wag about them. Anyway, as Lady Marianne knew from being an earl's daughter, it was the proper thing to have a lady's maid along. Daphne bent her own inclinations to keep as smooth a relationship as possible with Major Stoner's wife. Having a maid with her paid off on this occasion. Daphne could stay with the injured man in case there were some development with which she could help while Betsey rode for help. It never occurred to her to reverse the roles and go herself while Betsey stayed with the injured man.

The Major showed signs of reviving after what seemed to Daphne to be a very long time. He groaned and tried to move, an effort that only produced a loud yelp of pain.

"What happened?" he asked groggily.

"Don't you remember?" Daphne asked. "You tried to jump a gate that I thought was too hazardous, and you came off your horse."

"Did I? I don't remember any of that. Are you sure? The last thing I can recall is having a bang-up luncheon with you, Lady Giles."

"Well," thought Daphne, "he obviously doesn't remember the argument that led to his foolhardy attempt to jump the gate." What she said was, "I am afraid that you have had a bad bump on the head. Sometimes when that happens, one forgets what happened just before the accident."

"Is that so? Well, I'd better get up and find my horse, hadn't I?"

"Not on your life, Major. I think you may have broken your leg and possibly your wrist. Just rest quietly until help arrives."

It was not long before the rescue party began to arrive in the form of Mr. Jackson, the apothecary, who had a medical degree but did not want to be confused with the leech-dependent doctors in the area. He had been visiting a patient at one of the tenant farms on the way to Dipton, and Betsey had had the presence of mind both to recognize his gray horse and to tell him what the problem was before she proceeded to Dipton Hall.

Mr. Jackson opened the gate, passed through it, and then made sure it was safely fastened before striding down to where Daphne and the Major waited.

"Well, Major," Mr. Jackson said. "This is a precious pickle that you have landed yourself in! No, please don't move until I have examined you *in situ*, so to speak. No, I mean it, do not try to move. In a lot of cases, more damage is done after the event than in the original accident. Now, very gently try to turn your head — good. Now, the other way — good. Now, try to raise your head just a very little."

The major raised his head, not just a little but quite a lot.

"Did that hurt?" asked the physician.

"A bit."

"That is very good. Now let me try to get you sitting up — No! Don't use your arms! I will lift you, I haven't had a chance to examine your arms and particularly your wrists, and I don't want you to make worse any injuries you may have. — Yes, you have a large lump forming where you must have hit the ground. Let me feel. Tell me if it hurts too much."

Mr. Jackson ran his fingers over the Major's skull several times. "I don't think you have cracked your skull, but you have given yourself a big lump on your head. I am sure that you are suffering from a serious concussion. You are going to have a massive headache, I am afraid, and you may feel dizzy and forgetful for quite some time. I'll get you some laudanum and show Lady Marianne how to administer it. Only take it when you absolutely can't bear the pain anymore. It is based on opium, and you know from your experiences in the East how opium can destroy lives if you become dependent on it.

"Now, lie back again," Mr. Jackson continued, "and I'll examine your wrist and your ankle."

More gentle poking and prying followed, first on the Major's wrist and then on his ankle. When he had finished, Mr. Jackson again came close to the Major's face.

"All things considered, Major, you've got off lightly. Your wrist and arm are not broken, though your wrist is sprained. I have bandaged it tightly to try to immobilize it and to lessen the swelling. There is a danger that I have made it too tight. If you feel that your fingers are becoming numb or turning purple, you must have the bandage loosened. Otherwise, its tightness will speed healing and reduce pain.

"Now, your leg is a more serious problem, though it could be a lot worse. You have broken it, but only one of the two shin-bones, not both, which is very unusual. That has made it a great deal easier to get the broken parts lined up. I am going to splint your ankle and bandage it, but you *must* keep off it, or you may never walk properly again. Right now, I'll use these small sticks as splints, but when we get you to Dipton Hall, I will rebandage it with proper splints. It would be best if you stayed at Dipton Hall until I am sure that you can safely travel to your home."

Mr. Griffiths had arrived as Mr. Jackson was examining the Major. He had brought a cart and a stretcher with him as well as three stable hands to help as needed. While Mr. Jackson was completing his bandaging of Major Stoner's leg, the stablemaster went looking for the Major's horse, which he found a furlong down the cart track, grazing happily.

Mr. Griffiths brought the horse back in time to take over direction of getting the Major loaded onto the stretcher and positioning the cart to receive the load. Daphne rode ahead of the group accompanying the cart to make sure that Dipton Hall was ready to receive the injured man with the least amount of fuss and disorder. Only a word or two were needed to Steves to set everything in motion.

Daphne then retreated to her office, where she dashed off a note to Lady Marianne telling her the bad news and inviting her to stay at Dipton Hall until the Major could be moved. She wasn't very happy about having Lady Marianne as a guest, possibly a long-time one, having only recently succeeded in helping to engineer her marrying the Major as a way to get her out of Dipton Hall, but, without question, inviting her was the right thing to do. She also wrote a note to Mr. Summers, the President of the Ameschester Hunt, to tell him about Major Stoner's accident. Unfortunately, Mr.

Summers was a rather ineffective man, and most of the Hunt organizing was done by the Major. Now, even more of it would fall on Daphne, who was already responsible for the Hunt Ball and all that entailed. Luckily, Steves and her other servants at Dipton Hall would do much of the work.

Thinking about how Major Stoner's broken leg and concussion were likely to affect organizing the last hunt of the season and the accompanying Hunt Race and Ball made Daphne remember what he had said about the problems at Harksmouth. Now, she would have to go and find out what that problem was and soon. Otherwise, the smugglers would get a much firmer hold on the trade. Going to Harksmouth by canal would be far too slow, but there was no decent direct route. The quickest way would be to go to London and then back along the coast to the port. It would take several days. Surely, she could find someone else to do it.

Well, feeling sorry for how overburdened she was wouldn't get anything done. The cart with Major Stoner was arriving, and she should go and greet him, even though Steves and Mr. Jackson were perfectly able to get him settled comfortably. Anyone who thought that the mistress of a major house didn't have anything to do hadn't seen her at work! That's what was running through Daphne's mind.

As she turned to follow the servants carrying the Major upstairs, one of the footmen said, "Mr. Steves, there is a carriage approaching."

Daphne was tempted to ignore the information and hastily disappear up the stairs; Steves could welcome whoever had arrived and then look for the mistress of the house to tell her who had come to see her. However, Daphne decided to forego the rigmarole that attended a visit among the better levels of society because she wanted to see immediately who might be in the carriage.

Daphne stared as the carriage came to a stop in front of the portico. It was one of the vehicles that were for hire at the posting inn in Ameschester. There was only one person who would arrive unexpectedly at Dipton Hall using that carriage. Without pausing to collect her wits, Daphne dashed down the few steps leading to the ground. There was almost a race between her and the footman who came forward to open the door of the carriage. Out stepped Giles to be almost knocked over by Daphne. Luckily he knew her ways and had already braced in case she was forewarned of his arrival. He knew that she didn't care who saw her expression of love for her husband, not the servants, nor anyone else who happened to be there. He braced himself so that she wouldn't bowl him over. He was most definitely home!

Chapter X

The following evening Daphne sat at the head of the dining-room table, surveying the guests before the footmen started serving dinner. Giles was at the foot of the table, not very far away from her since most of the table's leaves had been removed because there were only a few guests, people who were close to Giles and Daphne. The guests were also people who would most like to hear about Giles's voyage.

Of course, Daphne reflected, she and Giles had already done a lot of catching up before this dinner. Indeed, it had taken several hours from the time that she had shooed the servants away as Giles began to get undressed for his bath and the time they emerged to visit the nursery. She had better not dwell on that period right now, or she would reveal her inner thoughts with a silly grin on her face when she glanced towards Giles. The sort of look her niece Catherine directed at her husband, Captain Bolton, whenever she glanced at him. It was strange: Daphne was not at all ashamed for the servants at Dipton Hall to be well-aware of how she welcomed Giles home, but she didn't want her guests to suspect what had been their first order of business. She noticed that Catherine Bolten was glancing at her husband in a way that suggested she was thinking of more intimate matters than what was being discussed at dinner.

They had indeed been busy since Giles returned. After he had got dressed following his bath and their protracted dalliance with each other, they had visited the nursery, where Giles had admired Christina and bounced her up and down. Then he had engaged in some silly game with Bernard on the floor until it was time for dinner.

"That's what you suspected, wasn't it, Daphne," her father interrupted her thoughts. It took a moment to realize what he was talking about — oh, yes, it was about why Giles had been sent on the mission to Spain.

"Yes, I was very suspicious how that report from Havana happened to come in right after we discovered what Mr. Edwards had been doing, and also about how they selected the three captains whom we knew that Mr. Edwards had been cheating. Maybe I was wrong, but I am pretty sure that having an ordinary person explain how they had been harmed would have done little to get Mr. Edwards convicted, and they might not have expected even that would happen. With the principal victims being at sea, lawyers might be counted on to so confuse the jury that Mr. Edwards would get off."

"I hate to say it, but I think you may be right about the source of that fool mission we were on," said Giles. "The more I think about it, the more convinced I am that it was bogus."

"Well, even if that's true, we did very well out of being ordered to Ferrol," remarked Bush.

"That certainly seems to be the case," agreed Catherine Bolton. "I couldn't believe it when Captain Bolton told me what our share of the prizes was likely to be."

"Well, that is still speculation, as is what our share of a galleon would be if there had been one to capture," Giles commented. That reminds me, Daphne, were you able to arrange for a different prize agent?"

"Yes, Giles. Mr. Snodgravel recommended Everett and Company as being a well-established and reputable company. They provide fewer services than Mr. Evans used to, but at lower fees. They should be ready to deal with the prizes you have just brought in. They couldn't take over your account at Mr. Edwards's agency. Something about the government freezing everything under his control until they discover all the larcenous things he may have done. You still have some prize money there which has not been transferred to us, and his agency still has all those consols* into which he put a lot of your money. Mr. Snodgravel will be looking after that aspect of things."

George Moorhouse, Daphne's uncle who had been half-paralyzed by a stroke, became agitated at this remark and started to scribble energetically on the slate he kept handy so that he could communicate with others despite being unable to talk coherently.

"What is it, Uncle George?" Daphne asked, taking the slate so that she could read it.

"Have Edwards's books checked," she read. "Get a good accountant to look for fraud. The lawyer should know who to get."

"Are you saying that Mr. Edwards may have been stealing from us in other ways, Uncle George?" Daphne asked.

This remark was met with vigorous head-nodding by her uncle.

"George was telling me how accountants have been able to get to the bottom of fraud that occurs through company books among the shadier businesses in Birmingham," Daphne's father chimed in.

Daphne knew that the two brothers, so long estranged through their father's actions, had been having long, slow conversations recently. In the winter days, when Daphne's father rarely ventured out, and Uncle George was, of course, house-bound, they spent the time in the library reading and the evenings discussing what they had read and aspects and reminiscences of the long years when they had been estranged. As a result, Daphne's father became much more knowledgeable about business matters, especially the tribulations and dangers of running a successful industrial company. In return, Uncle George had learned about the fascinations of ancient military history. She would not be surprised if soon her uncle joined her father and Captain Bush, debating the merits of Hannibal's invasion of Italy.

"I am afraid that I don't quite follow what Uncle Goerge is getting at," Daphne told her father.

"George believes that, very often, an examination of the records of the transactions of a company — in this case, Mr. Edwards's agency — can reveal any wrong-doing that has been going on," Mr. Moorhouse explained while Uncle George nodded in agreement. "We know that Mr. Edwards was cheating various men out of some of their earnings. He suspects that he may have also been embezzling from the accounts of which he has been in charge while giving their owners false information about their wealth. He thinks that your lawyer probably knows someone who is an expert at finding cases where the books have been falsified."

"I still find it hard to believe that Mr. Edwards was so crooked. I always thought that he provided excellent service and assistance," remarked Giles. "Didn't you find him very helpful, Daphne?"

"Yes, I did, though he was singularly unhelpful when dealing with the problem of your half-brother's house of ill repute. I am not sure that, deep down, he didn't feel that you should take over what Ashton had left you, at least in that instance."

"Do you think, then, Daphne, that we should act on Uncle George's suggestion? At least, we might write to your London attorney — what's his name?"

"Mr. Snodgravel — he's *our* attorney."

"Mr. Snodgravel to advise us on the best person to conduct the investigation for us."

"That's a good idea, though I would like to see what is going on myself next time we are in London."

"As you wish," Giles concluded. "I'll write tomorrow, first thing. Thank you, Uncle George, for your suggestion."

"I suppose that we should go to London soon," Daphne wasn't quite done with the related topic of when she might have a look at Edwards's accounts herself.

"I am afraid so. I have to report to the Admiralty before too long, and I have to arrange to take my seat in the House of Lords."

"I've told Daphne," Giles continued, "but I don't think that I have informed the rest of you that I am going to take my proper role as a peer of the realm by being an active member of the House of Lords and not just as a tool for the advancement of my interests as my father did."

"That's why we are reopening the London house," Daphne said. "If Giles weren't going to have an active and important life in the capital, I don't think we would bother with it. I'm looking forward to being in London much more frequently, but the reopening of Camshire House and then managing our two large houses is going to be challenging."

"Well, Daphne," said her father, "You know that you love that sort of challenge. So how soon will you be going back to London?"

"Not for another week or so," Giles replied for her. "I want to spend some time here. I've missed Daphne, and I want to get caught up with my children. I never realized how important they would be to me. Furthermore, I need to show the Admiralty that I am not entirely at their beck and call for improperly motivated assignments. I want to get reacquainted with our properties here and especially with the horses and the hounds. I also intend to learn more about our holdings so that I can take some of the burden off Daphne. She is the one who runs everything, as you all know, and she does a very good job of it."

Uncle George started scribbling on his slate again. Everyone waited for him to finish so that his brother could read aloud what was said in the message.

"You can say that again, Lord Camshire. She is also doing a magnificent job running my business in Birmingham."

Though he would have denied it if challenged, George Moorhouse was still rather overwhelmed to be sitting at an earl's table and finding out that the earl was a very pleasant and unassuming fellow, even if his name did feature prominently in some of the newspapers that George read.

"I'm glad to hear it," Giles replied, "though I am not surprised. If the Countess of Camshire could take the Earl of Camshire's seat in the House of Lords, I think I would ask her to do it."

"That's the first time I have heard of any advantage arising from how limited are the roles that women can take," Daphne quipped.

"Will you be active in the House of Lords, Giles?" asked his father-in-law.

"I am not sure. I have a lot to keep me away from London here in Dipton and in sorting out what properties and problems have come with the earldom. There are some things that Daphne can't handle or that I should relieve her of. I have arranged to have myself be introduced to the House of Lords on the Thursday after next. The Earl of Reeding has kindly agreed to take me to my place, and then I will give my maiden speech."

"What will the speech be about?" demanded Mr. Moorhouse.

"It will be in connection with the Abolition of the Slave Trade. It's not being debated yet in the House of Lords, only in the Commons, but there is quite a lot of latitude in what lords can discuss in Parliament, and that is especially true for newly seated members."

The conversation then turned to other matters having to do with what had been happening in Dipton while Giles had been gone. Daphne's custom in family gatherings of not leaving the gentlemen to their port in the dining room while the ladies withdrew to the drawing-room meant that the stories about local events and curiosities were much more complete than if only the men had brought Giles up-to-date without the ladies' contributions.

The diners did not linger overlong, and both Giles and Daphne were still wide awake when they were once more by themselves.

"I'm sorry that I am never here when there is a crisis," said Giles.

"There aren't really many crises, you know. Of course, I would like to be with you always, but what you do is important, both for who you are and for the country. I knew that you would have to be away a lot when I married you. I always wish you were here, but I am content to have as much as possible to do while you are away doing your duty."

"That is very good of you. But, you know, I hate that I lost touch with you even on this latest cruise. I didn't even know if you became pregnant the last time I was at home."

"Well, as you now know, I didn't either. Maybe we should try to make up for lost time — right now!"

"I thought that that was a chore that women had to bear as part of marriage."

"Wherever did you get that idea? Getting pregnant is no chore, quite the opposite; being pregnant has its disadvantages, but they are certainly worth the reward when a child arrives. I don't know why I didn't get pregnant last time you were here. All we can do is to try again and again and again while you are here. Oh, Giles, it is so good to be with you!

The next day, Daphne's first concern was to discover how Major Stoner was doing. Lady Marianne had come to Dipton Hall the previous afternoon and stayed the night, but, even so, Daphne felt a continuing obligation to make sure that the Major had the best care. Though she headed to the Major's room even before going down to breakfast — much to the consternation of the staff, she disliked taking her breakfast in bed as married ladies were supposed to — she went to the Major's room.

Early as it was, she found that Mr. Jackson was already there. The Major was awake and in a foul temper.

"What do you mean I have to stay in bed. I know I have broken some bones, though I can't say that I know how I did it," the Major was yelling at Mr. Jackson. "Happens all the time, all the time. Throw a bucket of water over the man, and he is good to go, definitely good to go. I have to check the race route with Lady Giles, or, I should say, Lady Ashton. Nothing the matter with me, definitely not, not with me!

"Ah, Lady Ashton, Daphne, here you are," continued the Major. "Tell this fool saw-bones that I am alright and can do whatever I want."

"I am afraid, Major, that I have to agree with Mr. Jackson. After all, you just got my title wrong. You've never done that before."

"What? Lady Ashton?" the Major sounded puzzled. Then he revived. "Lady Camshire, of course, Lady Camshire! Slip of the tongue; anyone could make it. Anyone! Nothing to do with this sawbones keeping me in bed. Nothing at all!"

The Major was about to make an even more bad-tempered response when Giles showed up. He had heard the Major's protests as he came down the corridor leading to the Major's room but decided to feign ignorance.

"Major," he said. "I was sorry to hear of your accident. Tricky things, bumps on the head. I imagine that Daphne is refusing to let you get out of bed. Probably remembers my tales of having been knocked out on *Glaucus* — that's my frigate, you know. Very nasty getting hit on the head! I know all about it."

"Well, my bump was nothing. Nothing!" replied the former soldier. "Only out for a few minutes, I am sure. Feel good. Don't need to be coddled. Not at all!"

"That's how I felt when it happened to me," Giles said soothingly, "but when I tried to get up, my head was reeling. I realized later that I couldn't remember anything that had happened just before I got hit on the head."

"Well, I don't think that's my case, and if it is, there isn't much I can do about it. It was just a simple case of my horse shying at something. The animal must have done so, though I don't remember seeing it. But it is strange that I don't recall his throwing me. Must have been distracted by something. Anyway, I'm all right now. Can't just laze in bed to satisfy that saw-bones, can I? Of course, I can't!"

"Quite apart from your head, Major, you have a serious break in your leg. Mr. Jackson tells me that he wants it immobilized until it starts to join together. Then he can put a cast on it. Until then, you are not st have had more minor breaks or cracks than you have, or a lot of them would have lost the use of their legs," the physician broke in. He liked to call himself an apothecary largely to advertise his disagreements with the medical establishment, but he was an exceptionally well-trained physician and surgeon. "I can't put your leg in a cast until the scrapes on your shin have scabbed up, and there is no danger of infection. Otherwise, you may get gangrene, and I will have no choice but to remove your leg. Now, Major, for your own good, stay still in bed! If you don't, I cannot be held responsible if you never walk again. That is the danger you would be running!"

Mr. Jackson left on that note, and Giles and Daphne accompanied him.

"Thank you for that help, Captain Giles," the apothecary said. "I am afraid that often the gentry tend to try to undercut my advice on things like broken bones or serious wounds or on whether a particular medication will do their condition any good at all."

"You're welcome. I hope that, between us, we have scared the Major into taking care of himself." Giles replied."

"Daphne, would you like to go riding?" Giles asked when Mr. Jackson had left.

"Yes, I would. After I have seen about Berns." She replied.

"Steves," she ordered, "can you send word to the stables to harness Dark Paul and Serene Masham and bring them to the Hall. Giles, I'm going to visit the nursery while we wait."

Giles felt a wave of guilt break over him. The previous afternoon, he had seen his son whose accomplishments had been demonstrated while Giles was playing with him. He had not thought of Bernard yet this morning, something he was not going to confess to Daphne. Instead, he said, "Yes, I would also like to see him, even if it does disturb Nanny Weaver's regimen."

Nanny Weaver did voice complaints that Bernard's schedule would be interrupted, and so he might be difficult to get down for his nap, but Giles and Daphne, and for that matter, Bernard, paid no attention whatsoever to her protests. They played with the child, devising ever more silly games while rolling around on the floor with him. Then, with him thoroughly tired out, they left Bernard to Nanny Weaver's care while they took to their horses.

Giles was more than keen to ride, just for the sake of riding. He had been on shipboard for a long time, and despite his significant captures and the blowing up a Spanish ship-of-the-line, he had doubts that his time had been well used by the government. For Giles's purposes, Dark Paul was an ideal horse to chase those thoughts away: powerful, swift, and with a hankering to try to see if his rider was really in control. Daphne's mount, Serene Masham, had proved herself in the past capable of keeping up with Dark Paul; her name fitted her personality well, except that she had a fierce desire to compete successfully, though she did do it with a minimum of effort.

Daphne and Giles covered a lot of ground on that ride, with Dark Paul careening wildly across their own fields and those of their tenants. Giles enjoyed pushing his rebellious horse, showing the stallion who was in charge, forcing him to race madly across the ground and take the many hedges and gates in stride. Surprisingly, Daphne on Serene Masham had no difficulty keeping up, the mare's gait being smoother and more efficient than the stallion's and requiring less effort to sail easily over barriers. This pattern of horse-handling went on until Giles felt that he had conquered his mount's determination to try to be in charge. Then he turned his horse towards home and eased off on the demands he was making.

"I don't know how Serene Masham was able to keep up with this powerful brute," Giles remarked as they were coming up to the Hall.

"She has a much lighter load, of course," replied Daphne, "and she has always been a very smooth runner, making less work of moving quickly than Dark Paul. She wouldn't do nearly as well if she had you in the saddle." Daphne didn't think it was worth mentioning that she had shortened the stirrups she used at Mr. Jackson's suggestion. He had pointed out that doing so moved Daphne's weight more onto the horse's withers* while she transferred more of her own weight onto her legs. She also found that this made it easier to ride the horse when galloping, cantering, or jumping. She just didn't want Giles to know about this development until the upcoming race was over, in which she intended to beat him.

When they returned to Dipton Hall, they turned their horses towards the stables, not the ones serving the mansion, but those that were part of the hunting-horse complex that Giles and Daphne had established on their estate. On previous occasions when he was at Dipton, Giles had become great friends with Mr. Griffiths, the stable master whom they had acquired when they moved the stud farm specializing in hunters from Saltan Masham to their own premises. Giles wanted to renew their friendship and to find out all the things that Mr. Griffiths might tell him that he would not mention to Daphne unless she asked explicitly. Daphne wanted to consult him on aspects of the race that she was not completely happy about. He knew far more about the problems of racing horses cross-country than any of the members of the Hunt who had taken on the task of planning the race. Mr. Griffiths was at his table in his room in the stables, about to take a break to enjoy some cider and tarts. He had seen his employers arrive and invited them to share his refreshments.

"Well, Captain Giles, I see from his condition that you gave Dark Paul a demanding run. Was he up to his old tricks?"

"Yes, but not as badly as the last time I rode him after being away. I think he is slowly realizing that he will be happier doing things as I direct rather than trying to get his own way."

"I see that Serene Masham looks much less tired than Dark Paul, my lady," Mr. Griffiths went on. "Did you not keep up with the mad antics of the stallion?"

"Oh, yes, I went the same route as Captain Giles. Serene Masham, of course, didn't waste as much energy trying to dislodge her rider. As always, she was very well behaved, and of course, I weigh a great deal less than my husband."

The talk then turned to the race.

"I heard about Major Stoner's accident," Mr. Grifiths said. "I hope he is recovering."

"As well as can be expected with a broken leg and a knock on the head. The good news is that the break did not come through his skin, so infection is not an issue.."

"How did it happen?"

Daphne explained what she and the Major had been doing and why he had tried a blind jump.

"What I don't understand," Mr. Griffiths said when Daphne had finished, "is why you were laying out a course in that way."

"So that the Hunt could run this new course."

"Fixed routes aren't usual for this sort of race, though one is starting to see special races with preset courses and required jumps, sometimes even artificial ones. But a good cross-country race, something that can be truly called a steeplechase, only needs a few places that the competitors need to go through. Let's see, if I were doing it, I would start at Dipton, then on to Upper Dipton, St. Mary's Underhill, Langfield, St. Paul's in

Copse, and then finish at Dipton. To make it more of a challenge of hunting skills and picking good routes across the countryside, I would only require that riders pass each of the churches — you could station someone at each place to record that they did go there — and otherwise not worry about how they went. That turns the race more into a question of how well the rider can pick out the best ways to a destination, rather than just how fast their horse can run."

"That sounds an exciting race, though maybe more complicated for those who only want to watch," said Daphne.

"Not really," replied the stable master." Usually, people want to see the start and the finish of a race, and they will be in the same place. Indeed, if it happens to be a good day and the race starts from Dipton, Mr. and Mrs. Carstairs at the Dipton Arms should do a fine business as people wait for the racers to return after seeing them off."

"Maybe we should take this up with Major Stoner," said Giles. "It sounds like a good idea to me."

"To me also," Daphne chimed in. I think I would enjoy participating in that sort of race more than one with a fixed course, with possible small deviations, such as the Major was thinking of. Of course, it would give us an advantage over others who don't know the countryside as well."

"Surely, you are not thinking of competing in the race, Lady Giles," said Mr. Griffiths.

"Yes, why shouldn't I."

"It's very bad form for the people who are putting up the prize for this sort of event and are involved in planning it to win the prize. That's how it strikes me anyway."

"I can see your point," said Giles. "Putting up one hundred guineas as a prize and then winning it, when the race is held to a large extent on our properties, might seem a bit peculiar. But I would be disappointed not to participate, and I know that Daphne has been looking forward to competing. I wonder what we should do."

"Try a variant," Mr. Griffiths suggested.

"What would that be?"

"Establish a cup for the best course time that could stand as a progressive challenge for future years. If this race is a success, it would be very advantageous if it becomes established as a major annual event. One way to do that is to have a challenge-time — the fastest the race has ever been ridden. To establish that, I suggest you two race each other sometime before the real race – maybe a day or so ahead – to establish the initial time. The cup would have engraved on it the name of the winning competitor of the race provided he — or she — also beats the mark for the fastest time achieved up to then. It would also give those who breed hunters a trophy to win to show the strength of their programs. I don't think we should be squeamish about one of our horses winning the cup.

"I would suggest that you set the initial standard by the two of you competing against each other a couple of days before the race itself. Then you are not competing against others who do not have your advantage, just setting a time that others can try to emulate. Of course, it won't hurt if your time remains the standard after this race. It will give a challenge for later races and attract attention and, hopefully, participation in future runnings of the race. With luck, the Dipton Hunter Race could become a major fixture in the racing season. That would be good for the stud farm as well."

"That is an excellent suggestion," said Daphne. "And if one of our times is faster than anyone's competing in the race, it will reveal that we would have won if we competed, without the embarrassment of actually winning when we are sponsoring the event."

Daphne and Giles returned to the mansion, intending to discuss Mr. Griffiths's ideas with Major Stoner. They found that Mr. Summers, the rather ineffective President of the Ameschester Hunt, had come to commiserate and consult with the Major. Daphne suspected that he was terrified at the idea of having to organize the race without the Major's assistance.

"Ah, Earl Camshire," Mr. Summers began, "I was just discussing with Major Stoner the route for the race. In view of his accident, I said that we must have a simpler, shorter track where there would be no danger of anyone taking a wrong turn. No cross-country sections, just keeping to the main roads, between Dipton and Harvey Hollow on the road to Ameschester would be best, I believe."

"Oh, I don't think that would do at all, Mr. Summers," said Daphne while Giles was thinking about how to answer without causing offense. He had already told Mr. Summers how he preferred to be addressed and was annoyed that his preference had not been followed, as well as being appalled by the proposed change to the event. "It is too short a course, for one thing, and too easy for another. This is a race for hunters," Daphne continued, "not a speed trial on a fixed path suitable for thoroughbred horses that are good for nothing else. What you propose won't be a test of the best qualities of hunting horses and their riders."

"But, my lady, Major Stoner's accident demonstrates that a course like you are suggesting is just too dangerous. We can't have people who have come to join our Hunt, as well as to race, breaking their legs. That is obvious! Major Stoner was trying to select a good course for the race, and his accident suggests that it cannot be done."

Giles had little respect for Mr. Summers, but he didn't want to upset the little man while Major Stoner was laid up. If the current President resigned, it was likely that Giles would have to take over his position, at least on an interim basis. He knew that would mean that Daphne would have to do all the work if he had to go to sea again before a better candidate for the position could be found.

"Mr. Griffiths, the master of the Dipton Hunting Stables, had an interesting suggestion," Giles broke in before Daphne could set Mr. Summers straight. "He said that the only requirement should be that the racers must visit a specified number of places before returning to the starting point. How they do it is up to them. For example, the starting and finishing point might be Dipton at the church. The other places that have to be visited could be Upper Dipton, St. Mary's Underhill, Langfield, and St. Paul's in Copse. Except for starting and finishing at Dipton, the riders can choose to visit the other four places in any order and by any route they want."

"That is what I suggested originally, but you over-ruled me, Mr. Summers. You just over-ruled me!" piped up Major Stoner.

"Your suggestion was quite different, Major, totally different in fact. Your places were all different from these, and you had to take them in a particular order." Mr. Summers retorted sulkily. Daphne suspected that he was not happy about having his plans coming to pieces and was damned if he would let Major Stoner take the credit. He also may have realized that, even though he was the President of the Hunt, he would have to give way to the opinions of the Earl, who was the strongest supporter of the Hunt financially.

"Won't it seem a bit peculiar," Mr. Summers continued, "if the sponsor of the race, where there is a distinct advantage to having local knowledge, should happen to win the race?"

"Oh, there is no worry about that, Mr. Summers: I shall not be racing, nor will Lady Camshire." Giles had recovered his voice. "However, we shall race against each other a couple of days before the race and the meeting of the Hunt to establish the starting point of a new cup awarded whenever someone can better the best previous times. The cup would then be held by him until someone else surpasses his time."

"Or her," Daphne added.

"What, my love?" asked Giles

"Not just 'held by him.' It should be 'held by him or her.' Women can race too."

"Quite right. 'By him or her,' and, I suppose, 'his or her time.'"

Mr. Summers knew when it was wise to acquiesce in what was being suggested. He did so, but with a parting shot at Major Stoner, "There you have it, Major. Just get better, and next year you might win the cup, provided that you don't fall off your horse again."

Daphne and Giles also took their leave of the Major, though only after Daphne had firmly admonished him to not get out of bed until Mr. Jackson authorized his doing so. They were well pleased with their day. Daphne, however, did wish that this would be only the first of a long line of successive such days that they could spend together at Dipton, but she knew that was not to be. They would have to visit London before returning for the Hunt Ball and all the other events at Dipton for which the Ball was the climax.

Chapter XI

The unfamiliar sounds of the city, so different from the muted ones at Dipton Hall, woke Daphne at an earlier hour than she would have liked. Struthers House, in Mayfair, was quiet by London standards; nevertheless, the noises were much more pronounced than at Dipton Hall, and they were of a quite different nature.

Giles was still asleep, but Daphne had no more sleep left in her. She rang the bell for Betsy to come and help her get dressed. The Struthers's servants had become used to this unconventional countess, who didn't seem to realize that it was an established right of noble, married women to have breakfast in bed, or to have the meal at a table in their room in the course of morning activities such as writing letters.

Giles woke up when Daphne got out of bed and promptly went to his dressing room, where he summoned the footman who had been assigned to help him dress. Giles could, of course, dress himself. Onboard ship, he did so, though some captains were known to use their servants for the purpose. Usually, he also shaved himself, but when Lord Struthers's own valet showed up in answer to the bell, Giles changed his mind. The man was an expert with a razor, and Giles would prefer not to have any nicks on his face today. He had important meetings and wanted to look his best for them, first with the First Lord of the Admiralty and then with the Earl of

Reeding. After a bit of thought, he decided to go to the Admiralty in the full uniform of a post-captain, including the star of the Order of the Bath. He would need the full regalia for his induction into the House of Lords, even though, for that ceremony, he would be wearing it under the elaborate, voluminous robe peculiar to the peerage. He would be picking up that costume from his tailor after his lunch with the Earl of Reeding.

Giles realized that he was dressing extravagantly for his meeting at the Admiralty to remind the First Lord that he was a man of substance, not very keen, unlike so many successful captains, to get more recognition and prize money. He had already had plenty of both. He would now only accept assignments where the reason for his being assigned the task was to further the war with France, but not ones based on the personal convenience of the individuals who ran the Admiralty. His recent experiences with the attempts to hide the full extent of what Mr. Edwards had been doing had made him lose faith in how devoted the Admiralty might really be to considering only how to defend the country and remove the threat of Bonaparte.

Then he realized that perhaps wearing his full-dress uniform was counterproductive, indicating his own uncertainty about maintaining his position and his nervousness about joining the House of Lords, an institution about whose customs and rituals he knew nearly nothing. Instead, he would wear his best civilian day-time clothes to emphasize that he was still the same no-nonsense ship's captain and country gentleman that he had been before rising to the peerage, but one that no longer required his naval career to meet his monetary requirements. He changed again, now presenting the costume that was most appropriate for his twin missions that morning.

Giles had taken an unusually long time choosing just the right clothes, for he had been half-dressed in his naval regalia before adopting the civilian garb he usually wore when he was in town. Even so, when he descended to the breakfast room, it surprised him to find Daphne there before him.

"My goodness, my lord," Daphne teased him, "you do look distinguished and important."

"That is the idea, my dear. I am going to tell the Admiralty that I will only accept assignments in home waters that are genuine. Not something like intercepting that supposed galleon, which was invented just to make sure that I couldn't testify against Mr. Edwards. Even if the treasure ship had been real, its capture could have been assigned to many other captains."

"Aren't you afraid that they will take *Glaucus* away from you?" Daphne asked

"Not really. First, because I am pretty sure that I would want to leave the sea if it weren't for my duty to protect this island in a time of danger. Second, I have come to the realization that I have much more influence than I ever thought I would have. Largely because I have been incredibly successful as a frigate captain, even though you and I know that that was more luck than merit. There is nothing like stumbling into a favorable and rewarding situation, like intercepting those Dutch spice ships on a mission that was supposed to yield nothing, to make one seem important. Third, I, or really you and I, since most of the work always seems to fall on you, also have control now of four seats in the House of Commons besides my being in the House of Lords; that gives me a lot more influence than I ever had before. I think, maybe, it is time I used some of that influence for things that we think are important and that can't be done easily while I am at sea, at least not by me, and it isn't fair to burden you with carrying everything out in my absence."

"I hope you succeed in getting what you want from the Admiralty. Don't worry about me. I quite enjoy being involved in important matters, and people are getting to recognize that I *do* have your complete backing. But I trust that you will deal with the Admiralty in ways that suit *you* best, not because you think that I am overburdened."

"Thank you. What will you be doing today?"

"I will start with seeing how the work on Camshire House is getting on. You remember that I got the name of a man who specializes in restoring houses after they change hands or need alterations for other reasons. Lady Clara told me that, when money got tight, your father rather let maintenance go to pot on his London House."

"Yes, he did. We were just lucky that the senior servants stayed as it went downhill, possibly because my mother had been a good mistress, though my father was never a good master. That meant that they were still available when he shut down Camshire House, just when I needed staff for Dipton Hall. Of course, neither they nor I realized at the time that I would be lucky enough to persuade the independent Miss Moorhouse to become Lady Giles, and therefore the Mistress of Dipton Hall, nor did anyone realize that that step would lead to you becoming the Mistress of Camshire House. I remember you telling me about this designer and seeing to setting the old house in order. I didn't realize that you had arranged a meeting for today."

"That's because I didn't know if I would have one at all until I got a note just a few minutes ago confirming it. After that meeting, I am not sure what I will be doing. Possibly go to Bond Street."

Giles left Struthers House as soon as he had finished breakfast. He decided not to take his carriage. It was not a long walk from Mayfair to the Admiralty in Whitehall. Dawn was breaking as he set out. Already the streets were bustling with all sorts of workers getting ready for the day ahead. Even as Giles pushed through the early morning bustle in Pall Mall, he had to dodge aside to miss the small groups of well-dressed but disheveled men, much the worse for drink, who were staggering along the sidewalk.

One of the rowdy and disheveled groups was coming from Green's Club. Giles was a member there because his father had owned the building in which the club was located. In fact, he must be the owner of the building now. He wondered if he could do anything about the club or, at least, sell the building. He would have to have Mr. Snodgravel look into it. Daphne might have to arrange that if he were sent to sea immediately. Of course, she seemed to know more about the ins and outs of the entailments involved in his father's estate than he did, and she probably knew more about disposing of property.

Giles arrived at the Admiralty with two minutes left before the time of his appointment. He was shown immediately into the Board Room where only the Second Secretary, Mr. Newsome, was present.

"I am sorry, my lord," he greeted Giles. "I am afraid that the First Lord and the First Sea Lord were called to Downing Street only a quarter of an hour ago. I didn't have time to warn you that your meeting had to be postponed. "

"Can't be helped, I suppose. Tell me, Mr. Newsome, do you have any idea what is afoot, though despite our long friendship, probably you can't tell me, even if you wanted to. And please, don't call me 'my lord.' In the Admiralty, I am still just 'Captain Giles.' "

"I can't tell you, Captain Giles, because I don't know. It is very unusual. We have received no dispatches which would require the immediate meeting between the Prime Minister and the Lords of the Admiralty. If the French have come out of Brest, we would be the first to know, and I can't think of anything else that would require such urgency. I have no idea when they will return, but if things are as critical as an unscheduled and immediate visit to Downing Street would suggest, they are likely to be very busy when they return. I suggest that you go. I'll send a note when your appointment is rescheduled. I imagine it will be tomorrow. Are you at Struthers House?"

"Yes. I guess that is the best way to proceed."

Giles found himself in Whitehall, outside the Admiralty, at a loose end. He could go back to Struthers House, but then it would not be long before he had to set off again to the club in Pall Mall where he was to meet the Earl of Reeding. That didn't make much sense. Instead, it was only a very short walk to the Strand, where he knew that he could find coffee shops and maybe a bookshop.

Giles settled with a newspaper into a corner of the first coffee house he found in the Strand. He hoped that the paper might give some hints about the likely cause for the suddenly urgent meeting of the Lords of the Admiralty with the Prime Minister, but he could find nothing of relevance. What he did find was a piece on how the cost of spices had been increasing and that several spice merchants were eager for the cargoes of recently captured Dutch ships to be auctioned off. However, the bulk of the article was spent retelling the story of how those ships had been captured. It also emphasized the oddity that the three naval captains involved had also been prominent victims of the swindling done by Mr. Edwards, for which the agent had recently been convicted in the Old Bailey.

Reading about Mr. Edwards's swindling reminded Giles of George Moorhouse's concern about the substantial funds he had left with Edwards. Daphne had written to Mr. Snodgravel on the subject, Giles knew, but she might not have time during this London visit to ensure that the lawyer acted as promptly as possible. Mr. Snodgravel's offices were not far away, and Giles had several hours before seeing the Earl of Reeding. He refolded his newspaper, called for his bill, and left the coffee shop to proceed along the Strand to Chancery Lane where Mr. Snodgravel had his chambers.

Mr. Snodgravel was in and would be very pleased to see the Earl of Camshire immediately. After introductory pleasantries, he got down to business, "I received a letter from Lady Camshire, my lord, about checking into your account, or I should say 'former account,' with Mr. Edwards. I immediately had my investigator, Roland Shearer, look into it. He is very good at tracing monies through financial records of complicated accounts and similar sources.

"I have just received his report, actually his preliminary report. Indeed, Mr. Edwards was stealing money from you and many of his other naval clients who left funds with him. His prime way of doing it was through an accounting slate of hand that can be traced through his books. As you know, Edwards usually invested monies received as prize money in Consols. His trick was to pretend he had overpaid for the securities. Most of your fellow officers did not know the prices of Consols and just looked at the guaranteed annual return. That is how people frequently report their financial wealth. So much per annum in Consols, so much per annum in rents on their properties, and so on. If anyone questioned the figures, he could say that there had been a clerical error and restore the filched Consols or replace them with others. Shearer is not sure why, but Mr. Edwards decided to buy an estate in Shropshire, near Shrewsbury. Possibly he was thinking of it as a retirement location, for there is a rumor that he was intending to leave his business and become a country gentleman, far from where his business had been centered. That happened at a time when his own funds were tied up in several different ventures — most of them unsuccessful, Shearer reports.

"What happened is that Edwards discovered a country estate for sale in Shropshire, near Shrewsbury. The property and the house had been let decline for many years, but, Shearer understands, it could be transformed into an excellent property for a country gentleman.

"How is this of concern to you, you may well ask. Well, that is where we became a little bit lucky. Mr. Edwards paid for the estate by selling your Consols. His clerk is a fussy record keeper, and he listed exactly which Consols had been used to purchase the estate. Of course, the bonds are numbered, and the ones that bought the estate in Shropshire were ones that Edwards had bought with your prize money and then sold from your account, though you were never told about them. You also wouldn't have been credited in the reports Edwards sent you if and when he returned them. Of course, his empire collapsed before he could do that, but he might never have returned the funds for all we know.

"It is probably going to take years to straighten out the mess involved in Edwards's stealing from so many people and hiding the theft in so many devious ways. It will take still longer to work out how to divide up whatever money is left after we lawyers take whatever we can extract from trying to settle things. But Mr. Shearer thinks that he can finagle things so that it appears that your Consols were used to buy you an estate, and only a technical glitch makes it appear that Edwards used the money for himself. The books do show several cases where he did similar transactions for clients, though the record had to be studied to realize that was what was going on and not a piece of skullduggery like the one involving your Consols.

"So you are saying, Mr. Snodgravel, that I have, possibly, bought a country estate in Shropshire and that I should take possession of it as soon as possible?"

"Essentially, yes."

Before Giles could respond to this answer, Mr. Snotgravel's clerk knocked on the door and followed it immediately by the announcement, "Sorry to interrupt, sir, but the Countess of Camshire is here."

"Show her in immediately."

Daphne paused when she saw Giles. "What are you doing here? I thought you were tied up in the Admiralty all morning."

"So did I. I discovered that the meeting had been canceled when I arrived at the Admiralty, so I came here to find out whether anything useful could be learned about Edwards's thievery. Mr. Snodgravel has some interesting news. Mr. Snodgravel, please tell Lady Camshire what you have learned."

It took only a few minutes for the lawyer to bring Daphne up to date on what had been discovered about Mr. Edwards's handling of the accounts entrusted to him.

"Do you mean to say that we have acquired an estate in Shropshire because he used Giles's Consols to buy it?"

"In essence, that is true, though there are also some other thefts from your account for which you can lay claim against whatever is still in Edwards's possession."

"Giles," Daphne said. "We already have too many estates that we can't get rid of. There is Ashbury Abbey and Ashton Manor, which came to you completely entailed. Then we have Dipton Hall, and I am not giving that up! And the ones in Norfolk that your father was trying to hide from you. And, of course, Camshire House here in London, and Green's Club and I don't know how many more places we own and don't need. So do we really want an estate in Shropshire?"

"Speaking of gentlemen's clubs like Green's," said Giles, "I really should leave to be on time for my luncheon meeting with the Earl of Reeding at Brooks's. I don't want to be late since he is doing me a favor. Daphne, you may want to stay so that you can go into some of those problems that you have been handling for my mother with Mr. Snodgravel."

Giles left at once, and he would have to walk fast to get to Brooks's on time. The rather unimpressive front door of the club was opened by a doorman. Inside, a factotum welcomed him, "Lord Camshire, it is an honor to see you in Brooks's. Lord Reeding is waiting for you in the small drawing room."

Giles had become accustomed to being recognized by total strangers, after likenesses of him, some quite accurate, and some not, had appeared at various times in the newspapers when his successes at sea had led to them reporting, with varying degrees of accuracy, about his activities. The man led him to one of the rooms off the foyer of the club and pointed out to him a middle-aged man engrossed in a newspaper.

"My lord, Lord Camshire is here," the superior servant declared before turning to return to his post.

The middle-aged man tossed his paper aside and rose to his feet.

"Camshire," he declared. "It is an honor to meet you. I knew your father, of course, but Struthers assures me that you are a different kettle of fish entirely."

"I hope so, my lord. I confess that I had not been an admirer of my father in his later years. Of course, I went to sea at an early age and saw very little of him after that, so I never really knew him well. I was a bit of an afterthought for him — his third son — and he never had much time for me or my younger brother."

"Ah, the fate of the extra sons. The first one is critical to the continuation of the title and the estate; a second is needed for insurance, but any more are superfluous. Though I was only a second son, not the third, I know it well, but my brother was healthy. My father expected me to become an MP to further his concerns in the Commons. Winchester, Queen's College, Cambridge, then the Middle Temple, but before I was called to the bar, my father and elder brother died of smallpox. I was away at the time and was not infected. So, instead of the Commons, I became a member of the House of Lords, though not a particularly active one.

"But that is enough about me. This club does a very good cold collation at this time of day. Let's go up and see what they have today."

The dining room was a bright, airy place, somewhat to Giles's surprise since he had expected a dimly lit place with heavy curtains. The head waiter showed them to a table by a window.

"We'll each have the cold collation and a bottle of that claret that I liked so much last time I was here," Giles's host ordered.

"They have a very good cellar here," Lord Reeding told Giles. "They took advantage of the short peace in 1802 to acquire and lay down some excellent vintages. I trust this one will be to your taste."

"I know very little about wines: not much vintage wine is on offer in the wardrooms of frigates or even in their captain's cabins."

"I suppose. One doesn't often think about the implications of gentlemen and gentlemen's sons spending long periods at sea. If you wish to know more about wines, the gentlemen's clubs in London are not a bad place to learn. Most of the best clubs have good cellars and very knowledgeable wine stewards like we have here. Are you a member of one of the clubs, Camshire?"

"I suppose I am. Of Green's, though I have never been there except once with my father years ago. I inherited the building it occupies, which seems to automatically make me a member. My solicitor is looking to see if there is some way to break the entail on the property."

"Yes, Green's does have a rather unpleasant reputation. Poor cellar, too, I am told. You would be better off being a member here. I'd be happy to put your name forward, but it might meet some opposition from men who remember your father with distaste."

"That's very good of you, Reeding. I can see the difficulty. My father did make a lot of enemies, I know, and I don't want to embarrass you."

"Oh, it wouldn't bother me, though it would disappoint me if someone black-balled you. We are a more easy-going club than, say, White's. It is a Tory haunt while we are more Whig, but we have many members who do not follow a party line, such as myself or Mr. Wilberforce. He is a member here, as was Pitt before he died, which gives you a bit of an idea of the extent to which we are a party club.

"That's a good introduction to what I wanted to talk about, which is the House of Lords," Lord Reeding continued. "You are joining a quite complex organization and one that is infuriating at times. There are, as I see it, four types of members. The largest group comprises peers who do not care much for attending the Lords and only show up occasionally, usually when the act under consideration might directly affect their rights or profits. Their interest is a bit unpredictable, which adds a measure of uncertainly to the passage of bills through the Lords. The second group consists of the peers who regularly attend sittings of the House, especially when votes are to be called, and who vote along party lines — Tories or Whigs, as the case may be — without fail. Next, there is a third group, somewhat smaller than the other two. This is composed of people who decide on how they will vote solely on the merits of the bill under consideration. I am one of them, though I tend to side more often with the Whigs than with the

Tories. Finally, there are those who are in it for their personal gain. I won't say that their votes are for sale, but their own self-interest can be used to steer their participation in directions desired by others. At least in his later years, when I was familiar with him, your father was definitely one of the fourth group."

"I have no intention of following him in that role," Giles replied. "I imagine I will be either in the first or third. I intend to take my duties as a peer very seriously, but I may still have an obligation to serve at sea, which will prevent my regular attendance."

"Very understandable, Camshire, very understandable. And I'll be glad to have another free-thinker as a colleague.

"Now, as you may know, when you are introduced to the House, you can make your maiden speech or leave that for another time. If you make it now, the speech can be on any subject and does not have to be about the bill, which is currently being debated by the Lords. Do you think that you will want to give one right away?"

"Yes, I want to get it out of the way. Future contributions will then be much easier."

"Quite right. I expect you will be talking about land husbandry, which Lord Struthers tells me is a great interest of yours."

"No, though you are right about my interest in that subject. I want to talk about an issue that gives me great concern and in which I am afraid that Britain is supporting an unjustifiable situation."

"What is that?"

"The slave trade, particularly the transportation of slaves from Africa to our colonies in the Caribbean. The conditions are appalling on the slave ships: we would never dream of transporting animals that way."

"I agree with you; it needs to be abolished. What about slavery itself?"

"I believe that it is wrong, but not such an awful degradation of humans. From reading the papers, I would guess that outlawing of the trans-Atlantic trade is much more likely to be possible than the abolition of slavery in the colonies."

"I think you are right about that," Lord Reeding concurred. "The plantation owners have a lot of interest, particularly in the Commons, where I know they have bought any number of ridings and are contributing in various ways to several other members. Of course, some of our peers also own properties in the colonies and are fiercely opposed to any hint that they will lose the slaves who toil on their plantations."

"I understand that though I regret it. At present, it is only possible, I believe, to stop the transport of slaves. Even that may improve the lot of those already enslaved: they may become more valued by their owners and thus be better treated."

"Good luck with that," replied the Earl of Reeding. "I look forward to your speech."

Their conversation drifted off to other matters. Lord Reeding was interested in progressive farming for his estate, though he had yet to enclose its fields. Furthermore, he was fond of music, choral more than instrumental, but, even so, they had a discussion that enlivened each man.

Giles returned to Struthers House to find that Daphne had only recently returned and that their hosts had arranged a dinner party to introduce them to more people who were prominent in London Society. Giles was not entirely happy about his aunt's wanting to show Daphne and him off to the men of distinction and power and the ladies who set much of the tone for Society, though not that of the rakish Prince Regent's circle.

Daphne was nervous about being expected to take the role of an important member of the aristocracy, especially as she still often felt herself to be the unpretentious Daphne Moorhouse, who had expected a quiet, unmarried life in the country. It was one thing for her to become the wife of the sea captain who had swept her off her feet. It was quite a different matter to find out that, instead of a quiet, country life, fate had dictated that they both had to assume greatly changed roles arising from his family's prominence as well as from his own achievements. But they could not object to being expected to play tonight's roles.

Lady Struthers had always been Giles's favorite relation, and she had been very good in welcoming Daphne into the family even though her newly acquired niece had little of the knowledge about the activities and habits of Society that was Lady Struthers's birthright. Although it was no part of Daphne's background, she could sympathize with Lady Struthers's disappointment at never having had daughters to bring out for their "seasons" and how, in a way, introducing Daphne made up for that disappointment to some degree. Daphne had decided to make the best of the situation, enter into her hostess's plans enthusiastically, and persuade Giles to take the same approach. They had to do it: Giles's position guaranteed that they would be thrust into fashionable Society repeatedly. They might as well make the best of the opportunities and enjoy them rather than showing that they were being dropped unhappily into a situation they could not avoid.

Chapter XII

Daphne left Struthers House a few minutes after Giles. She, too, did not take the carriage since her destination was only a few streets away. Of course, she went with Betsey, who trailed along behind her mistress as was the custom in London. Betsey much preferred when her mistress was at Dipton, where she only had to accompany her on rare visits to Ameschester. She knew that Camshire House would not be the last of their destinations this day and that she could expect to be trailing after her mistress on many crowded streets.

Both designer and the builder were waiting for Daphne, ready with suggestions and plans for what might be done. They were surprised by the definite ideas the new Countess of Camshire had about how she wanted the house to be improved. Several rooms that Daphne thought were too small were to be expanded by being combined with others. Daphne believed that they did not need a great many small rooms; she and Giles could expect far fewer guests staying there than the current layout permitted, and she felt that less cramped quarters would be more enjoyable for guests and leave fewer empty rooms to keep dusted.

Three of the senior servants at Dipton Hall had been recruited by Giles from Camshire House when his father had closed the establishment. Daphne had taken the very unusual step of questioning them about what improvements could be made to the house. They each had made suggestions for improving the kitchen and the serving areas. To Betsey's surprise, Daphne also examined the servants' quarters and ordered some improvements there.

The men who hoped to be in charge of the renovations to the house found that, while the Countess listened to their opinions, she quickly made decisions, some of which reflected her own ideas, sometimes in contradiction of theirs. They had come expecting to have a long period in which they tried to persuade a flighty woman to agree to renovations that would line their pockets nicely. Instead, it became evident that this Countess was not quite like the others they were used to working with. They had also hoped to be given orders to proceed at once with the work or to wait for the Earl's confirmation of her orders; instead, when she believed that things were clear, Daphne ordered them to prepare estimates for the job and to submit them to her solicitor, Mr. Snodgravel, before they proceeded with the changes. Daphne suspected that they had hoped to be told to proceed without first giving estimates for the work to be done, but she had learned from seeing tradesmen take advantage of her good-natured and not business-like father that without a firm agreement on price, they would invariably try to exploit wealthy people if they could.

As she had already told Giles, her next stop was on Bond Street, but not, as he might have thought, to go shopping. She was going to visit the artist, Michael Findley, who had done some work at Dipton and painted some possible family and individual portraits with Giles in them that just waited for him to sit while the painter filled in his likeness where needed in the scenes. Daphne wanted to see what Mr. Findlay had accomplished and learn when he could complete the work. His studio was in a house in Bond Street, opposite the music store where Daphne had bought Giles's violin. She had sent him a note from Dipton, making an appointment for that morning, but she was told that Mr. Findlay had gone out when she reached the house.

Daphne dawdled for a few minutes at the music shop across the street from the artist's house, but she didn't want to choose music without Giles. Instead, she decided to visit Mr. Snodgravel. Daphne hailed a cab to take her to Chancery Lane, though she might have made better time through the crowded streets walking. When she reached the lawyer's chambers, she was surprised to find Giles there ahead of her. He was in discussion with Mr. Snodgravel about how serious were the thefts that Mr. Edwards had made from the monies Giles had left with the agent. That problem had slipped Daphne's mind, so she was glad that Giles had remembered and been concerned enough to pursue the matter with the solicitor. The main news was that Edwards had been pilfering on a very large scale from the accounts with which he had been entrusted. Some of what had been taken from the funds held in Giles's name could be traced to the purchase of an estate in Shropshire. Daphne was alarmed to find that yet another estate had been acquired when they already had title to many others. When she was about to raise this concern, Giles realized that he had to meet the sponsor introducing him to the House of Lords. He left Daphne to deal with this and any other business with Mr. Snodgravel.

"This place in Shropshire, can't we just sell it and not have to have anything more to do with it?" Daphne asked after Giles had left.

"No. We would have to establish the title first before we could sell it. Mr. Edwards registered the property in his own name, and we will have to argue that that was a slip where he should have added that he was acting as your husband's agent, not for himself, in purchasing the property. Taking possession and either renting it out or running it yourself would help to establish your claim to it. After all, the old saying the 'possession is ninety percent of the law' is still true. I'm trying to get more information about the place. All I know now is that it is a few miles downriver from Shrewsbury on the River Severn."

"I didn't realize that Shrewsbury was in Shropshire. It's quite close to Birmingham, isn't it?"

"I believe so. I have the impression that it is only five or six hours by carriage, but I don't know the area at all. Why do you ask, my lady?"

"I am likely to have to go to Birmingham in the near future and might consider examining this property if I have a chance."

"I see. I had no idea you had any reason to go to Birmingham. Surely an agent, or one of our correspondents in the city, can serve your needs."

"No, I need to deal with my uncle's townhouse there, especially to make sure that some long-time retainers are well treated. He'll want an in-person report from me about the house and about how his gun-making business is going. What I do depends, of course, on what Lord Camshire wants, but I would like more details about this estate before we make any decisions about it."

Daphne and the solicitor then went on to discuss the Norfolk properties that had belonged to the late Earl of Camshire. Here again, Daphne's desire to get rid of the estates ran into legal objections. Her father-in-law had so tied up his holdings in leases of dubious value and other covenants that it would take years to get clear title so that the value of the holdings could be realized if they were sold.

"My recommendation is that you use an agent to manage the estates, my lady, until the confusion the late Earl left behind has been straightened out." Mr. Snodgravel asserted. "In addition, there is the point that thirty percent of the revenues will go to your mother-in-law, Lady Clara, if you hold onto the properties, while she would be entitled to nothing if you sold them."

That consideration decided Daphne to follow Mr. Snodgravel's recommendation. She knew that her mother-in-law was enjoying having funds over which she had complete control, even though Lady Clara's expenses were small and she was living with Giles and Daphne at Dipton Hall.

Daphne left the solicitor's chambers and returned to Bond Street. There she went to the shop and workplace of a fashionable furniture maker. The furnishings in Camshire House were not only old but old-fashioned, suiting the rather dreary style that the late Earl's first wife must have liked. Lady Clara had mentioned that her husband had refused to update the house while they were using it.

The furniture establishment fascinated Daphne. She was seeing for the first time real examples, not just sketches, of the styles that were spreading from France. Drawings of the new style had been smuggled in and were now causing a revolution in what was considered fashionable. Simpler, but also more exotic, was the impression that Daphne received about the new style, though that is not exactly how the enthusiastic designers she talked to at the shop described it.

She ordered the furniture maker who had been showing her the possibilities for furnishings, including material for drapes and suggestions for colors and even for woodwork in the principal rooms of Camshire House, to go and see the rooms in question and make suggestions about what furniture would be needed, and about drapes, and wall coverings. She would expect a report with plans, drawings, and swatches of any cloth to be used to be sent to Dipton Hall within the next three weeks, with estimates of the work and its schedule. As the work progressed, they could expect payment at various stages, and Daphne demanded a discount for prompt payment of bills. That last provision startled the man she was talking to. He had been worried that he might have great difficulty collecting his bills as with so many of the nobility. If Lord Camshire delayed payment excessively, he would still be very reluctant to take serious steps to get what was owed him since his other clients might take this action as an affront to themselves as well their class and take their business elsewhere.

Daphne returned to Struthers House quite satisfied with her day. She had to dress for the evening. Lady Struthers would take her and the Countess of Reeding to observe the ceremony where Giles would take his place in the House of Lords. Giles arrived at

Struthers House only a few moments later. He explained that he had no news about why his appointment at the Admiralty had been canceled; maybe he would learn something at the House of Lords tonight since it was likely that someone in the government would know what was happening, probably Lord Struthers. If his uncle-in-law didn't know, he could certainly find out.

Daphne then related what she had been doing about Camshire House and its furnishings. To her surprise, Giles was very interested. Maybe, he said, she could show him on the next day some of what she had decided. They could return to Dipton on the day after that. Daphne was delighted at the suggestion. Up to then, Giles had seemed to regard the improvements of his London House a matter of no consequence. Maybe he was warming to the idea of living there when aspects of the house were removed that would call to mind unhappy earlier times.

They had little time to dawdle getting dressed. Soon, Giles and Daphne descended to the entrance foyer to find Lady Struthers already there. She was going with Daphne to the Strangers' Gallery of the House of Lords. They were to meet Lady Reeding at the entrance, after which the carriage would carry Giles to the main entrance, where he was to be met by Lord Reeding.

Lady Reeding turned out to be a striking, tall, middle-aged woman. She was dressed in the height of fashion with a gown of sapphire blue, elaborately styled, and a matching hat. She looked like she had just stepped out of one of the magazines showing the latest fashions from Paris. She broke into a warm smile when she was introduced to Daphne.

"Lady Camshire," she stated. "I am so pleased to meet you at last. Gillian, Lady Struthers, has told me so much about you, and I have seen so many reports in the newspapers about your activities that I feel that I know you already."

"Lady Reeding, it is very good of you to welcome me here and for Lord Reeding to sponsor my husband's entry into the House of Lords."

"Nonsense. We are delighted to be of service. Lord Reeding was very excited to be asked. He remarked that it was an honor to introduce an earl who was such a prominent naval hero. I am dying to see your husband and hear his maiden speech. Let's go up to the Gallery, where I have arranged for one of the ushers to hold some of the best seats for us."

It was fortunate that Lady Reeding had arranged for their seats to be kept. When they ascended to the Strangers' Gallery, it was already crowded. Word must have spread that this would be one of the rare occasions when someone could hear a prominent war hero speak. Daphne and her aristocratic companions had only just settled into their seats when the ceremony began.

A man carrying a highly decorated and gilded club followed by another in a rich robe entered from the end of the chamber. Lady Reeding whispered that the club was called the mace and that the man with the mace was called 'Black Rod' while the man coming behind him was the Lord Chancellor. They were followed by men in scarlet robes. Lady Reeding explained that they were all wearing these gowns because the introduction of a new member was a formal, ceremonial occasion.

Behind the Lord Chancellor were the peers, in order of precedence, starting with the dukes, of which only two were present that day, followed by a single marquis. Then came the earls. They were, Lady Reeding whispered, in the order of the age of their earldom. With Earl Reeding beside him, Giles led that part of the procession because a Giles had been Earl of Camshire since 1074 when the earldom was created by William the Conqueror.

Daphne had never seen Giles in his Earl's robe, a bright scarlet garment descending almost to the floor, trimmed around the collar with white fur, that Lady Reeding told her was miniver. The same fur formed three wide bands on the front of the robe. When Daphne asked what miniver was, she was told that it was the winter hide of squirrels.

The procession moved down the center of the chamber until Black Rod mounted a dais and moved around a large cushion to place the mace on a table. The Lord Chancellor then sat on the cushion, which Lady Reeding informed Daphne was called 'the woolsack.'

The Lord Chancellor made a few introductory remarks to establish that the House was sitting. Then he called on the Earl of Reeding to introduce the new member to the House.

Lord Reeding's speech was brief and to the point. He mentioned how Giles was joining an illustrious line of peers, stretching back to the Conquest, who had contributed to the public life of the realm. He indirectly reminded the House of the long line of successful naval endeavors of the new Earl of Camshire by saying that he knew that the new Earl regretted not having been present for the opening of Parliament because duty had called him to sea. Finally, before sitting down, Lord Reeding stated that he was sure that, as his other duties permitted, the newly seated Earl would make major contributions to the business of the House, uninfluenced by the particular interests of persons with whom he had recently spoken. Instead, he would adhere to seeking what he saw as the public interest. It was a very clear jab at the behavior of the previous Earl of Camshire. The Lord Chancellor then formally welcomed Giles to the House and ceded the floor to him

Giles rose to his feet. He made a few introductory remarks before getting to the meat of his address. Daphne was amazed. She hadn't realized that he had the actor's trick of projecting his voice so that his words were clear in all parts of the chamber without shouting. His delivery was also loud enough to cut through the low babble as peers whispered to each other.

"My Lords," Giles began, "I know most of you expect that I will talk about the Navy, possibly about how important it is to our safety as a country or else about the shocking amount of corruption that pervades the various services that are supposed to keep the Navy afloat and effective. These are vital matters but more of an administrative nature than a legislative one. I will speak instead of an urgent wrong that it is in the power of Parliament to correct. I talk of the trade in African slaves."

Giles went on to outline the essence of the triangular trade quickly. He was scathing about the first stage, where cheap iron goods were transported to Africa to trade for slaves. He described the goods shipped from Bristol and Liverpool as 'shoddy,' 'a disgrace to British manufacturers,' 'an embarrassment to the country,' descriptions that had many heads nodding even as others, possibly Lords with interests in this aspect of the trade, looked angry at what was being said.

Giles then launched into a description of 'the middle passage,' where the slaves acquired in Africa were transported to the West Indies in irons. He related the terrible conditions as the cargo was transported in cramped conditions in the hold, with sores produced by the ill-fitting and badly finished shackles, again an implied criticism of the ironwork involved in the slave trade. Giles next spoke of the high death rate among the cargo, who were being transported in conditions far worse than those used for carrying horses or other domestic animals abroad. Of how the dead, and even the still living but seriously ill, slaves were tossed overboard without ceremony to be eaten by sharks.

"You may think," Giles said, "that the slave trade is necessary for the islands of the West Indies to be profitable. That is not true. I have seen well-managed plantations that rely only on their existing workers and the natural increase that occurs when the slaves are well treated and respected. Those who rely on the constant arrival of more slaves from Africa are not the most profitable plantations but are poor ones, reliant on shoddy practices of husbandry and inhumane treatment of their slaves. Stop the slave trade, and all planters will have to respect the value of their workers — their slaves — and by treating them properly, increase the profits of their plantations.

"You may ask how I know this, especially as I am sure that many of you think that, had my father ever owned property in the West Indies, he would have been among the worst of the slave owners. But I have experienced the islands of the West Indies myself during my service in our navy, and I have seen first-hand the terrible consequences of the inhuman transport of slaves.

"It was while I was Third Lieutenant on the frigate *Perseus*, 32, that I experienced the full horrors of the slave trade. We were returning from an unsuccessful eastward chase of a French privateer and approaching Antigua in a gale when we spotted a ship aground on reefs at the eastern end of the island. It was evident that the ship was a slaver. With the roaring wind and pounding seas, she was in danger of breaking up. We launched a boat to see if we could help while *Perseus* stayed well away from the hazardous reef. I was in charge of our longboat. As we approached the stranded ship, a small boat left her, fleeing for the shore. She yelled to us that the ship was being abandoned since it was about to break up. However, we could hear desperate screams coming from the wreck, and I decided that we should investigate. It may not have been the wisest decision in my career, but I felt that we must do what we could, a position that my captain supported when he reported the incident.

"We boarded the ship and found that the hold was packed with people, shackled on narrow shelves rendering them completely helpless. They didn't have enough space even to sit up! With the shackles, it was impossible for them to move off the shelves. We searched desperately for tools to undo the heavy iron shackles, but we could find none. There was nothing we could do. The water was rising, and the ship showed every sign of soon sliding off the rock that held it and sinking. We had to abandon her. We rowed to safety with the shrieks of the condemned people in our ears. It upset all of us terribly. The midshipman who was with me was so affected that he soon quit the service, fearing not the enemy but, instead, being confronted again with such a terrible situation. I myself still have nightmares about it and wake to find myself shaking and weeping.

"When *Perseus* reached English Harbour, we learned that the crew of the slave ship had all escaped safely and felt no remorse for abandoning their 'cargo.' Insurance would cover their losses and pay their wages. That their 'cargo' had all drowned was of no concern to them or the owners of their ship. The trade they were engaged in is inhuman, involving terrible and unwarranted hardship inflicted on innocent people. We would never dream of abusing the criminals who are transported to Australia in such a fashion. It must stop!

"Members of the Royal Navy are proud to serve in situations of hardship and acute danger for the good of the Nation. That is an expected, though regrettable, part of warfare. Our people should not, especially not the young men unhardened to the atrocities that can accompany service at sea, be exposed to sights such as we on *Perseus* endured that can scar them for life.

"A bill will soon be introduced, I am informed, in the Other Place to abolish the trade in slaves. I trust that when the bill reaches this House, it will receive the support that should be automatic in the legislature of any enlightened society. I yield the floor."

Stunned silence followed Giles's speech caused by the final description of his personal experiences with the slave trade. A murmur then arose as people, both sitting lords and the hoard of visitors, many of them from the other House who had been attracted as news spread that a remarkable piece of oratory was being delivered by the new Earl of Camshire.

As the next speaker rose to his feet, most of the lords started to leave. Daphne thought it was rather rude to the lord who was now speaking, but, clearly, it was the established way of proceeding. In fact, Lord Reeding whispered to Giles that they should stand and make their way to the end of their bench and then to the lobby. There they encountered a swarm of well-wishers, both from the Commons and the Lords. All supported the quality of Giles's address, and many supported the cause he was promoting. One of the most memorable of the latter group was the renowned champion against slavery, Mr. Wilberforce.

"An excellent speech, my Lord," the celebrated abolitionist declared. "You may have swayed some votes when my bill reaches the House of Lords and may even have helped in our House."

As the crowd of well-wishers thinned, Giles spotted Mr. Newsom, the Second Secretary of the Admiralty, hovering nearby. "Mr. Newsome, I did not expect to see you here to listen to me."

"My Lord, I was curious to hear what you might say in your maiden speech. I must say that I was very pleasantly surprised. Even your opening criticisms will strengthen rather than weaken the Admiralty's hand.

Well done! I had also been concerned about what you might say about the First Lord's and the First Sea Lord's involvement in the 'Affaire Edwards.'"

"Oh? What about them. And what is the Affaire Edwards?"

"Good heavens! You haven't heard the news?"

"What news?"

"There is clear evidence that both Lords were in league with Mr. Edwards in embezzling from prize winnings. So much so that they even ordered you and Captains Bush and Bolton to go on a wild goose chase to the coast of Spain. I confess that I was a bit suspicious of the 'information' about Spanish treasure when I first learned of it, but I didn't have any idea about what the motivation might be of those disseminating the news so I presumed that they might know more than I did.

"Things did turn out all right since Lady Camshire was fully able to cook Mr. Edwards's goose. The actions of the two Lords of the Admiralty only came to light when the detailed examination of Mr. Edwards's accounts was being conducted. That is why they were not able to see you this morning. They didn't confide in me about what your next orders might be. I suggest that you wait for a couple of weeks while the mess at the Admiralty is straightened out. Possibly, by then, we will know what the Admiralty hopes you will agree to do in the future."

As Mr. Newsome went away, Lord Struthers caught Giles's attention. "Richard, a splendid maiden speech. I am very proud of you. Now, we should be leaving so that we can get in reasonable time to the dinner that your aunt has organized in celebration. Reeding is, of course, also invited. We can all go in my carriage, which has returned from taking the ladies to Struthers House."

Almost all of the guests were present by the time that Giles reached his uncle's mansion. The first order of business was to introduce the guests to him. Most of them were unknown to Giles, and, of course, these introductions required a short pause filled with trite conversation. Many of the men had been at the House of Lords and praised Giles for his speech without dwelling on the specifics; their wives had not been present, and so the remarks were even less focused on anything important. Since Daphne had been at the gathering from its beginning, she did not accompany him on the tour of the room, and she only had a moment to tell him how proud she was of him before he was whisked off to accompany some other lady to dinner.

Daphne was seated on the opposite side of the table from Giles and at the other end. Her place was between two middle-aged peers who, Giles could tell, were boring her though he doubted that the noble gentlemen had any inkling of how she was feeling. Giles's luck was only slightly better. To his right sat a woman, considerably older than himself, whose only interest was the Season and how it was progressing. Though Giles had never seen why there was such interest throughout Society with the annual ritual in which noble and wealthy daughters were supposed to pair up with equally wealthy and noble gentlemen in an elaborate and expensive marriage market, the lady's interest did make some sense to him in this instance.

Lady Enderby, the lady on his right, had one daughter and a somewhat older son entered in the marriage lists, so her interest in who was charming whom and with what financial stakes involved had some direct and personal interest.

When he turned to talk with the Lady Farrel, who was on his left, Giles at first thought the conversation promised to be more interesting since the first thing she asked him was whether he hunted. Of course, he answered that he did and was about to continue by saying something about the Ameschester Hunt when his partner launched into a long tale about a hunt party that she and her husband had attended recently at some large estate in Berkshire. However, the only mention of the actual hunting was a side remark that her husband had returned in a filthy mood, having lost the pack completely. Instead, her harangue was about the social interactions among the ladies present as they jockeyed for prominence different from what resulted from their husbands standing in the peerage. Giles gathered that her husband, while only a baron and not a viscount or an earl, had an ancient title that should have given him (and so her) precedence over anyone else there, but some ladies had tried to diminish her status.

Giles rather regretted that his aunt had not seated him next to herself because she was well acquainted with him, while the purpose of the dinner was for him to meet others of Lord Struthers's political circle. Apparently, as happened often with the peculiar practices of the aristocracy in choosing their mates, Lord Farrel had married a petulant bride whose intellectual abilities were far less than his own.

Things picked up for Daphne when the conversation became more general. Lord Struthers opened the conversation by mentioning that Giles and Daphne were preparing Camshire House for reopening and asked her how it was progressing. It was a subject on which all the nearby ladies had an opinion and some of their husbands as well. Many were familiar with the residence from the days when Lady Clara had entertained there before the late Earl of Camshire's fortunes had sunk so low that he could no longer maintain it. They were sorry that the house had gone downhill so badly. There was no shortage of suggestions for what Daphne should do to restore it to its former glory and bring it up-to-date. While she suspected that she would not adopt many of the suggestions, which, in many cases, were contradictory, the discussion was helpful in suggesting to her who were the best tradesmen to hire for various aspects of the renovations and who could most reliably supply the work and the materials.

The general conversation also picked up at Giles's end of the table when Lady Struthers asked him about the plans for the Ameschester Hunt Ball. Several of the people near him were fox-hunters who had never been to the Ameschester Hunt. They had also heard rumors that the Ameschester Hunt Ball had recently become a very successful social event. Giles described the Hunt and then went on to mention the cross-country race that he and Daphne were sponsoring. Everyone at the table was interested, especially about the unusual rules. Before long, friendly wagers were being placed on the outcome of the special race, with the odds being established as five-to-one in favor of Giles, even though none of the participants had ever been to Dipton or Ameschester. And knew nothing about the horses. The highlight of this discussion came when Lady Enderbury refused to bet with her husband, arguing that he never paid his gambling debts.

When Lady Struthers decided that it was time to lead the ladies to the drawing-room while leaving the gentlemen to their port and nuts, the men all settled at the foot of the table with Lord Struthers. Giles soon realized that this was probably the real purpose of the gathering, to sound him out on political issues of the day and see how much he might want to be involved in the workings of government. He preempted much speculation on that front by pointing out that his father's estate was a complete shaambles and would require a lot of his time which was already scarce since he was still on active naval service. Despite the wealth that he had gathered, he had to hold himself ready if his services were again required by the Navy. On his opinions, Giles took the stance that he had to find out more before he could make up his mind. He quickly got the other men explaining and arguing about what the issues were without committing himself. On two fronts, however, he was adamant in his opinions. Now was not the time to try to make peace with Napoleon, despite the victory at Trafalgar. The French still had a formidable navy and could still be a much more important threat if Napoleon ever turned his mind seriously to naval warfare. The other was that the Navy needed better support from the various agencies, which were supposed to keep them afloat, were riddled with inefficiencies and corruption that were costly and inept. This situation seriously weakened the fleet.

Giles couldn't give a fig if some of the powerful men who benefitted from the present system were present in the gathering. When it was time to join the ladies, Lord Struthers congratulated Giles on his performance but warned him that his firm stand on corruption and cronyism could land him with the difficult job of trying to end these practices in the face of the interest of the perpetrators of the situation.

Daphne's experience, after the ladies had withdrawn, was similar to Giles's, for the other ladies were as curious about Daphne as their husbands were about the newly elevated earl. Their questions were directed towards Daphne's interests and her home rather than her political interests. Daphne knew better than to emphasize her participation in estate management or in defeating smuggling occupations that many would have considered unladylike, though she did let it be known that she would be overseeing the restoration of Camshire House if Giles was called to sea once again. She was naughtily amused when Lady Gillespie approached her about the Ameschester Hunt Ball, for which she wanted an invitation to stay at Dipton Hall. Lady Struthers had already told Daphne that while her husband was highly respected in Parliamentary circles, Lady Gillespie was the butt of jokes arising from her frequently expressed disdain for those who became rich through trade or exploitation of the colonies. Daphne explained that she regretted that all the places at Dipton Hall had already been taken, but she might be able to arrange an invitation for Lord and Lady Gillespie to stay with her father.

While he was not a member of the peerage, he was a very well-established gentleman, educated at Harrow and Baliol College, Oxford.

"My father owns the second-largest holding near Dipton," Daphne declared, "where he lives with my uncle. He might have room if I ask him. Shall I?"

"That would be very good of you, Lady Camshire," Lady Gillespie replied. "Lord Gillespie attended Eton and Magdalen, so they will have a lot in common. I shall so look forward to the Hunt Ball, and Lord Gillespie will be keen to participate in the Hunt itself."

Later in the evening, when Daphne and Giles had retired to their bedroom, she recounted the incident as they told each other about the events of their day. She had been afraid that Giles would be annoyed at her for the awkwardness she was planning for the supercilious lady. Instead, Giles roared with laughter.

"Oh, marvelous. Those two have it coming in spades! Luckily your father is now quite without embarrassment about his origins — not that there is any reason that he should be — while your uncle revels in his status as a successful businessman with no pretensions to gentility. It is a pity that George can't speak. I know he would delight in greeting them with a broad Midlands accent."

"So, you are not angry with me?"

"Of course not. I would have done the same if I'd thought of it."

Chapter XIII

Giles woke just before dawn and luxuriated in the pleasure of not having to jump out of his berth in darkness to take part of the clearing for action that was routine in his commands before dawn. Daphne and he were agreed that they liked to sleep with the curtains open so that they could enjoy the view from their bedroom when the moon shone or when dawn started creeping over their holdings. The skivvy who made the fires in the morning had strict orders not to enter the mistress's bedroom but to make sure that the fires in the Master's and the Mistress's dressing rooms were blazing strongly each morning before they woke up. Of course, their bedroom could get very cold in the night, but a thick mattress and heavy bedcovers kept Giles and Daphne comfortable. This morning, the temperature could only have been slightly warmer than freezing, but Giles was comfortable with only his head raised on the pillow exposed to the chill of the room while Daphne was curled up alongside him.

The rising sun shot pink rays over the house to illuminate the pond they had created at the bottom of the garden. Giles's eyes wandered up the rise of not closely mowed grass to the folly they had built at the same time that they had remade the gardens. He loved that view, and it was so much better than any to be had at Ashbury Abbey, the family estate where he had grown up.

Ashbury Abbey had been the principal estate of the Earls of Camshire ever since the time of Henry VIII, and before that, they had had a castle in that area which was now a ruin. Most of his ancestors were buried in the church there. Nevertheless, though Giles had been surprised to find that he was a lover of tradition, he much preferred Dipton Hall to Ashbury Abbey and the company of the people around Dipton and Ameschester to the society of Ashbury. He did reflect that it was odd that the two locations had such similar names; he wondered why that might be the case.

It might be a break with tradition, but there was no reason why the principal estate of the Earl of Camshire should not now be Dipton Hall. Of course, his mother still had claims to the dower cottage at Ashbury Abbey, but, like most of that estate, the dower cottage was a gloomy place and very run-down. Anyway, Lady Clara seemed to prefer living in Dipton, and she was getting on very well with Daphne, surprisingly so when one remembered the rocky start with which their connection began. Anyway, Captain Bush would soon be marrying, and he would not want to continue living in the dower cottage at Dipton, so Giles's mother could move there so that she would be close at hand to her grandchildren. Of course, Giles suspected that she might well marry Daphne's father, despite the vast difference in their social standings and the fact that she would then be giving up her independence.

Beside Giles, Daphne snuggled up against him and murmured, "Hello, husband, you're awake. What time is it?"

"Just after dawn. About six o'clock."

"Oh, Lord, we *have* slept in! We have to get up!"

"Why?"

"Jamison is coming at eight o'clock."

"Who?"

"You know, Jamieson, the new steward."

"Can't he wait? After all, he works for us."

"True, but 'punctuality is the courtesy of kings.'"

"Well, We are not king and queen, thank heavens."

"Yes, but we have so much to do today. The children, and seeing that plans for the ball are in place, and seeing Major Stoner, and reassuring Mr. Summers that everything is going well for the race and for the hunt and for the ball, and seeing my father and uncle, and I don't know what — seeing that the horses are ready for tomorrow — you remember that we are racing against each other tomorrow — and I don't know what else."

Despite these disclaimers, it was, in fact, a full thirty-five minutes before Betsey was summoned to help Daphne prepare for the day. After that, everything felt a bit hurried as Daphne and Giles tried to make up for the delightfully lazy time. Daphne drank her tea too hot at breakfast. She was a bit annoyed that Bernard got upset when Giles and Daphne tried to leave unusually quickly while playing with their children, and getting him back to calmly taking their need to depart ate up more time than she had wanted. Then Jameson and Giles got into a discussion about using the new fields on a more permanent basis for the needs of the hunters in training, which Daphne felt was a waste of valuable time on that occasion. She only felt less pressed when Mr. Summers sent a note to say that all issues concerning the race on the following day had been resolved, so he need not trouble the Earl and Countess (his capitalization, not Daphne's.)

Giles asked Steves if he knew why the president of the Ameschester Hunt had begged off meeting with them. Giles had learned as a boy with unlimited curiosity on a nobleman's estate that the servants knew far more about the doings of their masters than might be expected and had a very efficient network for transmitting news throughout the community. Of course, for their employers to tap into this network, the servants had to trust, respect, and like their masters. Giles knew that he and Daphne fell into that category. Steves or one of Dipton Hall's footmen would undoubtedly have had a word with whoever had delivered the note, and they would know not only the what but also the why of the missive.

"Steves, do you know why Mr. Summers has canceled our meeting?" Giles asked.

"Yes, my lord. The groom who brought the note told me that Mr. Summers was in a right tissy when Major Stoner had his accident and couldn't organize the race. So much so that Mrs. Summers summoned Mr. Jackson to see if he could give him something other than brandy to ease his worries. Mr. Jackson told Mr. Summers that he would deal with any problems caused by Major Stoner's accident. Mr. Jackson, who is not much of a sporting gentleman, as you know, discussed the situation with Mr. Carstairs at the Dipton Inn. Mr. Carstairs arranged for the inn-keepers at the other four points to verify that the contestants reached each place. Mr. Foster, the curate, will declare the winner and the time between different arrivals using the church clock."

"Surely that is not necessary for Lady Giles and my race," protested Giles.

"I believe, my lord, that most of these steps were taken not so much as being necessary for the race between Lady Camshire and yourself as a trial run for the general race that is planned."

"But I don't see the relevance of the arrangements. Surely, the race is a simple matter of starting together and then seeing who returns first. I suppose that the time can be judged by the church clock for setting a challenge to later races, but the rest of the provisions seems to me to be superfluous."

"Not really, my lord. Not after people started betting on the race."

"People are betting on our trial race? Surely not."

"Yes, my lord. You and Lady Giles are well known in the area, and so are your horses. There has been a great deal of interest in your race throughout the neighborhood, and this has led to many friendly bets, some for more than the bettors could easily afford to lose. That is why the need to establish that the conditions of the race have been met."

"I can understand the need to establish that we do, in fact, reach all the critical points, but why the timing specification?" asked Daphne.

"Well, my lady," the butler replied. "It is partly to establish the time criterion for the subsequent race and the ones that follow them, but even more it is needed to resolve the bets."

"I can appreciate the first point," commented Giles, "but why the second one. How is that relevant for the gambling."

"I am afraid, my lord, that many people wished to bet, but most were of one mind about the outcome, and the odds were hard to calculate for bets to seem fair. Instead, people started to bet not so much on who would win, but by how many minutes difference there would between the two of you."

"Good heavens, what an idea for making wagers. And what is the most common expectation?" asked Daphne.

"I am afraid it is that Lord Giles will win by eleven minutes, my lady."

"Good Lord!" Giles cried. "If it weren't grossly improper for me to wager on the race, I would certainly take that bet."

"Are you that confident of beating me that badly?" Daphne asked sweetly.

"You misunderstand me, Daphne," replied Giles. I would be betting that you couldn't possibly fall that far behind me."

"Well," Daphne replied, "don't expect me to take the other side of that bet! And you, Steves, are you involved in the betting?"

The butler, to Daphne's surprise, blushed a bright red. "Yes, my lady, I have little wagers with Mrs. Darling and Mrs. Wilson."

"Oh," said Daphne, surprised that the staid old butler was betting with the cook and the housekeeper at Dipton Hall.

"Er … er … I wagered with Mrs. Darling that the Earl would beat you by six minutes and with Mrs. Wilson that you would lose by five minutes."

"And what was the wager?" asked Giles.

"Er … the loser would take the winner to dinner at the Dipton Arms on our evening off."

"Well, I never!" declared Giles. "At least, Steves, you will get a good meal out of it. I hear that Elsie has hired a very good cook."

"Tell me, Steves, have you heard anything more about Major Stoner?"

"Yes, my lord, Lady Marianne sent a note asking if she and the major could come for dinner. In your absence, my lady, Lady Clara allowed it, and she also decided to invite Mr. Moorhouse and his brother as well."

That was perfectly agreeable to Daphne: it was sensible to have a family gathering to celebrate the return of Giles and herself to Dipton after their excursion to London.

"I don't suppose that Lord David is at the vicarage, is he, Steves?" inquired Daphne.

"No, my lady."

"Pity, we could have had even more of a family gathering if he were, but I will write a note asking Mrs. Bolton to join us."

"Is Major Stoner fit to travel?" asked Giles.

"I understand that he is, my lord," replied Steves. "Despite having his leg in a cast and his head still hurting, Mr. Jackson said he could go out if he used crutches. Lady Marianne will undoubtedly insist that he come by carriage, not on his horse."

The following morning found Giles and Daphne already out of bed and dressed. It was another fine day, with promise that the early morning chill would disappear before long. Giles found that the breakfast room was already occupied by Major Stoner and by the Moorhouse brothers. While he wasn't surprised to find the Major there — he had been in charge of organizing the race before his accident ad no doubt wanted to get to the starting place in lots of time — the other two were unexpected.

"Good Morning, Major. How is your leg today? Morning, Daniel and George." Giles greeted the three men. It had become clear very early on that addressing each of the brothers as 'Mr. Moorhouse' was tedious, and they suggested that he use their first names. Though Giles had no objection to being called by his first name, everyone always called him 'Giles.'

"My leg itches terribly," complained the Major, "but my head is a bit better."

"I suppose that you are up early because of the race."

"True. Can't loll around like an invalid when there are things one has taken on that need doing. Wouldn't do at all!"

"And why are you two up so early?" asked Giles. "Incidentally, I am very glad that you decided to stay the night."

"Thank you," replied Daniel Moorhouse. "It is a bit tricky to get George in and out of the carriage in the dark. It will also be much easier to take him to the church for the start of the race from here. Our footman, Thomas, can manage to push him there quite easily."

"But why are you up so early?"

"Daniel wants to get there in time to get a good place to hear all the others cheering and also to take a few more bets."

"More bets. Are you also betting on the race?"

"George is, but I am not. I don't think I should bet against my daughter."

"What time difference is he favoring?"

George started writing furiously on his slate. Giles and Daniel waited while the Major did not try to hide his curiosity. Then George held up his slate. It said, 'Daphne is going to win.'

"At what odds do you bet?" Giles asked.

"Oh, George will take any bet just about. Even one at evens."

"I hope he isn't betting too much."

"I think so far he has wagered £100. Well-spread out. He won't take bets for more than £5, and many are smaller."

The two brothers finished up after this, and Daniel pushed George from the breakfast room.

"Remarkable man, isn't he?" said Major Stoner. "I hope that I would be able to handle adversity as well, but I doubt it."

"Have you also been gambling on the race, Major?" asked Giles.

"No, of course not. Can't have the officials of a race betting on it, what? Must go, however. Can't have the start turning into a carnival before I get there, can I? Wouldn't do! Wouldn't do at all!"

As the Major left the room, Daphne entered. She stopped at the buffet to get some eggs, bacon, and a scone. As soon as she sat down, the footman on duty came with hot coffee and warm milk to pour into her cup. Steves had been horrified when he first served Daphne with breakfast to find that she didn't want the tea, which was the standard breakfast beverage of ladies if they didn't want small beer, but now he took pride in making sure that his unconventional mistress received what she wanted without having to ask for it.

"Giles," said Daphne, "I suppose that we have plenty of time before we have to be at the church."

"Yes, I think so. There is no point arriving early. The general excitement that we have been hearing about suggests that it might be awkward mingling with people beforehand, as we usually would, if everyone is thinking mainly about how fast our horses are."

In line with this thought, Giles and Daphne arrived at the church with only five minutes to go before the scheduled start of the race. Daphne was glad that she had authorized repairs to the ancient church clock while Giles had been away. Given how she had heard that most of the wages were concerned with the difference when the contestants finished, it would be highly embarrassing if the clock stopped before the race finished.

Soon the waiting ended. Rather officiously, Major Stoner lined the two competitors up on a little side lane that ran beside the churchyard into the main road through Dipton. That was where the starting and finish line was since the racers could leave Dipton in any direction. Some minor betting had even taken place about which way they would turn.

Major Stoner had brought a pistol with him to start the race (and he had told Daphne earlier that he would have a second one all loaded and ready to go if the first one misfired.) 'Bang' went the pistol. A startled Dark Paul surged away, with Giles already having to work hard to guide the slightly panicked horse in the right direction. Serene Masham, Daphne's smaller mount, started much more smoothly, and Daphne did not try to gain the advantage immediately. In fact, she slightly reined in her steed so that Giles had a lead of several strides in the first hundred yards. The road to Upper Dipton then curved to the right sharply and started to rise steeply. Dark Paul charged up the incline at full speed; it is doubtful that he would have allowed Giles to slow him even if his master had wanted it. Daphne, by contrast, turned her horse to the left to jump a gate onto a narrow track. She proceeded to ride cross-country towards Under Dipton, one of the places the racers had to visit. The track led through rather scrubby brushland before opening onto fields that had lain fallow for the past year and sloped downhill gently towards a large stream. It was perfect territory for Serene Masham's strengths, Daphne knew. The path she followed led to a place where the stream narrowed. Since the weather had been dry for the past several days, the stream was not in flood, and Daphne knew of a spot where her horse could jump it easily.

The road between Dipton and Under Dipton plunged down to the valley bottom, where it crossed the stream over an ancient bridge. Daphne's route would not go down nearly as far. If her calculation about the stream's level was right, Serene Masham would have no trouble jumping across the stream, and the increase in height to get to the village would not be taxing. Daphne was certain that she would gain a good deal of time over Giles if he intended to ride by the road from Under Dipton to Dipton as the last stage of the race. She was certain that he was not aware of the shortcut she was taking. This difference in their routes was one of the reasons that she was confident of taking less time than Giles to complete the race.

The next stage of the race was central to Daphne's plan to beat Giles. If one looked at a sketch of the area, the five villages that the riders had to visit were laid out in a rough circle, though with Dipton, Upper Dipton, and Three Laurels on the perimeter while Under Dipton and Lesser St. Luke were nearer the center, with the first between Dipton and Ashburough and the latter between Three Laurels and Upper Dipton. What the sketch would not have revealed was that Under Dipton and Lesser St. Luke's were at a much lower elevation than the other three and that while they lay in two distinct valleys, they changed from one to the other at a much more modest level than the locations of the other villages. To make choosing a route, the descents from Ashburough to Under Dipton and from Upper Dipton to Lesser St. Luke's were steep and twisty, while the rise from Lesser St. Luke's to Ashburough was much easier, though longer, than the other hills and had a shortcut that eliminated one large curve which was located on a fairly flat part of the road. Daphne planned to go first to Lesser St. Luke's after Under Dipton and then to Three Laurels before taking a fairly straight and even route to Upper Dipton. Daphne knew that she was taking unfair advantage over Giles, who was not nearly as familiar with the country around Dipton as she was, but she knew that he admired ingenuity and had commented that this sort of race should involve using the terrain to find the alternative paths that might prove faster. He had particularly liked the system of five checkpoints, without specification about how the riders were to reach them.

Daphne gave Serene Masham her head to dash through Under Dipton, waving at the small crowd gathered outside the tavern. She noted that someone had set the church bells ringing as she spd through the community. As she had planned, Daphne headed straight for Lesser St. Luke's next. This was country she had hunted over while Giles was away during the winters, so she had little difficulty finding what she thought would be a faster way to get to the next village than taking the established and badly kept-up road. When she reached the church, she paused to drink a tankard of ale pressed on her while allowing her horse to drink, though not very much.

She was relieved to hear that Giles had not arrived yet. She laughed as she thought about how surprised he would be at the news that she had come and gone, especially as he would not have met her on his way to their second checkpoint. She dallied no longer than was necessary for the good of her steed, and then off they went on the road to Three Laurels. To a very large extent, Daphne gave Serene Masham her head on the next stage of their journey, only being careful to let the mare know what route they were following. A couple of years of hunting with the horse had let Daphne know how to pace herself so that her horse did not become exhausted any sooner than necessary.

Serene Masham rewarded Daphne by taking the slope faster than Daphne might have allowed if she were trying to determine the mare's pace, but, at the top of the rise, the horse was breathing easily. They turned into the main street of the village to be greeted by a cheer. Giles had still not arrived. Daphne paused, and a tankard of ale was thrust into her hand while the mare drank at the horse trough. She gulped down a couple of draughts before handing the tankard back, and off they went again. The road to Upper Dipton — a track, really, not a road — went through mildly hilly country. With many curves designed to ease the grade for heavily loaded carts being pulled by teams of horses. Much more direct ways were available for a horse and rider who did not hesitate to jump over hedges and other barriers. Daphne had hunted over the area several times while Giles had been at sea and had no difficulty guiding Serene Masham across-country in a way that was much more direct and less tiring for the horse than taking the road.

Daphne arrived at Upper Dipton to be greeted by an impatient but rather boisterous crowd. They had been waiting for some time for her to arrive. With no church clock and only the sundial to tell time, it seemed to be a very long time since Giles had ridden through without pausing and Daphne's appearing from the other direction. They had been anticipating Daphne to arrive at almost the same time as Giles, after which most of the watchers had intended to march off to Dipton to verify the claim that Upper Dipton's ale also was a great deal better than Dipton. Instead, most of them had stayed at Upper Dipton, though now they were making sure that they were well and freshly familiar with the quality of the local brew. As Daphne swung up into her saddle, in her most unladylike way with which everyone in the area was familiar, most of the villagers set out to follow her to the larger town.

Daphne swept into Dipton to the amazement of the watchers there since she returned by the same road that she had left. Could she have had an accident that caused her to turn back? She didn't look like it, and she was riding hard for the finish line, after which she reined in her horse. Daphne then let the beast walk about for a few minutes before dismounting in front of the church.

"I hope that you noted the time I crossed the finish line, Major Stoner," she remarked as she passed the reins to one of the grooms from Dipton Hall, who was in the crowd.

"Yes, my lady," Major Stoner, even as he desperately tried to recall just what the church clock had said when he was fully engaged in watching the countess cross the finish line. It wouldn't matter, except for the record books. He had heard of no one betting that Daphne would come in first by any significant number of minutes. It didn't matter, he supposed, for the record. No lady was likely to beat Daphne's success any time soon.

Daphne accepted the congratulations from the people gathered to see the end of the race; even those who had lost their bets were glad to see the joy she took in having completed the race ahead of her husband. Elsie, who was the landlady of the Inn and had formerly been Daphne's lady's maid, got her to sit in the Inn's enclosure and enjoy one of the pasties that she had had baked for the occasion. Elsie knew that most ladies of quality would prefer to drink some lemonade or a dainty cordial. However, she knew that that was not the way of the Countess of Camshire: Her former mistress would want a flagon of beer — not small beer but her best bitter — and so Elsie should just enjoy and take pride in how her former mistress behaved when surrounded by common people, not worry about whether she was maintaining the standard which would enhance to the prestige of her lady's maid.

Daphne was enjoying the pasty and the conversation of some of her tenants who had dared to ask if they could join her. However, after a while, she started to worry about where Giles had got himself to. Even though she had outfoxed him by using her better knowledge of the area to beat him. That superiority would not account for the time it was taking Giles to finish his part of the race. She was about to suggest that they search along the road to Under Dipton when a tired-looking Giles appeared around the corner leading a Dark Paul who was limping badly. What in the world could have happened to him, Daphne wondered.

Giles had pushed Dark Paul on the ascent to Three Laurels. He suspected that he might be behind Daphne in terms of distance to the finish line as she was clearly ahead of him on this stage, but her further trip might be longer or slower. Three Laurels was probably the highest point on his route, so Dark Paul should make good time on the descent to Under Dipton. Three Laurels must be closer to Dipton via Under Dipton than via Upper Dipton, but still, he couldn't afford to dawdle.

The track to Under Dipton did not descend smoothly but instead alternated nearly flat stretches with some steep declines, often at a sharp bend. These places coincided with some loose gravel. Giles was not happy about having to rein his horse in, but Dark Paul had almost slipped at several places. Giles had to make the hunter go more slowly for fear that he would injure himself. Once through Under Dipton, where again Giles did not stop, the track seemed a bit better, and Giles let the horse have his way, even though it was evident that the creature was becoming exhausted.

Disaster struck when they came to the bridge, after which the track would rise to Dipton. It was approached at an angle, and the trees along the stream prevented a ride from seeing exactly where it was going. In fact, the track turned left almost at a right angle, with the land still sloping down. Had Giles known the area, he would have been aware that several carts had tipped over on this turn even though they were going slowly. To make matters worse, the surface of the turn was sand and loose gravel. Whether it was because of the conditions, or because Giles had not reined in Dark Paul, or because the horse was tired, Dark Paul stumbled when they came to make the turn and started to limp. Giles immediately stopped his horse and jumped off to see how serious was the injury. Luckily, the horse did not appear to have broken anything, but Giles was going to take no chances. He judged that the best thing for the horse would be to lead him on foot to Dipton, where a more expert evaluation could be made of the injury. Off they went. The race was now irrelevant to Giles, though ironically, he reflected that people who followed him in attempting the race track would have little trouble besting the Earl of Camshire's time.

Daphne jumped up from her chair and rushed off in a most unladylike manner to find out what was the matter with Giles's horse. Mr. Jackson, the physician, and Mr. Griffiths, the Stable Master of Giles's horse farm, set off at a run with Mr. Jackson lugging his medical bag. Though a well-trained physician, Mr. Jackson also served as needed as a veterinarian. When Daphne had teased him that attending to animals would undoubtedly reduce the number of patients he would get among the gentry, Mr. Jackson had laughed. "The animals don't complain and have serious problems, unlike my clients among the gentry. They are also more interesting." Mr. Griffiths had seen and dealt with all the myriad of injuries and ailments that horses could contract. Dark Paul could not be in better hands.

Mr. Jackson ran his hands up and down Dark Paul's leg a couple of times. Quickly and then more slowly. "He hasn't broken anything," The doctor turned vet said. "I think he as torn — sprained — some muscles and maybe ligaments in here. What do you think, Mr. Griffiths?"

"Feels that way to me," said the stable master after making his own examination.

"What should we do?" asked a worried Giles.

"I will bind it tightly to lower any swelling after rubbing in some salve and then keep him inactive, my lord. It will be very hard to keep this beast inactive long enough to heal. I'll see if I can't think of some method to keep his weight off his foreleg while he is walking. No galloping or cantering or even trotting for a while, I am afraid. He won't like any of it, I am afraid, and he may never be able to hunt again. What do you think, Mr. Griffiths?"

"I agree, I am sorry to say. I've seen this sort of injury before, though I certainly don't have Mr. Jackson's touch. Some horses do recover, though they usually have a limp and are no good except as riding horses who should never be pushed beyond a canter. I know that most owners would just shoot the animal."

"Oh, no!" cried Daphne. "He is a mean-tempered and cantankerous animal, who doesn't like most people, but surely that isn't a reason to kill him. What do you think, Giles?"

"I agree with Lady Giles. I have respect for the creature, even though he has spent a lot of effort getting me off his back. Especially as I am to blame for his accident. I knew how he was and should have reined him in at the difficult place where he stumbled, especially since I knew how poor his judgment of dangers was when he was going all out. I was just so annoyed that I was likely losing the race that I didn't consider Dark Paul's weaknesses."

"I would like to have him as a stud horse, with your permission, of course, my lord. We've been reluctant to breed him because of his temper, but that has been getting to be less of a problem and may be the result of being mishandled when he was young — before you got him. In some ways, he is the best horse I have seen, though, of course, Lady Camshire's Serene Masham is the best mare I have even raised when all aspects of the horse are considered."

"That settles it then. We are keeping him. Mr. Jackson, can you bind up his leg now?"

"I can put a temporary one on here, but I should treat the leg properly when he is in his stall."

"Good. Jenkens," Giles called to one of Dipton's grooms, who was on the fringe of the crowd assembled around the horse, "walk Dark Paul, *slowly*, to the stables and keep him inactive there until he can be treated fully."

The group around the horse returned to the inn. Giles would just as soon have snuck back to Dipton Hall directly rather than have to cheerfully accept the condolences of so many people who had lost money betting on his success. He kept it secret that, when he learned the time at which Daphne had completed her ride, he realized that, even without the accident, she would have beaten him handsomely. He had a position to maintain and didn't want to be known as a poor loser.

It wasn't until Sunday evening that Giles again felt all right in his position as leader of Dipton society. Giles had informed Steves that he and Daphne, as well as Lady Clara, would be dining at Dipton Manor so that there was no need for the kitchen to prepare a meal for them on Sunday evening or for any of the servants to hurry home after evensong to wait on them. He had arranged with Daphne's father to give the same message to the servants at Dipton Manor, except that, in this case, both he and his brother would be visiting Dipton Hall. Only the coachman and a footman to push Mr. Daniel's bath chair would be needed that evening.

Giles had also visited Carstairs at Dipton Inn to make sure that his best parlor would be reserved for his party for Sunday evening and that the second-best would be reserved for the senior servants from Dipton Hall and Dipton Manor. Giles knew that Steves was a connoisseur of wine. Originally, he had hoped to smuggle several of his best bottles to the Inn for the servants' party, but he had realized that it would be almost impossible to do that without Steves noting the loss. When he mentioned the problem to his coxswain, acting as publican, Carstairs told him that Elsie had secured several cases of the finest Claret that was now coming to Dipton by Daphne's canal company with the duty all paid. It should be a treat for Steves as well as for the other staff members. Elsie knew that Mr. Tisdale, the butler at Dipton Manor, also had a good pallet for fine wine, though Mr. Moorhouse rarely had bottles that matched the best at Dipton Hall.

Daphne had realized that with their being relieved from duties for the whole of Sunday evening, many would visit Dipton Inn, especially the parlor for the women. She had told Elsie to have the initial drinks paid for by Dipton Hall but not allow anyone too much alcohol. By the time that Lord and Lady Camshire visited their servants, all were in a mellow mood. Both in the parlor and in the taproom, Giles made a little speech about how much their devotion to duty was appreciated and how he realized that the coming week would put them on their mettle with all the extra work that would arise from the Hunt Race, the Hunt itself, and the Hunt Ball. In the parlor, his words were met with enthusiastic thanks; the parlor led to hearty three-cheers.

Lady Clara, who had had a great deal of experience with the ways of the aristocracy, had never seen or heard of anything like Giles's treatment of the servants and wondered to herself if it was a wise move. Daphne had seen the devotion that Giles had won from his naval crews; she realized that Giles had just guaranteed the continuing loyalty of their staff.

Chapter XIV

"My Lords, the matter before this House needs careful reflection," Giles announced in a loud, clear voice. Giles was used to making his words clear without shouting despite blustery noise. The House of Lords presented little challenge to his getting its members' attention.

Giles was on his feet to address enforcing the Navigation Acts. He had only decided to attend because he had to be in London and felt that participation in debates, when he could, was his duty.

It had been a busy two weeks since he had lost the race to Daphne. First had come the pre-hunt race for anyone who wished to enter other than Lord and Lady Camshire. The final hunt of the season had been held the next day, followed by the Hunt Ball that was hosted (and paid for) by Giles and Daphne.

The Ball had been a great success. The musicians hired by Daphne to come from London played all the latest dances. While only some of the debutantes from London had been able to secure an invitation among the gentry near Dipton, many more of the young men from London seeking brides with healthy dowries had come, so the young ladies of the neighborhood had been well displayed to the visiting gentlemen. They had all had several dances with eligible suitors. Further interactions might come due to these gentlemen from London becoming acquainted with ladies from a different milieu. A couple of marriages had arisen due to the previous year's Ameschester Hunt Ball; even more betrothals might result from this year's version.

The days after the Ball had been very busy for Daphne and Giles. Both knew that they might be summoned away at any moment, Giles to sea and Daphne to London, Norwich, or even Shropshire. Of course, unlike Giles, Daphne could stay at Dipton if she chose, but she felt that it was better to deal with serious matters in person when possible. In the meantime, they would mend any fences that needed looking after by having their neighbors to dinner as well as seeing their tenants before the farmers were so burdened with spring plowing and planting that having the Earl and Countess of Camshire visit would be more of a nuisance than a pleasure for the recipients of their favor.

As they had expected, all too soon word arrived that they were needed in London. Giles was summoned to the Admiralty, while Daphne was needed for decisions on the refurbishment of Camshire House. Most noble ladies would have left all the decisions about changes to their houses to the professionals hired to make the alterations, but Daphne was convinced that she was more likely to get what she wanted by overseeing the work in person when needed.

Giles was puzzled by his summons: it had been issued by Mr. Newsome in his own name, not on behalf of the First Lord as was usual. Nevertheless, Giles would treat the request as if the wording were the standard one, which no serving Captain would dare refuse. Anyway, He was not averse to visiting London at this time: Lord Struthers had sent a note to remind Giles that the House of Lords would be debating the enforcement of the

Navigation Acts as they pertained to the West Indies colonies. Giles's experiences with smugglers in the Caribbean while he was a junior officer meant that he felt he could contribute to this debate. Hence, Giles found himself on his feet expounding on points that he thought were relevant, supporting the side, the government side, that felt that lax enforcement was in the national interest.

However, after this participation in debates, Giles had no intention of revisiting the House of Lords again on this trip to London. The other main business before the House involved arrangements for the impeachment trial of the former First Lord of the Admiralty, who had done much to advance Giles's career.

If the summons to the Admiralty seemed strange, the reality that confronted Giles the next morning was much stranger. He was shown immediately into the Board Room, whose only occupant was Mr. Newsome, who was working away at the Second Secretary's desk.

"My lord," Mr. Newsome greeted Giles. "Thank you for coming."

"Come, now, Mr. Newsome," Giles replied. "You know that, in the Navy, I prefer to be called 'Giles.' And you know that when the Admiralty requests my presence, it is really an order."

"True, but in this case, the request came not from the First Lord but from me, acting on my own. As Second Secretary. The Admiralty right now is rather chaotic, with the First Lord and the First Sea Lord having being dismissed over the Edwards affair and the previous First Lord facing impeachment. May I ask if you are keen to take part in his trial?"

"Not really. I regarded him as a friend. He was also very good for my career, and I believe for naval operations. I don't know anything about any shady dealings he may have had or abuse of office, and I would rather not learn about them. However, I suppose if I don't have any pressing business elsewhere, it would be my duty to take my seat in the House of Lords for the trial."

"Well, there is a mission that I believe that you should undertake. It is a bit irregular since the request came directly from His Majesty the King without going through the usual government channels. That is because the newly named First Lord is a placeholder filling in while they find a seat for Admiral Longshaven to take over the duties, and the First Sea Lord has yet to take up his position. Therefore, there was no one competent to handle His Majesty's request except myself."

"Yes?"

'So I have taken it upon myself to satisfy the King's request, which is within my power in the circumstances, though it is most unusual for me to be in a position to exercise my authority.

"As you know, one effect of Napolean's recent push to the east is that Prussia has become, at least for the time being, a vassal state of France. Furthermore, Napoleon seized parts of Prussia that he thought were of strategic significance for France. In return, he offhandedly gave the King of Prussia some parts of Saxony, including Hanover. The King is, of course, the elector of Hanover, and he is not at all happy about the situation. There is no chance that we will go to war against Prussia about this, but His Majesty would at least like the presence of his navy in Hanoverian waters to show some sort of support for his authority in the area. So the duty of dealing with His Majesty's order fell to me — without pretending that I am just carrying out the First Lord's orders since there are none. I hope that you might be willing to undertake this mission, Captain Giles."

"What is it? I can't answer until I know what you want."

"I believe that we should investigate just how hostile the new regime is to us. I would like you to take *Glaucus* to the mouth of the Wesser to see what is going on there: any military activity, French or Dutch privateers, or Prussian naval ships – not that they have many – pirates too. More to demonstrate that we are still interested in the area and won't tolerate its turning into an actively hostile region. The cabinet still hopes to revive the coalition against Napoleon, even though the last one was ineffective, and Prussia abandoned the other members when push came to shove.

"Quite apart from that, *Glaucus* has been in harbor quite long enough and should go to sea to keep your crew sharp. Of course, if you think you should stay here, you are free to appoint a jobbing captain to temporarily take your place.

"In case you think this is a ruse to prevent you from taking part in the impeachment, I can assure you that it is not. After all, the government allowed the

House of Commons to vote for impeachment, and they are happy to let Lord Gordonston take his chances in the House of Lords without interference. They are pretty sure that he will not be found guilty, even though most members probably believe that he is."

"Well," replied Giles, "I would be just as happy to miss the trial as I told you, and you are right. *Glaucus* should be at sea, or else her crew will become less skilled. I am busy, of course, but I am not yet ready to give up the sea."

"All right, that's settled. I'll send the orders over to Struthers House. I hope that you can sail within the next two weeks."

Giles left the Admiralty, shaking his head in some bewilderment. He had never received orders in such vague terms from the Admiralty and with such a limited sense of urgency about them. Of course, in the past, Mr. Newsome had been transmitting orders that had been issued by the First Lord, even though rumor in the Navy was that most of the orders had been initiated by, or at least approved by, the Second Secretary. Now that he thought about it, the orders that had taken him on the previous fool's errand had not come from Mr. Newsome but from some other official at the Admiralty. That was something he had noted but thought nothing of it at the time. It was certainly the case that *Glaucus,* or rather her crew, would benefit from some time at sea. A short mission to the Wadden Sea* would be good for them, and he was starting to miss his frigate and being on the water. He didn't want a long voyage or to be tied to the apron strings of some admiral beating about in strategic waters, waiting for something to happen, so the suggested mission was most attractive. He would be gone at most three weeks, and then he would be home when spring was in full swing. He would not mention to Daphne that he had been given the option to simply refuse the mission.

Daphne was not at all pleased to hear that Giles was off to sea once more. Not that she wasn't prepared for it. She had married a naval captain in time of war. She could expect him to be home only rarely. And she had been very fortunate that he allowed her complete freedom to manage his affairs when he was away and never complained about her decisions. She reveled in the freedom and authority it gave her when he was away. But recently, Daphne had become interested and involved in so many different things that she was feeling overwhelmed.

Having Giles home for an extended period allowed her to spend more time on other matters, as he took on some of her tasks whenever she suggested it. But she had noted that he was getting restless, even though he never came out and said it, and she would rather lose him to the sea than to have him spend all his time in London clubs or in his study; not that he had done much of either. No, she just liked having him home, but she knew that she would be most unwise to press him to give up the sea: it had to be his decision. All she could do was gently point out all the interesting things he could do while at home.

Part of the reason for Daphne's disappointment was that she had discovered, only that morning, that she was pregnant. It was early days, of course. She had been expecting it; indeed, she had been surprised that it had not happened sooner since Giles had been home for some time. She wouldn't tell her husband until she was sure; she knew of all too many women who had thought they were pregnant only to have the belief unravel all too soon. No point worrying her husband for nothing. But she would like to tell him in person rather than by letter and to experience his support when the pregnancy became tiresome.

Daphne's annoyance was somewhat reduced when Giles explained that he did not need to take *Glaucus* to sea for another fortnight or so. That would give her time to attend to matters which she thought were best handled by the two of them together, or even in some cases, by Giles at her urging. She was particularly mollified when she learned that after his interview at the Admiralty, Giles had gone to a coffee shop on the Strand where he had written and had dispatched orders to his first lieutenant to prepare *Glaucus* for a voyage so he would not, as he usually did, have to go down to Portsmouth in advance of sailing to make sure that everything was ready.

Of even greater interest to Daphne, even though it confirmed how ready Giles was to relieve her of some tasks that she had to undertake when he was away, was that he had gone on from the coffee shop to see Mr. Snodgravel about the legal problems connected with his properties, particularly those in Norfolk and Shropshire.

The news from Norfolk was good. Two of the tenants involved in the late Earl's scheme had been willing to give up their false leases for what they had paid for them and were happy to sign new leases with the present Earl. The new ones included better terms about who shared what expenses for improvements, just as Daphne had wanted. Whether they were still entailed was a question for the Diocesan Court. When Giles asked her, Daphne agreed that the arrangement was acceptable, especially as it helped with the income to which Lady Clara was entitled. Both Daphne and Giles believed that it would be best if the Dowager Duchess could count on a more than adequate income in her own right rather than depending on Giles. If Lady Clara ever wanted to remarry, and she was not an old woman, it would be because she wanted to marry for her own sake, not to avoid putting a burden on Giles's resources. In addition to this good news, Mr. Snodgravel had told Giles that there would be no need for Daphne to visit Norfolk again if she did not want to; the lawyer Daphne had found and the stewards she had put in place should be able to handle things, at least for the time being. While Daphne would not have minded going to Cambridge again and meeting with more mathematicians there, Norwich had no attractions for her.

The Shropshire property was more of a problem, Mr. Snodgravel reported. The transaction had been done in Mr. Edward's name, though using money held in trust for Giles. Edwards had also started renovations for the house and improvements to the property, so it might look like he intended to use the estate himself. If that interpretation were accepted, it would greatly weaken Giles's claim that the property was registered in Mr. Edwards's name only by a clerical error in which the agent had been mistaken for the owner. Luckily, however, while Edwards had made it sound as if he were doing the renovations for himself, he had paid for some preliminary design work with money from Giles's account. To establish his claim, Giles should take control of the project, either by himself or using Lady Camshire. Mr. Snogravel strongly suggested that Giles and/or Lady Camshire write to the builder immediately to pause the work until they had a chance to inspect it and, if necessary, modify the planned changes themselves, stating that they were not convinced that Mr. Edwards's instructions really carried out their desires. In the near future, one of them should visit the Shropshire estate to help establish that it was theirs. "'Possession,'" Mr. Snodgravel had quoted yet again, "'is nine-tenths of the law.'"

"I asked Mr. Snodgravel to write the needed letter, and I signed a blank sheet of paper so that his scribe could write the letter in a proper hand and then send it," Giles told Daphne. "Mr. Snodgravel," Giles continued, "also said that it would be very wise when one of us visited the estate to make sure that it has a staff of servants paid by us. If they are still available from Mr. Edwards's time, they should be paid their wages for the intervening months. If they are not, they should be replaced with at least a skeleton staff, and it would be best if we did that ourselves, in person, since we have no steward appointed for the property, and Mr. Edwards may not have had one either."

"Well, I don't want to be apart from each other before you have to leave," Daphne declared. "It might be interesting for both of us to see what Mr. Edwards has left for us in Shropshire. We could go to Birmingham on the way. For settling my uncle's affairs, an earl might be more respected than a countess. Even though you are about to declare that that isn't the case, I know that the best business people of Birmingham, who are also leading engineers and scientists, respect someone who can handle the intricacies of a full-rigged ship, and deep down feel that a woman is less capable in handling business matters than a man. Even my uncle is not immune from that attitude. Several times he has written, 'For a woman, you are doing very well.'"

"That makes sense. I have been curious about your uncle's business and Birmingham ever since you sent those enthusiastic reports. I suggest that we go to Dipton for a couple of days, then on to Birmingham and spend several days. After that, let's visit this place in Shropshire. Say, two weeks in total. Then I can go down to Portsmouth and take *Glaucus* to sea."

"Yes, that sounds good, though I would like to spend one more day in London. Aunt Gillian has invited me to go with her to a lecture tomorrow afternoon, and I want to attend. Lady Berkensop's Ball is tomorrow night; we have an invitation, and it is one of the highlights of the Season. I am still fascinated by Society's courtship rituals, and I love to dance, and I could get some ideas for next year's Hunt Ball."

"So we are going to host the Hunt Ball next year, are we?"

"Only with your permission, of course, my lord."

"As if I'd dare say, 'No.' I think it is all a good idea, but there is one more thing I would like to do while we are here."

"What is that?"

"I'd like to talk to the man who designed the changes at Camshire House and also see the renovations that are going on. I think it would be useful for dealing with whatever is being done in Shropshire if I knew more about what you have arranged here."

"That makes sense. I will appreciate having the workmen see that I have your express backing. And that will be helpful in Shropshire too. So many men seem to believe that women are not capable of understanding anything to do with building or other practical matters."

"I know and am sorry for it. Tomorrow's lecture, for example. What is it about?"

"The latest developments in bridge building."

"There you are. I am sure that you will lap it up while I would have great difficulty following the lecture."

"Fiddlesticks, but you still have to go for that sitting for your portrait. I insist. You may not care about your portraits, but I do. The artist says all he wants is an afternoon with you posing to get all he needs to complete your role in the pictures. Though I don't see how just one afternoon can be adequate."

"Probably not. I think that the painter should just complete the picture with only you in it."

"Nonsense. And *I* want a picture of you that I can stare at when you are away. All I have is a miniature of you painted long before I met you.."

"All right, All right. Now we should get changed for dinner and the evening since Aunt Gillian has been so good as to get us all a box at the King's Theatre."

"You are right. I am really looking forward to this new opera by Mozart – new to London anyway – something about Titus."

"I am too, though I must say that I would rather see one of his lighter works. I am told that this opera uses one of those tiresome, old-fashioned librettos."

"Even so, Mozart's operas are supposed to be breathtaking. Anyway, I have only seen one opera in my life, and it was marvelous."

Chapter XV

The day after Giles and Daphne attended the opera produced more challenging events. They met with Mr. Beaver, the designer whom Daphne had selected, after asking for recommendations from Mr. Edwards and Lady Struthers. Mr. Beaver had a reputation for delivering imaginative, stylish, and practical designs for renovating the mansions of the aristocracy. Engaging him resulted in houses of which his clients could be proud. While they were going over the changes to Camshire Hose with the designer, the first surprise occurred. Giles had done what Daphne had not: examined the servants' quarters below stairs. When he looked at the plans for that part of the house, he immediately saw that the layout was awkward.

"Wouldn't it be better to have extra doors put in here and here, Mr. Beaver?" he asked. "That would allow the butler and the housekeeper to go about their duties with far less time required than using the present set-up."

"Let's see — yes, you are right, My Lord. I am afraid that I have not looked seriously at improving things below stairs or in the servants' quarters in the attic. My experience has been that my clients have little interest in such matters, even when considering building a new house, so I just don't waste my time looking at that part of a building that I am renovating. No one has ever before shown any concern about the physical arrangements for servants."

"Well, you must consider their facilities, and we can go over the changes you recommend together before proceeding, or, if I am away, with Lady Giles."

"That is a very good idea, Giles," Daphne said. "I confess I had never thought about the servants' areas at all."

"I will do what you want, of course, my lord, my lady. I am surprised a little," agreed Mr. Beaver.

"Why?"

"Well, I have also been doing the design work for the changes to the estate in Shropshire that Mr. Edwards commissioned. I know that he said it was for himself, but I started to doubt that after a while. I had great trouble getting him to pay his account on time; in the end, he gave me a draft for part of it that was drawn on an account at Coutts's Bank that had your name on it. So I guessed that it must actually be your estate, my lord."

"Ah, yes, of course! Did he say anything more?"

"Not really. But I stopped working on the project when Mr. Edwards said that he couldn't pay the next bill because he was strapped for cash right then."

"Ah, I see, Mr. Beaver," replied Giles. "I am afraid that Mr. Edwards was overstepping himself there. Do you know that he was found guilty of cheating his clients, particularly his naval clients, of large amounts of money?"

"I knew that he had difficulties with the law, but not the details. I make a practice of not paying attention to reports in the newspapers and scandal sheets. Too depressing!"

"Well, Mr. Edwards was convicted. His sentence was commuted from hanging to transportation. Needless to say, he is my agent no longer. Do you know what is the status of the work on that property in Shropshire?"

"I am afraid not, my lord. When Mr. Edwards stopped paying the bills here, I warned the builder whom I had engaged locally to carry out the work. He also had been unable to collect any interim payments from Mr. Edwards, so he had already stopped working on the project."

"Well, well, well! How Edwards's dishonesty has complicated matters! Send Mr. Snodgravel, my solicitor, the builder's name, and I will tell him to make sure that the account is settled as soon as possible. I don't suppose that you have a copy of the plans for that residence."

"Of course I do. I make a habit of having one of my apprentices copy the plans of any project I am involved in. I will be happy to send them to you."

"That would be very helpful, Mr. Beaver," Daphne broke in, "but I wonder if we could persuade you to come to Shropshire to go over the plans on the site. We will be there Tuesday, ten days from now. Would it be too much to ask you to meet us there?"

"A week Tuesday? Yes, I see no problem. I would like to review the site and the plans myself. Sometimes, the passage of time can make one see possibilities that escaped one earlier."

"That's settled then," replied Daphne. "Now, let's have a look at the rest of the servants' quarters, especially their rooms on the top floor. I have been very remiss in not thinking of them. I have learned from my father and my husband that the better you treat people who are working for you, the better service you get from them."

The rest of the discussion took almost no time at all. As Mr. Beaver pointed out, the layout of the servants' attic was very standard. What might be needed were coats of paint and better beds and bedding. Usually, that was the last thing owners thought of and something that was allowed for insufficiently in their housekeeper's budget, especially beds, which were often somewhat broken down. In Camshire House, both beds and mattresses looked as if they dated back to the time of Queen Ann. Daphne made a mental note to buy all new furnishings for the servants' quarters.

Giles and Daphne walked back towards Struthers House, talking excitedly about what they might find in Shropshire. They parted at the top of Bond Street, Giles to go to the studio of the painter, Mr. Findlay, to sit for his portrait, Daphne to meet with Lady Struthers to go to the lecture. They agreed that, rather surprisingly, they were enjoying their visit to London this time.

Giles was not looking forward to his visit to the artist's studio. The tedium of sitting for several hours as the painter laboriously sketched and drew and finally applied paint to the sketch held no appeal for him. He would have refused point-blank if Daphne had not told him that it was very important to her to have a good portrait of him as the man she knew and loved.

He turned down Bond Street and stopped for a moment to look into the window of Blackett's Music store, which was just opposite the house where the artist had his studio. Blackett's was the shop where Daphne had purchased the magnificent violin she had given him. It was a constant joy, especially when he was at sea. Giles was tempted to go into the shop to see what they had in the way of new music for violin and pianoforte, even though he and Daphne were far from exhausting the works they already had acquired. Indeed, he wouldn't mind skipping the appointment with the painter altogether. For himself, Giles couldn't care less about having his portrait painted, but he knew that Daphne was very keen on having pictures of him and of their family. Most of the tedious work had already been done on the family portrait; all that was needed was for him to sit so that the artist could fill the details about him in a picture whose composition was already chosen. With a shrug of his shoulders, Giles turned away from the display in the music store's windows to cross the street to the artist's house.

Giles was expected. Directly after he knocked on the door, a servant led him up to the top storey, where he was shown into a large attic room which was flooded with light from north-facing skylights. His first impression of the studio was of a haphazardly cluttered space with stacks of paintings, many with their reverse side showing or covered with cloths. A second glance told Giles that there was nothing haphazard about it. He had spent too much time in the highly restricted space of the midshipmen's berth and the lieutenant's wardroom not to know the difference between carefully placed items that could not be hidden from sight and actual clutter. This was definitely the former.

Mr. Findlay came forward from behind an easel, clutching a paintbrush. Giles noted that the paintbrush did not have any wet paint on it.

"Lord Camshire, what a pleasure to meet you at last! My condolences on the loss of your father."

"Thank you, Mr. Findlay," Giles replied. "Let's get on with the sitting."

"Very good, my lord. You might like to see what I have accomplished so far, though I usually don't show sitters any part of a picture until it is finished."

The picture, a large canvas, took Giles's breath away. Findlay had placed Daphne with Bernard playing at her feet with the foxhound that Daphne had rescued. She was looking down at her child with a fond smile on her face. Daphne was not conventionally pretty, though she was striking and, in Giles's eyes, beautiful.

The artist had captured Daphne's essence perfectly, not trying to make her look more beautiful in the standard way. Instead, he had brought out how unique her face was. Giles was delighted with the picture. The only flaw in the composition was a rather poorly sketched area near Daphne. Giles realized that that was where his portrait was supposed to go.

"That is a perfect likeness of Lady Camshire, Mr. Findlay," Giles remarked. "You have caught her expression perfectly. And the grounds of Dipton Hall as well. I just hope that you can do anything like as well with me."

"It will be a challenge, my lord; I agree," replied the painter, "especially as you do not look anything like I expected."

"Oh?"

"I confess I was expecting some rather self-important and self-satisfied man with his nose tilted slightly in the air and a bored look on his face. Bland self-confidence and giving me an order that if there are any scars or worry lines, they should be smoothed away, though the bit of a pot belly and spindly legs could be kept. Of course, such clients expect to be the center of the composition."

Giles laughed. "I've seen some of those pictures. The Admiralty is full of them, even of captains and particularly admirals no one has ever heard of. Just put me in my place as long as you make Lady Camshire the focus of the picture."

"Oh, I don't think I can paint you as I expected. You are much too natural-seeming a man to render you as a conventional, pompous officer. I see strength and worry, humor and sadness in your face already, and I would like to bring them out in this picture, but even more in the portrait that Lady Camshire has asked me to paint you by yourself. I'll have to think some more about the possibilities for that picture. I know she wanted it of you in your ship, though I haven't really thought about the implication of that difficult suggestion yet.

"Now, shall we get to work, my lord?"

"Certainly. Where would you like me to stand?"

"Over here, so that the light from the skylight is at much the same angle as in the picture. Are you all right standing, or would you rather sit while I concentrate on your face and head?"

"Yes, I am used to standing for long periods."

The painter picked up his charcoal and started sketching on the canvas. He worked quickly, but, even so, the clock in the corner of the studio had rung the quarter hour three times before he was satisfied. All the time, he chatted with Giles, mainly about what he had seen at Dipton Hall when he visited and how he had admired how well the farms were managed. Giles found that he was telling the painter about the various endeavors that he and Daphne were engaged in, even about their interest in the latest farming information and practices and how such techniques could be adapted for their use on their own properties.

"You can have a look at what I have done so far, my lord," announced Mr. Findlay as he laid aside his charcoal.

"I thought you people never let your clients see their pictures until they were finished."

"That's true when we are in the middle of filling in the details and blending the colors. The client will usually find it displeasing, and I would, too, since the colors are not right yet because they have not been blended properly, and the representation of the light is not correct.

"Now you can see how I have posed you, my lord. At first, I thought I would have you looking out proudly at your estate, but I think this is a better idea. I have pictured you gazing fondly at Lady Camshire as she is looking at her son crawling on the ground. Rather unconventional, I think, but suits what I believe are your characters.

"Before we start again," the artist continued, "could we discuss the painting that Lady Camshire wants of you on your boat? I am planning to go down to see it in a few days, but it would help if you have any suggestions for the setting."

"Well, I don't think that Lady Camshiree would really want one of those standard portraits with me standing on the quarterdeck looking out at the horizon with my nose in the air, looking as if I had smelled something vaguely unpleasant. I think she would prefer a representation of me in my cabin on a sunny day."

"The difficulty with the usual cabin portraits is that the lighting is all wrong. It suggests that there was a big hole in the ceiling."

"It's called the 'deck,' but that is not quite what I had in mind. I was thinking of representing me sitting at an angle to the windows. *Glaucus,* my frigate, has quite large stern windows. I saw a portrait of Admiral Nelson once that was posed that way. The light fell on his face as he was reading a book."

"Yes, I can see that that might work."

"Rather than a book, I thought it might be a good idea to have me holding my fiddle."

"Ah, yes, I can imagine it now. In fact, I think I have something a bit similar among my works in progress. Just let me find it."

Mr. Findlay moved to a dark corner of the room where many canvases were stacked. He started rummaging around, turning them up enough so that he could see what lay behind. After going through one small stack, he moved to the next one. Its top canvas was a landscape; the next one was of a reclining nude. Giles looked at it casually and then with more care.

"Isn't that Mrs. Bolton."

"Yes, it is," replied the artist. "I'm sorry, my lord, you were not supposed to see that."

"Well, I have now. How in the world do you happen to be painting my niece, Mrs. Bolton, in the nude?"

"It's at her commission, my lord, a portrait of the sort that is called a 'gentleman's dressing-room picture.' They are commissioned by gentlemen, or often by their wives, to enhance the gentleman's ardor. They are quite common, though rarely discussed, I believe, except among the women."

"And the one below Mrs. Bolton's, is it another 'gentleman's picture?'"

"Yes, my lord. That was commissioned by Lady Spense. She is a quite dashing member of Society, though her husband is rather an old stick."

"But there seems to be a very similar one below it," said Giles, who had moved forward and had started to turn the pictures himself.

"Ugh ... ugh ... yes, that is the same lady, though it is a somewhat more voluptuous one, as you can see. I rather enhanced her charms."

"But why did you paint the two pictures?"

"Ugh … ugh…it is a long story. Just between ourselves, you know. Lady Spense is not at all proper, though she sometimes gives the impression of being a prude. Lord Spense is not at all generous with her, though he is rich enough. Lady Spense originally commissioned the work in the hope of loosening his purse strings, but she couldn't afford my fee. I — well, I told her that I could find a ready buyer for another picture of her, especially if I enhanced her best features. She agreed, so that is why there are two of them. They just have to dry a bit more, and they can go to the places where they will hang."

"Where will the second picture go?"

'To Green's Club, my lord."

"Green's Club — really?"

"Yes, indeed. The special member's smoking room."

"So any member or their guests can see it?"

"I don't believe so. The special members are a club within the club. Only special members have access to the smoking room; regular members do not. I understand that the special members are among the most brazen womanizers in Green's. Rumor has it that much more goes on there than just smoking and enjoying salacious pictures."

"I see. Let me warn you, Mr. Findlay, that if Mrs. Bolton's face appears on any naked body, you will wish that you had never been born. Using courtesans for such pictures is one thing; using respectable ladies is quite another. Now, where is the picture you were referring to when this search began?"

After some more searching, the artist found the picture. It was of a man sitting in his library with the sun partially illuminating his face as he read a book.

"That is as far as I got with this picture, I am afraid, my lord," said Mr. Findlay. "The subject then canceled his portrait without paying me anything for the work I had already done. It is a hazard of my trade. And," Mr. Finddlay continued with a laugh, "there is no chance of selling this work to some gentleman's club."

"I suppose that is true. Don't worry about Lady Camshire and me. We pay our debts in full and at once. I think this basic idea would do for my portrait, but of course, you'll have to see the cabin on my frigate. She will be in Portsmouth for the next while. I'll write you a chit to gain access to my cabin.

"As I said, what I would like to have me doing, rather than reading a book, is playing my violin. Possibly holding my instrument as I reach forward to turn a page of music."

"Sounds brilliant. Let's start now if you still have some time."

Giles left after another hour of posing. He walked back to Struthers House, deep in thought. He wasn't horrified at the revelation that gentlemen's pictures existed or even that his niece had sat – or rather lounged – for one. He knew that some men needed visual stimulation to prepare for the conjugal act, especially if their love-making was conducted in the dark. That was, of course, Captain and Mrs. Bolton's business. The exposure of lewd pictures for the benefit of the rakes at Green's Club was another matter altogether. There must be something that he could do with that disgraceful enterprise that sullied his name by association.

Daphne had told Giles that Mr. Findlay had hinted that Giles might like to have a nude picture of her. She had thought the suggestion amusing rather than either tempting or disgusting, and she had told the artist that it was unnecessary without apparently explaining why that was so. However, Giles knew that Daphne was aware that imagining her had always been more than enough to arouse him, and she had never been inhibited about showing herself to him. He realized that he knew nothing about the private side of other people's marriages. All he did know was that he couldn't imagine anything better than his own.

Chapter XVI

"I have been looking into the lease on Green's Club, as you requested, my lord," Mr. Snodgravel announced.

Giles had had to cut short his trip to Birmingham and Shropshire with Daphne when a dispatch rider from the Admiralty had caught up with him in Birmingham. The message called him to London to meet with the King on a day so soon that he would only be able to comply with the order by leaving immediately for London, stopping for one night at Dipton. So Daphne was left with the task of going to Shropshire to meet with Mr. Bottomly. She wouldn't hear of postponing the journey until Giles could come too: Mr. Snodgravel had emphasized the importance of asserting their ownership as soon as possible.

When Giles received the King's summons, he immediately wrote to Mr. Snodgravel to look into the lease on the mansion where Green's Club was located. That property had come to him on his father's death and was entailed so that he could not sell it but had to pass it on to his heir. The more he heard about Green's Club, the less he was happy to be associated with it in any way. He had resigned from the membership that came automatically to him as the owner of the property. Still, after what he had learned from Mr. Findlay, he wanted to see if there was any way to abrogate the ninety-nine-year lease that Green's had on the property. Now, having had his royal meeting in an early morning audience where the King thanked him for undertaking the trip to the waters where the River Weser flowed into the Waldon Sea, which is the part of the North Sea where the shore turned northward to the Danish peninsula. Now he was free to pursue matters that were more important to him, particularly the Green's Club lease.

"The lease is a strange document, my lord," continued Mr. Snodgravel, "in containing rather unusual terms under which the landlord — that is you, of course — can break the lease. Of course, there are also the usual conditions about paying (and setting) the rent and the maintenance of the building, which falls mainly on the lessee, i.e., Green's Club. What is unusual, especially given the present reputation of the Club, is some provisions that were carried over — without much thought, I suspect — from the lease on the original building housing the Club. Green's is a much older club than I thought, and its initial landlord must have had a strong non-conformist inclination and was, I suspect, a Mason. Anyway, two clauses of the document are unusual. The first, which makes me suspect a Masonic background, is that if at any time the Club establishes different types or classes of membership, the lease will be considered null and void with the Club being required to vacate and leave the premises — that is, the mansion, of course — at once. The second provision is that the lease may be terminated if lewd or lascivious behavior or pornographic or obscene pictures or statues or other objects are allowed in the Club. If situations conforming to either stipulation are found, the Club must leave and vacate the premises, taking none of the offending items with them.

"It would seem, my lord, from what you wrote to me, that Green's is in violation of both these provisions since a special members' smoking room must indeed violate the first one while having pictures of naked women gracing the walls unquestionably can be considered both lewd and lascivious unless, I suppose, they are antiquities. The problem is to establish that these breaches and violations have occurred and are still present so that we can apply to have the lease revoked and terminated."

"I suppose that Mr. Findlay's report about his commissions for gentlemen's paintings would not be enough."

"Not by itself, no, especially as it is clear that the landlord — that is you — has been paying the artist considerable amounts of money."

"Yes, but those payments were for the portraits of us that he is painting."

"True, but you can imagine what a clever barrister could make of that transaction in court. But, no, we have to see the pictures *in situ*."

"What do you suggest then, Mr. Snodgravel?"

"Well, my lord, I took the initiative to raise and discuss the matter with the Chief Magistrate for Westminster. He already was not at all happy with Green's Club, he told me."

"Oh?"

"Yes. Partly he was worried about what was happening there, especially some wagering that involved unlawful actions. More than that, he was disturbed that having drunken aristocratic louts wandering the streets near Green's Club late at night invited criminals to the area to prey on them. In doing that, the miscreants were also making the streets unsafe for law-abiding people with valid and legitimate reasons to be on the nearby streets late at night, many of them tradesmen delivering in anticipation of the morning or servants on similar errands.

"The Chief Magistrate had had the Bow Street Runners raid the place a couple of times, but even though he considers that the special smoking room is actually a place of ill-repute, based on what they found and on the fact that some of the women found there were known prostitutes, he could not prosecute any of the gentlemen because of influence rather than lack of evidence. All the influence, some of it coming from the Bench — can you believe it? — was all on one side.

"So there is nothing I can do about the situation?" Giles asked glumly.

"Not quite. The Chief Magistrate told me he would be willing to have his Bow-Street Runners again visit the place to verify that the smoking room violates the terms of the lease, even if it does not cross the line into criminal activity and that there are pictures that could be considered lewd and lascivious. With it being a matter of terminating a lease rather than explicitly punishing a club for allowing improper behavior, Mr. Downing, the Chief Magistrate, believes that the same purpose can be served. By terminating the lease, shutting down Green's Club would be achieved unless you lease it to a similarly reprehensive establishment.

"Though the Runners would also be on his service, the Chief Magistrate believes it is in his power to cancel the lease based on the wording of the document and so to use his people for the raid, but he did emphasize that his men would appreciate being tipped the cost of drinking your health in a tavern."

"Quite right! Men should be rewarded for willingly performing extra service.

"Mr. Snodgravel, you have found the perfect solution to my dilemma. When can the raid occur? Will the magistrate be able to cancel the lease? Can the magistrate close Green's Club and restore the building to me without a long legal wrangle?"

"Easy on, my lord. Let me try to answer the questions and queries one at a time. You do realize, I hope, that many of the answers will be my best guess, and some courts might think differently.

"First, the Chief Magistrate is willing to sponsor a raid as early as this evening and join in himself.

Second, he believes that he has the power to close the Club indefinitely and thereby restore the lease to you.

"Third, he will also inform the scandal press of what is happening and what is found.

"Fourth, he will have his Runners ensure that the club vacates the property immediately without removing any items that help to account for the lease being terminated.

"Of course, if the raid produces incontrovertible evidence that the terms of the lease have been broken, Green's Club could tie the property up in suits in the courts for a long time, but that is not likely to happen."

"Why not?" Giles asked curtly. He was getting tired of Mr. Snodgravel's tendency to use three words where one would do.

"Green's Club is not in a strong financial state. In fact, they are behind on the rent that it owes you, though the period of delinquency is still within the traditional period of grace before we could take action against them. However, their members are by and large a group of wastrels who have unsettled accounts all over town and are sometimes only one step ahead of the bailiffs in keeping out of debtors' prison."

"So are you saying that if the magistrate raids and enters the place forcibly and finds that the terms of the lease are being violated and contravened, then he can rule the lease canceled and terminated?"

Giles realized with horror that the tendency to use pretentious synonyms seemed to be catching.

"Yes, my lord, though 'null and void' is how we would express it in the law. The property would still be entailed, so you couldn't sell or dispose of it."

" Yes, I see. Lady Camshire and I don't need another London residence, especially not one in St. James's when we have one in Mayfair, but I expect that we can find some other tenant for the property."

"I am sure that we can, my lord. Indeed, I have something in mind that may serve your needs."

"Well, let's not get ahead of ourselves. First, we have to get the current lease dissolved."

"Quite right. I suggest that we meet with the magistrate and his Bow Street Runners at 11:30 this evening opposite White's Club in St. James's Street. That is late enough that the more respectable members of Green's will have gone home while the illicit revels may well be in full progress."

The appointment left Giles with an empty day ahead of him. A visit to Hatchers for books, lunch at Brook's Club, where he had just been elected to membership, some time in the House of Lords, and then dinner with his aunt and uncle, and he would be ready for the raid on Green's Club. But first, he would have to return to Struthers House to alert Carstairs about the plans. Carstairs had kept in touch with many of his old shipmates who had left the navy for one reason or another. They had also been shipmates with Giles, of course. Carstairs had suggested he could always recruit some in London if Giles needed them. Now would be a perfect time to see if Carstairs could call in some of the promises.

The group assembled a bit before 11:30. It was just as well that Giles and the Chief Magistrate were among the first to arrive. Otherwise, the first arrivals would have been asking to be challenged as an unlawful assembly in the well-to-do neighborhood of St. James's. What the members of White's Club across the street thought of them could only be wondered at. No one left the club while Giles's gang was gathering. Giles did spot the watch huddling at the next corner, wondering what was going on but not prepared to confront the group. It was not their job to try to stop a mob.

Mr. Snodgravel introduced the Chief Magistrate, Mr. Downing, to Giles. Mr. Downing announced, "I am glad, my lord, that you are providing us with this opportunity to close Green's Club. It has been a thorn in our side for years. By various accounts, it is a gambling hell, a bawdy house, and a molly house where members commit unmentionable acts with each other. But its members have too much influence, often from highly placed parents who are unwilling to see their heirs belittled or arrested. Maybe now we can shut it down! And thank you for bringing some of your sailors to assist my Bow Street Runners. We will need to close off the back of the building if we want to make the most significant impact on the licentious doings of Green's Club."

"I will be relieved not to be associated with the place anymore," said Giles. "I knew that it had a bad reputation, but I had no idea how bad. So let's get on with closing down Green's Club. I see, Mr. Snodgravel, that you are carrying a portfolio. Is that for recording the events and what we find?"

"Yes, my lord. I would not be surprised if we find some members in compromising positions who may be willing to sign a statement confirming that the purposes of the club are being transcended. Such statements will ease my task of breaking the lease on your behalf."

Green's Club was located a couple of streets from the group's assembly point, though it was not on

St. James's Street, so no one at the target club could see them gathering. The club occupied a large, impressive building. It had a massive portico in a rather old-fashioned style that gave entrance to the three-storey-and-attic mansion that had once been the London residence of the Earls of Camshire.

"I had no idea how big the place is," Giles remarked to Mr. Snodgravel.

"It's actually even larger than it looks'" replied the lawyer. "After occupying the building for several years, the Club asked your father for permission to build an annex in what was then the garden between the house and the mews. That addition is where what is called 'the special members smoking room' is located, though the addition is much more than a smoking room. The old residence is used as a somewhat less raffish establishment, basically being a standard gentlemen's club with the upper storeys being used as bedrooms for members visiting from out of town. Even so, I have heard rumors that the club's chambermaids supplement their income by being available to meet all the desires of the members. Of course, some members only want a place to say without any special favors."

"That's true," added Mr. Downing. "We will try not to disturb them too much tonight, though I trust that such gentlemen will have to find different accommodations in the future. Now I'll send a few of my Runners and, if you agree, my lord, some of your sailors to the mews in the back to intercept those who want to disappear when we go in the front door. I expect some of them to be the doxies rumored to ply their trade in that part of the club. If so, I expect that the pillory will be full tomorrow."

After waiting a few minutes so that the contingent whose job was to block off the mews could get into position, Mr. Downing led the way to the front door, where he used the large knocker to demand entrance. The door was opened by a liveried servant who initially tried to deny entrance to the mob who appeared to be most unsuitable visitors to the club. However, his objections died when Mr. Downing produced an impressive-looking document that he stated was a warrant to verify that the premises were being used as a house of ill fame and criminal and other activities that were in violation of the terms of the lease on the property held by the Earl of Camshire.

Once inside the building, Mr. Downing confidently led the invaders to where he must have been informed that the entrance to the special members' smoking room, so-called, was located. However, one member of his team was posted to prevent anyone from leaving the premises by the front door, while a couple of Runners had been left outside to intercept anyone trying to leave the building by the basement exits.

The entrance to the restricted part of the building was easy to recognize; its name was written on the doors in elaborate lettering. In front of the doors stood two liveried servants who looked more like they were more suitable as denizens of prize-fighting arenas than as the largely superfluous doormen at a gentlemen's club.

"Here, governor, you can't go in there." One of these men greeted Mr. Downing.

The Chief Magistrate turned to the Runner immediately behind him, a very large and hard-looking individual.

"Mr. Latimore, arrest these men for obstruction of justice."

"Yes, sir. Come on, Red," said the Runner who, Giles saw immediately, was no stranger to brawling. Giles couldn't follow exactly what happened next, but in moments the two club servants were on the ground with their hands shackled behind them. Mr. Downing, without pausing to see what his subordinates were doing, strode up to the double doors and threw them open, shouting, "Magistrates' officers! Remain where you are!"

A stunned silence greeted this proclamation. The room was filled with groups of men at tables or on lounge settles that were scattered around. Some groups were playing cards, but others were simply talking and smoking. A pall of smoke hung over the area.

Even before a babble of voices broke out in response to the announcement, Giles noted a couple of men descending a staircase that ran up the side of the room to a gallery above. They stopped in their tracks and then reversed direction to go back up. Mr. Downing shouted something that sounded very much like a view halloo used by fox hunters when their prey is sighted and bounded up the stairs after the men, yelling, "Please organize things down here, my lord."

Giles would have preferred to follow the Chief Magistrate, but he could see the sense of the official's request. He raised his voice to inform the crowd in the room what was happening.

"As many of you know, I am the Earl of Camshire. I hold the lease on this property. I regret that you are all being inconvenienced, but it is necessary to investigate allegations of improper behavior in this club contrary to the terms of the lease on the building and possibly in contravention of the laws of the Kingdom. The gentleman you have just seen mounting the stairs is the Chief Magistrate of Westminster, under whose jurisdiction this property falls.

"Right now, following the instructions of the Chief Magistrate, I require that you give your names to Mr. Snodgravel here, where you reside, whether you are a special member of Green's club, and, if so, what makes you a 'special member.' After providing the information, you may leave the Club or go to your rooms if you are staying here for the night. While you are waiting to talk to Mr. Snodgravel, you may order further refreshments from the staff and continue your card games if you wish."

There was quite a bit of low-level grumbling at these requirements, but somehow Giles intimidated most of the people into abiding by what he demanded. It, of course, helped that he was backed up by men who gave the impression that they would be all too happy to put these toffs in their place.

Not having to ensure anymore that there would be an orderly processing of the information needed from the patrons of the special smoking room gave Giles a chance to glance around the room. The walls sported paintings of nude or skimpily covered women, usually in reclining or even more provocative poses. Definitely, they were what Mr. Findlay called 'gentlemen's pictures.' Indeed, one of these paintings was the salacious portrait of Lady Spense that he had observed in the artist's studio. Looking a bit more closely at the other paintings, Giles recognized the faces of several as ones that he had seen and, in some cases, been introduced to at some of the large social functions he had attended in London recently. Surely, they had not all had the same reason as Lady Spense to allow their improper pictures to be displayed at the raffish Green's Club. Could it be that unscrupulous artists had made copies of gentlemen's pictures to sell to Green's club? Possibly the painters had added the faces of well-known women to the bodies of other models who had provided the basis for the erotic parts of the paintings without their knowledge? Giles was relieved that none of the nudes featured the face of his niece, Catherine Bolton.

Giles decided that he should see what was happening upstairs. He had heard several high-pitched screeches coming from the top of the staircase, suggesting that that part of the gentlemen's club had been invaded by women. The scene that greeted him when he reached the top of the stairs was like a scene from Hogarth's paintings. There was no question that the terms of the lease on the property were being shockingly violated.

Even as he took in the scene suggesting complete debauchery, one of the Runners dragged in a couple in a state of undress. The woman, who had a heavily made-up face, was wearing only a set of stays and a strange, slightly diaphanous set of pantaloons, which Giles supposed must be the new-fangled item of woman's wear that Daphne had told him were drawers. The man, who was clearly in his cups, was struggling to fasten his trousers with little success. Even as the Runner shoved the pair into the room, the woman yelled to the man with her, "You still owe me a tip, even though you couldn't get it up." Some of the other people in the room were still in disheveled clothing, which suggested that they had also been caught in the midst of very improper activities.

As Giles stared at the scene before him, a woman who had been haranguing Mr. Downing, looked over at him and let out a screech. Unlike most of the other women in the room, she was dressed in what Giles took to be the height of fashion, though the crude, flamboyant makeup on her face did not correspond to what he had seen on any of the mature women he had met in Society. Now she stopped yelling at the Chief Magistrate to turn her attention to Giles.

"Look who's here: the goddamned flaming Earl of Camshire. I should have guessed that you would be behind this bleeding raid that is interrupting my business. Just like your bleeding, poncy wife, high and mighty Lady Ashton. She klept me out of a fortune, and now you, you goddamned mollyboy, are again disturbing my legitimate provision of services to the gentlemen of this club."

Giles realized that the woman must be the whoremonger that Daphne had tricked into releasing Giles from wretched entanglements with the seamy side of London's fashionable society that had been willed to him by his older half-brother.

"Madam, I imagine that you must be Mrs. Marsdon. My wife tells me that she thoroughly bamboozled you a couple of years ago. This meeting will be much more serious for you. Running a knocking shop on my property is intolerable. Mr. Downing, I hope you intend to charge her."

"Yes, indeed, my lord. I have known about Mrs. Marsdon for a long time, but she has so much influence that I could never hope to convict her before. Now what we have seen with our own eyes should be enough so that she can't get off. If I may, my lord, I shall emphasize that you favor prosecuting her to the full extent of the law. She won't hang, worse luck, not with all the influential men who are in her clutches, but she will be transported, I expect, if she survives the hour in the pillory to which I can sentence her myself. She has ruined enough young girls' lives that she may not survive that ordeal."

"I suppose that there is not much you can do to punish the men involved."

"I am afraid not, my lord. What the men were doing is not a crime, even though what the women were doing is. What I will do, however, is make sure that the scandal rags get all their names and the details of what we found here. Then, at least, they will feel some shame, I would hope, and the contempt of others, though I am afraid that many of these reprobates may know no shame or are already condemned in Society's eyes. Having their peccadillos widely broadcast might prevent others from risking the same embarrassment if they are tempted to indulge in the same pleasures. "

"With your permission, Mr. Downing, I will leave now that you have everything under control."

"Thank you for your aid, my lord. Especially for those sailors that you coxswain recruited. They were invaluable."

"I'm glad to hear it. They are former members of my crew, not in the Royal Navy at present, and good men all. Incidentally, I gave Carstairs some half-crowns to distribute to your Runners for their assistance."

"That was more than necessary, my lord; sixpenny pieces would have been plenty for them, but I am sure your generosity is much appreciated. That sort of concrete support makes my work easier. Good luck on this voyage that I hear you are about to take."

Giles and Carstairs made their way back to Struthers House. They slid into their beds immediately and fell asleep at once. They would have to be up before dawn so that Giles's carriage could reach Portsmouth the next day.

Chapter XVII

The left rear carriage-wheel fell with a thump into yet another hole in the road that led past Sallycove, the property that Mr. Snodgravel had said belonged to Giles. According to the landlord at the inn where Daphne had spent the night, the road was public, but it was supposed to be maintained by the owner of Sallycove. However, he had said that no work had been done on it for over a year, so the road was in very poor shape after the winter. While he had not said so, Daphne had the distinct impression that the landlord expected the Earl of Camshire, who, Daphne declared, owned the property, to have it fixed soon.

What a disappointment this part of the trip was turning out to be after the success of the past few days! Even though the pleasure of their excursion had been largely ruined by Giles's summons to return to London, Daphne felt pleased with the trip. She had been welcomed in Birmingham by the engineers and factory owners she had met previously. These people took her seriously, not as some beautiful, aristocratic lady with a fine taste in clothes but nothing of substance in her brain. They had even listened to her thoughts on the least-squares method. Best of all, Giles had been taken with them as much as they were with him. Perhaps they could share their interest in engineering and similar matters when he was ashore.

Things had also gone better than she could have expected in making arrangements for her uncle's house and servants. She had wondered how to find a buyer for the house and give fair treatment to her uncle's faithful servants. Of course, the latter concern was unusual for someone of her status; most servants could, at best, hope for a good reference on being dismissed with little notice, if any. These problems were solved easily when Mr. Heatherstone, whom she had met on the previous visit, approached her to explain that he was about to get married and that he would like to purchase her uncle's house at a fair price to provide a home for his new bride. He would also employ the existing staff, whom he knew to be excellent.

The turnpike from Birmingham had been smooth, and even after they had turned off it to follow the river, the road had been in good repair and offered pleasant vistas. The Woodbridge Inn where they had spent the night had a pleasant location, good food, and excellent service. Now things had deteriorated to the point that Daphne was wondering about the wisdom of visiting the estate just to show interest in Giles's new property. Would it really strengthen their case for ownership of the estate on which Edwards had spent their money? Anyway, this track was clearly not a sensible way to get to Sallycove, at least not in a travelling carriage.

Daphne knocked on the roof to have the coachman stop before another hole upset the carriage. It must be less than a mile to the estate. She could walk faster than the coach was moving. Besides, poor Betsey was looking distinctly ill, and Daphne did not want to have to deal with a lady's maid who had been sick all over the carriage.

As soon as Graham, the footman she had brought on the trip, opened the carriage door, Daphne climbed out and called to the coachman on his box. "Richards, take the coach back to the inn and then return with a horse that I can ride and one for Betsey as well, of course. This road is impossible!"

Daphne glanced at the side of the road where Betsey was throwing up the remains of her breakfast.

"Graham, get some water for Betsey," she told the groom. "She will, of course, have to accompany me to the estate even though she is feeling unwell."

When Betsey had recovered enough to be able to walk, Daphne set off with the maid limping behind her. Betsey's corns were bothering her. She should have had Mr. Jackson take care of them before they left on this trip, but she had been too busy, or so she had thought. And, of course, Lady Camshire could not send her back with the coach. For her mistress to be wandering around a strange countryside on the way to meet with two men would be unthinkable without a maid accompanying her. Even Betsey's unconventional mistress wouldn't go that far!

Fifteen minutes walking brought them to the turnoff from the road that must lead to Sallycove. The estate's drive was in better condition than the river road, but it also needed work. The junction with the road was in a copse of trees, so Daphne had yet to see anything of the house. Finally, after walking another hundred yards along the driveway, they came to a view that caused Daphne to pause.

The land sloped gently down to the river with open fields through which the drive passed before reaching the groomed area in front of the house. The residence was a large building made of warm, yellow stone. A forest of chimneys suggested that the mansion extended quite a distance towards the water. Though large, the house was very plain with no embellishments. This was true even of the main entrance, which was only a simple double door with almost no flat space before steps descended to where the drive circled in front of it the house. To one side of the house was a separate block of buildings in the same stone, presumably the stables and other outbuildings required by every gentleman's estate.

Standing near the house were two horses. Their riders had dismounted and looked as if they were waiting for someone. Daphne presumed that they were the builder from somewhere nearby and the designer, Mr. Beaver, from London. The men had probably been waiting for some time since Daphne had not allowed for the state of the road when setting out to keep their appointment. She was late, but she knew that they probably expected such behavior from a countess. With a final appreciative glance at the view, Daphne started down the drive to the house with Betsey limping along behind her.

"Mr. Beaver," Daphne called, "I am sorry to be late. I am afraid that I had not anticipated the state of the road."

"Shocking! Quite shocking, isn't it?

"My lady, let me introduce Mr. Worthington, who is the builder I told you about."

"Mr. Worthington, I can't see any work in progress here. What were you working on before the money dried up?" Daphne asked.

"I have not started doing any work on the front of the house as yet, my lady, nor on its riverside for that matter. I was about to start working on some leaking windows when Mr. Edwards said the sheds must have priority. He wanted me to fix up an old one and then build some new ones, which I have been working on. Their site is in some trees, down by the water near the dock. You can just see the end of the wharf at the river where the cleared ground meets the trees, my lady.

"Then Mr. Edwards didn't pay my bills, so I stopped the work until I got some money. I have been had by too many gentlemen who don't pay their bills for me to do much work on credit, if you'll pardon me for mentioning it, my lady."

"Very understandable. You will find that Lord Camshire pays his bills in full promptly. Now, what's this about storage sheds? What are they for, and why did they take priority?"

"My lady, there was a shed — actually, quite a substantial building — used for storing things that arrive by the river before they are taken to the house. It was also used for produce from the estate that was awaiting shipment. As you may know, the River Severn here is used for all sorts of traffic. That's one reason why the road is in such shocking condition; it isn't used much since travel by the river is faster.

"Mr. Edwards claimed that repairing the shed and building some other warehouses were very urgent tasks and had to be done at once. Anything that can be transported by water usually goes on the river in this part of the county, and Mr. Edwards claimed the sheds were needed before work could begin on the house. I had no idea where he expected to get the goods to put in the sheds, but that was his problem, not mine.

"That seemed to be a new approach for Sallycove. Things were different when this house was occupied. The previous owner, Sir Humphrey Little, kept the road in good shape, except in his last year, and used it for many deliveries that could have gone by water. For him, the old shed was more than enough. He didn't even keep it in good repair."

"Let's start with the inside of the house, shall we," Mr. Beaver interrupted. "I find in considering changes to a house like this one that it's best to first see what would be desirable alterations to the inside, including such things as windows and doors, even walls that may need to be moved. Then one can see how such changes would affect the appearance of the outside and consider any other alterations that would improve the look of the place. Next, one tries to harmonize the whole — the inside with the outside."

Daphne did not find the inside of the house attractive. There were many public rooms on the ground floor, but they were all small and dark even when the heavy drapes were opened. It didn't help that small windows let in little light. When she had Betsey take off the coverings, the furniture was old-fashioned and not of the best quality. Everything felt damp and chilly, not surprisingly since no fires had been lit and the drapes had been closed. Their quick exploration of the ground floor left Daphne appalled. This house would require a vast amount of work to bring it up to standard.

"What are you thinking of doing here. Mr. Beaver?" Daphne asked. "Let's see those preliminary plans you have brought with you. You can lay them out on the table."

"Well, I haven't got around to making many changes yet, my lady. Mr. Edwards was more concerned with the outbuildings than with the house.

"It seems that, in fact, Mr. Beaver, you have done very little about planning changes to this house. What you are showing me looks like a sketch you might have tried to make from memory. The dimensions shown for this room seem to be wrong, and you have drawn the fireplace on the wrong wall."

"I admit, my lady, that when I knew you would be looking at the place today, I quickly made these sketches. They were drawn from memory and are not very accurate."

"This house needs as thorough a redoing as is feasible. You can use those 'plans' to make notes. They do not seem to be much good for anything else. What were you thinking? Did you imagine that I have no ideas about building or what would make a comfortable as well as a spectacular house?"

"No, my lady."

"Well, redo your plans completely. I want every room to have a clear purpose, airy and light, and comfortable. Similarly, on the first floor, all rooms should be spacious. If that means fewer rooms, so be it. The servants' quarters above should be laid out with convenience and propriety considered. Draw up the plans and make sure that the outside will look very elegant. Let me know when you are done. I can examine them in London or Dipton, whichever is more convenient to me.

"Yes, my lady. I have to warn you that it will cost money."

"I'm sure it will. We are quite prepared for that. Lord Camshire's prize money could pay for several such properties."

"Now, let's have a look at what needs to be done on the outside of the house."

They started with the front entrance, which needed to be enlarged and to have a portico built over it. Next, with all the windows needing to be made larger, more ornate window frames would, Daphne thought, improve the house's appearance. Certainly, the too-small windows that the house had presently looked ridiculous with their minimal embellishments. On the west side of the mansion, which faced the river, Daphne wanted the terrace enlarged, and, since the land there was sloping down to the river, a stone balustrade and steps would be needed.

Daphne paused on the rather restricted terrace presently in front of the house. The land going to the river was covered by what should be a lawn, though now the grass looked like it was being mowed by sheep. Basically, this aspect of the house was pleasing; all it needed was some care and flower beds. The picture from the terrace was framed by rows of yew trees on each side. Across the river, the land rose again in what looked like grazing land. Daphne wondered who owned it. It was not an urgent concern, but the vista could be improved if the far side of the river could be harmonized with what lay on the house side; maybe a folly or suitable plantings would do the trick. She would have to think about that. Maybe Giles's niece, Catherine Bolter, could help with those plans.

"Mr. Worthington," Daphne addressed the builder. "Do you know who owns the land across the river?"

"I believe it belongs to Sallycove, my lady. Certainly, it did when Sir Humphrey owned this place, but it could have been sold without me knowing about it."

"How much land then does Sallycove have, do you know?"

"Not really, my lady. I know that it was a large estate, with holdings on both sides of the river; there is also quite a lot of land leased to tenant farmers, I believe, but I can't even guess at how much. Surely, Lord Camshire must have found out when he bought the place."

"Mr. Edwards bought the estate for us as an investment while the Earl was away at sea, and he did not think to tell me about it. I need to know more about these things if I am to make the right decisions so we can get on with the job until the Earl returns."

"I understand, my lady," replied Mr. Worthington. "I know that the land was not farmed properly last summer, and the tenants are not happy that Mr. Edwards made no provision for the owner's share of maintenance and improvements to their holdings. Furthermore, Mr. Edwards had disputes with the bailiff and the estate manager of Sallycove and dismissed them both. He certainly acted as if he owned the place. We had no idea that he was acting for the Earl of Camshire."

"I'm not surprised, really. Mr. Edwards was Lord Camshire's prize agent — my husband is a captain in the Royal Navy — and was acting without proper instructions on how to use the funds coming as prize money. He has since been transported to Australia for stealing from Lord Camshire and other naval captains. We only realized recently the extent to which he had not been ensuring the proper maintenance of this estate. At present, I am acting for Lord Camshire in these matters since he still has duties in the Royal Navy that have taken him to sea.

"Do you know what happened to the former bailiff and estate manager of Sallycove?"

"Yes, my lady, they are living in Sutton Maddock, where they have a smallholding. It's quite adequate to keep them going until another estate needs them. They are brothers."

"Do you suppose, Mr. Worthington, that they might be interested in resuming their positions?"

"I am sure that they would be."

"If this Sutton Maddock is on your way home, could you stop by and ask them to meet me at the Woodbridge Inn this evening, please."

"Certainly, my lady."

"Good, now what is this about storage sheds at the water? All I can see is a bit of a dock beside the river."

"The buildings are behind the trees on the right-hand side. The track from the dock to the house also runs behind those trees. Mr. Edwards wanted me to make three new sheds, in addition to the one already there. I have completed two and the repairs to the existing one, but I stopped work on the third one because he hadn't paid me."

Daphne was getting more and more suspicious about what might be going on at Sallycove. First, Mr. Beaver seemed to know nothing substantial about the house. Now there were sheds whose existence did not seem to be explained, far too much space for an estate with agricultural produce in which Mr. Edwards did not seem to have been interested. Daphne would have to be cautious about committing funds to this property until she knew more about it.

"Let's go look at them. What did he want these sheds for?"

"That was never very clear to me," said Mr. Beaver. "He talked about storage for coal and other things that could come by the river and shipping the produce from his estate by water, but I couldn't see the need for them. However, he was adamant, so their practicality was no concern of mine."

Mr. Beaver's answer did nothing to relieve Daphne's doubts. "Since we are already on this side of the house," she said, "we might as well see these sheds before looking at the stables up here."

Luckily, Daphne's boots were suitable for venturing into a meadow, and so were Betsey's since the way down to the river had no well-defined path. They had to walk through what should have been a lawn, but instead, the long grass had patches of muck in various places. Rather to Daphne's surprise, when they reached the river, they discovered that the towpath ran on the house side of the river. Daphne thought it would have been better across the river instead of passing in front of this prominent mansion. Maybe there was some pressing reason for it being on the east side, but, right now, she was more interested in discovering the nature of these buildings.

They emerged from the trees that hid the storehouses to find an old wooden structure and two new-looking ones made of the same sort of stone as the mansion. All the buildings had wide double doors that could accommodate a large cart or wagon, and each of the doors had a large, shiny new lock. Muddy tracks leading up to the doors suggested that they had been in use recently. Even as Daphne wondered what this was all about, she noticed a rowing skiff pulling up to the dock. It had two rowers resting with their oars out of the water as the boat slid towards the landing and one man curled up in the bow. In the stern sat a figure that she recognized: it was her friend, Sir Titus Amery.

Sir Titus was a High Court Judge who seemed to spend most of his time on government assignments rather than on the bench. Daphne had met him when a nearby landowner had tried to steal the parliamentary seat at Dipton and again when she had become involved with smugglers. What in the world was he doing here?

She wondered how much he would be willing to reveal about his activities.

As Daphne and her two companions watched, the lead rower shipped his oars and moved to the bow. Mr. Worthington ran over to catch the bowline when it was thrown. In minutes the boat was tied up, and Sir Titus scrambled out.

"What are you doing here, Sir Titus?" Daphne demanded.

"It is always a pleasure to see you, Lady Camshire," replied Sir Titus. "I could ask you the same question."

"I have come to inspect the estate that Lord Camshire has acquired."

"Has he? I understood that this property was owned by a man called Edwards."

"Ah, yes, Mr. Edwards spread that falsehood," rejoined Daphne. "He was Giles's prize agent and used our funds to buy this place. Edwards registered the land under his own name even though it was paid from Giles's account. Edwards had wide discretion to use our funds for our advantage, dating from the days when Giles was single and usually far away, at sea, so it is not unreasonable to suppose that Edwards simply was sloppy in registering the property transfer."

"Oh, so he is *that* Edwards. The one at whose trial you testified so effectively to the delight of the papers. I should have realized, but Edwards is such a common name in these parts that I didn't connect the one here with the one who stole from you. So you own this place now, do you?"

"Yes, but we only discovered that fact recently. I came here today to assert our ownership since, if it belonged to Mr. Edwards, its value would be divided up among the many people he swindled. In Giles's view, those men are mostly greedy, incompetent admirals and their undeserving cronies."

"So you — or Lord Camshire — knew nothing about these sheds until today?"

"That's right, but what brings you here?"

"Many loads of goods that were shipped up and down this river have gone missing in the last few months. Some of them were going down river for sending abroad or for towns along the way while others were coming up river. Since the alcohol and tobacco among the goods that have gone missing had their duties all paid, the revenuers are not interested in the problem. The scope of these disappearances is such that their investigation is beyond the resources of any of the local magistrates. So the government asked me to look into the situation. I have borrowed a couple of Bow Street Runners from Westminster, and I can use the militia here to help. They are from Nottinghamshire and so have some experience with rivers and river traffic. When I discover just who is behind these disappearances, I can call on them to round up the perpetrators and have them dealt with by the assizes at Shrewsbury."

"So, what are you doing here, at Sallycove, Sir Titus?"

"I reckoned that, for such a substantial operation, the thieves must have a base on the river where they could hide their stolen cargos. People talk, of course, so I learned about the new sheds on this property that seemed to have no purpose. I hired a skiff and had my two Runners row me here to look into it. I'm told that the river is a much better way of getting here than the road that, I imagine, you used, Lady Camshire."

"And the third man with you, the one you have chained in the front of that boat?"

"Ah, that is Smith. He is a skilled locksmith, expert at opening locks for which one doesn't have the key. He is helping me so that his sentence can be changed from hanging to transportation to Australia. I want to find out what is in the sheds without warning the crooks that we are onto them, as would be the case if we had to break in."

"Hendricks," Sir Titus addressed one of the men who had been rowing the skiff. "Take Smith and his bag over to the first of the sheds. We might as well find out what those shiny, new locks are protecting."

The Runner manhandled the shackled man out of the skiff and over to the first shed. The other rower picked up a leather bag that was in the skiff and went along with them. When they reached the door of the first shed, the locksmith started to examine the lock.

"Can you open that lock, Smith?" asked Sir Titus.

"Don't know yet," replied the locksmith in a surly voice. "Can't do much with these shackles on. I can't even reach the lock properly."

"Hendricks release the prisoner's hands but keep the ankle shackles in place. That will prevent him from trying to see if he can outrun you two." Sir Titus ordered.

Hendricks complied. Smith bent down and took some sort of tool from his bag. Then he shuffled over to the door and started to examine the lock carefully. "Can you open it?" asked Sir Titus.

"Yes, I certainly can get it open, though it will be a bit tricky: it is a very good lock, and I haven't seen many like it."

"Well, get on with opening it; we don't have all day."

Smith turned his attention back to the lock. Somehow, while holding the lock in one hand as he fumbled to align his tool with it, he succeeded in dropping the tool.

"Bloody hell! I've dropped the lock pick."

"Well, pick it up. Do you expect one of us to be your servant?"

Smith bent down to pick up the tool, and, in doing so, he succeeded in tripping over the chain that bound his ankles together. Down he went, screeching as if he had broken his leg.

"Oww! Bugger it! Owwie! God's Bollocks! I have sprained my bloody ankle!"

Smith rolled on the ground holding his ankle and continuing to swear.

"Get up, you lazy idiot. Your ankle isn't broken, and I need that lock opened," ordered Sir Titus. "And I'll thank you not to swear when there are ladies present."

Smith levered himself to his feet again and shuffled over to the door. He spent some time with his lock pick until the lock opened. Then, with the lock still in place, he bent down as if to restore the pick to his bag. When he straightened up, he had in his hand the chain that should have been joining his ankles. In one motion, he turned, swinging the chain as he did so. The end of it caught Sir Titus across the forehead and continued round to hit the Runner, Hendricks, a solid blow across the back of his head. Both men collapsed.

Daphne was horrified, but, nevertheless, she responded immediately. As a child, she had taken a great dislike to crows and became very proficient at hitting them with rocks. At her feet was a hand-sized stone which she had noted when she almost tripped over it as she moved to see around Smith's shoulder to where he had been working on the lock. Without thinking, she picked up the rock and flung it at Smith's head with all her strength. Her target was so close to her that she could not miss, and down the locksmith went.

Glancing around to see what the other members of their party were doing, Daphne was horrified to see that Mr. Worthington was fighting with the other Bow Street Runner. Without thinking, she rushed over to see if she could help the peace officer. It is as well she did. Just before she reached the struggling men, the builder landed a knockout blow and, even while his opponent was collapsing, turned to see what was happening elsewhere. There was only a moment before Daphne would have reached the fighters. She tripped and went head-first into Mr. Worthington's middle, knocking him down. She was first to recover but saw that her opponent was only winded and would soon be back in action. Before that could happen, Daphne rose to her knees, picked up a short board lying close to her, and hit the builder on the head with all her might. He collapsed again, this time to stay down, unconscious.

Daphne forced herself to stand, even though she was feeling very shaky, and turned to see what was happening elsewhere. Much to her surprise, she saw that Mr. Beaver was also lying on the ground, writhing in agony, with Betsey standing over him. As Daphne stared open-mouthed, wondering what had happened, Betsey aimed a well-aimed kick at the designer's chin that knocked out her opponent. Betsey promptly sat down and rubbed her boot.

"Well done, Betsey!" called Daphne as she ran toward her maid. "Not many women could do that."

"I grew up with five older brothers, my lady. Once, when they were rough-housing, one of them got hit in the bollocks and collapsed just like that. I asked what had happened, and my oldest brother took me aside to explain how men are sensitive between their legs. He told me that I should knee a man between the legs if ever I had trouble with him being too familiar with me. My brother also told me that kicking the man in the jaw would keep him from recovering soon. He didn't tell me how much that would hurt, especially when you have a corn on your toe."

"Have you ever done it before?" Daphne asked curiously. She had not known about this way of dealing with troublesome men, but then she had never had brothers nor any close female confidantes while she was growing up. She wondered if Giles knew about his vulnerability.

"Yes, my lady," Betsey replied. "Do you remember that footman called Philip at Dipton Hall a while back?"

"Yes."

"Well, he got fresh with me in the back pantry once, and I kneed him between the legs. What a racket he made! I was sure that Mrs. Wilson would dismiss me, but all that happened was that Mr. Steves sent him packing immediately."

"Good for Steves! I never heard about the incident at all. Well, we can't just stand here chatting. These men will recover all too soon. So let's start with seeing if we can get that locksmith back in shackles. None of the others seem to be moving yet."

Daphne had noted that Sir Titus had the key to Smith's restraints in his pocket. The judge was still not moving though he was breathing quite smoothly. The Runner, Hendricks, was also showing no signs of recovering though he was breathing noisily. So Daphne's first step in avoiding a repeat of the mayhem was to get the key from Sir Titus's pocket. Then with Betsey's aid, she rolled the locksmith into a ball and, using the chain that had been his weapon and the locks he had so conveniently opened himself with his lockpick, Daphne locked him in a position where he could not move at all. Next, she turned to Mr. Worthington.

The builder was still out cold, but the Runner whom he had felled was recovering. The man sat up, shook his head, staggered to his feet, and surveyed the scene.

"He took me by surprise," the Runner complained. "Otherwise, I would have nailed him. Did you subdue these — these thugs, my lady?"

"With my maid's help, yes, I did, Mr. ... ?"

"Butcher, my Lady."

"Well, Mr. Butcher, do you remember if you have any rope in that boat that we could use to tie these men up?"

"Yes, my lady, we do."

"Then fetch it before any of them come to."

Butcher headed off towards where the skiff was moored, stumbling a little as he went. Daphne noticed that Mr. Beaver was stirring. Betsey saw it too. She had learned her lesson about the consequences for her corns of kicking him in the jaw, so she hit him with a board, left over from when the sheds were built, that she had selected for the purpose. Her victim lay still again.

Butcher returned from the skiff with two lengthy ropes. Daphne realized that she had never tied someone up. When she asked her, it turned out that Betsey had no idea either, and Butcher was equally inexperienced. So Daphne would just have to do her best. The others looked up to her, which she thought was silly because being a countess gave her less insight into this problem than the others had. Daphne reasoned that the important thing was to tie the men so that their hands couldn't reach the knots. Maybe if she tied their wrists behind them, it would be impossible for them to get their fingers on the knots. Maybe tying their ankles together would make it even more difficult for them to get loose, especially if she then tied their ankles to their wrists.

With Betsey and Butcher helping, Daphne rolled Mr. Worthington onto his front. Rather roughly, they pulled his arms behind him so that his wrists crossed, and Daphne wound the rope around his wrists and knotted it tightly. It was, however, a very messy-looking knot, and she was doubtful if it would hold. Taking the other end of the long rope, Daphne and her assistants tied Mr. Worthington's ankles together. Despite her winding the rope around his ankles several times as she had his wrist, the knots did not look all that tight. Might her victim wriggle out of the bonds or untie the knots when he recovered consciousness?

Daphne took the center of the sprawling rope and pulled it between Mr. Worthingrton's arms above where she had tied up Mr. Worthington's wrists. She did the same between his ankles and pulled the ropes tight. One more loop pulling ankles towards wrists, and then Daphne tied that part tight. She still wondered if the builder could struggle free though she noticed that her latest addition had certainly pulled the binding about his wrists much tighter than it had been. It should serve until the others recovered consciousness and could make sure that the captives did not get loose.

Daphne then turned her attention to Mr. Beaver. He seemed to be recovering from Betsey's treatment and was trying to sit up. Betsey put an end to that with another kick to his jaw. Daphne worried that her maid might have killed the man, but then she reflected that he was bound to hang anyway. With help from Betsey and

Butcher, she secured the unconscious Mr. Beaver in the same way she had Mr. Worthington.

Now that the immediate threat was dealt with, Daphne could turn her attention to the two victims of Smith's wildly swung chain. Sir Titus was starting to recover and to become vocal.

"Oh, bloody hell! Oh, my head! Bugger it!" he mumbled as he struggled to sit up.

He noticed Daphne, who was standing over him. "I'm sorry, Lady Ashton," he mumbled. "Shouldn't say that in front of a lady."

Sir Titus grimaced, turned his head aside, vomited on the ground, and lay back again. "God's bollocks, it hurts! What happened? Ow! Bloody Hell! Where am I? How can I see two Lady Giles?" His speech was badly slurred, and he became unconscious again.

Daphne bent down to examine the man. Blood was coming from a wound on his forehead where a swelling was already very prominent. The chain that had knocked him over might have done serious damage. Daphne thought of a farmhand at Dipton who had lost most of his mind after being kicked by a horse and was never the same again. Surely this could not have happened to Sir Titus.

The wound on Sir Titus's head needed bandaging. Unfortunately, Daphne had nothing with her that was suitable for the task. Without even thinking about the propriety of her action, she pulled up the bottom of her skirt and then tore a strip from her petticoat. She wrapped it several times around the judge's forehead, tightly enough that the makeshift bandage should reduce the bleeding and allow the wound to clot.

While Daphne was trying to help Sir Titus, Butcher went to the skiff to fill a bucket with water. He brought it back together with a bailing crock which he filled.

"Give him some of this, my lady. It might help," he suggested, giving Daphne the crock. Then he emptied the rest of the bucket on Humphries's head.

Humphries responded to this treatment. The shock of the cold water had worked. He started to sit up, shaking his head to remove some of the water soaking him. Then, the Runner got to his feet, staggering a little in the process, and felt his head.

"What happened? I thought we had him under control and then —. Damnation, my head hurts! Sorry, my lady, shouldn't have said that. What hit me?"

"The chain that was supposed to be locking up Smith."

"Smith?"

"Yes, the locksmith that Sir Titus brought with you to get into the shed."

"Shed? — shed? — now I remember. What happened to him."

"I knocked him unconscious, and we shackled him again. He's over there" Daphne pointed at the bundle that was Smith.

"And those other two," pointing at the tied-up men.

"They seem to be colluding with Smith in whatever is going on. One of them attacked the second Runner, Mr. Butcher, and the other one attacked my maid, Betsey."

"And you subdued them?" Humphries asked incredulously.

"Yes. Now we have the problem of what to do with them and how to take care of Sir Titus. He seems to be more seriously hurt than you two Runners," remarked Daphne.

"Oh, God! Sorry, my lady. Let me think. Butcher and I could row him back to Shrewsbury, but it will take a long time, especially as it will be against the current, and there is no room for you and your maid. Moreover, I don't like leaving you here, not by yourself, since we don't know what other ruffians may appear. Do you have a carriage up at the house?"

"No, I had to send it back to the inn because the road was so bad. But my coachman and groom are supposed to be returning with horses for us. I am surprised that they are not here yet.

"What we will do," Daphne continued, "is to place Sir Titus in your skiff and make him as comfortable as we can. Then you two can row him upriver. I would be happier if you took him to the inn where I am staying rather than going all the way to Shrewsbury. It's a place called the Woodbridge Inn. The sooner we can get him into a bed and arrange some proper nursing, the better. The Innkeeper or his wife can arrange to provide a room for him and send for a doctor and the local magistrate. We will need him to sort this all out. There should be people at the inn who can nurse Sir Titus, maids or such."

"I don't like leaving you here by yourself, my lady. It isn't proper."

"Well, nothing much about this situation is 'proper,'" Daphne retorted. "Let's get Sir Titus loaded into your skiff so that you can leave before our horses arrive."

The four of them stared for a moment at the figure of Sir Titus lying on the ground. It was one thing to say, 'let's get him loaded into the skiff' and quite another to do it with the subject unconscious. Where to put him once they had taken him to the skiff might be another problem since he couldn't sit up in the sternsheets, and they could hardly jam him into the bow without quite possibly worsening his fragile condition.

"We'll need something for him to rest on in the boat," Daphne declared. "There must be a mattress or some pillows in the house. Come on, Betsey, let's get some."

"But, my lady, isn't the house locked up?" protested Betsey, whose mind was more on her corns than on the problem of moving Sir Titus comfortably.

"Yes, but I noticed that Mr. Beaver put the key in his pocket after he relocked the house," Daphne replied. "Get the key, Betsey, and come with me."

Painful corns or not, Betsey had to comply, of course. She found the key in Mr. Beaver's pocket without trouble, even though he had revived and was writhing around and groaning expletives that were most improper in the presence of a woman. Betsey gave him another good kick in response, her corns be damned. She had never before, and probably would never again, dare to kick a gentleman, no matter how much they might deserve it.

Daphne, with Betsey trailing along behind her, returned to the mansion. Daphne selected several cushions from a couple of the more hideous settees, which she and her maid carried back to the river. Then, with the aid of the Runners, they made a nest for Sir Titus in the stern of the boat. The two Runners took their places on the thwarts, pushed off, and started rowing upriver.

Daphne checked their three prisoners. Smith was awake but had not succeeded in shifting any of his bonds. Just to be safe, Daphne took his bag of tools and moved them a good distance from where the locksmith lay. The other two captives were awake and had apparently thrashed around a bit since they were not quite in the positions they had occupied before the two women went to get the cushions. However, the two men were still effectively tied up, and they were far enough away from each other that they would not likely be able to roll together to jointly try to work on the knots that secured them. Daphne suspected that Betsey wanted to give Mr. Beaver another good kick but gave her maid such a stern look that Betsey resisted the temptation. After all, Daphne could hardly encourage Betsey to assault her betters, even if they did deserve it. Then they went back to the house to await the arrival of Richards, the coachman, with the horses.

Chapter XVIII

"Mr. Matthams," Daphne addressed the proprietor of the Woodbridge Inn, "Where is Sir Titus Emery? I noticed that his boat is tied up to your dock."

"Is that really his name? Those two ruffians who claimed to be Bow Street Runners, whatever they are, said that was what their injured man was called, but I have never heard of him, and he didn't look like much of a gentleman to me. I did put him in the lounge on a couch, though I was tempted to tell them to take him away in their boat. But that would not have been the Christian thing to do," the innkeeper stated self-righteously. "I suspected that he only needed to sleep it off."

"Well, that is who he is. A very important man. Sir Titus is a high court judge who is presently engaged in very important work for the government. I will see him immediately. Have your best room prepared for him, and we'll move him there when it is ready."

"Yes, my lady." Mr. Matthams did not think it wise to inform the Countess that it would be his second-best room since hers was the best one.

"Good. Now have you sent for the magistrate and a doctor?"

"No, my lady. I don't summon important people on the word of two rascals who looked like they had been in a fight."

"Well, send for them now. No, wait a moment. Betsey, get my writing case. A note will be more effective than sending some servant to say that they are needed."

Daphne had learned that, indeed, rank had its privileges. A demand written on her crested notepaper with an impressive-looking seal would be much more likely to get immediate attention than a message delivered orally by the Inn's servant. Daphne, Countess of Camshire, got far more attention than plain 'Miss Moorhouse' or even 'Lady Giles' ever had.

When the messages had been dispatched, Daphne was tempted to have something to eat and some tea, or even something more substantial. But she had to see to Sir Titus first. The innkeeper had yet to fill her order to have Sir Titus shifted to another room; Daphne found him in the lounge, stretched out on a settee with a cushion under his head. He was awake and tried to sit up when he saw Daphne in the lounge, but he immediately sank back, looking groggy.

"How are you, Sir Titus?" asked Daphne.

"Very well, my lady," the jurist said as he struggled to sit up.

"Nonsense, I can see that that is not the case, though I am glad to see you conscious. You have had a very nasty bump on the head. You are going to have to rest here for some days — no, I insist. Being active too soon after such an injury can lead to long-term problems — or so Mr. Jackson says."

"Ah, Mr. Jackson, the Sage of Dipton," retorted Sir Titus dismissively.

"Yes, he is!" Daphne retorted. "He knows a great deal more about treating this sort of injury than most doctors, but I have sent for a doctor, though he may not do much good, and the local magistrate."

"Why did you send for the magistrate, Lady Camshire? For that matter, what are you doing here?"

"Don't you remember? We met at Sallycove, where there were those suspicious sheds."

"We did? I don't remember."

"You don't? Well, don't worry about it; it will probably all come back to you. You have had a very nasty knock on the head. I have arranged for a room for you at this inn. It is quite a nice place, much better than most inns. Once the doctor has been, you must rest for the night. Tomorrow you should feel a bit better and maybe remember why you are here."

"Where is here?"

"The Woodbridge Inn in Shropshire. It's on the River Severn."

"Is it? I confess that I wondered what I am doing here. I don't seem to be able to remember anything recent. Let's see: I can remember being in the Home Office, something about the Severn, but I don't know what it was or how I got here. Oh, but my head does hurt!"

Sir Titus collapsed back on the couch.

Had he fallen asleep or passed out? It didn't really matter, Daphne thought. She just hoped that that innkeeper would get Sir Titus to his room soon. She didn't know what to do about the situation.

The period of waiting for the doctor seemed endless, even though Daphne took the opportunity to have a meat pie and a mug of cider in the inn's parlor after the innkeeper's wife had supervised the shifting of Sir Titus to a bedroom.

Daphne was draining the last drops of her drink when the doctor arrived. He was a portly, fussy, self-important, servile man who announced that he was Dr. Davies who would have her ladyship know that he had abandoned what he was doing to attend to her immediately. He somehow succeeded in getting Daphne's back up the moment he appeared.

"What is it you need, my lady?" Dr. Davies asked. "Some female problem, I am sure. I will have just the cure for you when you have described your symptoms, and I have examined you. Possibly my own special elixir."

Daphne explained that it was not she who needed the doctor but a man who had been struck by a chain and knocked unconscious.

"Ah," said the doctor. "Your servant must have experienced a concussion, as we term the ailment. It is quite common among the lower classes, and sometimes even the better class of people suffer one, especially when they have had a fall while hunting. It is often cured by throwing a pail of water over the victim, though more stubborn cases may demand my attention. Was your man loading a cart when the injury occurred, my lady?"

"No, he was not. And he is *not* my servant. Instead, he is Sir Titus Emery, a distinguished High Court judge. It has been several hours since he was hit in the head, and he is far from being recovered. He is in a room down that corridor. You should look at him right away."

Sir Titus was awake, though lying down. The innkeeper's wife had replaced his bandage, but blood was already staining the center of the white cloth.

"Sir Titus," said the physician, "I'm Dr. Davies. I hear that you have had a knock on the head. Feeling unstable, disoriented?"

"Yes."

"Good, that's to be expected with a concussion. Let me look at the wound now. You," he said, nodding at Betsey, "take off that bandage."

Betsey complied even though she was not used to being ordered about so abruptly by strangers. Dr. Davies ran his hands over the affected area, presumably to see if he could feel any cracks in the skull. The wound was no longer bleeding, though there was a very pronounced swelling.

"Good," he announced. "Sir Titus, as nearly as I can tell, you have not cracked your skull. You may feel disoriented and wobbly for a few days, but, in a couple of weeks, you should be fully recovered, maybe sooner. Now, I'll just bleed you and let you rest."

"Dr. Davies," Daphne interrupted, "Sir Titus has already lost quite a lot of blood. There is no need to bleed him."

"But, my lady, the humors! the humors! he must be bled!"

"No he does not! My personal physician forbids bleeding in most cases, and I also forbid it! It will do more harm than good."

"Have it your way, then, my lady. And on your head be it!"

"Fine! Now, doctor, do you cut corns."

"Yes, my lady, in exceptional cases, such as yours, I do."

"Oh, it's not for me, but for my maid Betsey."

Dr. Davies drew himself up to his full height.

"My lady, I only treat *servants* with the most serious of ailments. I don't treat *corns* for *servants*!"

"As you wish, Doctor. You may go now."

"But my bill."

"Give it to the landlord here, and I'll settle it together with his when I leave."

When the disgruntled doctor had left, Daphne turned to the innkeeper's wife. "Tell me, Mrs. Matthams, is there someone here who cuts corns?"

"Yes, my lady, Robert Jones, the farrier, does a very good job. Gets them first time and hardly ever draws blood."

"Could you ask him to come to attend to my maid, please?"

"Yes, my lady. He is in the taproom right now. I'll send him to you right away."

Betsey was surprised. Lady Camshire had become rather bossy recently, though still not as much as she was told most noble mistresses were, but now she realized that her mistress's thoughtfulness had not disappeared. How many other mistresses would even know that their maids suffered from corns?

Daphne was waiting for the farrier when Mr. Matthams sent word that the magistrate, Mr. Richard Clarke, had arrived.

Mr. Clarke looked to be the epitome of an English squire as drawn by cartoonists. All he lacked was a red coat, and his nose was not as red as usually portrayed. "Lady Camshire," he stated after they had been introduced, "I had a message from Sir Titus that warned me I might be needed. So, when I got your note, I gathered up two of the parish constables in the area and sent word to a couple of others whose parishes are farther away. Where is Sir Titus?"

Daphne explained why Sir Titus was not available and also told what had happened at Sallycove. She took the magistrate to see Sir Titus, but he had lapsed into a very fuzzy state. Daphne wasn't at all sure how much Mr. Clarke got from talking with him.

"Ah, I knew about the missing cargoes, of course, but not that such an expert as Sir Titus had been sent to look into the problem. It is a pity that he is feeling so confused since time is of the essence in stopping these criminals, whoever they may be. Did I understand that he had arranged for help from the militia?"

"So he told me."

"Then, I think that we should alert them of the developments and ask them to send troops to help us protect what he found at Sallycove as soon as possible. I'll dispatch a note to Major Hallam asking him to send troops to guard the storehouses if the criminals have not emptied them before the militia can get there. Hallam seems to be a good man, especially for a militia officer, so we can hope that he will respond quickly. But they can't get here *that* quickly. I had better go and take charge of those prisoners of yours if they have not already been rescued by the scoundrels. Lady Camshire, I will take those two Bow Street Runners with me: I don't think you will be in any danger here at the Woodbridge Inn.

"I'll put out word for men to join me," Mr. Clarke continued. "We'll leave in a half-hour to give men in the immediate neighborhood a chance to join us. I am sure there will be many who will want to come with us: we haven't had this much excitement for a long time."

"Well, you can add my coachman and footman to your group, Mr. Clarke. Mr. Matthams seems to have a good stable here so that they can ride along with us. They have a pistol and a musket which may come in handy. Have you thought about sending those two Runners by boat ahead of us in case our prisoners are finding a way to get loose before we can get there?"

"No. I don't want to endanger Sir Titus's men. It is quite possible that some members of this thieving gang have already found your victims and would be prepared to treat the Runners very harshly.

"But there is no 'we' about this expedition, my lady," the magistrate added. "It would be completely unsuitable for you to join us. This isn't some picnic jaunt along the river to have lunch, you know. It is serious business, men's business, and could be quite dangerous. You shall stay here."

"Mr. Clarke, I protest most strongly. I own — that is, my husband owns — Sallycove, and, in his absence, I must be there to protect our interests."

"No, my lady. It is too dangerous! I forbid it!"

"Do you, Mr. Clarke? Well, I'll have you know that I have had quite a bit of experience in dealing with ruffians when Sir Titus helped me set up our canal enterprise in Ameschester. I am sure that you have heard about that incident; it was in all the papers. I am quite prepared to take the risk."

"My lady, as I recall, the papers all agreed that it was a Viscountess something or other who was involved in that case."

"Quite right! It was. That is the incident I was claiming. My name then was Viscountess Ashton. Captain Giles, my husband, was Viscount Ashton, but when his father died, he became the Earl of Camshire, so I became Lady Camshire. If you don't let me join your party, I shall go by myself with my maid. You can't stop me from going to my own property!"

"But, my lady …," Mr. Clarke said. He lapsed silent for a moment and then said, "All right, I'll take you, but I won't be responsible for what happens to you."

"Good. You said we would be leaving in half an hour?"

"Twenty-five minutes, now. We'll meet on the other side of the bridge."

It was a rather rag-tag group that met across the bridge from the Woodbridge Inn. Only four of the dozen or so men had guns: three fowling pieces and one ancient pistol. Mr. Clarke had a hunting rifle while Richards, Daphne's coachman, had a blunderbuss while Daphne's footman had a pistol. Mr. Clarke had arranged for a horse-drawn cart to accompany the group. As evening was closing in, they set off at a good pace, with the cart following more slowly. The condition of the road was no easier on the cart than it had been on Daphne's carriage, though the cart's lack of springs meant that it did not sway quite so alarmingly.

Mr. Clarke gathered the group together when they reached the turnoff to Sallycove. "We don't know the situation," he stated. "The thieves may have arrived first, and they could still be around. The mounted men will go ahead, and the rest of you follow closely. I'll hold up my hand, like this, when I want us to stop and evaluate the situation. Let's all try to be quiet."

Mr. Clarke set off again. Daphne fell in beside him.

"Not you, Lady Camshire," the magistrate said in a horrified voice.

"Why not? I am the only one here who has been on the property recently and knows exactly where I left the men we captured."

"It's too dangerous! I can't have a woman coming with me into such an unknown, hazardous situation! It is my job to maintain the peace, not yours. You must stay here until I discover what lies ahead.

What in the world would the Earl of Camshire say if I allowed his wife to go blithely into danger?"

"Mr. Clarke, you can't make me. This is my property, and I have a right to go onto it. Don't worry about Lord Camshire: he knows that you would have to tie me up to prevent my coming with you, and he would like your doing that a great deal less!"

Daphne knew that, in fact, Mr. Clarke had the legal power to prevent her from accompanying him. She also guessed, correctly, that he would not dare to cross a peer of the realm to demonstrate his power.

The group proceeded at walking pace until they came to the spot where the house became visible together with the vista down to the river. Mr. Clarke stopped to examine what lay ahead.

"Where are those sheds you told me about, my lady?" he asked Daphne.

"Over to the right, behind that row of trees, beside the river. Incidentally, that row of trees hides from us not only the sheds but also an open field."

"George," Mr. Clarke addressed one of the men on horses. "Take a couple of men over through the trees over there. There is an open field, and the crooks may try to escape that way — if there are any crooks, of course."

"Very good, Dick." responded the man. "Walters and Shepherd, come with me."

"Were you in the army, Mr. Clarke?" Daphne asked. "You seem to be used to planning and giving orders."

"Only the militia, my lady, and only for a short time in '95 before my father died and I had to come home. The experience does help in being a magistrate. Let's go before we lose the light completely, but at least there will shortly be a moon just a day past the full."

They set off down the slope to the river, with the other men close behind them. When they reached the water, Daphne pointed out the path through the trees, and they quickly followed it. As they emerged from the trees, a sudden scurrying noise came from where Daphne had left Smith, the locksmith, tied up. There was little light in the gloaming, but that didn't stop Mr. Clarke from shouting the view-halloo and riding off with the other mounted men in pursuit. Daphne was left to go over to where she had left Smith all shackled up. He was still there, though he was conscious now. As Daphne dismounted to check on the man, the full moon came over the eastern hill and gave better illumination to the place. Daphne saw that Smith's leather bag was on the ground near him, and lock-picks were scattered about.

"Were they trying to unlock you?" asked Daphne.

"Yes, damn fool idiots. They had no patience and wouldn't listen to me. So they couldn't get me free. We had a deal! Idiots! They've cost me the whole business, and now I'm for the high jump."

"Let's look for the other two men, Betsey. Get off that horse," Daphne said to her maid.

Betsey wasn't too happy with the order. Didn't her mistress know anything about corns? They stopped hurting badly soon after Mr. Jackson attended to them, but that farrier might be less skilled. The corns weren't bothering her now, but how agonizing would they become when she slipped off her saddle to land on her feet? Well, she would just have to find out, wouldn't she?

The two women stumbled over the rough ground to where they had left Mr. Worthington. He wasn't there, but, even in the poor light, they could see clearly the marks where he had maneuvered himself uphill towards where Mr. Beaver had been left. The moonlight was getting stronger, and they could just spot their first prisoner only fifty feet away. He was still firmly tied up. Then, a couple of hundred feet further, they came upon Mr. Beaver. He had moved very little from where they had left him, but he certainly seemed to be wide awake and squirming about.

"Don't you dare kick him again, Betsey," Daphne said. "We don't want to kill him."

Betsey had looked to be taking aim at the builder's jaw again. Her feet were bothering her far less after the farrier's treatment of her corns. She was delighted: the farrier was every bit as good as Mr. Jackson, and Daphne paid his bill without thinking about taking the sum out of her maid's wages. How Betsey looked forward to boasting about it to the other lady's maids when they gathered in Ameschester on their afternoons off!

Daphne started examining Mr. Beaver's bonds to make sure that they were secure. She was not going to untie him, at least not until Mr. Clarke and the others had returned from their chase of whoever it was that had been on the property when the magistrate's party arrived. The bonds were holding well and needed no attention. The designer's temper was another matter altogether. He was swearing at Daphne, calling her names, and cursing the day he had met her. Clearly, he realized that his situation was hopeless: the noose was now looming in his immediate future.

"Betsey," Daphne announced. "I said that you could not kick this cretin, but you may gag him. I've heard too much from him already."

Betsey was delighted to comply. She had a couple of rags used to clean up Daphne's effects when they got dusty on the trip, and she was more than happy to hold Beaver's nose until he opened his lips so that she could stuff one rag into his mouth and secure it by tying it tightly in place with the other one.

While this was going on, Mr. Clarke rode up and dismounted. "That is quite a cat's cradle of knots you used to tie up this man, my lady. I hate to think what Lord Camshire would say about them, him being a naval officer."

"Mr. Clarke," Daphne retorted tartly. "These knots succeeded in restraining this man, Mr. Beaver, and the other one, Mr. Worthington, for hours and hours while they were trying to get loose. What more could you want from knots? Now, what will happen to these criminals?"

"I'll load them in the cart while they are still tied up and take them to my barn where I can lock them up for the night. That locksmith too. I'll give them some water and food, of course. Then, tomorrow, I'll get the other two magistrates together, and we will decide their fate. Both the fate of your captures and of the ones we just caught trying to leave here. One of those, I am afraid, was the son of one of my tenants. Provided they tell us who sent them here today, I imagine we will give each of the men an hour or so in the pillory. Your three and any others who won't cooperate, we'll have to hold over for the assizes, I expect. The judges will be busy. I'll check with Sir Titus first before I do anything. I expect he knows far more about what is going on than I do and can advise me."

"Will I have to testify before the magistrates or the judges?"

"No, I don't think so, my lady. Even in my limited experience, gentlewomen do not testify no matter what they may know."

"Good, though I probably know nothing useful. I am not afraid of testifying if needed, but I don't want to unless it is absolutely necessary to get the criminals all convicted.

"I'll take my driver and my footman together with my maid to the inn now. I don't know how long we will stay there. I only planned two nights, but Sir Titus and his injuries have rather upset those plans."

When Daphne and her servants returned to the Woodbridge Inn, Mrs. Mattham quickly prepared a late-night meal of cold lamb, bread, and pickles. After eating, Daphne sat down to write Giles a letter as she always did when he was away. She told him all about what she had found out concerning Sallycove and very little about her adventures there. She only mentioned that her meeting with Mr. Beaver had not been at all satisfactory, that they would have to find someone else to do any work they wanted, and that she had run into Sir Titus. She would tell him more in her next letter. She didn't tell him that today she had for once felt out of her depth. She did tell him that she wished he had been with her. It was tricky for her: she didn't want to worry Giles when there was nothing he could do about the situation, but she had indeed wished that he had been with her that day.

Chapter XIX

The end of the forenoon watch did not produce the usual flurry of activity on *Glaucus* that happened when the Master and his mates and some of the midshipmen took the noon sightings. She was at anchor and had been for the past few days, so they knew where they were. Anyway, it was drizzling as it had been intermittently for the last while, so there was no sun visible to take the noon sighting. Even so, there was an eruption of activity as hands to dinner was piped. All messes could eat together since the harbor watch only involved a very few men who would be fed later.

Giles stood at the taffrail contemplating the gloomy scene off a mud bank at the mouth of the River Weser. They had brought *Glaucus* as close to the city of Bremen as they dared without a pilot to take them through the shifting mud banks of the river's estuary. To Giles's surprise, no pilot had come to guide them, and no official recognition of their presence had been made. After waiting a day at anchor, Giles had himself rowed up to Bremen in his barge. There, his reception had been chilly, to say the least. 'No,' had said the highest-ranking government official in the town who was willing to talk to him when Giles asked for a pilot to bring his ship to Bremen. As far as Giles could make out, in a conversation that, at times, was reduced to sign language, the bureaucrat was forbidden to assist foreign warships even by providing a pilot when a war was on in which Bremen and Hanover were neutral, and Great

Britain was not. At least, that is what Lieutenant Macreau also guessed the official was trying to convey.

Giles had taken Mr. Macreau with him to Bremen, knowing that French was probably the language most likely to be available for communication since no one aboard *Glaucus* spoke German. After talking to the official, Giles and Mr. Macreau weren't even sure whether Breman was part of the King's holdings in Germany or an entity separate from Hanover.

The subsequent discussion with the official went no better. Could the official recommend a boatman who would take Giles to Hanover to present the Elector's message? No, he could not. In fact, he could not allow Giles to proceed upriver without explicit permission from the Hanoverian officials in the capital. Hanover had to demonstrate it was neutral since Prussia was, and Bremen wasn't taking sides. Would the official send a request to the officials in Hanover to allow Giles to go there? He would if Giles would pay for the expense. Giles should send the King's statement with the request that it be approved for public dissemination. He repeated his willingness to pay for sending the message to Hanover, though he had little hope that it was money spent wisely. He did it in the hope of somewhat appeasing the poor King whose German neighbors showed no respect, probably reflecting the view of his subjects in Hanover.

Now Giles would have to wait for the result of sending the request to Hanover. The reply should arrive soon, provided that the officials in Hanover dealt with the matter promptly. Based on what he had learned so far, Giles would not be surprised if he was denied access to the river system leading to Hanover. That would effectively wreck his mission.

Giles's voyage to the mouth of the Weser River was shaping up to be a complete failure. That he could already admit to himself, but he was starting to doubt that the Admiralty would find any more useful employment for him. The use of frigates remained primarily as backup to the lumbering ships of the line that were taken to be the *sine qua non* of naval power. Otherwise, the fifth rates were largely used as commerce raiders by the admirals in charge of them: licensed pirates in Giles's view even though he had profited greatly from taking enemy commercial ships over the years. His own view was that frigates should now be used principally to prevent enemy privateers or pirates from capturing British commercial vessels, but that was not a job he relished performing. If he were tied to some admiral's apron strings, as frigates on most assignments were, his views on anything would carry little weight.

If Giles remained a frigate captain, he would not be making any great contribution to defeating Napoleon; he wasn't even needed to man the ships of the Royal Navy. There were more post captains than there were berths for them. All he was doing by holding the command of *Glaucus* was to condemn some other poor fellow to being on land on half-pay. Never before had Giles dwelt on the value of what he was doing. He found it very distressing that now such thoughts were plaguing him.

Giles had work that was more worthwhile and satisfying as a member of the House of Lords and a very prominent landowner than as a frigate captain in distant waters following the whims of some time-serving admiral. Daphne was capable, more than capable, of handling the running of his properties. Still, she had repeatedly stated that she would much prefer to have him taking his proper role on land than to his being away at sea, even though she understood and appreciated the necessity of his doing his duty. It was also the case that their estates and other ventures were becoming more and more complicated, and he was not really fulfilling his obligations as Daphne's husband by being a ship's captain. Furthermore, Daphne could not fulfill his duties in the House of Lords, and surely that was a more important role for him now that the danger of invasion had lessened.

Giles's sad reverie was interrupted by the sight of a boat rowing toward them. In the stern sheets was a man dressed as a gentleman, not as a boatsman. At that distance, Giles couldn't be sure of his identity, but it looked like the rather obnoxious official he had been dealing with in Bremen. The man did not appear to have brought an interpreter with him.

Giles was tempted to be as churlish in welcoming the official as had been his welcome to Bremen. Then he reflected that such behavior was petty and that he never could tell when it might prove advantageous not to make an enemy. Instead, he would even welcome the emissary by having him piped on board and met at the gangway as if he were an important government representative. After the ceremony, Giles showed the envoy to his cabin and offered the man a glass of wine, a decent Rhenish vintage that he had acquired before leaving England.

Before Giles could go below with his guest, Midshipman Bush sidled up to him.

"Sir, a small boat is approaching from upriver. It is smaller than the one you just greeted and seems to be hanging back to avoid the people you just welcomed."

Giles looked to where the midshipman was pointing. He could see a small rowboat with a gentleman in the stern-sheets. The two rowers were resting on their oars. Checking angles in his head, Giles realized that the newcomer was hidden from the envoy's boat, which was still moored to *Glaucus*. The visitors from Bremen might not be aware of its presence.

"Mr. Bush," Giles ordered quietly, "invite that boat to come alongside us on the opposite side from our other visitors. Have them wait there until I get rid of the group that has just gone below. I'll see the newcomers when the coast is clear."

The preliminaries with the man from Bremen were ended by the envoy offering a toast that Giles thought was to his health. He responded by one to "König George von Great Britain und Hanover."

The look on the envoy's face made it clear that he understood the meaning of the toast, but he still surprised Giles by lifting his glass to drink to the King. Then the official got down to the business of this visit. Word had been received from Hanover. An English translation had been provided so that there could be no question about what was meant.

Giles read the English version. Its meaning was indeed crystal clear: Giles's requests were all denied. King George III was not recognized as the ruler of

Hanover any longer. Hanover was neutral in the war between Britain and France.

The official from Bremen then shoved another document to Giles. It was in English, quite comprehensible English. This one was from the authorities in Bremen. That state, the document called it the Republic of Bremen, was also neutral, and *Glaucus* had no further business in that country. *Glaucus* must leave Bremen's waters within twenty-four hours of receipt of this communication.

Giles was very angry at the abrupt, indeed rude, way in which these messages were presented, but he restrained his anger. "I shall have to report all this to King George III, and it will be up to him how to respond," he announced coldly. "I can understand how the threat of Napoleon might cause the officials to act in this way, but I have no doubt that he will deal with the perpetrators of this insult appropriately after his forces have defeated that upstart emperor, Napoleon."

The German official, whose English had suddenly improved greatly, rose to his feet in response and drew himself up to full height. "I can assure the English captain that Bremen, like Hanover, is not subject to the French emperor. Not surprisingly, given that your monarch has never visited Hanover during his long period of alleged rule, that state is no longer under the control of the English king or of some ignorant committee in London. It is now fully allied with Prussia, and its allegiance is owed to King Frederick. I must now take my leave to make sure that our shore batteries are instructed to fire at you if you are still in our waters at three in the afternoon tomorrow."

With that, the official turned and flounced out of Giles's cabin, for all the world looking like a dowager aristocrat who had been offered stale cake for afternoon tea. Giles followed along behind, still seething. Seeing Midshipman Bush reminded him of the earlier development.

"Mr. Bush," Giles said as he paused for a moment next to the midshipman. "What happened to that other boat?"

"It is alongside, sir, to starboard."

"Good. Have them stay there, making sure that the visitors who are now leaving can't see them. When the coast is clear, bring the newcomer to my cabin."

Giles went below. He started to write his log while the events of the afternoon were still fresh in his mind. He would not be surprised if his account were shown to the King, and he would have to watch his wording more carefully than usual since the bearer of bad news all too often had to endure the anger of a disappointed superior. He was particularly careful not to report the gybe that King George had not visited Hanover in the more than forty-five years of his rule over the kingdom.

Giles's task of trying to placate his monarch was interrupted by Midshipman Bush, "Captain Giles, may I introduce Mr. Jonathan Westerby? He is the passenger on that rowboat you had moor on our larboard side."

Giles looked up from his task. Slightly behind Mr. Bush stood the visitor. He was of medium height and thin, dressed in the clothes of gentlemen. Something about him told Giles that he was an Englishmen even though he had the pale face of a man who spent most of his time indoors.

"Mr. Westerby, welcome aboard," said Giles, rising to acknowledge his visitor. "Mr. Bush, you may leave us. What can I do for you, Mr. Westerby?"

"It is a delight to meet you, at last, Captain Giles," the visitor began. "We are related, you know."

"Are we? How?"

"Our great grandmothers were cousins, I am told."

"Ah … I am afraid that I was not aware of the connection. Your father is?"

"Baron Westerby of Taflonton."

"I am afraid that I have yet to meet him. I am only newly elevated to the House of Lords and have yet to meet many of the members."

"That's understandable since he is rather remiss in his attendance at the Lords. I am, of course, only his fourth son, so I have had to make my way on my own."

"I quite understand. I was a third son and never expected to be the Earl of Camshire. Now, what can I do for you, Mr. Westerby?"

"First, let me explain my position. My father had me educated at Shrewsbury and then at Brasenose College, Oxford. He intended me for the Church and indeed had a living available in a small town in Staffordshire. However, I did not fancy the life of a country parson, and, instead, my father got me a position with Barings. I had learned German from my governess, who was from Hanover, so I was sent to Bremen, where

Barings maintains an office, largely for historical reasons since they now have much larger fish to fry than helping trade with the German states. My territory included Hanover, even though the Electorate was supposed to be ruled from London's Hanover Office. In fact, however, it was managed by people in Hanover itself. My dealings in that city were with the local officials without reference to London.

"When Napoleon and then Prussia took over, things changed very little, except now they do not recognize the role of our King in the affairs of Hanover at all. I was in that city when news came of your arrival in Bremen and then word of King George's petition or proclamation or whatever it is that you are supposed to deliver. I was not surprised that they turned you down flat, knowing that there was no possibility of your bringing this ship anywhere near the city. Even so, the news caused quite a bit of confusion or, at least, it somewhat alarmed the Prussian officials who were just beginning to understand what the situation was in Hanover.

"I was in the office of the main administrator, trying to facilitate a shipment from Neinburg to Stockholm, which Barings is financing, when I heard of your presence here. The functionary was called away urgently for some unknown reason and left some documents open on his table. Curiosity got the better of me, so I looked at them. The administrator was someone whose loyalty was believed to be to both the French and the Prussians, a practical man who would not benefit from war between them. While he had been in office when Hanover belonged, in theory, to King George, but not to Great Britain, he was known to prefer either of the other powers to being controlled from London and hoped there would be no war between them.

"The document was from an official in Holland. It was asking, unofficially, on behalf of the French Government, for the opinion of the Hanoverian official. Did he think that Prussia (meaning Hanover) would stand aside should the French march through Saxony and Schleswig-Holstein to invade Denmark? The purpose of that maneuver would be to make sea trade between England and Sweden, as well as with Russia, very difficult. I don't need to tell you that such a development would not be good, either for Britain or for Barings!

"I suspected that the British Government would have no inkling that plans for such an invasion were so far advanced. I pocketed the papers and left. I was sure their absence would be noticed, so I promptly hired a rowboat to take me downriver. I was sure that the disappearance of the document was noted, but I don't know if there has been any pursuit. I bypassed Bremen to come here. Now, I hope that you can take me to England."

"I see," said Giles. "Well, my business here is finished, and I should return to England. I can take you with me. It will be about as quick as any other way, though you could try Cuxhaven right now to see if anyone is going to England. Currently, the wind is foul for us, and the tide is rising. The estuary here is filled with shifting sandbars, and we have no pilot. *Glaucus* won't be sailing before dawn tomorrow, if then. You might do better by going on to Cuxhaven in the hope of finding transportation to England."

"I would prefer to take my chances with you. Of course, Cuxhaven is a more likely place to find a ship going to England. Therefore, it is a much more likely place for the authorities to look for me if they believe that I have come this way. My rowers are, I think, loyal to me and can disappear until you have sailed."

"Good; well, welcome aboard, Mr. Westerby. It may take some time to work our way out of here, but it should then be straight sailing to Sheerness. It is quite easy to alter this cabin to have two separate sleeping areas, so you should be comfortable."

"Thank you, my lord. I am sure that I will be very comfortable, and I very much appreciate your willingness to take me with you."

"That's settled, but onboard ship, you must call me Captain Giles rather than "my lord." Like you, I was a junior son when I started to pursue this career in which I have achieved some success, so here I am known by the title that describes my role."

"Henderson," Giles called in a louder voice to the marine sentry at his cabin door. "Pass the word for the bosun and my servant,"

"Mr. Shearer," Giles addressed the bosun a few minutes later, "This gentleman is Mr. Westerby. He will be my guest on the voyage back to England. To avoid crowding the wardroom, I have asked him to sleep in my spare cabin. See that the partitions are rearranged so that it is readied for him.

"Aye, aye, sir."

"Henderson," Giles continued when his servant had slipped unobtrusively into the cabin. "Mr. Westerby will be traveling to England with us, bunking in my other cabin. I am going on deck now, but we will have some of that Welsh rarebit you and the cook prepare so well and one of the bottles of that excellent claret at two bells of the second dog watch. Mr. Westerby, I imagine you wish to see your boatmen away and then get straightened up. We'll get together at seven o'clock to exchange news and views."

On deck, Giles consulted with the Master. The sky was overcast, and the mist was thickening. The wind was light from the north-north-west, and the tide was flooding. These were not conditions in which to contemplate moving *Glaucus* before dawn. Giles ordered extra sentries to be stationed throughout the night in case any attempt were made to attack his frigate.

Giles went below with time to wash up before supper. He was rather looking forward to the chance of chatting with someone who was not subordinate to him. The rarebit was quite edible — 'edible' was high praise for *Glaucus*'s cook — the 1796 claret more than drinkable and the conversation pleasant. Giles and Mr. Westerby turned out to have more in common than would be expected, not just in being younger sons but more in how they had overcome that problem.

Mr. Westerby had heard about Giles's exploits, including his recent interception of the Dutch spice ships. He had been in Amsterdam on business for Barings when the news of the capture had trickled through to that city. Barings office there was furious, for they were involved in financing the trade and had lost money over what the Dutch regarded as a disaster. Mr. Westerby felt quite differently. He had been quite happy at the news of what happened to the Dutch spice fleet, even though it had not been good for Barings. Indeed, he had become somewhat disillusioned with his position as his role became more and more to help Napoleon by enabling trade between France and the German states since it was now quite clear that Napoleon was a menace to all of Europe as well as Great Britain.

Barings allowed their employees to trade on their own account in promising ventures. Mr. Westerby had not participated in the spice-ships venture though some of the men in the Amsterdam office had done so. They had been furious when Mr. Westerby had declined an invitation to become rich through the venture, and somehow they blamed him for the ships being captured. His friends had lost heavily — disastrously for some men who had borrowed substantially to participate in the venture. Somehow they appeared to believe that disaster had struck because he had not joined the doomed venture.

The resentment of the Barings representatives in Amsterdam had been unforgiving. Westerby was not at all confident about his future with the financial house. Anyway, he had grown disgusted at how Barings profited from the war, helping both sides just to make money for themselves, even at the expense of the country that had nurtured them when they moved from Bremen and of the German states where the company had originated. He had been particularly unhappy at how Barings gained a fortune by arranging that the fledgling United States buy Louisiana from Bonaparte, a transaction that could hardly be considered in Britain's interest since the money helped to finance Napoleon's wars.

"Will you stay on at Barings now?" Giles asked.

"I don't think they'd keep me after this. Getting the Dutch and the Prussians angry at me, not to mention the French, would not be seen in a good light at Barings. Anyway, I've had enough of them."

"So, what will you do?"

"Oh, I've made a tidy fortune while at Barings. I think it is time to leave banking and become a country squire."

"In Yorkshire?"

"I think so. I know the County well. It is, of course, a long way from London, but I've seen all I want of London for a long time."

"It sounds as if you have a place in mind."

"Yes, I rather think that I do. It's a fairly modest estate, with a charming house that was rebuilt about fifty years ago. It comes with a bit of a park, and home fields, and some tenancies. Not as grand a house as my brother's, but it will be more comfortable and profitable."

"Sounds as if you are well-positioned for a change in your life. Are you married?"

"Not yet, but I have my eye on a lass. Daughter of a local squire. Not much dowry, but also not many expectations. I think she'll suit me and I, her. Not nearly as flamboyant a marriage as the papers indicate that you have, Captain Giles."

Giles laughed, "Daphne — Lady Camshire — flamboyant? I am not sure that that is the right term. She is the daughter of a landowner near Dipton and managed – and still manages – her father's estate. And, in fact, ours too, though she pretends that I manage it except when I am away. She is very intelligent and capable and does not let anyone push us around. She also is fun-loving. Those traits have caught the eyes of the papers and much of the aristocracy, but I would not call her flamboyant. In fact, she hates to draw attention to herself. You must visit us to see for yourself."

The two new acquaintances talked long into the night, and one bottle of wine turned into two. It had been a relief for Giles to talk with someone who ranked neither above nor below him in the navy and had no desire to prove how important he was. He reflected on this as he sat down to add to his letter to Daphne. It would be very pleasant to have someone like Weatherby near Dipton. He had his circle of friends and acquaintances there, of course, Bush and Bolton and Mr. Summers and the Major, and also Carstairs and Mr. Griffiths, but the number of people with whom he was comfortable was limited. He had never been able to break through the aura of superiority that the gentlemen near Dipton had attributed to him when they did not know him at all, so he had no close friends in the area except for Bush. Maybe he could persuade Weatherby to move south with his bride.

Giles's addition to the letter to Daphne that night had included some of these thoughts. He realized that it might be taken as foreshadowing his giving up the sea. Should he delete the addition, which was on a new sheet of paper, so that he did not set her hopes up if he changed his mind? He hadn't decided to leave *Glaucus*. Would it sound too much as if he had? But then he realized that they had never started to edit their letters so that their thoughts would only appear in a favorable light. He wasn't about to start now. If he set some hopes up that he would disappoint later, so be it.

Chapter XX

Light spread slowly over the men on *Glaucus*'s deck. Everyone, not just the lookouts, but everyone on deck, scanned the sea as far as they could see for enemy ships or other problems. There was clear water all around the ship, but visibility was severely limited by rain squalls and fog banks where low clouds descended all the way to the water

"No bottom with this line," came the cry from the bow chains. The officers on deck relaxed slightly. They had been without a chance to get a fix for two days when they had left their anchorage in the river Wiser near Bremen. Dead reckoning could only be considered to provide a wild guess when they could see no landmarks, and there were currents whose strength had to be estimated based on little knowledge. At least, wherever they were, they were not about to go aground.

"Captain," the lookout at the quarterdeck rail called out, bypassing the line of command, "I think I see something — a ship, maybe — in that squall to larboard."

Giles had only just turned to scan the area indicated when a hail came from the top of the mainmast, "Deck there. Topsail, half a cable away on the larboard beam. Could be a ship-of-the-line or an East Indiaman. On a parallel course to ours. Disappearing into the squall again."

"Helmsman," Giles bellowed, "hard a larboard. Mr. Miller, we are tacking. Mr. Abbott, load the guns in my cabin with round shot and run out. Mr. Miller, when we have come about, set the topsails and royals. Bosun, pipe all hands to action stations."

Seeming chaos erupted on *Glaucus*'s apparently placid deck. Giles knew he was courting disaster by risking missing stays* by putting the helm down to come into the wind before the sail handlers were ready. However, if the stranger were a Dutch ship-of-the-line, which was all too likely in these waters, he risked being blown out of the water by her broadside. The Dutch had a reputation for being meticulous sailors, and it was highly likely that any Dutch naval ship would be at quarters at dawn, possibly even with their guns loaded, run out, and ready to fire. *Glaucus* could be blown out of the water if she didn't induce the enemy ship to sail ahead of her so that she was somewhat out of range of the enemy's guns.

The helmsman turned the wheel clockwise; the rudder moved to the starboard side of the stern. *Glaucus* turned her bow in the same direction. The tautness left the sails, and they started to flap. The frigate was slowing and swaying to starboard. Everyone not hauling on the lines controlling the sails seemed to be holding their breath as the bowsprit came right into the wind, with the ship's turn slowing. Would the bow continue to turn until the wind was on her larboard side, or would she stall, stuck until sternway allowed her to complete the turn? At last, *Glaucus* passed through the eye of the wind, and her turn started to happen ever so slightly more quickly. The sailors still had to keep hauling furiously on various lines, but *Glaucus* had come about smoothly.

A loud, sustained boom burst out astern of *Glaucus*. The ship-of-the-line had fired her broadside, not evenly because each gun fired the moment its captain thought that its shot would damage *Glaucus* most. Even as the sound of the explosions reached *Glaucus*, cannonballs raced past her larboard side, far too close for comfort though the eye could not really follow them. One shot had been aimed high, and a hole immediately appeared in the mainsail. One ball must have been low, for it skimmed off a wave, its course redirected towards the frigate and slammed into *Glaucus*'s stern, right where the stern joined the larboard side of the vessel, luckily well above the waterline.

The carpenter was about to order one of his mates to examine the damage when two guns roared out directly under Giles's feet. Even though he expected it, the sound startled the captain. Both the special stern chasers had fired, one only seconds after the other. Their aim was surprisingly good. All that Giles could have hoped for was that one of them might damage the rigging or scatter killing splinters all over the battleship's decks. Instead, the first ball slammed into the Dutch ship's mainmast after demolishing the head of a seaman standing in front of it. That blow was probably not enough to sever the huge wooden pole, but, amazingly, as Giles was still trying to absorb this hideous event, the second ball clipped the mast about a yard above where the first one had hit. That was too much for the spar. Slowly, slowly, still somewhat steadied by its stays*, the massive edifice that was the mainmast, sails, and shrouds swayed first one way and then the other, then back again but this time keeping going and speeding up as a noisy breaking of countless lines and splintering of wood heralded the disaster. The mast had gone by the board.

The Dutch ship-of-the-line was no longer a threat to *Glaucus*: long before her broadside could be made to bear again on the British frigate, Giles's ship would be out of range. Giles was about to enquire how serious was the damage to the stern when the masthead lookout called again, "Deck there. Frigate four points off the starboard bow, flying Dutch colors, close-hauled on the starboard tack. Seven miles distant."

Giles rushed to the starboard rail. He didn't need his telescope to see the enemy frigate emerging from a rain squall. She looked to be a thirty-two, somewhat smaller than *Glaucus*. Normally, Giles would have tried to engage her, but he did not yet know the damage to his ship, and, anyway, it was important to get Mr. Westerby's document to London. The two frigates seemed to be on courses that would intersect each other several miles ahead. Whoever got there first would have an advantage, but not a great one. Even as Giles raised his telescope to get a better look at the stranger, the distant frigate loosed her furled topsails and royals.

"Mr. Brooks," Giles called to the master. "Keep an eye on the enemy to determine which of us will be in front of the other when our paths cross."

"Aye, aye, sir."

The carpenter was waiting to talk to Giles.

"Mr. Evans, what is the news about the damage from that cannonball?"

"For a single ball, it did a lot of damage, sir. Of course, it was a very heavy one — a 32 pounder likely.

I've heard that they sometimes double charge their initial shots. The ball hit just where the side planks join the stern. It went right through and even made a hole on the starboard side. That damage wasn't of great concern, but the break in the corner is serious: it has weakened the whole structure there since it severely broke the last rib that strengthens that whole corner. There is a great hole in the corner of your cabin, sir, that works with every movement of the ship."

"Can you repair it?"

"Not really, sir. It is a dockyard job. I am having my mates jury-rig and brace it now, sir, but the ship is seriously damaged. I am not sure how many broadsides we could fire before that corner starts to come apart disastrously. The same is true for the stern chasers, but we could possibly fire them half a dozen times before they produced further serious trouble. Of course, any firing of the cannon may affect that weakened joint. I also don't know how it would stand up in a bad storm."

"Thank you, Mr. Evans. Carry on."

The race between the frigates was on. The carpenter's news convinced Giles that he should avoid a fight if he could. Of course, that also depended on his opponent and her capabilities. If *Glaucus* could be the first to reach the invisible point where the two courses met, and if she could sail faster or closer to the wind than her opponent, she might be able to avoid the battle entirely. If not, then *Glaucus* could try some other ruses to escape or else try her luck by attacking the rival frigate when they met. *Glaucus* should be stronger, and since she was larger, she was also likely to win a duel between them. But first, he would try to outrun her.

"Mr. Miller. Let's see if we can carry the mainmast royal to squeeze a little extra speed out of her," Giles ordered. "Helmsman, steer by the wind. As close as you can without pinching."

No sooner had these orders been given than another hail from the masthead altered his calculations again: "Deck there: another frigate's topsails off the starboard quarter."

"Mr. Miller," Giles called, "I am going aloft to see what this latest development is."

Giles climbed to the masthead, noting that he was a bit out of breath before reaching his destination. He should take more exercise, he thought a bit sourly. That reflection was forgotten as he trained his telescope on the stranger. Even as he watched, she unfurled her topgallant sails, and a pennant broke from the top of her mainmast. She was Dutch, a thirty-two like the first one, so also less powerful than *Glaucus*. However, if the two attacked together, they would spell trouble for Giles's ship.

As Giles studied the new enemy, he saw the ship alter course to meet with the closer Dutch frigate. She wouldn't arrive before the first ship crossed *Glaucus*'s course; the arrival of the new frigate would not be a close-run thing. However, if *Glaucus* were delayed by having to fight the first frigate, the second one might arrive in time to change the course of the battle. Giles looked behind him. Should he turn towards the land? Seek the shelter of the rain squalls in the hope of then eluding the enemy. There were two weaknesses with that course of action, even though the ship-of-the-line was clearly no longer a threat. He didn't know just where they were. Heading towards shore, especially towards a coast where mudbanks might be extending far out to sea, would be hazardous, and he really still had little idea of where *Glaucus* was. Mr. Brooks had been hinting that he would be happier if the captain would order that *Glaucus* stand away from shore before trying to outsail the other frigate, and his worry had been a valid one.

Furthermore, the wind was finally chasing the rain away, so Giles could not count on disappearing from the enemy if he turned downwind. No, Giles would hold this course until he got a better idea of the capabilities of this new enemy. He knew that he did not want to engage with the two of them simultaneously, especially as *Glaucus*'s weakened hull might not stand up well to the strains of rapid maneuvering that could be called for if a simultaneous battle with the two enemy frigates were to occur.

When Giles returned to the deck, he promptly took Mr. Brooks aside to discuss his worries. After telling the master his thoughts, he asked about his particular dilemma. "Mr. Brooks, can we increase the speed to the crossing point by altering course or sails?"

"I can see the problem, Captain Giles, though our best course of action cannot be known without seeing how much the enemy can improve their ship's performance. We are doing about as well as we can now. Steering any higher will slow our progress. The helmsmen are getting as much speed to windward out of her as there is to get. We cannot carry more sail, but I think the balance of the sails might be made a bit better."

"Oh, how?"

"Well, that main royal is not drawing as well as it might. We might go faster if you set up the fore and mizzen royals as well and put one or two reefs in all of them. I think we will go a quarter of a knot faster and point just as high."

"Mr. Miller, did you hear Mr. Brooks?"

"Yes, sir."

"Make it so."

"Aye, aye, sir."

"Mr. Brooks, continue to monitor the situation."

"Aye, aye, sir," the master replied in a tone that seemed to add, "What else did you expect me to do?"

Mr. Brooks returned to taking sights of the opposing ship and the angle to which she bore using his sextant for the purpose. After the other two sails were set and reefed, Giles had a distinct impression that *Glaucus* was going faster through the water. Would Mr. Brooks and his sextant, which he was using horizontally, very awkwardly, be able to verify that impression? Time would tell. At least another hour would pass before the two frigates could engage. Giles ordered that the guns be secured.

Now there was nothing for Giles to do but wait for the race to develop to the point where they could predict who would be ahead when two ships' courses came together. Except for more tiny adjustments to the course and keener attention to the lines controlling the sails than usual, *Glaucus* returned to normal, as if nothing out of the ordinary were happening. Giles did not interfere with the sailing of his ship, letting Mr. Miller, as the officer of the watch, and Mr. Brooks fret over pulling in and loosening sheets and letting out or taking in a reef in the royals. The concern was about who would be ahead when the ships finally got close to one another, and Giles had already formulated plans for what to do depending on their relative positions when it came time to act and how to respond to his opponent's initiatives.

By six bells of the forenoon watch, the enemy frigate was much closer, but it would be at least half an hour before they met. He ordered the hands to dinner a little early but did not authorize an extra tot in preparation for the battle. His crew all knew that this captain only ordered extra rum after they had won a battle, not before. It showed their good nature that Giles heard several jokes to the effect that they did not need Dutch courage though their opponents probably did.

Giles asked Mr. Westerby to join him for a quick lunch in his cabin. Of course, with the partitions stowed in the hold along with the furniture, it was really a picnic rather than a proper meal though at least they had chairs and a small table. When their meal was finished, Giles told Mr. Westerby that he should now go to the orlop to be safe. His guest protested that he would prefer to see the action.

"You will only get in the way, I am afraid," Giles replied. "Fighting on ships is skilled business, both at a distance and when it comes to hand-to-hand combat. In the orlop, you can be much more help aiding the doctor, for I am afraid that there are bound to be casualties."

Giles was relieved when his visitor agreed to go to the orlop. He had had too many guests in the past who seemed to think that they would be looked down upon if they did not stand around waiting to be killed or wounded in a battle while getting in the way of busy crew members.

On deck, the situation had not changed greatly since Giles had gone to lunch, but now the enemy frigate was much closer.

"How long before we meet, Mr. Brooks?" Giles asked the master.

"Ten minutes, by my calculations, sir."

"And will she pass in front of or behind us if we both hold our courses?"

"She'll be ahead by a half cable, I predict, sir."

"So she will be able to rake* us?"

"I am afraid so, sir."

"Well, we'll have a bit of a surprise for her, won't we, with our bow chasers?"

Everyone on board stood waiting for the encounter.

"Captain, do you see that strong gust coming at us?" asked Mr. Brooks. "It should hit just before the enemy crosses our course."

"Yes, I see it," said Giles. "Mr. Miller, stand by to ease the sails at my command. When that gust comes, let out just enough to veer downwind for a few moments. Immediately after, we will come about."

"Aye, aye, sir." The first lieutenant started shouting a string of orders so that Giles's command could be carried out when the captain gave the word.

"Bow chasers, fire when you bear," Giles roared. "Mister Miller, stand by for the course changes."

Nearer and nearer to each other came the two frigates. Just as the gust arrived, the Dutch frigate crossed *Glaucus*'s bow. The wind tipped her over. The broadside aimed for Giles's ship went into the water before reaching *Glaucus*, losing much of its power, though some balls deflected off the water to hit the British ship. Only one was aimed high enough that it slammed into *Glaucus* directly. Ominously, that one struck her close to the already weakened stern. At almost the same moment, *Glaucus*'s bow chasers fired.

"Now!" Giles bellowed.

Glaucus turned to starboard a little. Her broadside came to bear and rippled out as each gun fired the minute its captain calculated that it would hit the target. The damage being done as the balls crashed into the enemy, leaving lethal splinters zipping every which way, was hard to judge. As the last gun fired, Mr. Miller followed Giles's order to bring *Glaucus* about. Round she came, with the sail-handlers working ferociously to ensure a quick and complete tack. Giles had expected his opponent also to tack following their initial meeting so that she could have the weather gage and herd *Glaucus* towards the second Dutch frigate. By dodging downwind and then immediately tacking when he did, Giles hoped that he would be able to rake the Dutch frigate, doing enough damage to get away from her. If that didn't work, he would be in a strong position to board her and have her under his control before the other frigate could come to her aid.

The Dutch frigate did indeed turn into the wind as if to tack, but somehow, whether because of Giles's unexpected move or because of damage suffered from *Glaucus*'s broadside, the Dutchman missed stays*. Seeing this, Giles immediately backed *Glaucus*'s principal sails so that she could be blown onto her opponent. The Dutch ship had her starboard broadside ready, and it fired before Glaucus's larboard guns could reply. Both broadsides damaged their targets, how much would remain to be seen after the battle ended. *Glaucus* again suffered a hit right at the point where the larboard planks met the stern.

Glaucus's most effective shot came on an uproll. One of the cannon hung fire, the flint-lock not sparking properly. The gun captain quickly took the slowmatch, kept for just that eventuality, and applied it to the touch hole. The cannon fired, but the delay meant it fired high. The ball hit the Dutch mizzen topmast. It swayed back and forth once before toppling over away from *Glaucus*. Any hope of the enemy ship tacking went by the board with the mast.

Glaucus drifted down on her rival. The well-trained and prepared gun crews on *Glaucus* had been able to switch to grapeshot. Before the ships came together, her broadside wreaked havoc among the waiting crew. Grappling hooks were thrown, and *Glaucus*'s crew started to swarm over the railings to overwhelm the less battle-hardened enemy crew. A

Dutch officer bellowed surrender and had his ship's flag hauled down. That particular fight was over!

Giles's crew changed what they were doing without pause. This was not the first enemy frigate they had taken by any means. The rival crew had to be locked up, their officers with the other sailors unless they gave their paroles. The destroyed mast and sails had to be cut away, and everything made ship-shape so that they could sail again. The same held for *Glaucus,* where already repairs were being made, and the carpenter was having the bilge sounded in case she had started to leak. He then evaluated the other damage and decided how to repair it.

While all the other officers and crew were fully employed, Giles had little to do. As he waited for reports, he filled the time by visiting the orlop to get the doctor's report and visit the newly wounded. The butcher's bill was less than he had feared, though it was still significant. Three members of *Glaucus*'s crew were dead, and four had received wounds that required amputations, so their survival was still in question. Mr. Miller, who had taken charge of the Dutch frigate, sent word that the dead on her numbered twelve, with another five men whose condition was highly critical.

Mr. Westerby was visibly shaken by what he had seen in the orlop. The reality of war — the gruesomely injured and dying for whom often the surgeon could offer only drastic and even more painful help — had shaken him, as such scenes had affected others reared on the myths of glorious and heroic deaths in war. Giles wondered how long Mr. Westerby's shock would last. With other civilians who had been on board Glaucus during a frigate action, it had disappeared quickly when they concluded that, of course, such awful things only happened to the lower orders. Somehow, even Nelson's gruesome death had not caused anyone to think of the generally horrible price of warfare on those who waged it. He himself, Giles ruefully reflected, had come to take the "butcher's bill" for granted, not as a statement of horror.

It was well over an hour after the Dutch frigate's flag had been lowered before Mr. Miller returned from the captured frigate. "*Rijswijk*, that's the name of the captured frigate, though I am not sure of how to pronounce the name, is ready to proceed, sir."

"Very good, Mr. Miller. You take command of —what did you call her?"

"*Rijswijk*, sir."

"We'll get underway. I'll stay upwind of you, and we should sail as close to the wind* as possible. *Glaucus* should be the faster of the two, so carry all plain sail up to the royals, and we'll adjust to your speed."

"Aye, aye, sir. What about *Alkmaar*?"

"The what?"

"*Alkmaar*, sir. That is the name of the other Dutch frigate."

"Is it? Well, she's in for a stern chase. However, injured as we are, she will be up to us well before nightfall, so we will have to be prepared to take her on. Take the starboard watch with you and Mr. Stewart as your lieutenant. The larboard watch and Mr. Fisher will stay with me.

"When that frigate gets close, reduce sails to only topsails, so we don't need so many sail-handlers. *Glaucus* will tack, and you will wear* at the same time to face her, staying so that we can catch her between us her unless she comes about. If she does tack, we can waste time maneuvering until nightfall. There will be no moon, so we can then, quite probably, get away from her in the dark. Be ready to grapple with her at the same time *Glaucus* does if we can get her between us. Otherwise, grapple with *Glaucus* and board across us."

"Aye, aye, sir," was the first lieutenant's only reply.

Giles again was left with nothing to do while he waited for action. At least the rain clouds had disappeared, and the late afternoon sun still had some warmth in it. Slight adjustments to *Glaucus*'s course, mirrored by *Rijswijk*, ensured that *Alkmaar* continued to sail into the trap he was laying. Since Giles's two frigates were coasting along under reduced sail, it would not be long before the Dutch frigate caught up with them.

Closer and closer, *Alkmaar* came. Giles waited and waited to make his move until she could not escape him. The signal to engage was actually given by *Alkmaar* when she fired her bow chasers in a ranging shot. Giles did not observe where the shot went; the minute he saw the gun smoke at his enemy's bow, he gave the order to come about. Mr. Miller must have been anticipating the order, for even as Giles roared to his crew, his first lieutenant shouted to his own men. Round the two frigates came, one turning downwind and the other circling upwind. Then the two moved towards the

Dutch ship, with one ship aiming to pass to starboard and the other to larboard of *Alkmaar*'s bow. She was nicely caught in Giles's trap. Whatever she did, she would have to engage one of Giles's ships, with the other joining in quickly. Possibly she could have escaped the trap if she had been able to change course the minute the rival frigates turned to face her, but she turned out to be unable to do so. By the time she could have got her sail handlers to their stations, it was too late. Or so it seemed, but maybe her captain never even thought about doing this. What *Alkmaar* actually did was continue on her course, and, like Giles's frigates, she reduced sail before manning the guns in preparation for the encounter.

Now the gap between the ships was closing rapidly. *Glaucus* altered her course slightly so that her massive bow chasers could bear and then reversed her course as the cannon were being swabbed out for the next shot. *Glaucus*'s guns had little effect, though their cannonballs did sever some jib stays* before sending slivers all over the Dutch foredeck. They may also have hit some of the crew of *Alkmaar*'s bow chasers, for those guns made no response. *Glaucus*'s weapons got in one more shot before the bows passed each other, but they did not seem to have done much further damage.

Giles had anticipated his next maneuver, for he had ordered the broadside guns to be double shotted with grapeshot. Though he hadn't discussed it with Mr. Miller, he expected the commander of *Rijswijk* to do the same. *Glaucus*'s crew, including the officers, took shelter behind the hammock nettings, except those immediately handling the guns. The precaution was certainly needed, for even before *Glaucus*'s guns had been secured, a wave of grapeshot crossed *Alkmaar*'s deck and thumped into the nettings. That was the signal to board. Grappling irons were thrown from *Glaucus*, and she was hauled up against *Alkmaar* as the crew sheltering behind the hammocks surged onto the enemy ship. The men on *Glaucus* hardly noticed as *Alkmaar*'s broadside pounded into them. The Dutch cannon had been loaded with round shot, most of which, surprisingly, was absorbed by the hammocks behind which most of the crew who were going to board the enemy huddled. The hammocks also protected many of them from the vicious splinters caused by cannonballs hitting the railings. Only one Dutch gun misfired, but that problem was fixed with slowmatch. Unfortunately, the delay meant that its ball went full speed into the starboard side of Glaucus near the stern, opposite to where already too much damage had been done.

Rijswijk's attack with *Alkmaar* went in much the same fashion. In both cases, when all the cannon had fired and before the Dutch crew had any chance to recover, *Rijswijk*'s crew members stormed across the barriers separating them from their opponents. The combined British crew was actually a little smaller than the Dutch frigate's one, but Giles's men were hardened by repeated experiences of taking ships by storming aboard them, while this was the first time most of the Dutch sailors had encountered battle. Only a couple of moments was needed before the Dutchmen broke and began to plead for mercy. *Alkmaar*'s captain himself hauled down her flag. *Glaucus* could add two enemy ships to the total she had captured in her career. All that remained of this voyage was to get her prizes and Mr. Weatherby's document to Sheerness, which should not be very challenging. Giles was deeply satisfied with this part of his cruise. *Glaucus* and her crew were once more victorious. They were the epitome of British naval power in 1806.

Chapter XXI

A little after ten in the evening, the coach carrying Giles and Mr. Westerby from Chatham pulled up in front of Struthers House in Mayfair. Slightly over twenty-four hours ago, *Glaucus* and her prizes had dropped anchor at Sheerness following a voyage across the North Sea. It had been an uneventful trip, the wind from the north-northeast being steady if somewhat cold. Aboard Giles's ship, the clank of the pumps draining the bilge had been almost constant. Somehow, Mr. Evans announced gloomily that the last round of cannon fire had been just too much for the old girl. Putting that together with the carpenter's dire comments on how the final battle had affected the damaged corner, Giles feared that it would be a long time before his frigate could return to active service.

The admiral at Sheerness had not been helpful. He resented that Giles sailed under Admiralty orders, so no admiral, him in particular, got the one-eighth share in any prizes *Glaucus* had taken. Somehow, the admiral, about whom Giles had never heard good things, felt he was owed one-eighth of the value of each thirty-two gun frigate that *Glaucus* had captured just for being an admiral near the German coast.

The Chatham dockyard personnel were no more helpful than the admiral until Mr. Westerby informed them that the captain of *Glaucus* was also the Earl of Camshire, a man who could do irreparable harm to someone who needlessly prevented his vessel from being fixed promptly. Even so, after surveying the frigate, the chief shipwright declared that there was no rush to have her repaired. She could stay at Sheerness, waiting for him to assess the damage thoroughly before taking her into the dockyard.

Only a desperate message from Mr. Evans that the leak at the larboard stern of the ship was rapidly getting worse and was not now contained even with all their pumps, regular and emergency, in operation prompted any action. Then, just in time, a drydock was cleared out. It had had a brig in it for over a week after work on its hull had been finished. *Glaucus* could go directly into it when she had been towed up the Medway. Giles had been afraid that they might not get there before his frigate sank. However, when drydock had risen so that the hull could be examined, the shipwright made it clear that even before he surveyed her properly, he was doubtful if she would be worth repairing.

Giles had done everything he could to arrange for the wellbeing of his officers and crew during *Glaucus*'s lengthy repairs. The strings he needed to pull to keep his sailors together and get them substantial leave were better handled in London, where the Earl of Camshire had more influence with the naval authorities than he had in Chatham, where he seemed to get little respect. Giles also knew that, as soon as practicable, he should report to the Admiralty and possibly the King the dismal failure of his mission. So, by eight bells of the afternoon watch, Giles was ready to leave Chatham.

The wind had backed into the west since Giles had arrived at Sheerness and was blowing harder. Often Giles's quickest way to get to London from Chatham would be to have his barge row or sail him up the

Thames. With this weather, however, he was better off taking a coach.

Mr. Westerby had declined Giles's offer to get him to London as quickly as possible when *Glaucus* reached England. The former Barings employee had no easy way to contact government officials or get them to give priority to the news he carried. Giles was much better placed to get the information to the proper authorities. It would be best for Mr. Westerby to accompany Giles to London, where Giles's connections could provide a proper and speedy reception of the secrets brought from Hanover. So they hired a coach to take them to Westminster. They would arrive sometime in the evening, far too late to do anything that day with the news about Napoleon's plans.

When Mr. Westerby said that he would stay at an inn near Charing Cross since his brother's London House might well be closed, Giles objected. His Aunt Gillian and her husband, Lord Struthers, would insist they stay at Struthers House if they knew that their nephew was visiting London, no matter the hour at which they arrived. Furthermore, Lord Struthers was the man who would be most likely to bring the information to the eyes of the proper authorities more quickly than any others. These developments explained why Giles was knocking on the heavy door of Struthers House so late in the evening.

A footman opened the door. Were Lord and Lady Struthers at home, and, if so, had they gone to bed? Yes, they were home, but no, they were in the drawing room. Would my lord like the footman to announce them? Yes, that would be convenient. The footman made quite a production of knocking on the drawing-room door, throwing it open, and crying, "The Earl of Camshire, my lord and lady, and Mr. Jonathan Westerby." He must, Giles thought, be preparing to become a butler.

Lady Struthers jumped out of her chair to embrace her nephew enthusiastically but quickly remembered her manners. "Who is your friend, Richard," she asked, turning towards the stranger.

"This is Mr. Jonathan Westerby. He came with me from Bremen because he has some important news for the government. Westerby, let me introduce you to my Aunt, Lady Struthers, and my Uncle, Lord Struthers."

"Westerby? ... Westerby? ... Are you related to Baron Westerby?" broke in Lord Struthers.

"Yes, my lord, I am his son, his fourth son."

"Well, well, well. Welcome to Struthers House. Any friend of Richard is a friend of ours," declared Lord Struthers.

"Did you know, Mr. Westerby, that your mother is my second cousin," asked Lady Struthers, "though I don't think that I have ever met her."

"Yes, my mother told me, though she is not much of a pursuer of family connections. I am delighted to meet more of my relatives. There aren't any nearby in Yorkshire, and I confess I never looked up possible family when I was in London. Indeed, I am even rather distant from my other brothers."

"That is a pity. Still, we can start setting that straight right now. Since your father, mother, and brothers have not been taking part in the Season this year, I hear that they have closed their London House almost completely. So you must stay here while you are in London."

"That is very good of you."

"That's settled then,"

"Lord Struthers, Westerby, is in the Government as I told you," Giles remarked. "He might have some good ideas about what you should do with that document you discovered."

Lord Struthers and Mr. Westerby were soon deep in conversation about the situation among the western German states and Denmark. It continued even while they waited for the footman to bring the portmanteau that included the purloined letter.

In the meantime, Giles and his Aunt Gillian were catching up with Giles's affairs. The first bombshell was at the start of the conversation.

"Richard," said Lady Struthers. "It is fortunate that you stopped here rather than going straight to Dipton."

"Why is that?"

"Because Daphne is here, in London, staying with us, of course. If you had gone to Dipton directly from your ship, as you usually do, you would have missed her."

"Good heavens, where is she, and what is she doing in London?"

"To answer the first question, she is at a lecture on some mathematical topic that is quite beyond me. She should be here any moment. Lord Struthers and I were waiting for her before going to bed.

"To answer the second, she is in London to try to straighten out the mess that she discovered in Shropshire. It affects both Camshire House as well as your new property in Shropshire. You really shouldn't leave her with such a large set of complications to deal with when you go to sea, Richard, though she does enjoy it. But I think that there has been far too much for her to take care of recently. If I were her, I'd be getting fed up with your going off to sea and leaving her with all the problems that arise from your previous cruises, especially when she is with child."

At that point, the door to the room again opened, but without any special announcement, so no one in the drawing room was aware that Daphne was in the doorway. That situation did not last long. The moment Daphne saw Giles, she gave a joyful hoot and rushed over to embrace him. Totally ignoring everyone in the room, she gave him a huge kiss.

"Richard!" she exclaimed, "You're here. That's wonderful! Oh, I'm glad to see you! I have so much to tell you! Are you all right?"

"Daphne, dear, of course, I'm all right. I am also tremendously delighted to see you. You are looking wonderful, and pregnancy becomes you! Are *you* feeling all right?"

"I am, Richard. I can't wait to tell you all about everything, but there are others here."

Giles saw that Daphne had spotted Mr. Westerby. She released Giles immediately and flushed bright red at the realization that a stranger had just observed her most unladylike, unrestrained enthusiasm for her husband.

"Daphne, Lady Camshire," Giles pronounced formally, getting to his feet as everyone else in the room did. "May I introduce Mr. Jonathan Westerby, my new friend who accompanied me from Bremen in *Glaucus*?"

Daphne curtseyed while Mr. Westerly bowed.

"I am pleased to meet you, Mr. Westerby," is what she said, though she was wondering where in the world Giles had found this man. "I trust that my husband gave you a pleasant trip."

"I am not sure pleasant is the right word, my lady. Exciting, possibly, or terrifying. He captured two Dutch frigates on the way, and our cabin was wrecked."

"But you are unhurt, I hope."

"Yes, my lady. He bundled me off to the orlop deck, where I tried to help with the wounded."

"Oh, dear," Daphne replied. "I was once there when Giles fought a French frigate. Being there really brings home to you how horrible the side effects of war at sea can be, doesn't it?"

"Giles," interrupted Lord Struthers. "Am I to understand that you have captured two more enemy frigates?"

"Yes, sir."

"That will do you some good. Many in the government are not happy about the Navy's initiative in the matter of the King's communication with Parliament. When you report on your mission, I suggest that you stress that your trip resulted in the capture of enemy ships; it would deflect attention from the main purpose of the voyage. Was your mission to Hanover a success?"

"No, it most certainly was not."

"Then, if I were you, I would go to the Admiralty first thing tomorrow. I'll be taking Mr. Westerby to see the appropriate ministers and permanent secretaries. Though it is quite fortuitous, his news should make the government look much more favorably on your trip, especially if that fool of a new First Lord is not blowing his own horn about it."

"Lord Struthers," said his wife after ringing the bell for the butler. "It is time we go to bed. Richard and Daphne undoubtedly have much to discuss. Mr. Westerby, Leadpole here, our butler, will show you your room and take care of any needs you may have. Come along, Walter. I see Richard is about to protest, but that is just his being polite. Daphne and Richard want to be together after their separation. Let's go now.

"Good night, Mr. Westerby. I hope you will be comfortable. Good night, Richard and Daphne."

With that, Lord and Lady Struthers left the drawing room. Leadpole took charge of Mr. Westerby and hustled him through the door unobtrusively, closing it behind them. The noise of the door closing was the signal for Daphne and Giles to indulge in a very long and very passionate embrace. Following that, they sank into one of the settees to have a long talk, though their conversation was interrupted frequently by the need to embrace.

Daphne started by reporting how the children were doing and what the latest developments at Dipton were. Then she went on to tell him about the dreadful situation she had discovered in Shropshire and how it complicated things concerning renovating Camshire House. Indeed, that was why she was in London now: to see Mr. Snodgrass about the various difficulties with which Mr. Edwards's treachery had saddled them as well as Mr. Beaver's treachery. Daphne hadn't intended to make Giles feel guilty, but that was the effect her words had on him.

Their conversation then switched to Giles's latest voyage. It was very clear to Daphne that Giles was less pleased with this latest venture than with previous cruises. Even the capture of two enemy frigates did not delight him in the way that earlier prizes had. It wasn't that he didn't like the money that would be coming their way as a result; he was still very happy to become richer. It was that he was not sure with the present situation in the war that depriving the enemy of two frigates was important. Indeed, Giles was not at all confident that naval action in home waters would have any decisive effect on Napoleon's defeat or survival. Possibly naval operations in the eastern Mediterranean or the Caribbean or even in the East Indies might weaken the tyrant. However, but Giles was not even convinced of that, and he had no desire to go on assignments that might take him away from England for several years on end.

Daphne suspected that the uncertainty about the future of *Glaucus* might have something to do with Giles's despondency about naval service. She was not about to express her deep desire that he leave the sea unless she became sure that Giles's feeling was not a temporary aberration. But secretly, she hoped that it might lead, at least, to Giles's remaining at home for a longer period than ever before in their marriage.

Daphne did state her belief that Giles could make real contributions through his membership of the House of Lords. She also mentioned that her disdain for the Season had been tempered by finding out that it concerned not just society balls, dinners, and soirées, but that it also was a time for lectures, plays, concerts, and operas, all of which she also enjoyed in moderation, more, in fact, than the social events that were supposed to be the highlight — indeed the *raison d'être* — of the Season. Having to be in London when Parliament was sitting might not be so undesirable after all.

Only after they were snuggling up together in bed in preparation for sleep did Daphne murmur to her husband one of her great desires. Giles had missed the birth of their two children. Daphne had always claimed that that had been no special disappointment for her, even though, in fact, it had been. Now she murmured, "It sounds as if you can be at Dipton when this child is born."

"I don't see why not," Giles replied. "If you want me there, I can promise you that I shall not take any assignment from the Admiralty until the child is born and both of you are out of danger." With that, he rolled over and fell asleep. Daphne stayed awake longer, delighted with the promise and wondering if he would have stayed home for the earlier births if she had told him how much his presence would have meant to her.

Author's Note

A lot has changed in the more than two centuries that have passed since the fictional events in this tale took place. Policing and maintenance of law-and-order were very different then, especially outside the London area. The basic law enforcement structure involved magistrates appointed by the central government, usually prominent land-owners serving without remuneration, and parish constables whose duties were as much concerned with implementing and enforcing some laws, such as the poor laws, as with apprehending wrong-doers. In cities, they were supplemented by the watch – essentially nightwatchmen primarily on the lookout for fire. In London – or more precisely Westminster — the Bow Street Runners had been created as a proto police force by the chief magistrate. Their members could be hired privately for law-enforcement jobs or other tasks. The Home Office issued instructions to the magistrates and was responsible for operation of the secret service. The fictional Sir Titus was likely working on instructions from the Home Office.

The militia were a domestic armed force stationed throughout the country whose primary job was maintenance of law-and-order. When magistrates had to read the riot act, it was usually the militia rather than the army who were brought in to quell disturbances. Because of this function, while organized and recruited on a county basis, the militia did not serve in their home county but instead were assigned to counties not close to their homes. They could also be brought in to enforce magistrates' orders relating to civil law on a rather *ad hoc* basis.

Estate and property law was at least as complicated during the early 19th century as it is now, especially with the complications added by entails which could severely limit a property's owner's options for its use and disposal. The limitations on Giles's ability to use and sell the properties in Norfolk arising from entails on the properties, seem to have been quite different from those in the building in Green's club and Camshire House. One suspects that some of the complications arose from Giles's father skimping on legal services. The oddity that the legal aspects of his father's estate were handled by the Arch-diocesan Court of Canterbury (which had its offices in London.)

Forensic accounting was far less developed in the Georgian Period than now, which is partly why sorting out what was left after Mr. Edwards's embezzlements appears to have been so complicated and why establishing ownership of real estate which was registered in his name by occupying it was important.

While the universities were closed to women, and academically inclined schools for girls were few and far between, a significant number of gentlewomen did become proficient in mathematics and the sciences, as Daphne Giles did. The method of least squares, which fascinated her, has become (in the form of both simple and multiple regression) probably the most frequently used (and abused) analytical tool in economics, though its calculation has only become entirely routine in the last fifty years. The "beta" coefficient routinely reported in financial evaluations of stocks is the central calculation of the least-squares method. It is only in the last fifty years that that least-squares calculations have been easy. Calculating the least-squares coefficients with any accuracy using only pencil, paper, and non-electronic calculating machine is a formidable task. As recently as the late 1950's students of economics at Cambridge were taught how to calculate them using a slide rule, a procedure that rarely produces accurate results.

King George III did petition Parliament about the loss of Hanover, but not with the consequences with which Giles was involved. His trip to Bremen and his encounters off Ferrol are entirely fictitious. Napoleon did not try to invade Denmark in 1806. Instead, when the threatened invasion would have occurred, Napoleon decided to march on Prussia, winning the battles of Jena-Auerstedt, though Auerstedt was the more important one and Napoleon was not present at it.

Napoleon abolished the Holy Roman Empire and incorporated Hanover in the Kingdom of Saxony. The Congress of Vienna reinstated King George III as King of Hanover, but the British Monarch lost that position when Queen Victoria ascended the throne. George III never did set foot in Hanover.

Glossary

Board(ing)	(1) Refers to attacking another ship by coming side to side so that men from one ship can attack the other one in an attempt to capture it.
	(2) in 'on board' it means present on a ship.
Boarding-nets	Loose nets hung from the spars of a ship to prevent enemies climbing aboard from boats.
Brig	A two-masted, square-rigged ship.
Close to the wind	A ship is sailing close to the wind when it is going upwind as much as it can
Consol	A bond issued by the British Government with no stated redemption date, paying the holder a specified amount per annum. The term is short for Consolidated Fund.
Cutting-out	Entering an enemy harbor in boats to capture a ship and sail her out to sea where the warship would be waiting.
Entail	A provision that the inheritance of real property would go to specified members of a family (or another specified group) usually to the closest male relatives. An entail typically prevented the present owner from leaving the property to someone else, and it was usually put on a property to prevent the immediate heir from dissipating the inheritance but would pass it intact (more or less) to the next generation.

Larboard	the left-hand side of the ship looking forward. Opposite of starboard. Now usually called "port."
Miss stays	the failure of a ship trying to come about to pass through the eye of the wind.
Quarterdeck	The outside deck of a ship at the stern.
Rake (a ship)	Fire a broadside into the bow or stern of an opponent who would not be able to return the fire.
Shrouds	A rope ladder formed by short lengths of rope tied tightly between the stays of a mast.
Sheet	lines controlling how much a sail is pulled in.
Stay(s)	(1) A line used to prevent a mast from falling over or being broken in the wind (2) Corsets
Stern sheets	the rear part of a small small boat.
Tack	(a) Change the direction in which a ship is sailing and the side of the ship from which the wind is blowing by turning towards the direction from which the wind is blowing. (b) (as in larboard of starboard tack) The side of the ship from which the wind is blowing when the ship is going to windward.
Taffrail	Railing at the stern of the quarter deck.
Wardroom	The area in a ship used by the commissioned officers of a ship when off-duty.
Watch	(1) Time: A ships day was divided up into fur hour watches with one further divided into two. The watches were

First watch: 8 p.m.- 12 midnight

Middle watch: 2 midnight - 4 a.m.

Morning watch: 4 a.m. – 8 a.m.

Forenoon watch: 8 a.m. – 12 noon

Afternoon watch 12 noon – 4 p.m.

First dog watch 4 p.m. – 6 p.m.

Second Dog watch 6 p.m. – 8 p.m.

In each watch, time was marked off in half-hour segments so the one bell of the First watch would be 8:30 p.m., two bells would be 9:00 p.m., and so on.

(2) Division of the crew. The crew was divided (usually) into two watches, the starboard watch and the larboard watch, which alternated when they worked (in normal circumstances) and when they were at leisure or asleep.

(3) the time when officers were on duty. Referred to as "being on watch" or "watch."

(4) Police force on land.

Wear (referring to a ship)   The opposite of tack where the maneuver of changing which side of a ship the wind is coming from is accomplished by turning away from the wind. Sometimes spelled ware.

Main Characters

Barbas, Captain Sebastien	Portuguese smuggler
Betsey	Daphne Giles's lady's maid
Bolton, Mrs. Catherine	Giles's half-niece and married to Captain Bolton
Bolton, Captain	Married to Giles's niece Catherine
Beaver, Mr.	Designer of the changes to Camshire House
Brooks, Mr.	Master of *Glaucus*
Bush, Captain Tobias	A Royal Navy Post Captain, formerly Giles's first lieutenant
Bush, Midshipman	Nephew to Captain Bush, midshipman on *Glaucus*
Carstairs	Giles's Cockswain, operator of the Dipton Arms Inn
Chapman, Mr.	Lawyer in Norwich
Clara, Lady Giles,	Dowager Countess of Camshire Mother of Giles and Lord David Giles
Cogswell, Mrs.	The Late earl's concubine
Darling, Mrs.	Cook at Dipton Hall
Downing, Mr.	Chief Magistrate of Westminster
Dunsmuir, Mr.	Midshipman on *Glaucus*
Edwards, Randolph	Giles's former agent, guilty of embezzling funds.
Emery, Sir Titus	A High Court Justice, who spends much of his time as an agent of the government
Evans, Garth	Carpenter on *Glaucus*.
Findlay, Michael	Portrait and landscape painter
Forsythe, James	Giles's agent in Norfolk
Giles, Daphne	Countess of Camshire
Giles, Captain Sir Richard,	Captain in the Royal Navy and husband of Daphne Earl of Camshire
Griffiths Mr.	Stablemaster at Dipton Hall
Hatcherley, Lord	First Lord of the Admiralty
Jackson, Mr.	Apothecary/physician

Jamieson	Steward at Dipton
Little, Sir Humphrey	Previous owner of Sallycove estate in Shropshire
Macreau, Lieutenant Etienne	Second lieutenant on *Glaucus*
Marianne, Lady	Giles's half-sister and Major Stoner's wife
Marsdon, Mrs.	A bawdy house keeper and procuresse
Matthams, Mr.	Proprietor/ innkeeper of the Woodbridge Inn, Shropshire
Matthams, Mrs.	His wife
Miller, Lieutenant	First lieutenant on *Glaucus*
Moorhouse, Daniel	Daphne's father, Owner of Dipton Manor
Moorhouse, George	Daphne's invalid uncle, owner of a gun factory in Birmingham
Newsome, Mr.	Second Secretary to the Admiralty
Philman, David	Giles's servant on *Glaucus*
Shearer, Bill	Bosun on *Glaucus*
Snodgravel, Mr.	Lawyer in London, starting to become Giles's agent in place of Mr. Edwards
Steves	Butler at Dipton Hall
Stoner, Major Ralph	Retired Indian Army Officer, married to Lady Marianne
Struthers, Lady Gillian	Giles's maternal aunt
Struthers, Lord Walter	Giles's uncle in law, a member of the government
Stewart, Lt. Daniel	Officer on *Glaucus*
Summers, Edward	President of the Ameschester Hunt
Westerby, Jonathan	Representative of Barings Bros. in Hanover
Wilson, Mrs.	Housekeeper at Dipton Hall
Worthington, Mr.	Builder in Shropshire

Printed in Great Britain
by Amazon